SHE RISES

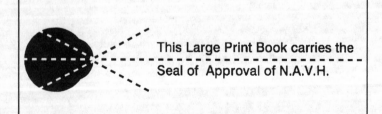

This Large Print Book carries the
Seal of Approval of N.A.V.H.

SHE RISES

KATE WORSLEY

THORNDIKE PRESS
A part of Gale, Cengage Learning

GALE
CENGAGE Learning®

Detroit • New York • San Francisco • New Haven, Conn • Waterville, Maine • London

GALE
CENGAGE Learning·

LIBRARY OF CONGRESS CATALOGING-IN-PUBLICATION DATA

Worsley, Kate.
    She rises / by Kate Worsley. — Large print edition.
        pages ; cm. — (Thorndike Press large print reviewers' choice)
    ISBN 978-1-4104-6294-7 (hardcover) — ISBN 1-4104-6294-3 (hardcover) 1.
Sailors—Great Britain—Fiction. 2. Great Britain—History—George II,
1727-1760—Fiction. 3. Harwich (England)—Fiction. 4. Large type books. I.
Title.
PR6123.O67S54 2013b
823'.92—dc23   2013024062

Published in 2013 by arrangement with Bloomsbury Publishing, Inc.

Printed in the United States of America
1 2 3 4 5 6 7 17 16 15 14 13

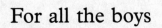

For all the boys

I shall sleep, and move with the moving
  ships,
Change as the winds change, veer in the
  tide,
I will go back to the great sweet mother,
Mother and lover of men, the sea.
I will go down to her, I and no other,
Close with her, kiss her and mix her with
  me.

Algernon Charles Swinburne,
'The Triumph of Time', 1866

CHAPTER ONE

It's the singing that wakes him. He does not move, he cannot move, there's a body pressed heavy against his left side. He won't be opening his eyes neither, his head hurts so.

Every note strikes like a clapper, sends the pain clanging round and around. It's a bitter little tune, spat out in gobbets, sung so thick and crudded he can't make it out. Damn it's cold, but there's a damp warmth too, blowing on his face. The singer's breath, close, and sour, like an unscoured milk pan.

He gasps and opens his eyes. Nothing but a solid, choking dark. A cellar? Please not a prison. Then the singer's heavy body lolls away, for there's a shifting and a rolling to everything like he's never known. His wits are addled, he thinks. As he lifts his head he feels a throbbing at the back of his skull. He reaches out to steady himself and finds his

9

wrists are cuffed. A prison then.

But the swaying goes on, and on. His stomach wallows and the gorge rises. He's panicked now, tries to cover his mouth because he can hear himself panting with fear but the hand that presses against his face is wide and clammy and not his. He beats it off, twists about, he'll drown if he can't see.

'Whisht,' a voice is saying, gruff and coaxing. 'Whisht!'

Held fast by the shoulder, held back against slime and cold, the boy can't stop himself crying out.

'H'way there, lads! Here's a squealer.'

There's a muttering and a grumbling of deep voices. A sharp, gleeless bark followed by a fit of coughing, some feet away. How many are here? What place is this? And how can he escape?

He sits small as he can, pressing back into the dark. He knows the weakness of his own body, how small and helpless he is. This place, wherever it is, is no place for the likes of him. His own breathing is panicking him. It's quick, tearing, like that of a cornered animal.

Thick fingers prod at his arms and shoulders. And the voice again, right by his ear. 'Not much meat on you, lad.'

He does not speak. He cannot speak. He will give himself away. He twists and turns instead. What holds his feet?

The burr comes closer. 'Ma-mmy need you home? Or did you no tell your bint you were off? Hmn. Big-bellied bint is she? Like as not notice you'd slipped out —'

Straightways the boy grows sharp too. 'You'll leave her be or —'

'Woah, Hotspur!' the man chuckles delightedly, and slaps the boy's shoulder.

The boy hears him settle his bulk back in the dark, but now he's thinking yes, I remember her, my god I remember her, but nothing else. How he came to leave her, how he came to be here, that he don't know.

'Come men, can't any of you sing? Sing now and raise the dead. *Cheerily, lads, cheerily! There's a ganger hard to windward.*' None takes up the tune and the man starts to hum again, like a big cat purring.

The boy waits, sweating.

'Fine mardle, man,' the man says finally, in a bright tone.

The boy has no idea what he means.

'Damned gangers,' says another, off in the dark, and hawks hard.

He hears the spittle land, and a lapping of water, close by his ear. Something begins to stir in the back of his mind. He struggles

11

again to stand.

'Dinne fash, man, they've snaffled you good.'

'Who?' he cries now. His legs are trembling, his heart racing. 'Who?'

'Whisht, the gangers, man!' The hot rank breath blows close. 'You're pressed, my lad. Welcome to His Majesty's damned whoreson Navy.'

There is a crash and rattle overhead, and raised voices. Hard white light floods upon him and he curls up like a grub and hides his eyes. It's been many hours since he first woke, but still he can't believe he is here. He has shivered and coughed and cried as silent as he can, and he has longed for light, for air, but the sudden brightness wakes a deeper dread. We are in hell, he thinks, this is a hell house and god has ripped the roof off.

'Bastards!' shouts the heavy man still slumped against his side. 'Damned bastards!' He spits, then sinks back, duty done.

The boy screws up his eyes against the light to sneak a glance at his neighbour.

The man must be over six foot and built to match. His bare chest is solid and wide, wide as a sack of wheat. A mat of red-gold hair bristles all the way up to his collarbone. About his well-larded neck slides a glinting coin on a thong. His jawbone is that of an ox. The boy watches his eyes close and his huge red hands clasp over his belly. As his jaw sinks the coin disappears into folds of ruddy flesh.

The other men are stirring. They rub their faces and clear their throats, squint upwards into the light. The boy stays on his bench and draws up his knees to hide his face. Hollering and cursing rise in waves over the drag and rattle of the chains that bind them all. There must be over a dozen men here, close packed in this dank and dripping space that he now sees to be the hold of a boat, and a mean and scurvy little boat at that. They rise up, in ragged smocks and muddied breeches, bruised and bleeding, mostly young but none so young as he.

Overhead, a hatching of light, and the dark shapes of two men squatting, and another standing, with a hanger by his side, all three peering in.

His foot is trodden by a squat tawny fellow who struggles to stand but falls to his knees and cries out to those above, 'Sweet Jesus release me, my mother is dying at Thorpe and I must go!'

'Damn your Navy I'll cut your throats you

poxy bastards!' calls another.

'Here take this kerchief and bring us some gin!'

' 'Tis nigh noon my girls will want milking bad, now release me I say!'

Their shifting sets the boat a-heaving and the boy clutches out for balance. A chunk of timber splits off in his fingers, black and soft as rotten fruit. Then something spatters hard against his face. It is a squirt of tobacco juice, hot and sticky.

'Damn the lot of you mutinous dogs,' growls a voice from above. 'Choke off your howling. You'll find release soon enough aboard the *Essex,* this very day.'

'Or the next. You've caught us a nest of country vermin. How are we to raise sail with this sorry lot?'

'Scooped the fair. Caught 'em all caterwauling in the alleys after dark. Came like rats out of a hole, the drunken sots. Got your numbers though ain't you?'

It's dark again, but there's noises everywhere and splinters of daylight that stab and confound him. He shuts his eyes against it all. Everything he has seen since he woke has made him wish himself dead. The tawny lad had shouted on and on, climbed up, even got a grip on the hatch edge but they stamped on his hands and then a fellow above pissed on his head for good measure. The grating was drawn across and something laid atop to muffle their protests. Then the men about him set on the shouting lad and the singing man roared and knocked him down and whether he breathes still, he don't know.

He hears again the droning song that woke him to the chill dark, sees again those sudden looming figures, the hard white square of sky. And he holds his tongue while all about curse their mothers for having born them into this wicked world. He tries not to flinch when other men piss and shit on the very benches where they lie. At the sound of a scurrying and a gnawing in the timbers by his ear he starts, but shifts away quietly and stills his trembling limbs. He buries his nose in his sleeve to keep out the stench, for he lies on boards only inches above the bilge. When he can hold it no longer he finds he must piss his own pants and does so, silently, and weeping, at the welcome warmth, the familiar scent.

And he waits, and he prays. For he knows he is safe here, at least safer than he will be the moment he is hauled out through that hatchway.

CHAPTER TWO

Was I happy before I met you?

I think now maybe I was happiest before I met you, back at Handley's farm. And happiest there, perhaps, making butter, with my fingers in the cream. I loved to feel the flakes form, the way they caught around my wrist like a bracelet, how they slipped between my fingers. Doing it with my bare hand like that, I knew just how the butter was coming, and when it came. And I liked that, knowing. It made me happy.

Course I was happy. I knew who I was then.

I was young Louise, Squire Handley's dairymaid. And a very dutiful little dairymaid I was too, trained up from the age of twelve in the dairy work, in cow milking, and the buttermaking, and the cheesemaking, and getting up the wheys and the syllabubs. I had other duties, of course; for all that Handley's was the finest place in the district, it weren't Lawford Hall. I had the chickens to chase and their necks to wring, I had bread to bake and all the rest of it.

But when I got back to the dairy, and nudged the door shut behind me, I'd always let out my breath with a sort of relief. It was the place I liked to be the best. It was quiet, it was clean, and it was neat. It was safe. The air was still and cool. We kept the windows shuttered against the sun and the dirt and the hot air, and dowsed the floor and walls regular with fresh water. After I'd strained the new milk and emptied it into clean pans, I'd take the crocks and pans to the scullery to scald them and when I'd emptied the strained milk into the clean pans I'd skim off last night's ripe cream and sit down to make butter. I could get more milk out of those cows than anyone and I could get butter to come cleaner too. I had the knack of it.

Yes we had a barrel churn then, the end-over-end, we called it. It did the job all right, and least you could keep your mits on in winter. But oh all that stopping and starting, and taking a peek, and what a bother to scald and always breaking. You never knew how it was coming, when it would turn. You'd have to keep on turning, and it

17

never come, or go on too long and it be too late.

No, I liked to do it the way I was first taught.

'Shut that door for the flies,' said old Mary Gould when my mother first prodded me over the threshold, 'and mind your feet.'

We was both scared of Mary, with her thickey brows like charred sticks. Mother stepped aside and set the latch back sharpish. After a moment I heard her clogs skit away on the cobbles.

Mary took up my fingers and sniffed them.

'My, look at the size of these pats,' she exclaimed, turning my hands back and forth.

I blushed like anything then. I always knew the size of my hands, and my feet too. You're more frog than girl, my sister used to tease me, and I'd never forgotten it.

'Chilly too. But that's good. Anyways,' she added, seeing my face. 'Cool hands, warm heart, that's what they say.' For she was not without heart herself.

'Let's see how you do's, young Louise. This here's ripe.' She passed me a crock of reddish earthenware. It was tall and heavy and when I tilted it to look inside, cream lapped halfway up the side in a thick wave. She wedged the crock between my skirts.

Then she took my right hand and slipped it inside the crock, right up to the wrist in the smooth, cool cream. It was like sinking my bare feet into the river mud.

'And flip that over the top,' she said, snatching down a muslin from the rack beside the window. 'You don't want none on your bodice. Got my reputation to keep up, and yorn.' She wiggled her black brows at me. 'Mind you, nothing like the whiff of a dairymaid to keep the boys off.'

That made me blush again, for I thought of boys much as I thought of flies, to be kept outdoor and well away.

Mary had a little stool she used to prop her feet out of the draught, but being so small I had to tuck my toes behind a rung of the chair instead to get the right angle. I'd settle the crock between my skirts, press my fingers together and cup my palm slightly, to the shape of a paddle, and set to sculling.

'Always start at a goodly pace,' said Mary, 'or else why bother.'

She would settle herself at the other end of the long deal table and take up her pats while I'd let my eyes rove around the place. That north window was set rather high, and when I started there I couldn't see anything out of it more than what the weather was doing and the rooks in the tops of the elms in the back field. Course, this was in the old dairy, just one room off the brewhouse and most unsatisfactory in many ways. The brick channel in the floor never drained properly and although the window to the west was blocked up with bricks and stones the walls weren't never thick enough and it was often too warm in summer to get the butter to come. The blue was always flaking off the walls and the flies came anyway on account of the mash next door.

My wrist would be aching and my arm would be stiff from holding the crock. So to distract myself, I would run through all that Mary was trying to teach me. Were there enough clean muslins hanging on the hooks by the door? The pans scalded and dry? Enough sand in the scouring bucket, the pats set back in pairs, matching flowers, matching acorns, and so on. Was the whey from the cheesecloths splashing on to the clean crocks there, and had I remembered to fetch fresh angelica?

Before I knew it the flakes would be thickening like a blizzard and when I clenched my fist I could scoop them into a clot. If I squeezed it too hard it would split and slide apart, like the stones on the shore that were not stone at all, but a sort of solid clay made that way by a secret spring down-river. So I would hold it lightly, like you'd hold a living thing.

After a while I would close my eyes as I churned. My tasks ran through my head more in the way of a lullaby I sang to myself, to the tune of the cream tossing and tumbling about deep in the crock between my legs. Yes, I was happy then.

But then often as not I would hear a familiar shuffle of clogs round the corner and the door unlatch.

'Stop out there!' Mary would call, rolling knobs of butter the size of pigeon eggs between her pats. 'You'll turn the milk.'

It would be my mother, come to see how I was getting on. And already my heart would sink like it was a lump of butter let go. For it hadn't taken long for me to start seeing her through Mary's eyes, and those of the other women of the farm.

She would be craning at the small screened window in the door, angling for a peek at my white bonneted head. I wouldn't look up. I hated to see her raw and red cheeks, her nose swollen and pocked and always dripping, her hair thicketed with dust and straw. I was ashamed of her, God forgive me.

She was the only woman as worked out in

the fields, with the men and the animals. She'd got me into the dairy and my sister Susie into the kitchen, but Mrs Handley wouldn't have her in the house. She wouldn't give a reason but, it was whispered, it was on account of everything else mother'd had to do to make ends meet back home. Until she couldn't splice us a living any more and came up and over the hill to throw herself and her girls on the good graces of the Handleys.

My mother would come straight from pulling turnips, with the clag thick on her feet and splatters on her face, her fingers cracked and her eyes reddened, staring off like a goat's. Or she'd turn up on a hot afternoon, straw and dust floating off her like a cloud and on to everything I tried so hard to keep clean. She'd got me away, she'd done her best for me, but I wouldn't look at her.

This day I'm thinking of, when I heard the latch go, I cursed under my breath. We were in the new dairy by then, Mary and I. Oh that was a fine place, did you ever see it? I watched it built, long and low below the brow of the northern hill, across from the brewhouse. It had smooth whitewashed walls, thick as anything, that glowed like moonlight, and a fine flagged floor. Like a chapel it was. I said as much to Mary and she said that if our Lord was to pay us a visit then he was welcome to a bit of the famous Handley butter with his loaves and fishes. I was proud to work there, there was nowhere better. I was dedicated to that clean pure milk as a novice nun is to dear old Jesus. I thought to spend the rest of my life there, listening to the cream rising.

And sweet Christ how many days since have I wished, wished with all my heart, that I had.

My fingers were numb to the knuckles, paddling away inside one of the little old crocks. I know I said I liked to feel the butter come, but I had any number of pans to do on account of the new calf, and the end-over-end did twice as much. I was cross with my sister Susie too. I knew she'd been in the day before, which was a Sunday, with one of the field boys. Though she swore they hadn't, they'd leant on the end-over-end and now the arm was broke. And I had twenty quart to do that day all on my sweet own, for Mary was off visiting her sister — as Susie well knew.

It was a blustery February morning, and when the latch went, the door swung wide open and banged. The cream wrinkled, the cheese shook and flakes of plaster dropped from the wall. A gust of wind took up the flakes and I jumped to my feet, for fear they would settle on the cream and the curds not covered.

But when I turned to the door the figure I saw was not my mother. Nor was it Susie, nor even Mary back early. Well, you know who it was. He was tall and heavy, not young even then. Very well dressed, though, in clean tan breeches and a frogged black coat. He wore his own hair, loose, and its dark shanks curled about his face. And there was that beard, thick and stiff as a broom. I knew him first, though, by his high black boots. He was the only man I'd ever seen in the yard without a spot of mud on him.

I heard his horse being led away. I didn't know why he'd come, or why he was standing here, and I wished heartily that Mary were back. I set down the crock on the table, pulled out my dripping hand and wrapped the muslin tight about.

He plucked his hat from his head and made to duck inside the door. I forgot all my manners on the instant.

'You can't come in,' I said.

He stepped in anyway and shut the door behind him. He must have ridden hard for I could feel the heat come off him in waves, see the beads of sweat on his forehead. The room I had thought so cool and airy suddenly felt quite close. I reached a fresh muslin from the rack and turned to cover the cheeses. Then I put the table between us and faced him. It was as though one of the bulls had wandered in.

'You know who I am?' he said, and his voice filled the place.

'I do.'

I'd watched him through the side window last Easter. Mary had said Mrs Handley made him come up to the farm to do business, wouldn't let her husband go to him. He strode about the yard as though he were aboard his own ship, arm in arm with his brother, like a raven strutting alongside a thrush. Sam and the other boys laughed behind their fingers. He didn't walk like other men, see, he rolled. They kept out his way though.

'You'll be Louise Fletcher.' He didn't talk like other men either. His voice was tuned to blast through gales.

I nodded.

'Where's Mary?' he asked.

'Hadleigh.'

'Shame. It's you I want anyways.'

If I'd had my wits about me that day in the dairy I should have remembered that old

Mary had a soft spot for the Captain — she had loved a sailor boy once but he was gone and drowned, and the master's brother was the only sea dog who came wagging about our place. I'd have remembered her going to the door to watch him dismount last Easter, and turning away all red in the face when he cocked his head and whistled at her, long and low. Our Mary, blushing. And later, just before he left, the pair of them standing close in the shadow of the barn.

Yes, if I hadn't been so froused about with the door banging and the flakes falling, my first thought should have been that he had come to see her. I would have turned him out on the spot, got all that butter made up, the churn mended and everything wiped down. And when Mary was come back I'd have giggled, wanting to see the old girl blush again, and told her the Captain had come sniffing after her.

But of course it weren't Mary he was after that day, was it?

'He wants you?' My mother put one hand to the small of her back and straightened up. I can still remember the look on her face: as though I'd just told her I'd made the moon out of cheese with my own fair hands. I remember how that look made me feel.

And I'd gone to find her, for once. My mother, who I thought I was so ashamed of, she was the first I wanted to tell. I'd wanted her to be proud of me. Soon as I'd bobbed my last curtsey I'd run back to the dairy — in those days I never ran — slipped on my clogs and headed straight off to the top field where she was lifting turnip. We stood there now, in the shelter of some blackthorns, for the wind was scouring in from the north-west and whipping my apron up about my ears. I never came this far out into the fields, and it seemed to me then an awful barren place, all weather. There was a storm brewing over Stutton, the other side of the river; the sky to the north was dark as pewter. I couldn't see the colour of the river, though, for the Rigbys' young oaks on the hill between. I couldn't remember when I'd last seen the river at all.

'He wants me, yes. That's what he said,' I answered, quite out of breath, but I could hear the triumph in my voice. Oh I was full of myself. I had something to tell her now, didn't I? I felt my soul billow like a sheet on the line. Great fat drops of rain burst against my cheeks, the splattery outriders.

'The Captain asked for you?' she repeated.

27

And I knew what her next words would be. 'Not Susie?'

How sweet it was to be able to reply: 'No. I don't recall him mentioning her.'

'Now, Louise, are you sure?'

I grew impatient. 'Yes, Ma, he come to the dairy himself.'

Her mouth tightened.

'He did, did he? Well, that's typical Harwich, that is. Why, the lady of the house what's making enquiry should consult with the lady of the house where the girl resides. Even I knows that.'

'His wife's dead, Ma. Six, seven year ago.'

'You think I don't know that neither? You should have sent him straight indoors to Mrs Handley. Shows no respect for you.'

'That's where we went, directly. And Ma, he told me he had great regard for me. Had heard sound report of my character.'

She snorted, and wiped her nose with the back of her hand. Now her face was smeared with earth. 'Did he indeed. And no doubt he was quite surprised to find a Fletcher of sound character. A rare creature indeed. So he flattered you?'

She said this with such feeling that now I couldn't tell her all that he had said, as I was dying to do. All the smooth quick flow of delight at being told how smart and diligent and neat and clean and eager and willing I was — confirmation that all that I had striven for I had achieved — choked right up. I knew what she meant, that he had seduced me with words and how that was no different from what all men were after.

But however bad I felt, it was too late, you see. All my dairymaiding notions seemed thin as whey just then. I had never thought to leave where I was. But now that the wider world had come knocking, how could I turn my back, retreat to my chill little cell?

My mother's eyes narrowed. 'Which one is it?'

'Which daughter? Rebecca.'

'She the elder?'

'No, no, that's Hester, she runs the household now, has done since their mother died. This vessel needed a steady hand on the tiller, he said.' Oh how I was bursting with all my new-found knowledge. 'No, it's Rebecca, her younger sister. She hopes to marry a Mr Henry Wilmington. He's a midshipman out on His Majesty's something or other. And she wants, well, he wants, the Captain wants, to find her a good clean dairymaid to train up to mind her person and keep all her things in order.'

'And why is this Rebecca not come herself

then, or Hester?'

'Rebecca is indisposed, he said, and Hester cannot spare the time, on account of the spring tides.'

'Is that so.' She sniffed. 'What sort of household does the woman run, I might wonder. And when is Hester to be married? What sort of girl takes on a lady's maid before her elder sister is fixed up?'

I took a breath: how little did my mother know!

'If Mr Wilmington gets his commission, as he's been promised, and he marries her, as they all hope, Rebecca'll be a gentlewoman. That will mean a great deal for the whole family: Hester's own prospects will be great improved. And after the wedding, Rebecca'll need me still, for her new position in life, you see. They'll want me well trained too, before Easter at least, for that's when Mr Wilmington is expected to return, and when he does, and then they marry, then —' I took a deep breath, 'then they'll be off to Wapping.'

'To Wapping? To London?'

'Yes, to Captain Handley's sister, her Aunt Tabitha.'

'Aunt Tabitha?'

She was like my echo. I wanted to shake her.

'Are you sure? You won't come back here, back to the dairy?'

I took a breath. 'No, I'll go with them, if I please her, if I please Rebecca.'

Then she squeezed my hand hard and pulled me to her. Her fingers were cold and grimed. 'You? Please the Handleys?'

Young fool that I was, I took the doubt in her eyes for lack of faith in myself, and said hotly: 'I learnt to be a dairymaid, Mother, I can learn to be a lady's maid. Didn't you always say we must improve our lot, that however humble we start out, every day we must strive to better ourselves? I shall learn all the ways of a lady, Ma. Why, with luck, I'll be part of the household of a naval gentleman by Christmas!'

I rubbed at my arms. I was shivering with cold now.

'I suppose,' she said slowly. 'I suppose he thinks he's doing right by us.'

'It's a great honour, if that's what you mean. Mrs Handley told me so herself. Captain Handley is the most respectable sort of sea captain, one of those that has the licence to run a packet boat over to the Low Countries, you know. He is a figure to be reckoned with. His is the finest establishment in Harwich.'

'Oh I know, Louise, I know.'

She let me go, didn't she? Despite everything else she knew and never told me,
never can tell me now. She saw there was a
chance after all. And she could see the heat
in my cheeks: her pale little Louise, all fired
up out of nowhere. Why did the Captain's
proposal carry such charge for me? Weren't
I simply swapping a life of servitude on a
farm for one in the town? All I can say is,
that's not how it seemed then.

But she only nodded, as I ran on about
the Captain's establishment and how I
should learn all about a lady's linens and
amusements. She wasn't looking at me no
more. She was looking back down to the
farm. I'd never seen it from such a distance
before. There was the farmhouse, with its
four new sashes at the front, and my dairy
behind it, peeking out the barns. With the
vast ploughed fields all about, the place no
longer seemed my safe little sanctuary;
rather it was as I imagined a ship stranded
on the ocean, a sort of floating prison.

Then she took a breath, wiped off her
hands on her skirts, for the dinner bell was
ringing. We walked back down the hill.

'Ah, feel them fingers, they're right down
frorn,' she said and the old words made me
think her quaint, and almost lost to me
already. She draped her thick workaday

shawl about my shoulders, and twisted its ends round my fingers like a ragged muff. As we walked she asked me what Handley would pay me and what would be my days off and when might I be able to visit; and I could not say that he had not told me these things and I had not thought to ask, and only said that these were details to be decided with Rebecca herself, when I met her.

Whenever a cloud burst over Stutton way no one at the farm ever ran to take in the linen, for by the time a storm crossed the river it had usually dropped its worst. But the rain was coming on hard now. My mother tugged the shawl over both our heads and we half ran, half skipped along. Most times, if we were any place the others might see us, I would never even walk by her side. But that day I leant into her, hugged my arm about her waist and breathed in all the sharpness of her sweat. It weren't just on account of the rain. It was because I was leaving.

Susie was stood on the straw by the pump, with a couple of buckets at her side. She watched us come in together under the shawl. Then she smiled, a funny little smile, and raised her chin at me that way she had.

'It'll be another's cast-offs you'll be wearing soon enough, I hear.'

I never knew how to handle my sister. Whatever I expected her to say or do, she always sidestepped me. She snatched up her plashing buckets and was away to the kitchen door before I could say anything. My mother sighed and went after her. I watched the back of Susie's red bodice wiggle away. The way she tugged her stays in so tight, you could always tell her figure from any distance.

Poor Susie. She was so jealous that day she could barely look at me. Of course the word had got all about the place afore I was halfways up the hill. And if anyone were thought likely to be off to Harwich it was Susie.

Yes, she was the one to watch. She was always impatient to get away, yearning for Harwich and the great wide world beyond. 'Call this a life,' she would say, sluicing a dish back in the grey water she was always up to her elbows in. 'This place's as dead as a mitten.' When the moon was full and we were all traipsing over to the Merrits' for a fiddle and a dance she'd lag behind and mutter: 'Don't know what you're all roused up about. It's always a scram of a do.' But when we got there she'd be out in the middle first, dancing afore she was even asked, and dancing still when I was falling asleep in the hay.

She was that bit older than me, see. She could remember life down at the town by the river, where twice a day the salt water surged upstream to mingle with the fresh and soak the marsh. She missed the smacks and the barges coming in and the stacks of brewhouse barrels, the whole place overflowing on market days.

No, she weren't ever cut out for the Handleys' scullery. She'd been walking out with Jemmy Jenkin, the cooper's son, and she was all for him setting up in Harwich, where his uncle lived. She'd been going up there on market days with Old Joe, asking for work. You never seen anything like what they get up to at Harwich, she'd tell me. That place never stops. You wait, I'll be dancing all the way into next week.

So when I caught up to her by the kitchen door, the best I could come up with was: 'Just think, Susie. When you and Jem are married, I can easy come visit.'

'Well, won't we be honoured,' she said harshly.

'Susie!' said my mother indignantly.

But Susie was all roused up now. 'Why couldn't you have took us all up to Harwich, Ma? Why did you bury us here?'

My mother did not reply. But I knew the run of her thoughts. She reckoned the sea was where all our troubles flowed from. Us Fletchers have too much salt in our blood, she'd tell us. It made her weep to think how many fathers and brothers and sons had been drawn away by the moon and the tides and the winds, and left their women to starve. Men always leave, she'd say. Men always leave, and the sea never gives them up, once she's got them.

She had wanted us girls up and away from men like that, and out of sight of the glinting waters. She hoped that the land would hold us fast, succour us. Whenever I saw her at work, it always seemed she was digging to anchor us with her spade. Leastways I'll always have my girls with me, she would tell us. Here every season has its crop; hard work reaps its just rewards.

'I wanted you all to be safe,' she said, finally.

'Safe!' retorted my sister.

'Yes, safe.' My mother grew fierce herself now. 'Lord knows what would have become of you my girl if you'd fetched up in Harwich back then! Lord knows what'll become of you now the way you carry on!'

They were heading for one of their set-tos when Sam snuck up behind Susie and slipped his bare arms about her, all wet from the pump. 'Who didn't get asked to the dance then, eh?'

Sam was a stable hand and most times he knew just how far to go. Susie would just giggle, whether Jem were around or not. But this time she slapped him away.

'Nasty! No wonder the Captain don't want a piece of yous.' He came round in front of me and leered: 'Fancy, Miss whey-face here getting the whistle.'

I never had no answer for the lads, as Susie did. My way was to keep my hips steady and my eyes low, and hope they'd tire. But he stood there still.

'Watch them sea dogs don't catch a whiff, Lou.'

He bent till his nose came close to my bodice, where crusted smears of buttermilk had run in the rain. I stiffened, backed hard against the scullery wall. He was so close I could see the dirt on his neck. Don't touch me, I was praying silently, don't you touch me there, no lad touches me there. He sniffed. Then he looked up and pulled a face.

'Oh yes, you're on the turn, all right. You'll scare the bleeding gulls you will.'

And he grinned, and went off with the other lads, hungry for their dinners.

■ ■ ■ ■

'Well now! Off to Harwich!' cried Mary, putting her arms about me and smacking a great kiss on my cheek, fumed with spiced vinegar and sweet berry wine; her sister's place was stuffed to the rafters with preserves and cordials and she always came back having sampled a good few.

I'd been quite scared to tell Mary. I'd always swore I'd never leave and she'd said that was the least I could do; all the trouble I'd given her she didn't have it in her to train up another. But if she were angered, or even dismayed, she didn't show it. Even when I started by saying she had missed a visit from the master's brother, I watched, but she only shrugged and carried on unpacking her jars and bottles.

'They want more of your sort down at Harwich. You're the cream of the girls on this place, I'll say that for you. Your mother done well setting you up here, you should be thanking her.'

She fetched two beakers and wiped them inside and out with a muslin. Then she uncorked a tall thin bottle, poured out an inch or so of the thick red liquid into each beaker, and held one out to me.

'Cream rises to the top,' she began. It was one of her favourite sayings. I'd heard it countless times. 'But the milk must be untainted, the vessel spotless and the air pure —'

'— lest the whole mess be spoilt,' I said, taking the beaker and tucking my toes under the rung I had worn smooth as china over the years. I took a sip. It was her sister's sweet damson wine, juicy as the fruit itself.

'They don't say Harwich is a spotless place, Mary.'

'No, indeed, and the air certainly ain't pure.' She tossed hers back and toasted me with her empty beaker. Her eyes twinkled. 'But you'll do well. A little bit of salt never did good butter any harm!'

That last night before I left was awful. I lost all my pride and hope. I lingered in my chill, clean dairy, unable to pull the latch to for the last time. My mother was right, I thought, I have been safe here.

After we'd done all there was to do, Mary fetched out six stone jars for me to scald. The new calf was still making more butter than we could eat and she had to lay some up. It could have waited till the morning. But she pressed the butter into the jars as I cut out the muslin to top them. Then she fetched the scoop and we sprinkled a thick layer of salt on top of each, all the way up to the rim. We worked in silence. It was growing dim all about and the rush of the grains was very loud. I wiped off the daubs and swabbed out the rinsing vessels for the last time and even when all was done I fussed with the butter stamps, lining them up with the handles to the rear of the shelf so all the pictures were level.

Our market stamp was a swan, but none of them was quite the same. One showed a rather stringy bird, with long legs that looked to be paddling furiously. Another looked more like a duck. My favourite had always been a rather stout swan tucked up on grass, or maybe it was its nest, I could never decide. The handle was cracked and it was hard to set in straight, but the breast of the swan swelled so smoothly it set our butter off proud, I thought.

Mary was stood by the door. I wondered miserably if they used our butter up at Harwich. Did they make their own? I thought not. Perhaps sometimes they bought ours.

'Fetch two jars to take along with you,' Mary said sternly. 'But leave them stamps alone.'

My mother turned to me in bed that night

as Susie slept beside her. I had thought her asleep too. She stroked the hair from my face and kissed my forehead clumsily.

'I would not see you spoilt, Louise,' she whispered.

I curled right into her then. I had not told her how he had handled me, that Captain, after he took me into the parlour and stood me in the light before Mrs Handley. How he looked me up and down, and then came from behind that small round table set by the fire and took my face firmly — but not unkindly — in his hand, turning it this way and that, so the room blurred and the green plastered walls slid by and the gilded mirror over the fireplace flashed.

No man had ever handled me like that. I flinched, didn't I? Couldn't help myself. He had chuckled, like he was teasing a pet. I could still smell the rankness of tobacco on his yellow-stained fingertips. See the smear of spittle at the corner of his wide and weathered lips. His teeth were edged brown like rotting fence posts. I had never seen a nose so long and narrow, so burnished by sun and wind it looked like cheese rind.

When he dropped my chin and turned away, all he said was: 'A freshwater creature indeed.'

Beware of men, my mother had always

told me. Beware of men young and old, but especially those of the sea. Their stories are tall, their manners rough, their desires unruly. Give them a wide berth if you wish the course of your life to run smooth.

She was stroking my face, her hand as cracked and hard as his. 'Harwich is a wicked place,' she said. 'You take care, Louise. Heed your new mistress. Watch her carefully, do whatever she wants of you. Make yourself over anew for her, as you did here. All shall come right. And think of your mother, and all her labours for you, won't you, as you sit by the fire in those fine rooms?'

I could not speak.

She lay still so long after that, I thought she slept. But presently she said: 'And Louise, if you ever get word, if you hear any news —'

I opened my eyes then. I stared into the dark. For I knew straightways who she meant, though she never spoke of them any more. To her mind my feckless brother were as long dead as his dad, and good riddance the pair of them. Or so she always said.

For the sea had sucked up my father soon after I was born, and while I was still a girl she drew off my brother also. I didn't remember nothing of my father, and scarce

anything of Luke — 'cept the swooping dizzying feeling I got when he would scoop me
up on his shoulders, sat me so high I felt I
could stroke the clouds.

'Your father,' she began. And I listened
hard, for I'd never once heard her say his
name if not to curse him, for being a fool to
set to sea in that weather, in that boat, with
those boys, not one of whom came back.

But she only scratched briskly in her hair
and cleared her throat, as if to say, no, never
mind him. Her hand clenched hard about
mine, and then I hardened too. What's she
want from me now? I thought grimly. A
good word put in at the Captain's house?

'When you get up Harwich, Louise,' she
said. 'I know it's a long time back now, but
still. When you gets a moment, I wouldn't
bother the Captain or nothing, but happen
you could ask about, see what anyone knows
become of Luke?'

Oh didn't she say it casual, like she were
minding me to ask the mistress for a fresh
candle on the morning. And so didn't I
agree, just as carelessly: to keep her happy,
to stopper my guilt, to staunch my tears. I
was a little relieved, even, that she wanted
nothing more. For I could agree to that easy.
My big brother Luke? He meant nothing
more to me then than one of the cracked

old vessels back at the dairy: familiar once, now never used, and rarely thought of.

So I took her rough, warm hand and held it to my cheek — like you would hold a sea shell to your ear — and I promised her. It was the least I could do.

CHAPTER THREE

Somehow he must have heaved himself up through that hatchway, and taken the leap from the rocking, pitching deck of the tender. Then an endless, pell-mell climb up the ropes, and a sprawling fall on to the deck of the *Essex,* as the foot of the man swinging up behind him landed square in the small of his back. His arms and legs still shake. The ropes have burnt his palms and swollen his fingers. Men with sticks and pistols fix the cuffs back on their wrists and beat them into a sullen huddle. The tawny lad is his nearest companion and when he's not muttering to himself or poking at his bruises he's thwacking his head with his hand.

And so he stands, the noon sun pressing down like a hot iron, trying to catch his breath, and his balance.

He has never been on a ship of this size. What's a hoy or a tender, a barge even, next to this monster? But he don't take in the vastness of the deck, the height of the masts, the quantities of goods and the crowds as raucous as a marketplace on saint's day. He steadies himself, against the pitch and roll of the deck, and looks for escape.

The *Essex* is anchored far out in a steady swell. A broken-down old hulk lies close. Beyond and all around lie a great variety of vessels, big and small. But beyond them, the vastness of the salt waters. He watches as a stiff breeze whips up flinty waves, on and on they go. He cannot swim, never even tried.

He turns his head to the splash of the oars as the tender pulls away and there to the south now he can see land, a low hazy strip sloping down to a town, sprawled under a pall of smoke. There are many masts, and chimneys and a spire. His heart leaps. Is that St Nick's? And yes, he recognises the cries of the bumboat women, in the small boats that come and go to shore. They do nothing for no one unless it be for money. For a wild moment, he feels for his coin in the bag he had slung around his neck.

His hand clutches at nothing. It is gone.

The sickness rolls deep in his belly with every pitch of the deck. He has not drunk or eaten for hours. Touching his fingers to the pulpy lump at the base of his skull, they come away red.

When he opens his eyes again, all he can see above are ropes, dozens of them, thick and thin, stretching up into a deep blue sky like pillars. It's as though they are holding up the heavens. High up on the ropes bodies cling, and crawl up and down. He grows dizzy. The ropes twist and shimmer, wings sprout from the climbers' backs.

A voice bellows hard by. 'Damn your eyes, boys! Bring us a can of flip can't you?'

The burr is familiar. When he looks up, past the coin glinting on its thong, and meets the man's red-rimmed eyes, he jerks away, grazing his elbow. But it's too late.

'Boo,' breathes the man softly, and belches in his ear. 'You got anything to drink, Hotspur?'

He shakes his head.

Then there comes a scream, high and piercing, then suddenly muffled, from somewhere below deck. It awakes a deep, animal alarm within him. She screams again, and again. Now he cannot hide the trembling of his limbs, he jerks like some newborn calf. He shakes his head, his eye watering, his nose in his sleeve.

The man nudges his shoulder like a playful beast. 'Never mind her, Hotspur. Last boatload of cunt before we sail, I reckon. Lads'll be getting money's worth is all, by the sound of it. By Christ, even a pint of purl would set me right.' He prods him in the shoulder. 'Any baccy?'

The boy may have lost his coin but he knows he still has his unopened prick of tobacco hidden under his shirt: he can feel the rasp of its string slung over his shoulder, the bulk of it against his side. Does this man know it too? He has not missed the sly trading between men and officers, a kerchief for gin, a cap for baccy and beer, the trading — and taking. He well knows how little he has to bargain with. He has the cap still, he has the shirt and the trowsers, the belt. And her red kerchief, stained and torn perhaps but knotted about his neck still. But no shoes, no flask of gin or brandy, no coin. And no knife.

No, he cannot lose the tobacco, barely opened and such a prize, so early. He remembers the buying of it, his first, the triumph of it — and he wants to weep at his own keen foolishness. The woman below decks is sobbing now, on and on. And something of who he thought he was sounds like an echo inside him. He will not crumple now. He will face this out. He will be Hotspur.

He looks the man in the face and shakes his head again, more firmly this time.

The man's smile vanishes. 'Give it over.'

He does not move, does not look away, willing this moment gone, and himself invisible. When the short stubby blade flashes at his neck he jerks his chin up, panting. His throat closes as the knife presses into the knot of his kerchief, then pushes it aside, like a skewered dumpling. The man chuckles, and taps the blade against the top tie of his collar. When it rasps at the threads he loses his nerve and reaches frantically underneath his shirt. He yanks down hard. The string cuts painfully into his shoulder before it breaks. He holds out the tobacco without looking up, and only breathes again when the knife is taken from his throat.

'Generous soul, ain't you?'

Tight cuffed as he is, the man cuts the rope binding and offers the boy a hunk of his own baccy on the tip of his knife.

'Call me Nick,' he says, and smiles, his strong yellow teeth veined with brown. 'Pardon me. Nicholas Stavenger, if you please. Named for the saint in Berwick twenty-nine long year ago god help my blessed mother. How'd they get you? Come on, your name at least?'

He hawks on to the boards as the boy

mutters something.

'Eh? Come now, you speak like a mouse in a cheese. Your name.'

The boy buries his face in his hands.

'Tell you what, lads. I've trapped myself a pretty harvest mouse here, aye, and all his stores. What else you got?' Nick reaches out to rummage under the boy's shirt. 'Cheese maybe?'

But the boy is up and standing before he knows it. Ducks under an arm and out of reach. Black specks whirl before his eyes, and the deck feels soft as a bed beneath his bare feet. He is squealing, hears himself, turns even paler.

'Gad!' Nick leans back in mock alarm. 'The mouse squeaks!'

CHAPTER FOUR

Most folk as arrives at Harwich for the first time see it from the sea. First the long low lip of land, that has Walton to the south and Felixstowe to the north. And then — they clutch at a rail or a rope, or a hand — for their gaze has snagged on a snarl of masts, and look, that's the spire of St Nick's piercing through. They can make out the vessels that cluster round the navyard, and the sags of smoke from dozens of chimneys. And then the land splits in two right there and the channel opens up before them, the best and most commodious harbour in the land, full of warships and merchant ships, packets and riggers and numberless more unnameable vessels.

The harbour splits again, into the two rivers that carry the little boats and barges on up to Manningtree and to Ipswich. But these folks aren't planning on staying afloat a minute longer. No, they're gazing greedily at the near shore, at the boats drawn up and the nets spread before those fine merchants' houses with their widows' nests and glittering glass; they're listening out for the hammering in the yards and the yells from ship to shore, watching for a flash of skirt. And as the fort of Landguard swings round behind them and they settle into the bay they catch the reek of fish and tar and there is Harwich full square before them, huge and teeming and as beset by vessels as a woman feeding fowl.

Many is the time I've dreamt of coming upon Harwich so. Sailing home to the smell of land, into her most ample of harbours. But that weren't my Harwich, not that first time. No, little Lou snuck up her backside, as it were.

I was bundled off along the turnpike early in the morning, with the ruts as hard as iron, and jounced about in old Joe's cart like a load of frozen cabbage. After about an hour we came rattling along the ridge to Ramsey and my teeth rattling too, fit to fall out. I felt as sick as I imagined any seasick traveller would be, and it only got worse the closer we got. I kept my mother's best red shawl close about my mouth, but it smelt unpleasantly of her rickety box, and a little of lavender, not of her at all.

Old Joe grinned. 'You looks like a frorn little calf, girl. Here, let Old Joe give you a squeeze.'

And do you know, I let him. Old Joe, as stank like a bird's nest. But his eyes were kind and twinkling and I'd known him since I was a girl. And soon, I thought, I would be among strangers and no one to hold me then.

He tugged the shawl from my face. 'Now, my little Louise, look out there, and tell me what you sees.'

I looked. And if I close my eyes I can still see it now. The landlubber's view of Harwich. Wide flat fields falling away to a low spine of land, flanked by puzzles of salt marsh and mud flats that glisten like pocked pewter when the tide is out. A spit of land that turns its back on the sea, as though straining to meet the peninsula of Shotley, and choke off the flow of the estuary altogether. And there it is, at the very tip, that fans out like a fish tail to contain it. More houses than I'd ever seen in my blessed life, the solid smudged mass of Harwich. About it, a veritable thicket of bristling ships' masts, a-flicker with pennants. And scattered in the channel beyond, great numbers of vessels large and small, roaming and at anchor. The mass of them, trailing off to the west, like a flock of birds, a three-master in full sail leading the way.

The wind freshened, lifting my shawl; there were seagulls above, dozens of them, and with every creak of the Ramsey mill sails came my first lungfuls of sea air. Oh, the smell of it — fresh yet rank — how it stung my nostrils and roused my heart. It was mineral to my vegetable, as fertilising as seaweed spread on soil.

'Oh Joe,' I breathed, and clutched at his cape. 'That's Harwich?'

I was done for then, had I but known it. For as the sea mists rolled back I saw beyond the town and her harbour the great wide sea, water as vast as I had ever seen. Harwich now, that great port, was by contrast a mere blot, of green and brown, drowning in a silvery blue sea. How huge is the world, I thought. Where is its end? But wherever I looked, glittering sea merged into dazzling sky. I watched vessels diminish as they departed and then they would flicker, vanish, reappear: or was that another returning?

My head throbbed with the strain. It was the lack of boundary that stunned me. I had never seen water so wide, distance so unbounded. And my heart, quite frankly, leapt, even as my land-bred spirit quailed.

Joe chuckled to see my eyes widen so and my breath quicken.

'Here be life, girl!' he said, his eyes a-twinkle. 'Here be entertainment aplenty!'

But first there was the narrow bar of mud and gravel to cross. And stinking, black-veined estuary mud it was too: poking its fingers into the marsh, sucking at our wheels and making the clag that frilled my mother's boots look genteel as lace. We joined a sullen crowd of handcarts, waggons and riders jostling for passage over a wooden ramp at the town gate. Joe begged a light from a drayman and sat back to puff on his stinking pipe.

I looked up at the new tile roof of the gate-house, at the high stockade and the wide watery dyke. And now I grew alarmed, for I could see the waters bubbling and pressing through the grasses, to lap over the very foot of the ramp. 'Is Harwich an island, then?' I asked Joe. 'Will she be cut off?'

'What and sail away with you? Maybe, maybe,' he nodded soberly. 'No, Louise. Spring tide, she's on the rise.' Then he chuckled. 'Best watch your footing, girl. You'll be lifting your skirts here sooner'n you'd know it!'

I sat straight up then and stared ahead, clutching at my seat as the wheels slipped on the ramp, hearing only the screech of the gulls and the honking geese. And through the open gates we went.

I don't need to tell you what Harwich was in those days. What with the seamen and the shore women, the travellers and traders and chancers and no-hopers, how could she be otherwise? But born to it as you were, did you know how it took your young Louise?

Your town was as overwhelming to me as the vastness of the sea that surrounded it. Warehouses, three or even four storeys high, towered over me. The houses were rackety as a row of sties, for all that some had squeezed out a many-paned bow window here, or pinned on a pair of painted columns to frame a drunken doorway. And the smell of the place! Tar and fish and beer and far worse. I saw why Susie had scoffed so. Harwich was fine for the likes of her as could take it. I didn't belong here. Why had I not listened?

Yells and shrieks and the rumble of wheels echoed off the houses and across a stone-flagged marketplace wide as a field but choked with stalls. The people milled about Joe's cart, seeming not to know or care for each other, each intent on their own business.

And right there at my elbow went a pair of sturdy, well-weathered men, the strangest men I'd ever seen. I knew them for ocean-going seamen upon the instant. Their dress was quite as strange as I had been told: they wore not breeches but outlandish canvas trowsers that seemed indecent womanish to me — wide and flapping as skirts and reaching nigh to their ankles — and shocking short blue jackets that showed their arses. Each neck was knotted about with a jaunty kerchief, glaring, gypsy bright. Both wore thick woollen caps pulled down tight over their ears and out from under stuck long shiny cues all stiff as dog tails. And here came yet more of them, moving in a pack, who all shouted and called to each other in penetrating, alien tones. They sported their shore-going best, were scrubbed up dandy clean, yet I shrank from them as from a gang of beggars.

What repelled me the most that day was not their looks but their ways. They all of them had the Captain's rolling gait and his long staring eye. Stared at every woman who passed, their eyes pale in their rough dark faces, drinking all of her up — her walk, her hair, her figure, her face — as they bit on their short pipes and turned slowly to stare still long after she'd went. I did not want them to stare at me so, not never.

And then, what was worse, I saw strewn about the corners and begging among the crowds, the casualties of the oceans. The men the seas had sucked up and spat out, too wrecked to reach their own shores again. That old man there, bowling along on a crutch with his right foot quite gone, why — I realised of a sudden — he could have been my reckless, selfish father. And that young man, barely more than a boy, wandering alone and hugging his arm in a sling, his face sun-scorched and his eyes dazed: was he not yet another sea-loving fool like my brother? Theirs was the fate my mother had long feared for her men, to end stranded and broken on some foreign shore. Oh how my mother had wept, how she had wept herself dry.

But as I saw them now, for what they were, what they had become, I found my own heart hard as flint. I would keep my promise to my mother, I would, and I would ask after my brother as and when I could. But I had no longing to know his fate, not then. I felt no kinship for sea-loving men such as these, who had been so reckless with their own lives and the livelihoods of their families. I felt no pity, no curiosity even. Only revulsion. They were fools, all of them, and they were everywhere. A wrinkled old man bared his loosed teeth and wagged a crude wooden figurine in my face and I gasped with fright.

'Treat your little miss there, eh?' he leered at Joe.

Joe knocked out his pipe on the man's bald head and drove a path straight through the crowd and out of the marketplace. A wide paved thoroughfare now stretched a great distance to a hazy chink of sky. The air was chiller here, and we rode in the shadow of many-storeyed houses that leant out over our heads as if swelling with pride. Emblazoned on their plastered bellies were coats of arms, and dates, and animals formed in plaster as are pastry leaves on a pie.

I noticed one in particular: three huge plaster squirrels chasing each other's tails. 1675, it read, and below the motto 'in gode we truste'. The windows were dark with smoke and the air infused with strong beer. This must be a tars' tavern, I thought, one of those that had drawn my father so. A muscled brute of a man stood at the door, swinging a cudgel by his side. Quickly I looked away. And again there, on the huge painted sign hung low above his head: the Three Squirrels.

How strange, don't you think, that I should have noted that tavern — of all taverns — that very first day? There's a queer churning in my chest at the very thought of the place, even now.

Joe picked up speed, just keeping his wheels from spraying up muck from the kennel. Then we turned sharpish into a crooked side passage and halted outside a low doorway, lanterns ablaze either side. Joe ducked his head inside. I glimpsed a spreading puddle, on red and black chequered floor tiles.

'Yo, my bully boys!' yelled out Joe.

A stout fellow in undone breeches stumbled to the threshold. 'The gang's all in, Joe! Come on in, take your pick.'

'Have baggage to deliver, don't I?'

The man peered up at me and grinned. 'Well bless you, Mother Joe.' As he turned away he shouted back to Joe: 'You want 'em fresh, man, don't faddle about!'

We came out the other end of the alley and turned right but I did not look up again, until the wheels slowed to a halt.

'Here we be, Louise.'

I took the shawl from my head and straightened my cap. So this was West Street. It was wider still, yet more sheltered. Shouts and yells and bangs and rumbles echoed from the furthest end, where a barricade of hulls and rigging blocked the view. The houses there appeared staggering towers of sheer lapboard. But Joe stopped before we reached them, stopped where the fronts were plastered smooth, though none quite flush with its neighbours. He nodded towards one to our right.

It had the prettiest set of steps I could have imagined: five softly curving slabs of scrubbed pale stone escorted upwards in a quarter turn by a fine iron balustrade. I admired its door too, wide and shining black, with a large, polished knocker in the shape of a fat fish. A ruddy glow spilled from the skylight above. Either side of the door glinted two large sashes, both flanked by heavy shutters. Up I looked, and up: for there were three more storeys.

I could not have seen any of the attic windows from there, of course. But might I not have sensed something, even then? And if I had, would I have stared up so meekly, in such awe?

No, all I felt then was a fearful surge of reassurance, on finding that this elegant mansion was indeed Captain Handley's establishment. For it was the finest house I had seen, by far; and clean and well swept too.

Joe jumped down to set my small box before the steps. Two barred grilles were set in the paving either side of the steps, and I could see lights moving below. He rubbed his hands together, looking right and left. I got down slowly and went to stand by him, letting my bundle rest on the lowest step. I thanked him.

'I'll be off,' was all he said. 'You watch yourself, eh girl?'

He swung up into the cart and turned it around. Empty now, it rattled and bounced in and out of the gulley. Then he turned down the alley and was gone.

I had not thought to have come to the front of the house. I would have gone about and found the kitchen door but there was no break in the frontages I could see, no passage. So I went up those five fine steps and stood before the door. Should I knock? Must I announce myself? As I stood exposed on my stone pedestal, a periwigged gent marched past, gazing at me curiously. He was followed by a couple of drunken rolling fellows with trowsers at half mast, who joined arms on sight of me and redoubled their efforts to walk up the street, as though in a high wind.

I turned away to take up the tail of the great knocker. It fell with a loud dull thud.

As I waited, I gazed curiously after them. Then I gasped. For there was the sea coming up the street: the spreading waters darkening the stones and filling the gulley. It was not yet beyond the lapboarded houses but it was creeping closer as I watched. The spring tide rising, Joe had said. But surely the sea could not advance into the town itself? I grasped that great leering fish to knock again and again.

'What is it?' asked an uncommonly tall fellow who creaked open the door a tad and stood in its shadow.

I steadied myself. 'Louise Fletcher, sir, if it please you.' He looked at me blankly. 'Louise Fletcher, sir, come from Squire Handley, to serve the Mistress Rebecca Handley.'

'Serve? Mistress Rebecca?' he repeated in a mightily quizzical tone. He drew the door full open, to reveal yet more of his great length, and the total absence of an orb in his right eye socket.

I recovered my wits enough to nod, and pull a swift curtsey. He stared, snorted and beckoned me in.

Inside was dark and stifling hot. The air was thick with a heavy spice, like rotting stems and fresh nutmeg. It stung my eyes, and sent me into a fit of sneezes. When I recovered myself the fellow was gone; I was alone, in a long narrow hallway all panelled and painted a shiny black. At my feet were wide boards chequered black and red, like the tavern passageway. It seemed a hellish cavern, and flickered with a bloody light from somewhere towards the back. A clock ticked loud and fast.

I felt the blood drain from my head. What to do now? Then I remembered, with a lurch, that I had left my box in the street outside. Surely it would not be safe for long in this town. I set off to find someone, anyone, the boards creaking alarmingly under my feet, and walked hard into a low pile of crates. This was where the smell came from: as bitter as bay, but syrup sweet. The pain in my bruised shins made me sweat. And it was so hot, my numbed fingertips were swelling like chestnut buds. For here was the source of the heat. To the right of the stair, the passage widened to accommodate the biggest coal fire I'd ever seen. Framed by glowing white marble, it rumbled and burnt like a furnace, and set my apron fluttering.

I dropped my bundle to tug off my gloves and backed away to look up the wide stair. Firelight rushed up the walls to a large sash at the turn, set with panels of red and yellow glass. But above that, and all about, all was dim, and silent. Until I thought I could hear booming sounds below, and in my alarm feared it was the very ocean come to suck me away. Something shifted and rustled loudly inside a wicker cage hung up by the coloured window. Then a great clatter of boots came, from under my very skirts, it seemed. A jangling curtain to the left of the fireplace was pushed away to reveal a narrow stairway leading down, and there was the tall fellow again, charging up with a slopping bucket in his hand.

'You get her down here, Skeggs, and sharpish!' came a high, querulous female voice after him.

He did not pause, only muttered as he passed, 'Nels wants you,' and disappeared to the back of the house.

I went to the top of the cellar stair. A wave of chill air broke on me, thick with mud and mildew. There was a right old commotion down there, candles moving, agitated voices, wooden objects being dragged. I took a hold of the iron handrail. But before I had taken a step, a wide figure bustled up and blocked my way. Her cap was off and her mass of reddish hair dishevelled. This must be Nels.

'Louise?' she said, panting heavily. 'Thank

heavens. Well now, keep your pattens on and — no, no, take them off, you must fetch her down.'

'Fetch who?' I said stupidly.

'Why, Rebecca of course.'

'Miss Handley?'

'Yes, yes for all she's such a fine lady these days, we need her down here now. Where's Hester got to?'

And what a reception, I thought. But the poor woman was so obviously troubled and dismayed I found myself only wanting to reassure her.

'I am sorry,' I said hurriedly. 'I've not seen Hester. I've not seen no one. That man opened the door but my box is still in the street and —'

Nels uttered a little cry. 'I despair of the man, I do really. Come on. Come on!' she called again as she banged out the front door.

Together we hoisted my box up the steps and into the hall. A great mound of a woman she was, with a beaked nose and watery eye. The bottoms of her skirts were hitched up about her bare calves and dripped greenish water all down the steps. A quick glance at the spreading waters down the street, then she kicked the door shut behind her and nodded at the stair.

'Better get up there now, girl, and fetch her.'

So off I set up that crowded stair in a panic, only remembering to kick off my clogs on the third step. Before I reached the turn, Nels had tromped back down to the cellar without another word. All I could hear was the tick-tick-tick of the clock and the swoosh of the fire below. I felt myself to be the only person in that strange tall house. Dairy Lou would not have gone on, I'm sure. But here I was, alone in the world for the first time, and there was a sort of freedom to it. I felt the urgency of my task, that I was needed, and it gave me boldness too.

On the first landing I saw two doors, both closed. I must not delay, I said to myself, and went straight to one and turned the knob firmly. Here was a fine sort of with-drawing room. A large round polished table stood between the windows, there were curtains, sofas and mirrors. But it was quite empty. I went out and knocked on the other door. Nothing.

Up the stair I went again, steeled myself to knock on two more doors, and stay to listen. Nothing. I did not know what to do. I cursed myself for not asking Nels which was the right room. In the end I opened one door, only a crack. This was a gentle-man's bedroom, there was a coat on its stand and breeches on the bed. And a pistol, half wrapped in soft leather.

Up I went again. I paused for breath on the third landing, where the air was cooler and the ceiling lower. Clear bright light came in through a large sash at the back of the stairwell, picking out all the motes swirl-ing in the air. Here I could hear distinctly all the hammering, shouts, rumbles and sawing that had filled the streets. All I could see outside, though, was a jumble of brick walls and tiled roofs, chimneys and masts. And the sea, just a patch of it. I felt light-headed. The Squire's attics weren't near so high as this.

I was at the final landing, with no more stair to climb. There were two doors ahead. I chose the one on the left.

The door knob was warm, I remember, made of softly ribbed wood. Perhaps it was the warmth, a sense of it, that made me choose that door. This time I did not knock. I turned the handle slowly, the latch clicked, and the door fell open an inch or two. Inside it was dark, as dark as the hallway had first seemed. The shutters were drawn, the curtains too. Then I saw it was lit only by firelight, and a low, sunken fire it must have been, for the reddish light came and went. The air in there was heavy, but not with spice this time. It was thick, clogged with stale, syrupy, almost meaty odours. I listened, and I could hear breathing, slow and steady.

As the light spilt in from the landing, I saw the bed before me. I remember the quick gleam of silken bedhangings, and a stirring in the humped bedclothes. You made a little groan then, I think. So I pulled the door to, behind me, to shut out the light and the draught.

What was I thinking, sneaking into your room like that? Any lady's maid worth her salt would have rapped hard on the door, parroted Nels's request and stood back on the landing to tap her foot and wait. But I was scared and I was nervous, everything about your house was strange and alarming to me. Yet, yet: I shut myself in with you and breathed in your air, as though we were family.

Still, I knew I must speak, but no words came. You did not move again. I listened to you breathe, in and out. I breathed you in myself.

'Miss?' I ventured finally, and my voice came out cracked and dry. 'Mistress Handley?'

You shifted a little, gave a small cough.

'Please, miss,' I tried again, and louder. 'You are needed downstairs. They says it's urgent.'

I saw the plump outline of your bare arm against the firelight as you put your hand to your dark hair, which was loose.

'What on earth?'

Your voice was so thick and full, so merciless even in tone, that I quite lost my head again. But, of course, you did not know me, did you? You could not see me in the dim. I turned and tugged the door open for the light.

'Heavens now, what a draught.'

With every low, drawn-out, uncaring word, I grew more afraid. I had spoken barely a word, yet I had managed to offend from the very start. How would I make amends? My heart was pounding as I shut the door again and rested my burning forehead against it.

'Well, what is it?' you demanded. I had to force myself to turn and face you. All was dark beyond the gleam of the bedcurtains.

'Please, Nels says —'

I heard you sink back down and pull up the covers. 'Oh,' you said, slowly, carelessly, dismissively. 'Tell Nels to go to hell.'

■ ■ ■ ■

'Well?' demanded Nels. 'And what have you done with her?'

I looked down at the ripples about my skirts, for the cellar was inches deep in foul water. A lantern dangling from the brick barrel vaults lit the figures of a young girl and boy and that man Skeggs. All were wading about, furiously pulling out barrels and crates, sacks and boxes with curses and grunts.

I found I was trembling in my agitation. I could not say I had found you asleep, that I had shut myself in with you and stood there in the warm dark and listened to you breathing. I could not tell Nels how you had spoken, what you had said.

'Oh, can't I guess. Just hitch up them skirts and give us a hand.'

Nels tumbled a great package wrapped in sodden canvas into my unready arms and nodded to a whitewashed doorway behind the stairs. Here stone steps led to a higher space, already almost filled with goods. The Captain must indeed be rich, to own all this and such a fine house on top.

'Back cellar almost never floods, let's get it all in there.'

There was no time to think. I shed my stockings and tucked up my skirts and set right to again. Skeggs and the other two never stopped, nor spoke to me neither. So in I plunged. Back and forth we went after each other, taking everything that crowded the three large vaults and heaving them into the back room. After a time the five of us moved quickly and well together. I was happy to do it, too, happy not to have to puzzle my head about you, lying there in that dark, hot room.

After a while, when I was quite out of breath, a young woman came down the kitchen steps. She moved with authority, and her figure was taller than Nels's, and almost as broad, but neater and straighter. The lantern was behind her and I could not see her face. But my heart quickened. Was this you, come at last?

'Thank heavens you're here, miss!' cried Nels. 'There's one vault cleared, but lord she's coming up fast. I ain't never seen anything like it. What was they thinking? I don't know what's worse, it all being ruined or them finding out what's —'

The woman patted Nels's arm firmly. 'Don't worry. Father's on his way with some fellows from the *Dolphin*.'

I felt a queer sort of disappointment. Her

voice was low and firm, like yours, but it was not yours. It was duller somehow, flatter.

She ducked under the vault to look about. Her face was square and handsome, her complexion good. 'You've done well, you and Skeggs and Hannah, and —' She peered at me.

'Young Louise Fletcher, up from your uncle's, miss,' said Nels.

'You brought her down here?' She spoke sharply.

Nels bridled. 'Well, I asked her to fetch your sister, miss, but she never come. You see how we're fixed.'

She held Nels's gaze for a moment before turning to look me up and down. 'Your very first day and we might as well have sent you to sea, you're that soaked.' She was attempting a joke, I could tell, and I could see she meant it well, but it did not come off, she merely sounded abrupt. She smiled a stiff little smile and held out her hand. 'I'm Hester Handley,' she said. 'Rebecca's sister. We're very pleased to have you here, Louise.'

Hester pointed to various items she wanted Skeggs and the boy to take up and elsewhere. She sent Nels upstairs to get dinner started and then she hitched up her skirts and worked on in the cellar with myself and the girl she had called Hannah until the Captain came with three grunting seamen. They stank of drink, but they heaved and tossed the rest of the goods as though they were feather parcels wrapped in paper. I was glad to leave them when Hester bade Hannah and me up into the hallway, aching and tingling, my numb fingertips grateful now for the heat of that fire.

We stood close by the hearth to wipe off our feet and pull on our stockings. Hannah was small as I, wiry and quick. Not, I thought, one to be fooled for long. When she held out her bony hands to warm them she never looked at me once, but when she spoke she spoke kindly. 'Not a bad job, Louise,' she said, and she threw me a quick, crooked smile.

I smiled back, and held my hands out to the fire also. Her name was Hannah Sheperd, she said, the Handley housemaid of four years, Harwich born and bred. Yes, Hannah was civil enough, but her eyes were black and secretive. She didn't say much more to me, then or later.

She did tell me the other fellow what wasn't Thom Skeggs was young Billy Price. He looked straight through me when the pair of them rejoined us in the hallway. He

was short and jumpy, and I took him for a
bit of a dodger from the start; as he went
off to the kitchen ahead of me I saw he had
something in a cloth hanging out his pocket
I just knew he had swiped from below.

The kitchen was out the back and down a
couple of steps. How high and dark and narrow it seemed to me, who was used to the
Squire's straw-strewn kitchen, the door
always open to the yard and the fields. This
place smelt of damp and coal dust and fish.
But there was the fancy copper moulds
hung about and the dresser loaded with
dozens of fine china dishes. And a sugar
loaf, so whittled about it could have been a
piece of driftwood stood on end, but still
the tallest I had ever seen.

I sat down with Nels and Hannah across
from Skeggs and Billy to platefuls of
spatched eel and potatoes with persil and
small beer and very fine they was too, since
I was famished. No one paid me much attention: at first the talk was all of the tides.
Billy swore this was the highest spring tide
in the history of the world and Nels scoffed
and said her uncle remembered before the
West Street houses had storm cellars built
to take up much of the flood. When the
spring tides came back then, he said, he'd
see the rats float up and go to sea in old

piss pots.

They laughed, but it was all very strange to me, frightening even. How would it be, I wondered, to live so near the sea, to depend on it so? And then to feel it come at your very feet and fear that it might lift you and your life away?

'Now then, Louise,' said Nels, who had been watching my face a while. 'What do you say to Harwich?'

'It's very fine, ma'am,' I said as polite as I could. Billy spluttered.

'Tell me, Louise,' asked Hannah, all smiles, 'where was you afore Miss Rebecca? Who was your lady?'

I stiffened. Somehow I knew that if I told this wily girl the truth — that I was delivered here straight from the farm, with no experience at all — I would be at her mercy. I could not pull rank; I must at least prove myself above reproach, 'fore I let anything slip. She was watching me close. I was about to dissemble, allude to Lady Hargreaves at Lawford Hall, when Nels plonked down a boat of sauce between us and asked: 'Any family here, Lou?'

And so it was with a sense of relief that I found myself fulfilling my promise to my mother on my very first morning in Harwich.

'Not exactly,' I said. 'Perhaps.'

I sat up very straight, then, and told how Harwich was where first my father and then my brother had come away to, and where the last had been seen of the pair of them. I told how we knew my father must be long lost, in his grave for sure, watery or otherwise. But my brother had been so young — younger than myself now. He might live yet, we had hopes. So many years it had been, though, with no word, no news at all.

'My mother has charged me with finding out what I can, now I am here,' I explained. 'Only I don't know where to start.'

'Well now!' said Skeggs, who had been sawing away at his eel with elbows wide and head low — just like my mother used to do, for it was always her favourite dish. 'Well now!' he repeated, swallowing hard. 'If a body goes to sea, happen he don't want to be found no more.'

Nels tutted. 'Come now, this poor girl's mother —'

'Fair do, fair dos. Now!' he continued. 'That old water looks fair big enough to get lost in, don't it, girl? But it's a small world out there, that's a fact. I was a-roaming out there twenty year. I could ship with a lad out to Africy one spring, and then meet him on the stair in Calais three year later.

Course, after *he* went —' and he pointed one dirty finger at his empty right socket, as if he would ream it out.

Quickly, because I did not want to hear that particular tale, I said: 'Luke Fletcher was my brother's name, Mr Skeggs. Did you ever sail with a Luke Fletcher?'

'Young lad, you say?'

'Scarce fourteen when he went, and that must be six or seven year ago.' I was going to say, shortly before mother brought us to the farm, but stopped myself. Hannah was watching me steadily.

Nels had me describe him, best I could, and Skeggs thought a while, but in the end he sucked his teeth and shook his head.

'Well now,' he said. 'Boys come and boys go. But there's a place in every port a body can go and be sure of meeting any of the boys fresh in. And if a body's in Harwich, and he wants news of a tar, God damn him for a fool if he don't know where to go, directly!' He said this triumphantly, as if he had uttered an oracle.

There was a pause, while his one frightful eye stared so long and hard at me I trembled anew.

'Why,' he said refilling his cup. 'Many's the time I've sat there myself, telling the lads my tales. The time I nearly lost me port

78

eye, for instance. And the time I lost him on larboard side, of course. There was the tattooed piece I nearly married at the Cape. And the Dutch bitch what took seven year to shake off.' He chewed on his lip.

Billy burped, and asked him, all snide: 'Where is it then, Skeggers? This place?'

'Haven't I just said? Young Louise, you want to find your brother, you want to get yourself down Church Street, down the Three Squirrels, and sharpish. All the fresh boys ends up at the Three Squirrels. Anything you want to know, you just sit there a while, and you'll meet a man as can help you. Course, the wench there are biters —'

'Drink up!' ordered Nels, thrusting a full cup of beer under his nose. 'Don't you listen to him, Louise. You don't want to get within twenty feet of the Three Squirrels, or any of those places. You keep well away from the lot of them. Think of the family's reputation! No place for any sort of respectable girl, let alone a Handley girl. Tell you what, Louise, I'll see if I can't have a word with the Captain for you. Can't have your poor mother fretting herself sick, now can we?'

She refilled my plate, while Skeggs muttered on under his breath to a grinning Billy and Hannah gave me the wink. I realised I had passed muster, for now. The talk turned to the ships that were in, and one that was just announced to be built, for the new war against the Spanish. Skeggs brightened, and launched on a tale of an officer called Jenkin, what had his ear cut off, saying he was the cause of it all.

And all of a sudden, despite Skeggs, despite everything, I found myself smiling. I was very glad to be sitting there with them all, in my damp stockings, however odd it was. Oh yes, Susie, I thought, as the hot potatoes warmed my belly, I'll make a go of Harwich all right. Show that Hannah. I did wonder, though, what I might say to my mother of the Captain's household, with all its damp treasures and strange inhabitants. And my courage ebbed as I remembered you, lying upstairs in the dark. The shape of you in the bed. The sweet, close air. I knew I would not want to speak anything of you to mother, however curious she might be. Not even to Mary.

Then I remembered the butter jars, that I had left in my bundle in the hall. But before I had the knot half undone I knew them spoilt. The heat from the fire had melted most all the butter to a scummed, oily liquid, the jars were almost empty and what was worse, half my garments stained and rancid. Billy sniggered, poking at them with his foot, and Hannah stared primly. Oh what a waste, said Nels with a grimace, what a shame now.

CHAPTER FIVE

'Look lively, boy.'

Nick prods him awake. He is chilled and lying in shadow, for the sun is going and the wind has picked up. The men were given the cans of purl Nick called so loudly for, but while it cheered the others, him it dazed still more, and finally sent to sleep. Now, as he struggles to sit up, he recalls seeing the women leave, half a dozen or so, seeing the blood on their legs as they were helped over the side. Hearing the men about him whistle and holler. He tries not to think too hard about Nick's rapt face as he told them all the hoary tale, of the scut he and his shipmates hid in a closet until they sailed with the tide, how they'd kept her there all the way to Brazil until she could fuck no more and they sent her over the side before the Captain ever knew.

Nick cups his hands to his mouth, singing out: *'Cheerily lads, cheerily, there's a muster-*

man hard to windward.'

The main deck swarms with men and stores and animals still but, beyond them, an officer stands alone, on a higher deck. The setting sun is full on him. He looks like a manikin: smooth dark hair tied back and a trim beard, a narrow figure in a blue coat and white breeches. This must be a very superior sort of officer, thinks the boy. Alongside the working crew, the dozens of tars who roam the decks and rigging with their rampant beards and ravaged complexions, their long roving gaze and thick muscled limbs, he might be a doll, a china puppet. The boy watches him make a turn about, bend neatly from the hip, and nip shut a pair of low doors at his back. Straightening up, the man shields his eyes to look about.

'Who is he?'

'Lord you are a field mouse ain't you? It's the surgeon's mate, one of 'em. Keep your eyes open. He came on late, like us. Fancy, ain't he? Not too fancy to douse our cods though.' Nick feigns a grab for the boy's privates.

Someone turns about and hisses back at them. 'Calls himself Gilles de Clare, they say.'

'A Frenchie?' splutters another.

'Ha! Jill, meet Jack Nasty Face!' leers Nick.

'Sam here says he's a Jersey fellow.'

'Damned Jack in an office is what he is.'

The boy strains to catch a glimpse of this puppet. He looks benign enough, tranquil even, like the ancient knights clapped out on stone tombs. And, for all the floating sawdust and flying feathers, he is very clean, as though come straight from his gentleman's closet. He takes several steps up the stair right by them, rests his hand on the rail and looks down upon them all. The gleaming whiteness of his necktie, tied neatly in three equal folds, draws the boy's eye. Above this his complexion is dark but smooth, like brown soap. His eyes are black and steady and unsmiling.

'What are we in church, fellow? Get to it!' yells Nick and several men turn and laugh. 'Give us the sermon, man!' Nick folds his palms together and bows his head. He sneaks a look about, grinning. He has become the joker of the pack.

Neat little Gilles de Clare ignores Nick. When he has seen enough, he orders them to be given another can of flip each, and goes to stand behind a tall barrel beneath the main mast, facing the huddle of pressed men. A frail boy brings him an inkwell and quills and he places them on top of the barrel. Then he takes possession of a new leather-bound ledger, finds a page, and lays it down open. His boy is tiny: must reach up on tiptoe to press back the pages when the wind threatens to take them, his pinched face expressionless. His master starts to speak but his words are blown away and lost in the hubbub.

'What's he saying?'

'He's saying you must choose.'

He has to ask. 'Choose what?'

Nick turns in surprise. 'Choose what, jingle brains? Why, choose whether to sell your soul or give it to them.'

They catch a snatch of the speech '— I would ask you to think of your country and join us of your own free will.'

'Free will!' scoffs Nick.

De Clare nods to the tar who guards them. The tar pushes forward a bent old man dwarfed by his huge yellow beard, shirtless and shivering. Stepping up on to the stair, the boy clings to the rail so he can look over the heads of the others. The old man drops to his knees.

'Sir, I beg you.' His voice is high and keening. 'I have more than fifty summers and shall not last one more if you keep me aboard this vessel.'

'This will not do,' orders de Clare. 'Stand please.'

The tar cuts at the old man's exposed soles with his starting stick and he hops to his feet.

'You think we can do without you? Here, take this rope.'

The old man grasps it. When it is tugged away he staggers and nearly falls but does not lose his grip.

'Dirty bastard,' mutters Nick. 'Had enough practice holding his pecker.'

De Clare asks the old man his name, then: 'You will volunteer, Simon Wivens?'

He mutters and wails and seems not to hear.

'Very well. You may be old but you can grip a rope and we need every hand we can get. You'll join the waisters. Make your mark here.'

And so it goes on. Nick has turned his attention to the other pressed men. He gives one a nod, stares another out, exchanges a few words with another. He jiggles on his toes, scanning the crowd. The tip of his tongue flicks in and out, like a lizard's.

But the boy is watching de Clare now. Four, six, ten men are inspected and all pass muster. De Clare comes forward, converses a while, then orders a shirt removed or a smock lifted. He squats with his back against the barrel to wait while a man drops his trowsers and the others halloo. Once he takes out his handkerchief, wipes his hands and shakes his head. The man is led away.

What makes him reject a man? What happens to him then? 'Too poxed, too old,' Nick tells him. 'Should get sent back to the poorhouse, or the clink. Near all end up stopping here, though. Navy needs its numbers, see? Don't worry. Young monkey like you. Take the money. You'll want to be in funds if's we get another boat load of cunt before we sail. No? Suit yourself. Any roads, yon bint'll be glad to have you back with a jingling pocket, she will.'

'I cannot do it.' He has spoken aloud.

'Bah!' says Nick. 'Turn down all the drink you can neck? And the bounty? This is the life, lad. We may take a prize, whip some greezers, dock their wenches, and some. Whisht! And what else would you be doing?'

'I cannot be here.' His voice trembles.

'And don't I wish I was back doing the jig with my lass? Don't we all, lad. Harwich has the finest nest of whores on the whole east coast, I'll say that for it. But we're here now. None of us true tars is getting off. Best take what you can, while you can.' Nick's tone turns quite fatherly. 'Ah, it's that lassie, ain't it? Damn, if she won't wait, I'll buy ye another meself.'

He cannot answer.

'Hell's teeth I'll buy ye two. Hey now, come along. Don't go all soft on me. Old Nick'll look after youse lad. You can mess with me, eh? We'll hope for some sturdy lads. And for a joker, and a butt. A happy butt will cheer the hardest day. But not every mess has itself a pocket mouse, do it?' And he squeezes the boy's shoulders till they crack.

A tall man in a bloody smock is shouting into de Clare's face. A butcher, perhaps, for he still bears a link of sausage about his neck that whirls about as he appeals to the men watching, spreads his arms wide, sags at the knees. 'Tell me they cannot do this, lads. We are not cattle, to be herded so.'

He spots the boy, sees something in his face and comes up close, takes a deep, shuddering breath before he speaks. 'Halfways up East Hill, the bastards took me. Look here, she said, our Samuel, only five weeks old. They laughed in her face.'

The boy stares at his wild eyes, his wet red lips. This man is as scared as I am, he sees, as lost as I am. For all his brawny shoulders, that strain at the seams of his smock, the reach of his big droning voice.

The butcher's face creases up with despair. 'She will starve without me, they will be turned out.'

A young lad at the boy's side jabs him in the ribs and whinnies with amusement, his gummed eyes half closed like a sick rabbit.

An officer has the butcher by the wrist and is speaking loudly and firmly into his face. 'Powell. Powell! Listen to me. Volunteer, and you can send the bounty home directly. There is a Jew about someplace.'

Powell's face shines with tears, but he is shaking with anger. He twists and turns away, yells back: 'Keep your damned dirty money. You have no right. No right!'

'Take the damn bounty you sad put,' a man spits on the deck. It is disgust, at Powell's naked need and sorrow.

'We only christened the boy two week since,' Powell intones, as though he hasn't heard. 'At St James.' He wipes his nose and then he spits at the officer's feet. 'I will rot in hell first,' he says deliberately. 'And god damn your hide.'

The officer brings his stick down across Powell's neck.

'Daft bastard,' says Nick.

When it comes Nick's turn he swaggers forward and leans on the barrel, staring into de Clare's face. The barrel tilts and de

89

Clare's boy makes a grab for the inkwell.

'Able top-man Nicholas Stavenger,' he proclaims. 'Old Nick, born of Berwick, schooled in the colliers, steeled in every manner of vessel, familiar with all the oceans of the globe and at your service.' He pauses before adding, 'Sir.'

De Clare stands steady.

'I am glad to hear it. You will join us?'

Nick looks to the men now turned volunteers, and being handed their pay.

'Took pity on ye lads, didn't I? Couldn't leave you all now, for sure.'

De Clare nods slowly, noting Nick's trembling jaw and reddened eye, taking all in.

And soon, too soon, it is the boy's turn. He can barely breathe now, surrounded by so many grown men, the reek of them, their hard eyes upon him, watching. He walks before the barrel and only then lifts his head, pleading silently. De Clare is a little taller than he. But he is bent over his book.

'Your name?' Now the muster man looks up. His eye is dark and fathomless, it makes the boy warm and wary at once. Afterwards, when he runs this moment through his mind, again and again, he will swear that look said: I know you, I know you through and through, I know who you are. And I knew from the moment I spotted you huddled at the back of the crowd, down the side of the stair, right under my feet.

But all the man says is: 'Come now. Your name please?' His tone is light but he's not smiling.

The boy finds himself helpless before that steady gaze. De Clare has a mole, just above his left eyebrow, it is perfectly round. He notes the fine lines around his eyes. A strand of his hair has blown free and the boy watches it stray across his cheek. This is the moment. He can speak the truth. Now.

'What's that?' asks de Clare. 'Luke, you say?'

The boy searches the man's face for the right answer.

'Luke what, boy?' De Clare waits, and watches.

Eventually the boy cannot help himself. 'Fletcher,' he says. His heart is plummeting, like a stone in water. 'My name is Fletcher. But sir, I —'

'Luke Fletcher,' repeats de Clare. 'Your age?'

This time the answer comes easy enough. 'Fifteen, sir.'

The pen scratches.

'Sir, please, forgive me, sir, you are mistaken —'

De Clare pauses. 'Mistaken? I think not.' He raises his voice: 'Luke Fletcher, welcome to the *Essex.*'

The boy takes a gasping breath. The moment, this was the moment, and it is gone. And over and over for years to come, he will ask himself: why did I not tell the truth? Was it fear? Surely fear might be forgiven. He will remember how young he was, how foolhardy. How very little he knew of the life. Of himself. To begin with he tells himself it was that man, de Clare, his deep dark eye upon him. Made him lose himself, throw himself away. Some nights he may even admit to having even as he said it a sort of longing — to follow, to know, to be sure. One day, he will understand only too well. But now, as his knees dissolve beneath him, he cannot tell what he has done, let alone why.

De Clare points his quill at Luke and, drawing it up and down in long strokes, says to the tar at his side: 'The boy comes with a fine set of sailor's slops. We are in luck!'

And he looks at Luke, and smiles.

CHAPTER SIX

It was seagulls woke me. Opened my eyes, there they were, moaning oh, oh, oh at each other, and squawking and swooping right at the window with their great hooked beaks. The sky was lurid with dawn and the air filled with the clamour and rumble of the port — the cries and bells and shrieks and crashes that I had heard all night long and thought would never let me sleep. Yes, I was up at Harwich all right.

Hannah snored on in the bunk below mine. I'd never slept up so high before. I wasn't sure how I'd get down again. My feet were heavy with cold but oh the fluttering in my chest. For that very first morning, as it was to be every morning thereafter, I found my first thought was of you. That morning it came with a pang of shame, fear even. What was I to make of my new mistress? You had been sleeping past noon, you had dismissed me on sight, and I had not seen you since. Yet all the household did not seem to think it in the slightest strange you had not roused yourself to inspect your new maid.

I hid my disappointment and dismay from myself, and I felt myself merely affronted. Did you do nothing but lie a-bed? Was I to tend an invalid? A cross, no, a *rude* invalid? I saw myself at your beck and call, with never a kind word. 'Ladies change their dress regular,' Susie had told me with relish. 'You'll be at her laces till your fingers bleed.' Well, I would work hard, I told myself, I would do my duty; for I was not about to give up, to go back to the farm to face Susie and Sam and all the rest of them. I had my pride. But if you were to behave so always? Then, I thought, well then, fine clothes, fine ways, were all very well, but I would learn what I could from you and move on. And so I dressed, and would not let myself think of home either.

I'd asked Hester after supper when I was to meet you proper and start my work, but she'd only looked at Nels and said with a sigh: 'When indeed?' Nels tutted.

'My sister,' started Hester carefully. She paused. 'My sister is accustomed to sleep late, and so you will find, most mornings, you must occupy yourself with other things

94

until she wakes. Take up any mending with you when you go to bed, you can bring it down here in the mornings.'

This didn't answer my question, but Hester talked me through my duties, which took quite a while as she didn't like to leave nothing out, even had me sign a paper against the small pox, saying I would leave straight off if ever I got it. It was late by then, and we all grew sleepy by the kitchen fire after our exertions in the cellar, and Nels rubbing at her back and making little sighs.

Then Hannah brought me up here, Skeggs staggering behind with my box. We came all the way up the main stair — I only realised after, this was on account of the box — and when Hannah paused by your closed door I thought for one dizzy moment that I was to sleep there with you. But she opened what looked like a cupboard door in the panelling and there inside was a fantastically steep and worn wooden stair, narrow as a ladder, but curved like a barley twist around the bare brick of the chimney and up into the attic. Skeggs rolled his eyes and cursed.

'Get on up there,' Hannah said to him, slapping his arse like he was a donkey. She turned to me. 'This ain't nothing. There's tunnels here you'd have to be a rat to

95

squeeze through.'

'Tunnels?' I said wonderingly.

'Tunnels. From house to house, from shore to cellar. Famous for 'em, Harwich is. Half the attics connect too. Smuggling, rendeyvoos, all the hush-hush stuff,' she giggled. 'Where you been?'

At the top the stair split into a pair of even narrower steps that served two low doors either side of the chimney. I was to sleep together with Nels and Hannah in one attic, Skeggs and Billy in the other. Hannah unlatched the door to the right and there was a pair of servants' bunks, with straw pallets and woollen blankets atop and pot beneath, and a table with jug and ewer under the small, high window.

It was back down this secret stair that I followed Hannah early that first morning, all the way down to the kitchen, for it twisted on down the sides of the flues, past all four floors, with a little hidden door on each. Hannah slipped down almost silent. I, though, had never known anything like it, and staggered, near slipped, in my haste.

'Take it easy, girl,' she called back to me, 'they won't want to hear you clattering about. You can hear your neighbour pick his nose in a Harwich house.' I slowed right down then, stopped, and put one hand out to the brick of the chimney, the other to the panelling. And yes, I could hear a myriad tiny noises, all of the life of the house. Someone humming, quite close. A teaspoon knock distantly against china, boots clamping on floorboards below. I listened on. Perhaps you were just there, on the other side of that wooden wall, sleeping still? I was suddenly aware of the grain of the wood against my bare palm. Carefully, quietly, I felt my way down, until out we came by the hearth in the hall, now dead and cold, and went into the kitchen.

Here were Nels and Skeggs and Billy all busy about their doings. And despite my resolve to try my best and learn, I was uncomfortable all over again and did not know what to do with myself, and was grateful when Nels told me to set myself down on the stool to watch the griddle. When Hester came in I started to my feet.

She looked pale and overworked, I thought, as she thanked me again for my efforts yesterday. I didn't know how to speak back to her. I'd never met someone so formal. And her manner was almost as gruff as her father's. I recalled the Squire's wife singing about the kitchen, taking up someone's baby and laughing at Sam's cheek. These are but town manners, I told myself,

I shall have to get used to them. And I could not dislike Hester, for she seemed awkward in her own way, and to be doing her best to settle me.

'We wage a constant battle against the salty element here, I'm afraid,' she said wryly as she took up the kettle. 'I do wish, sometimes, we lived out of town. You never know where the water's coming out next here. These houses are perishing damp, down below is quite honeycombed with tunnels and vaults.'

Hannah gave me a knowing look as Nels nodded emphatically, and I made some polite reply.

'Hope you don't suffer with the rheumatics, Louise, dear,' said Nels, her chest shifting like a sack as she sat herself down to sift flour. ''Cos you'll get it bad here, you will.'

I stayed in the kitchen most of the morning, for as long as Hannah worked upstairs Nels seemed to want my company. I had almost forgotten there was any more to the household than that dark narrow kitchen and was helping her take down one of the large moulds when I heard a light slapping step in the hall, as of bare feet. And then I heard your voice, rich and slow. You called out, in a penetrating tone: 'Why has this fire been let out?'

I froze. But Nels took the mould from my hands unperturbed. 'Hester never likes that hall fire lit,' she said. 'Never likes no fire lit at all, 'cept when the Captain's home. Just tell her Hannah will do it later and let's hope Hester will be back by then to stop her.'

I straightened my apron and cap, nervous all over again.

'Go on,' said Nels. 'Hope she's dressed.'

I will face you, I said to myself, I will not be afraid. For indeed I was afraid then. Afraid of what you might say, what you might see, in this little country maid come to help you play the fine lady. Never had I felt my ignorance, the smallness of my life, more keenly. I straightened my cap and apron and made my way to the hall door.

At first I saw only the shape of you. You stood with one hand on the newel post and the other on your hip. The yellowed light from the sash at the turn of the stair coated you in a glow as of summer sunlight. Then I saw your dress, and that struck me as most strange. For you wore only a pale morning wrapper, the like of which I'd never seen, with wide bunched and ruffled sleeves, cut low under the lightest of collars. Your hair was up somehow, but you wore no cap. You wore no shoes, or slippers even, as if you had come straight from your bed.

But how stately you stood, with what poise. Despite your undress I thought you the very picture of a lady. A gentlewoman discovered at home, I thought, and wondered where the phrase had come from.

Yes, you are Hester's sister, I remember thinking. You are of a height, your build similar. But poor Hester's made of solid stuff, rough hewn like a block of soap. I could see now why the midshipman had favoured you. You're as the same soap well handled, all soft curves and melting lines, made to be grasped tight in the hand lest you slip away. I followed the lines of your neck and shoulder and waist, over and over, and they seemed perfect to me.

I could not look at your face. I fumbled a quick curtsey, and waited, my face lowered, my cheeks burning.

'Hannah!' you said impatiently, and I heard the Captain in your voice as I had in Hester's, the easy command, the certainty. 'For heaven's sake.'

I realised then, as I stood on the kitchen threshold, that I must show myself. And the thought also came that perhaps you had mistaken me for Hannah last night also? And that had been the reason for your coldness? I came forward into the light, my movement stirring up the ash still in the hearth. Up you stepped quite close and you looked down into my face, stern as a judge. I worried you would catch the whiff of rancid butter off my skirts. The light was behind you, your features indistinct, and all I saw were your dark eyes, huge and un-blinking.

'Who are you?'

I swallowed. 'I'm Louise Fletcher, miss, from the Squire's.'

'It was you who —'

I nodded.

You frowned, pulling your wrap tighter, and took a step back. I saw your face was pale, sallow even. Your forehead high, and your features large but regular. 'Hester!' you called loudly up the stair. 'Hester! Is this the girl?'

Then Hester was there behind me, with her marketing basket on her arm, her damp hood still up. 'What is it?' she said evenly. But I could tell she was annoyed.

'Is this what I asked for?' you demanded, as if I were a dish you had ordered at an inn.

'Father will be back for dinner, you can talk to him then.' Hester went back into the kitchen and set her basket down on the table.

You stared after her a moment, then you took my shoulder and turned me briskly about.

'Let me look at you.'

I could see now your gown was primrose yellow silk, it rustled as you moved, and off it came sweat, and cloves, and oranges. Your smell.

'You've never been off my uncle's farm before, have you?'

I could make no reply.

'No, no of course she hasn't, look at her,' you said, as though all your lady friends were there, to laugh and whisper about me.

I flushed at that.

Hester came and stood beside me. 'Aunt Charlotte recommended her highly, said she was just what you require. And I think she will suit us very well. I am going down to the *Dolphin.* I shall be back well in time for dinner.'

Sleety flakes of snow swirled in the front door as she closed it behind her.

You laughed then, a great guffaw that made me jump, and that was not at all lady-like. 'Wait till I see my father. The old nigmenog.'

You looked hard at me again. Then you

took up my hand to squeeze it between yours, and all I could think was how soft and unworked your hands were, how small and warm and plump. Then you pulled me close, so suddenly I gasped, and your brown eyes flashed with amusement. 'We'll show him though, won't we, Lou?'

CHAPTER SEVEN

'Take it, Fletcher.'

Luke hears the officer, but he can't respond, or even look up. The officer cuffs him over the head with one hand and holds the coins out in the other. If he takes the bounty, he will hold in his hand more money than he could earn ashore in several year. And when he's paid off, even more, enough to set them up. But until then he will be a paid-up tar, bound to serve on His Majesty's ship and with all His Majesty's officers, for as long as they damn choose. And if he don't like the life, if he can't take it? If he runs, they will look for him. And if they catch him, they will string him up and what will his riches be worth then?

If he refuses, they will not let him leave. He has been passed fit. Welcomed even. If he refuses, he will have nothing to bargain with when they sail. What sort of life will that be? Even after one day he knows he would not survive. And if he cannot take it, if he jumps ship, he will die penniless for they will hang him anyway. But his brain is like a frozen pond, even these thoughts barely stir beneath its surface. He has no future, no past.

'Sblood.' The officer finally loses patience, and tips the coins at his feet. Luke watches them chime and spin off the caulking. Straight off those around him clutch and dive, like birds after grain. Watching the mêlée of cloth and flesh, hearing the bitter curses, some instinct kicks in and sends him down on his knees too, scrambling and fumbling. If he is to survive at all he needs that money. He is elbowed hard in the eye, kicked in the stomach, trampled on the shin, before a strong grip hauls him up and out and Nick has him by the shoulder. The officer bends over the scrum of bodies, yelling and shoving and kicking and tugging at his sword in its scabbard.

'Whisht, lads, come now!' Nick croons like he's coaxing pigeons, but they all see the set of his jaw. The deck clears before him. Four coins lie scattered upon it.

'Take the damn coins, lad, take 'em!' pants the officer.

Breathing hard, he bends to pick them up. His heart is pounding frantic, he wants to yell out now, for yes, Luke lives inside him after all. Throbbing in his veins, he feels him. His brain works furiously. He will survive this. Better than that. He will hoard this money, bargain with it, gamble with it, double and triple it. And if they take a prize he will have a share of that too, and his wages on top, and then what a figure he will make, by god.

One, two, three and four. Where is the fifth? He needs every one. He folds his fingers over the metal discs in his palm, feeling them warm in his hand like living things, and scans the deck hungrily, tracing every caulked line. Where is it, the last coin? Now he knows how he needs it he must, must have it.

'My last coin?' Luke finds voice at last. 'Who has it?'

Nick's great bulk looms by his side. Nick, with his own glinting disc about his neck, which Luke now sees is not a coin at all but a sort of polished shell, shaped very like a heart, that gleams and glistens and swells out at its centre. But Nick is looking beyond him. He is staring out the little old man with the long beard, Simon Wivens.

'Dear souls, I'm sure I don't know! Lord, I was shoved about so, an old man like me, and what with this weeping eye I can scarce see my own hand —'

The old man chatters on. Nick says nothing, just waits. Eventually, ducking his head like a gobbling turkey, the old man holds out a trembling hand. It is the last coin. Nick takes it, tosses it in the air and slips it into his own pouch. He grins at Luke. 'I were right, laddie, you are a generous soul.' And off he walks.

Luke knows there is nothing he can do. Nothing at all. His four pieces of metal grow hot in his fist as he watches how the other men disappear their coins: into jacket pockets, soft drawstring bags looped back over necks and tucked out of sight. But he has no pockets, no pouch. No shoe, even, to slip the coins inside. A short and nastily pocked man with a close-cropped head moves in front of him, whistling softly, tries to catch his eye. Those powerful hands could squeeze his bounty from his shrew's paw as easy as shucking a beech nut.

'Hey, pretty laddie.'

Luke holds his gaze, keeps his mouth firm, his jaw steady.

'Daddy gone away, has he?' He closes in, sucks his teeth.

Luke shrinks back, and back, hard up against the bulwarks. The man puts out one foot. At last, desperate, Luke twists away.

The deck is so crowded it is hard to move fast. There must be hundreds of men aboard. The stench of their sweat overwhelms him, rank cat piss and wild onion. When he knocks his hand against a spar he almost loses the coins. Frantically he untucks one of the front tails of his shirt, ties the four coins into it and tries to tuck it inside his trowsers. It makes a small bulge. After a moment's thought, he reaches down and pulls the knot back out again. He ties a second knot around the first. Then he pushes the knotted shirt-tail down below his belt once more, right into his groin. And looks about again, sweating.

Thanks to Nick he now has four of his five coin. Thanks to Nick he is still missing the fifth. And now, thanks also to Nick, he knows himself set apart. The action has been noted, a contract made apparent. What this contract may be exactly he does not know. But he feels marked.

CHAPTER EIGHT

Those early days and weeks in February and into March, as the weather thawed and the sea brightened. I want to remember how it felt. I need to know: when did it start?

Was it that very first morning, when you took me back to your room, saying it was too cold and damp for anyone but tars and whores to walk out? When you led me by the hand into your fuggy darkness, thick with the night pot and stale bed linen? But I hung back this time, hating the closing of the door behind me. I could not breathe. I released my hand from yours and went straight to tear open the curtains and unhitch the shutters and turn down the bed. For I did not understand you. I did not like you at all. I wanted to be away. I wanted to fling the window open, to let in some morning air, to see Ramsey and its windmill and the hills beyond. There was just the tall house across the street, all dark inside.

When I turned about, you were sitting quietly on a low chair by the hearth. As the chill air flowed in and the curtains swayed, I realised how forward I had been. I readied myself for more harsh words. Your expression was sceptical now and cool, your fine eyebrows slightly raised.

'Well now, Lou,' was all you said.

It was Lou from the start with you, wasn't it? Never Louise. You made over my name, turned Louise into Lou, without asking or pausing. New minted and yours from the start.

I wasn't to know you'd never had a maid of your own before me. I thought you commanded me as you always had and I had better watch I did right. So I made sure to do everything you asked from the very beginning. You sent me down to fetch up some of Nels's little cakes as you had not breakfasted. I took six still warm and turned back to ask Nels for a clean warm cloth to wrap them in. 'Louise, watch that —' she started to say, then thought better of it. I stood as you ate and when you let the cloth slip from your lap I picked it up and I picked up your crumbs from the carpet with my fingertips and threw them in the grate.

You had me fetch Hannah to set a new fire in your room and I watched her closely, for this was to be one of my tasks, to keep your fire going. I had never set a coal fire before, never seen one before yesterday, and thought you most extravagant for having one of your very own, and for no special occasion I could tell. But how the heat came off it, how hard and bright the flames. I knew my face was reddening and put the backs of my paddle hands to my cheeks to cool them. What with being nervous and all the to-ing and fro-ing I was as heated as a haymaker.

'Let me see how you work, Lou,' you said, as you tugged a low padded stool to you with one foot and, setting both feet atop, pointed your toes at the flames. I saw then your feet were not bare at all. You wore fine white stockings, soiled about the sole, and clocked red all up as far as your knees, which I thought very daring. 'Go on. Set the place straight, as a lady's room should be.'

Of course you had no more idea than I how a lady's room should be, did you? But I did know that no Christian, self-respecting woman, whatever her rank, would let her room fall into such disarray. The back of the spindly chair by your bed was piled high with discarded chemises. Odd slippers, trodden down at the heel, peeped from under the bed. Your table mirrors were dimmed with powder, the turkey carpets stained brown where a tiny cup and saucer lay overturned between the windows. And there were gnarled old nosegays, roses and carnations, pinned drooping all over the chimney breast. A dozen at least. Petals came away as the updraft of the fire caught them. How many dances had you attended? No wonder you slept late.

This family has too much than is good for it, I remember thinking often in those early days, every time some strange-smelling package appeared on the stair or on the parlour table, half opened then left there for days for the kitten to tear at. And there was my mother, all that she had brought to your uncle's farm was in that one box she had pressed on me. What had she got since, in all these years, perhaps a new comb, or some stockings for church? Her best shawl, a parting gift against the damp Harwich air, had only been in the Handley household a few hours before it was ruined.

I did not remind myself that it was I who had left it there with the butter by the fire. No, I blamed you Handleys all. It was true, what she'd always said about sea folk. It's all easy come, easy go with them. They treat their possessions like something the tide washed up, and could take away again at the turn of the moon. Watch they don't treat you the same, Louise.

I straightened my shoulders, conscious all the time of your eyes on me as I went about the room, bending to pick up and set straight, fold and tidy. I blush now to think how fierce I disapproved of you, who had so much, but was so careless. Yet I must own myself awed, too. The sun-yellow silks about your bed glistened. The smooth linen of your sheets flowed heavy in my hands. Three tiny flowers, of wire-thread and deep violet yarn, fallen from some head dressing and crushed underfoot, I nestled in my palm as if they were my own. In taking up a white kid glove and looking about for its partner I spilt a fine powder from the cuff, that gave off a heavy, stunning scent. I breathed deep. I made the pair and then I stroked them once, twice, just to feel the softness of the kid, before I closed them in a drawer. I was startled, as if from a dream, when you spoke, in that drawling, mocking tone.

'Do wake up, Miss Fletcher. I see I were right. I'll warrant you've never set foot in civilisation before this week.'

Immediately I bridled. 'Indeed I have. I was born down at Manningtree, miss. And I have been to Wix.'

You did not have to reply. We both knew Wix to be a mere half-dozen miles from Harwich.

'Before I was eleven I had been to the Low Countries most every other week, and to France and Spain. Have you no spirit of adventure?'

'Yes I do, miss. That is why I am come here.'

'Here?' you snorted. 'Harwich? The arse of Essex?'

I turned away, quite shocked. As I picked my way about, you wriggled your toes before the fire and asked me questions. Endless questions. How old was I? Why did I look so much younger? You knew me not to be a true maid on the instant. So what work had I done? Heavens, how unpleasant. But did not dairymaids grow plump on cream? What did a cow's teat feel like? Where was I born? Why had I not been back? Who were my family? Did I have a sister? Was she as tiresome as hers?

I kept my eyes on my tasks, answered as best I could, but you were staring full at me, smiling and nodding now as though you thought my small life the most fascinating tale you had ever heard. I couldn't look at you.

Did every mistress question her new

servant so? Back at the farm I could have been a three-legged stool for all anyone ever asked of me. I'd never got the habit of talking of myself at any length, or at all. Though I tried my best I felt my answers to be abrupt, my manner even more rigid than Hester's had been. You listened so hard, too hard, your eyes never leaving my face. It made me tremble. I stumbled over my replies. And I felt myself softening, my reserve slipping. Your queries were so direct, as bold as the flames licking over the coals. You are so like your father, aren't you, I thought, recalling the way he had come straight to the point, made it impossible to say no. I had pleased the Captain, I reminded myself. But I had yet to please you. I am not sure I even wished to please you just then. But please you I must.

Still your curiosity was not satisfied. And my mother, you asked. What was her work? Now I grew angry in some obscure way, but dared not show it.

'She works on the farm, miss.'

'Not in the dairy?'

'No.'

'Where then?'

I shook out your night chemise, that was still warm, and folded it again and knew that my hands were trembling. How hard I had worked at that dairy, and all the order I had made was a swilled sink with the broken curds picked out, a scrubbed cold floor, a dull row of thick earthenware. Here I had made for you — and I looked about me, anywhere but at you — a swelling primrose counterpane without a crease, a bright-patterned carpet, clear gleaming mirrors, and soft spotted dittany and scarlet wool in neat folded piles: a room of sumptuous, harmonious comfort the like of which my mother would never know. I took up a pile of your torn garments to mend later. I would tell you no more. Already you knew almost all there was to know of me.

'I don't know of what account my mother is to you, miss,' I said shortly. You raised your eyebrows sharply. I flushed up and inspected the pile. 'Will there be anything else?' I said, as stiff as Hester.

When you did not reply I looked up and at you. I took in the strong lines of your open face as if for the first time. Your broad forehead and pointed chin. I saw how smooth your skin was, how creamy and unblemished; not flushed by the close heat of the fire but an even, tawny caramel. I saw your eyebrows fine and arched, almost invis-ible. I saw your brown eyes, dark and steady, how they seemed to drink me up. Maybe it was then.

When you spoke next your voice was quite different, as though everything you had said before had been some sort of act.

'Perhaps because my mother,' you began, and then stopped.

I watched you look down and fumble your hands in your lap, all girlish. Are you trying hard too, I thought suddenly, to be someone you want to be, but are not at all sure of? I felt as common in my judgements as a cottage hen then, ashamed of myself and my ridiculous pride. For I had forgot your mother was dead, and mine alive, yet I would not even own her. And I was about to compose some sort of reply that might let you know my contrition when you rose to your feet with great determination and pulled out a small bundle of newspapers and pamphlets from the drawer where I had stowed them so recently.

'Now,' you said with a smile that showed all your straight and even teeth, and so cheerily I was quite confused. 'Let us start your education by studying these, fresh in.'

You beckoned me to kneel by your chair and we bent over pages of the most delicate engravings, some tinted, some plain, of young ladies in various states of fashionable dress. To my eyes they looked outlandish, each in their huge skirts and tiny caps, like so many ruffled pigeons. You turned a merry, social, questioning face on me. I could see that you expected me to speak. What could I say now? I smiled back cautiously and said the first, ignorant thing that came into my head: 'What makes their skirts so marvellous wide?'

'Why,' you replied with an incredulous giggle, 'hoops!' And you told me a delicious story about a woman in a hoop and a bun seller, with gestures that made me blush, and laugh too. I was still awkward, kneeling so close, trying not to let my sleeve touch yours. Susie should be here, I thought desperately, she would tell you another right back.

Then you pulled out a letter from your Aunt Tabitha upon which she had sketched a sack dress she had seen at a soirée, and bade me sit on the bed at your side. You wished to have it made up, should it be in cambric or silk? This was another test but again, what could I say? Even Susie hadn't a hope when it came to the fashions. 'You would look well in either,' I muttered and you rolled your eyes in a sort of mock despair that warmed me through and through.

None of it felt real. Little Louise Fletcher,

sat here in a fine bedroom, with a young lady hanging on her every word and a coal fire burning, looking idly through the latest almanacs direct from London Town. But all the time I was thrilling inside. For I lost all my resentments as I looked at you, so close at my side. None of those society drawings was half so fine as you, I thought fiercely, in your yellow gown that was crumpled and spotted about the neck, and missing some stitches where the lace attached. I was itching to fix it, take it away and press it. You did not wear stays, I saw that, but still the curve of your shoulder and breast pressed up against your bodice, spilled slightly over like twice-raised bread. And that sugary soft skin. Yes, she will make a fine naval gentleman's wife, I thought. Wouldn't it be something, to tend someone as fine as her?

There was a knock at the door. I sat up straight on the edge of the bed. It was Hannah come up to call you for dinner. You lay in the litter of papers, your head close by my lap. Swiftly I slipped off the bed and bent to pick up those on the floor.

'It can wait a while, Hannah,' you said, without looking up.

'Meat's on table, miss,' said Hannah firmly, before she closed the door.

Out on the landing the air was chill on my

burning cheeks and you tutted as we reached the bottom of the stairs, for sure enough the hall fire had been let out. There was a smell of meat that made my mouth water. When you opened the door to the eating parlour, broiled trotters were steaming and savoury on the plates already. And there were Hester and the Captain around a large table, laid with a white cloth and fine blue-and-white china and much glassware. The Captain sprang to his feet as soon as he saw you and pulled the door wide.

'Come in now, come in, let me see you.' That voice again, booming like the barrels I had heaved in the cellars. Before I came here, I realised, it had been the Captain who had loomed largest in my thoughts. Now he was quite diminished. Let his voice boom, his beard wag. What did he matter to me, with you at my side?

He scrubbed at his beard with his napkin and wiped his hand on his waistcoat before he reached out to clasp yours greedily. It seemed to me he looked at you as eager as though you were his own wife. 'So, sweet-pea, what do you say?'

You pressed yourself against his side as a cat would, and glanced coolly back at me. 'I'd say she is very — fresh, Dadda.'

I didn't know how to take this. Your tone

was droll, yet your eyes were unamused.

He nodded hard. 'Quite so. Very young, very neat and very clean. Just what you need, Becca dear.'

'Dadda, this is not your best work, is it?' You detached your hand from his and walked round to tug petulantly on the back of Hester's chair. You addressed the room at large: 'Give him a crew to muster, and he could bring you a dozen or more brawny tars within the hour. Ask him for a lady's maid and he brings me a milkmaid dressed in her own cheesecloth!'

Hester set down her water glass and I drew back to the doorway, feeling suddenly faint. Where was the sweet, confiding, curious Rebecca who had giggled beside me on her bed only moments before?

'If your mother —' began the Captain, but Hester spoke louder.

'Becca knows very well she is unfair to you both,' she said. 'Louise is most willing — God knows she did her share down below — and she will do well enough. There will be plenty of time to train her up. Indeed, Becca is very fortunate to have a maid at all.'

'Oh, don't I know it,' you fired straight back, 'and to not be a sour old one!'

'Hester, please,' said the Captain, quite

unfairly I thought, for it was clearly you who'd been rude. He was all red in the face and twitching with discomfort. I could not believe it: this harsh commanding fellow, brought to this pitch of anxiety by his squabbling daughters. And it was he who had dragged me here. 'Hush, girls, hush, do,' he urged. 'I'll be gone again soon enough. Don't quarrel now.'

Hester continued to glare at you. The Captain backed away and pulled out a chair. He bent over you as you sank on to it, and patted your shoulders.

'Run along now, young Louise,' he said without even looking at me. 'No, stop,' he said, pulling out his kerchief to wipe his face. 'Ask Skeggs to fetch me up more of the Canary.'

Nels had kept some potage warm and I ate alone at the kitchen table, all that poring over prints had kept me from dining with her and the others. The light was fading outside already, the yard walls dark and louring, as was my mood, for I knew well enough this would be my last meal here. I cursed my mother, as Susie had, for shutting me up so at the farm: perhaps, had I been more worldly, I would have seen what I had done wrong. And how could I bring her news of Luke now, sent home in disgrace and after just one day? I was in the scullery swilling my dish, imagining Susie's face when she saw me home again so soon, when you appeared in the doorway. I set down the dish carefully and wiped my hands, fully expecting you to tell me to pack my things and go, you would find yourself a real lady's maid. But you smiled, and held up a small blue cloth purse.

'See, Lou,' you said, tossing the purse so its contents chinked. 'I can bargain just as well as my father. What he saved on the goods, I shall get back on the dressing.'

You took me straight back up to your room and bade me draw the shutters and light all the candles and build up the fire well. Then you asked me to bring down what clothes I had. I tried to lay them out so the stains did not show, nor touch the bed. Atop I placed my summer bonnet, good side to the fore.

'Well that was a waste of time,' you said, picking up the hat and letting it drop with a sigh. 'Get them off my bed, they reek of the country.'

Then you turned your back to me.

'Well, come on,' you said impatiently, lowering your chin.

I knew, of course, that you meant me to

unlace your dress. Dressing and undressing you, this would be all part of my work. But so soon? How could I touch you, who spoke to me so fiercely, who mocked and teased me? I knew my fingers would fumble, I would displease you once more. I loosened your ties quite easy, though you complained my fingers were chill. I had been right, you were not wearing stays. I could only pretend to look at the creases in your smock when you turned back to face me. You prodded the warm gown I held in my arms still, that I had just slipped from your shoulders.

'Well, take it.'

I was slow to understand.

'Come, Lou. If you're to be my maid you must look the part.'

When still I did not move, you said impatiently, 'in there,' and nodded me behind the screen. It was dark there, with the shutters closed, and I was all alone with that dress, still warm and smelling of you.

But when I came out, you laughed in my face. 'My, what a puppet,' you said. 'Look at you. Oh my goodness, take it off directly!'

I was too ashamed to care about anything then, and pulled on my old skirt and bodice again right there in front of the fire. But you were out on the landing calling to Hannah.

Before long I had an armful of your discarded bodices and petticoats, torn stockings and a couple of bonnets, even a cape. 'See what you can do with these, Lou,' you said, 'I'm off to keep the old man sweet. He'll be away tomorrow if the winds are right, and then we'll have us some fun!'

You had me lace you tight into a jauntily striped gown and then, at the door, you told me to throw away everything I had come with, even my mother's best red shawl. 'Nels will burn them.'

'She said what?' Hannah almost shrieked. Nels huffed over.

'Nels will not,' she said, her hands on her hips. 'That girl is more extravagant than royalty. And I'm very glad her mother isn't here to see what she wastes every day, god rest her.'

She set my stained old clothes to soak and I carried my new finery up to the attic. I did my best, but I had only the one candle and little or no elbow room. Hannah found me and took me down to the kitchen and together with Nels we looked it all over.

Hannah shook the cape out and examined it closely. 'Ah, there is a rip here,' she said. 'But I wouldn't bother. You'll get a good price for it anyways. I can take you if you like.'

I was shocked, and said so. 'But Miss Rebecca gave them to me.'

'Exactly. How's you think you're going to make any money at this lark? You can't wear them all.'

'I would not think to sell a single one of them. It wouldn't be right.'

She looked at me quite puzzled, then shook her head and handed it back. 'Like to know what she's paying you, Louise.'

Nels took up a sprigged lawn gown that I thought would need the least taking in, and looked up at me in surprise: 'She gave you this? I remember her in this when she was eleven or twelve. You done something right, Louise, for that was made up from one of her mother's.'

The look on my face must have been encouragement enough. As she unpicked the placket and I pinned up the hem, she told me how your mother had suddenly sickened when you were eleven, after a hard voyage up through the Bay of Biscay. This was before the Captain had settled in Harwich for good, when he had sailed as far as China, trading in silks and all sorts. The Captain's negro man — a fellow called Peter who had been your father's closest

companion through most of his time at sea
— applied some outlandish treatment. It
had killed her, Nels said with dread relish,
her eyes wide. In a rage of grief the Captain
sent the evil man away. Ship's company near
finished the poor fellow off, right there by
Angelgate. Hester at seventeen had taken
over the running of the household, took on
Nels soon after. The Captain never sailed
the oceans again, and set about working his
way into the packet trade. And you? Bless
the girl, said Nels sadly, Miss Rebecca
would come into my bed nights and curl
about me. Pined like a kitten.

CHAPTER NINE

'Make way, make way there!' shouts a grim-faced tar.

'Heave!' comes another voice from up above in the rigging.

A huge iron-bound chest swings towards Luke out of nowhere, a solid dark mass that fills the sky. Gasping, he presses himself back to allow the men to guide it on to the deck. Then he hears the bosun's whistle and a shouted order cuts through the crowded air. 'All pressed men, all pressed men, to the forecastle if you please!'

There are grumbles and curses, but in ones and twos, and then in a constant stream, men take the steps up to a raised deck at the bow of the ship. Luke spies the pocked man and hangs back. There's Powell, his cheeks grey and his eyes glittering with anger. No Nick. And with a start he recognises the silent, dapper officer standing close beside him at the foot of the steps:

for it is the man who mustered him, the surgeon's mate. Another officer comes forward and curtly shakes de Clare's hand. This man is taller, but his shoulders are narrow and lopsided. He bends to address de Clare over Luke's head.

'By god am I glad of this.' His lips barely move and his whole stance is rigid. 'The men stink. When the wind changes the stench from the gun deck is fouler than the Augean stables.'

De Clare nods, with an air of great understanding and regard. 'Certainly, Tremmel,' he says, clasping his hand fondly over the officer's. 'It is a welcome sight.'

Tremmel's mouth twitches and he withdraws his hand from de Clare's, as from a mess of cobwebs.

'Can't say I'm looking forward to this voyage,' de Clare continues blithely. 'Weevils after three weeks, the flux after six. And then the scurvy. Sailing at the end of the season like this, there'll most certainly be storms. Men lost, or fallen. Crushed thumbs —'

Tremmel turns to glare. 'Damned unpatriotic of you, de Clare.' Then he spies Luke and his ire spills over. 'Come now, boy,' Tremmel says crossly, 'no dallying.'

Luke has no choice but to join the crowd

mounting the steps. At the top he stops dead. For the pressed men, dozens of them, have been stripped quite naked. They stand around steaming buckets of water, set to wash each other down. He cannot take his eyes from their swaying shrivelled privates, their white buttocks that wobble like shelled eggs. They will do this to me too, he realises. My god, they will strip me of my rig and I will stand here naked among them all, alone.

He sees Nick, his hands braced against his knees as another scrubs and swabs at his shoulders and back. The brush raises red welts on his skin as dirt streams off in great flushes and scribbles. He sticks his finger in his ear and shakes his head, sending pellets of water all about. Then he makes a grab for the bucket, empties it over the man's head with a yell, banging it hard against his skull for good measure. The others jump back and curse and double up, a milling pack of bedraggled dogs.

Luke takes a step or two back. His feet feel like they are lifting away from the deck, like he is floating off to heaven.

'Off with them now,' a man yells in his face. He points his stick to where two men are dropping clothes from the pile in front of them into two smoking braziers. 'All shore clothes to be burnt.'

Luke clutches his collar together.

'I said strip, lad.'

He shakes his head.

'Damn you into next week, get over there!' and the man prods him with his stick over to where men are pulling their shirts over their heads. Simon Wivens is there, shivering and naked, his body speckled grey with hair like some obscene fledgling.

Luke tries to sneak across to the other ladder. But he has only gone a yard or two when Tremmel bars his path and without breaking off from his talk with another he kicks Luke viciously in the thigh, knocking him over.

Luke bites his lip against the pain and scrambles to his feet again. He cranes his neck to scan the crowd. Dimly, he knows that he looks for Nick. Someone grabs the back of Luke's collar and starts to tug him towards the braziers. He twists and struggles, kicks out as effectually as a kitten.

'I have my sea rig,' he shouts. 'Look you!'

But the tar is dragging him by his shirt, as though to pull it from his back. Luke hears the rip of the cloth and screams. The sound comes from his throat as from a distance: it is high and unearthly, a screeching wail. His strength fails him and he crumples. The deck seems very big and very unsteady. Above him the seagulls swoop and the sound of their cries seems to echo in his skull.

'I have my rig, see,' Luke pleads. 'This is my rig.'

'You lousy bastard.' The man bends over him. 'The surgeon gave orders to strip you all. You're a pressed man ain't you? You sat in the tenders with all that lot from the prisons and poorhouses. Then you're as dirty as them.' He hoists Luke to his feet.

Then Luke sees de Clare, at the bow with some officers. He is uncorking a big earthenware bottle and peering inside. Luke twists out of the man's grasp. 'I am summoned to the surgeons,' he says, with as much dignity as he can muster. 'I have a wound, here, that must be dressed.'

Touching his hand to the back of his head, he shows his fingers to the man: they come away red with blood. Without waiting for his reply, he breaks away to stand before de Clare.

The man yells after him: 'Oi! They don't want to touch your scabby head.'

Luke holds out his bloodied hand to de Clare. He is panting and shivering. 'Sir, you must treat my wound, sir.'

'Must he indeed,' splutters one of the officers. 'What is this nonsense? We cannot spare men to go sick.'

'We should have sailed a week ago,' says another.

'We have not the men to raise sail, nor yet the medicines to treat half of those who claim to be sick!' scoffs the first.

'Why we delayed for this sorry lot I have no idea. Half of them will have to go straight back to the poorhouse.'

The pair of them have turned away to dispute among themselves. De Clare regards him gravely. Once more, Luke cannot hold his gaze. His head begins to swim. De Clare reaches out a steadying hand. 'I shall see to him,' he says to his fellows.

'Snivelling like a girl!' The spluttering officer turns on Luke with renewed venom. 'Call yourself a sailor? Ever been to sea before? Thieved your damn rig too, I shouldn't wonder.'

De Clare stoppers his bottle and sets it down. He smiles at Luke, a private, amused, reassuring smile. Luke looks into his dark eyes. They seem so warm, so sustaining. They tell him he is safe, for now. So why does his stomach clench, why does he feel as exposed as if he were already stripped naked?

De Clare conducts Luke down through

the ship, touching his elbow to give him a steer as a gentleman might conduct a lady at a dance.

'Fletcher, is it not?'

Luke nods. He does not trust his voice.

'Yes, sir,' de Clare prompts.

He swallows. 'Yes, sir.'

'Already the air is so foul below, I hesitate.' De Clare makes a face. 'We have been so long at anchor out here, waiting for you men. Still, there is much to do. I have need of at least one more cabinet with key and lock.'

His speech is so precise, so formal. But his manner is relaxed, conversational even, as though addressing an equal. Luke is confused, when did anyone last speak to him so polite?

They come up against a file of marine and as Luke stops short, inches from de Clare's back, he is startled to smell the man. He don't reek like the men, steeped in their own puke and soil. Nor does he ooze, like the other officers, sweat or spirits or tobacco. Cautiously, Luke lets himself breathe it again. What fills his lungs is the sharp, sweet, mouth-watering scent of limes.

The sick bay is a small room, oddly shaped. Luke stares about him. Most odd of all is a great rounded bulge as thick as a tree trunk, bound about with iron bands, which rises at an angle out of the far wall down by the floor. It stretches across and up and disappears into the ceiling, like some great sea serpent intent on squeezing itself through the ship's timbers. All manner of jars and bags and bottles are stacked on every surface. Straw pokes out of an opened barrel; clearly unpacking and sorting has barely begun.

With the door firmly shut behind them, the place fills with the lime scent. Sweat prickles on Luke's back. In the corner a stove burns furious, and beside it kneels the feeble boy who attended de Clare on deck. He looks about nine, thin and pale, with dark shadows under his eyes. He wears only a grown man's shirt, the ties dangling to his knees. As he pokes the stove open with a stick, its light spills into the room and everything seems edged with fire.

'Come, Fletcher, sit here, if you please.'

Luke sits down, grateful for the kindness, the warmth, the attention, but wary still. Always wary now.

'Was that the gangers?' De Clare indicates his wound.

What does he know? How he got here, still he cannot recall, there is just a blackness. He keeps his head down, rubs at his stained fingers.

'Quite a blow.' De Clare pours a bowl of water from a kettle on the stove and tests it with his finger. 'Give it time.'

He speaks to his boy in a rapid, liquid flow of foreign words. The boy gets to his feet. He is smaller even than Luke.

'This is Dominique,' says de Clare. '*Mon petit* loblolly boy. I picked him up at Brest. He speaks no English. Or very little. *N'est-ce-pas,* Do-Do?'

Dominique looks from de Clare to Luke. There is nothing to see in his eyes. He looks half dead.

'But I teach him, no?'

Dominique nods.

Without warning de Clare reaches out and removes Luke's cap. Luke clutches for it, but too late. His hair falls about his shoulders, clumped and rancid. De Clare scans his face and frowns. Leaning forward, he touches his fingertips to Luke's left brow. Luke winces and closes his eyes. He had not known he had another injury there, this one swelling as hard as a nut. De Clare sighs.

Then Luke feels fingers graze slowly across his jaw and he opens his eyes again in alarm, only to see de Clare turn away and reach inside one of his soft bags. When he turns back his face is impassive, smooth as the sleeping knights'.

'Now, if you please?' He places his finger-tips just above Luke's ears and tilts his head forward. Luke sits very still. He looks at de Clare's shoes, soft and black, their polished buckles glinting in the light from the fire. De Clare picks apart what's left of Luke's pigtail, parts the hair at the nape of his neck and drapes it over his shoulders. Luke hears him dip a length of rag in the bowl. He dabs at the wound gently, so gently Luke thinks of his mother. He shuts his eyes against the tears. As de Clare works he enquires whether Luke has been given his station yet. He will try, he says, to ensure he is given a landsman's post, with such an injury he must not be sent aloft just yet.

The boy has filled another bowl and is washing Luke's Monmouth cap. No one speaks. Luke listens to the trickle of water as the cloth is lifted from the bowl, the crackle of the stove.

CHAPTER TEN

We stood in clouds of our own breath at the top of the five stone steps. The sleet and rain had cleared but the air was cutting cold. I had hardly slept, and my eyes felt raw and gritty after a long night of unpicking and stitching. I shivered in the sprigged lawn and the black silk cape, despite having mother's red shawl trussed tight underneath. Your cheeks glowed. You'd had me fetch you the warmest dress and cloak in your closet and never mind what it looked like for who was there to see you in Harwich?

'See,' you said, surveying the chill and windswept street. 'The town is as dead as a mitten.'

'That's what my sister Susie says about Wix,' I said, my tongue loosened by nerves. You raised your eyebrows and I was compelled to add: 'She would always be on to

138

come to Harwich and have herself some fun.'

'Have some fun? The only fun to be had here is teasing the tars, and I may'nt even do that now I'm to be respectable. But —' you added, gathering up your skirts and taking my hand to steady yourself, 'Mrs Fressing is to start up a masquerade at the Assembly Rooms in George Street next month. Dear Henry's ship is due in then. So we shall have some excitement at last!'

And when you smiled at me, and slipped your arm through mine, it was as it had been that first day when you took my hand in your warm soft fingers: I think I would have done anything for you, anything at all.

That's how it went, that dance of ours. You'd draw me to you, and then turn away.

Our task that day was to spend the money your father had gifted you in the small blue purse, and the prospect of the masquerade gave us ample opportunity. But first you walked me up the sea end of West Street, to where dozens of vessels large and small, whose creaks and moans had haunted my agitated night, lay tied up and at anchor. The noise, the bustle there, was tremendous to me, for the ships swarmed with men, sat close packed as another town. It seemed another world even, floating so close yet so apart.

Was this what had drawn them away, my father and brother? How they lived, who they became? No, I simply could not understand. And it angered me, suddenly, that they had both gone so blithely from their home, abandoned us women without a backward glance, and for such a makeshift life, such a motley set. As I stood and looked, the tide sloshed over the edge of the quay and I scurried back several steps.

'Honestly, Lou, anyone would think it was coming to get you.'

'Won't it be coming up in the cellar again?' I called anxiously.

But you were away, stepping rapidly in and out of puddles, and soaking your slippers. I followed a few paces, then faltered as half a dozen tars who lolled against the wall roused their whole bodies to look us up and down. They might have been a pack of gulls for all you paid heed.

You walked me along to the packet pier. From here, you told me, your father's hoy sailed back and forth to the Low Countries and beyond, carrying the mail and any paying passengers. You pointed to his vessel, the *Dolphin,* flying a blue flag that signified he was soon to depart. 'And see beyond there, that frigate?' On the deck of a large white ship at anchor some way off, dozens of tars in beribboned hats and piped jackets strained at the rails, and waved handkerchiefs to the bumboat women.

'They've won a prize, or else been at sea so long they just want ashore. Look at them. Pricks like pokers. Come now, don't blush. It's true. They're here to spend everything they've got and don't Harwich know it?'

Then came a long whistle from the tars behind me. I turned to see four or five girls in bright spotted muslins and great ringleted wigs come halloring across the quay, armstrong.

'Don't you love a rolling sailor,' they sang out in crude unison, *'don't you love my rolling boy.'*

They poked their tongues at the sad penniless fellows who leered after them, made eyes only at the new boys.

'Tedious, ain't it? What bores me most about life in a sea port. Simply can't go out when there's a rout on, and the carousing always turns sour, you must step over them in the street the next day, sozzled and half stripped and picked over by those lovely girls. It's why father moved us away from the King's Quay. Oh yes, Mr Winston is building a fine house down there now, with

141

a grand aspect across the lanes, but we're so much the quieter in West Street, more genteel by far.'

I kept my eyes low. 'Can't we go back now?' I asked. But you squeezed my arm to indicate a stocky sailor boy stood close behind us. He watched you silently, his candid blue eyes half furred by thick blond lashes. You held his gaze. Then he touched his cap, and made to approach us. Giggling, you pulled me away. 'Come on. Let's make the circuit.'

There was a great commotion about a huge treadmill crane ahead, the people blocking the street, and so we skirted out along the shore a way. But the wind cut in bitterly here, reached cold fingers under my garments, seemed even to rake at the pebbles as if it were invisible surf, and blew us almost to a standstill. After fifty yards or so you gave up and turned your back on it. Then you crouched down suddenly and I feared you had been taken ill and came staggering after you. But you rose with a handful of pebbles and picked them over. Then you placed them in my palm. I would have thrown them down on the instant had you not cupped my hand to hold it steady.

'These, they say, are all that is left of men taken by the sea.' You put your face close to mine lest the wind take your words. 'Their bodies grow cold and hard, the creatures nibble at them, and then parts fall off. Like these.'

I stared in horror. They were like nothing I'd ever seen before: stubby little tubes that were pale as cold, brine-soaked flesh; one short and wide as a thumb, the rest longer and knobbled. They were tipped with dark ovals the blue-black of bruises, of congealed blood.

'Dead men's fingers,' you whispered in my ear.

I thought of the maimed seamen I had seen in the marketplace. I imagined what terrible accidents had befallen them. And I thought of my father, of my brother, their broken bodies sinking slowly to the bottom of the ocean. I emptied my palm with a shudder. 'What are you about?' I cried. 'How heartless of you. My own father was lost at sea. And my brother too perhaps.'

You pulled back then, and the wind whipped your ringlets over your eyes, into your mouth. 'Look,' you said quickly. 'Look again.' And you picked one up again. It was but a short tube of flint, coated in thick white chalk and showing dark and translucent at one end with an oval patch at the other where the chalk had flaked and worn away.

You closed my reluctant hand over its chill smoothness. 'Come now.' As we walked on, you put your arm lightly about me, but you did not apologise; or ask, as I expected, after my father and my brother. 'Why, Lou, I think I shall make you a present of it.' You slipped it into my pocket. 'Won't you say thank you?'

How you confused me. You affected boredom and disdain for port life, but your eyes lit up whenever a likely tar passed. You talked of respectability but then also of men's pricks. You loved your fires high but lingered on a forsaken shore to play with pebbles, with my feelings. No, I could not make you out. You were not the nice young mistress I had imagined, not at all.

When we reached the lower light house, you turned me around to look back at the town, seeming even more of a bleak island now, almost encircled as it was by sea.

'So, Lou, what do you say to Harwich?'

I could not answer you politely, as I had Nels. I was very cold now, and much disillusioned, and on my mettle. 'Not so very genteel, miss.'

You nodded, seemed not to notice my pique. 'Indeed. Know you Ipswich is a far superior place, despite the lack of naval offi-cers. Heavens, they even have a pavement or two.' Then as you gathered your skirts to walk on, you asked: 'And Lou, what do you say to your new mistress?'

How could I answer? That I found you cruel and indifferent to those who loved you? That your talk offended me, your ways alarmed me? That in truth I found you care-less and thrilling and marvellous and I wanted nothing more than to attend and assist you, to be at your side always? In the end I gripped that flinty pebble tight in my pocket and spoke without thinking.

'I find you not so very nice neither, miss.'

You pulled a face of mock dismay.

'Why then, young Lou, you'll just have to make a lady of me, won't you?'

You led me back into town and to a warehouse beyond the marketplace, and into a back room where a small man in a fur hat pulled out bale after bale of stuff for you to choose from. The stuffs were beauti-ful, I'd never seen the like, but after a while my feet grew numb and I did not under-stand the talk at all. So when the bell of St Nick's tolled twelve and you gave a great gasp, clutched at my hand, saying 'Lou, oh Lou, what shall I do, you must help me!' — for it was nigh the hour your father was to depart from the packet pier, quite the other end of town — I was very happy to run back to the house to ask Nels to make up a dozen of her hot cakes for you to take to him before he sailed. 'My father must think of me with fondness while he is away, you see, else what sort of present might he make me on his return?' You laughed. 'Thank heavens I have you!'

'She'll be along soon,' I said importantly to Nels, as she bent over the griddle, and I sat down to wait for you. When Nels handed me the cakes all wrapped in a cloth I went to stand by the front door, expecting you at any minute. But the cloth grew cool in my hands and still you did not come. Nels showed me the small door in the back wall of the yard and off I set towards the quays, looking for the packet pier.

It was the first time I had ventured out alone and I kept my eyes averted and my shoulders hunched. But I could not help what I heard: the foreign curses, the startling shouts and cries, the sudden laughter. I thought to avoid the busy main quay by cutting through a short alley but I knew my mistake immediately, for I came out opposite two drunken tars scuffling in a doorway where an evil-looking man stood guard. He swore at them to be gone, and me also, and brandished his cudgel wildly. From within the doorway came the sounds of a drum banged fast and loud, a fiddle sawed up and down, up and down, to the thumps and whoops of frantic dancing. I fled, but not before I noted the huge sign that swung low overhead: the Three Squirrels.

Nels had been quite right in her advice to me that first night. It had been ridiculous to imagine I might do as Skeggs directed, and enter that filthy tavern to ask for news of my brother. But I could not forget your flinty pebble, still rolling in the pocket of my skirt. My dead man's finger. And the very thought of it determined me to do something to relieve my mother's thoughts, and soon. I would not ask you for assistance, that I knew perfectly well. And while kind Nels had said she might speak with the Captain on my behalf, why, he was leaving today, and for I knew not how long.

Then I remembered what I held in my hands. Surely the Captain might look kindly on me, today of all days, come as I was with a parting gift from his beloved Becca. Yes, I decided, now was my chance. No doubt he would know nothing of a feckless young Fletcher who disappeared years ago. But I would have tried at least, and discharged

147

my duty to my mother. How conscious I was then of fulfilling my duties. I think I prided myself on it a little. Certainly I chided you, silently, for your carelessness in such things.

By the time I arrived at the packet pier I was quite out of breath. As I approached the *Dolphin* I saw that for a figurehead she had a great swollen fish, the very same form as the door knocker on the house in West Street. And there by the gangplank was your father: hard to miss, all togged up in a gilt-buttoned greatcoat and a heavy black hat. There was your sister too, close at his side. When she saw me and my bundle her mouth set itself in a thin and unflattering line.

'My sister always brought these herself,' she said curtly, as I dropped an awkward curtsey and the Captain looked anywhere but at me.

I swallowed hard, and recited with great care the greeting you had instructed me in while swearing blind I would not have occasion to use it: 'Your loving daughter regrets she is unavoidably detained, and says please for the Captain to accept these hot cakes that are as warm as the love she bears him.' And I held out my damp, deflated parcel.

The Captain cleared his throat and looked

to the sails.

Hester took the cakes from me. 'I see,' she said.

And then my moment was lost, my screwed-up courage all for nothing, for before I could open my mouth again to ask after my brother she went on in her firmest tone: 'I thank you for your trouble, Louise. Now would you be so kind as to go home and see what you can do for Nels.'

CHAPTER ELEVEN

'Get yourself a jacket,' de Clare is telling him. 'Shoes, if you can. We sail south, but it's late in the season, there'll be weather in the Bay.'

Luke's walking in a daze, his veins buzzing with relief. De Clare has passed his rig: he will not have to strip before them all. The man has dressed his wounds, eased his pain, and may yet find him an easy station. But still Luke has that floating feeling, as though he's not really here.

And now the gun deck is become a sea of cloth. He is quite astonished to see it. Scraps of scarlet and buff and indigo stretch into the shadows, covering every surface, like the rucked bedclothes of a hundred huddled sleepers. Fresh clothes, navy issue. But none look new. Rising from them all is the harsh odour of stale sweat and tar and mildewed cloth too long stored. Luke fingers a pair of long trowsers, torn at the knee and the cuffs ragged.

'Hands off there!' yells a man, his face almost obscured by the pile of clothes he is carrying. Luke jumps back. 'Bain't enough for bastards like you to have a frigging spare.'

The noise is tremendous, the yelling of complaint and orders fills the air. Most all the pressed men had their heads shaved as they were washed, and badly too. Luke touches his hand to his neat new cue and swallows hard. He looks at all the farm boys and paupers and wights and mongers disappearing into their navy slops. When was the last time any of them had a fresh set of garments? How eagerly most of them now seem to cast off their old selves along with their clothes and the memories they held; the shirt a mother mended, the breeches a girl threw after them from a window. Already they look more alike, whatever their age or condition, or the fit of their rigs.

Then it comes to him. We all look alike now, he thinks, surveying his own sailor's rig. The long trowsers swamp his legs, the loose shirt billows out over his belt. He realises he too is disappearing inside his clothes, and feels a sort of relief. I am not so very different after all. Would she even know me, if she saw me now, among all these men?

151

But he cannot think of her now. It is too hard. He cannot think of where she might be, what she might be thinking, or how he came to leave her. He must be one of them. He must summon up all that is Luke within him, a true-born tar. This is what he tells himself. But he knows himself an elver among pikes.

The word is the Captain likes to mix pressed men with old hands, boys he knows and trusts. Keeps a ship manageable. So when Luke and Nick are eventually assigned to the seventh gun larboard on the middle deck, they find themselves mess mates with a set of old hands who distrust and despise them on sight.

All five stand shoulder to shoulder and look them over, don't say a word, don't have to. Luke tries hard not to shrink from them, these sea-hardened men he must eat with and work with and spend every moment with when he is not on watch. But Nick leads the way. Bigger and louder and brasher than any of them, he is the first to break the silence, to proffer a flask about and insult them each in turn while filling their cups. Luke sees their eyes flicker but none of them demur. Then Nick positions himself at the centre of their little world: leaning against the aisle post, his leg cocked and his feet crossed, hemming them in between the two great guns, and makes them captive.

Before long Nick's a happy man indeed. Turns out Simon Burton and Henry Little are his sturdy lads, both of them seventeen and ready for a ruck whenever anyone gives the nod. There's weary William Winn, almost ten years older, a silent fensman, deeply tanned. He keeps his big round shiny head down and out of trouble. Lolling on his fine blue-painted sea chest is Nick's joker, Peter Bramley, a tall sniggering fellow from Kent. And astride the gun barrel swings young Tobias Fleet, a broad-faced sixteen-year-old up for anything, who's told them all to call him Hogmarsh.

And Luke? Luke's part of Nick's repertoire now. 'Meet my little pocket mouse,' he roars, clapping his shoulder. 'What a generous fellow he can be. Why' — and he wags the hacked-about prick of tobacco in their faces — 'just look at what he had hidden away!'

The sturdy lads are practically sitting at Nick's feet by now, like dogs. Tobias Fleet makes a giggling grab for the baccy. Henry Little gets him in a headlock, and Simon Burton piles in after. All three roll about and knock Luke off his feet. Then the three of them lay in to Luke with barely disguised venom. He kicks out with his feet, tries to scrabble away. Straight away Nick is there, jabbing his finger in their chests, warning them off. Luke gets to his feet, his face burning.

Nick clasps him close and jabs and punches him rapidly up and down his ribs, ends by goosing his buttocks. He pulls Luke's head close against his chest. 'There's my lad,' he mutters thickly in his ear. 'There's my lad.' Luke's eyes fill with tears. Nick slaps one cheek and pinches the other hard before he lets him go.

'Right then, Hogmarsh,' he shouts, as a bell starts to ring. Tobias Fleet beams and stands up, he never hears a sneer. 'Off to the stores,' and Nick shoves him so hard he has to clutch at a post to stay upright. When he comes back, with a bag of parched peas as big as his head, Nick tosses it to Luke and sends him off to the cook. He goes with a sense of release, and with his bladder bursting. He cannot find a square foot of solitude in which to relieve himself, and the ship's stove does not light so he must return the peas to William Winn, chosen mess cook for the week.

Nick sits up in mock alarm. 'Whisht, mousey. Youse made us jump! See him creep, boys?' Luke has not yet spoken a word to any of them. It becomes his own joke, the longer he goes without speaking the more it amuses them all.

'Eek,' needles Fleet. 'Eek, eek.'

Bramley lifts his fingers by his ears and scampers his feet about. He stops, though, when Nick fixes him with a look.

And now it's early evening, and here they all sit about the seventh gun larboard on the middle deck, with their one lantern swinging and smoking close above. The bosun's mate squats against the aisle post, the last striped waistcoat tucked under his arm, the last jacket at his side.

'Come now lads, settle down.'

He looks ready to wrestle them all to the deck if that would quiet them. For the shoving and shouting has started up again. There were not nearly enough slops for them all to have a full set, and the cook's stove still will not light. The chill and the damp are seeping into their bones, and in the flickering rushlight their cheeks hold vicious shadows. Above the grumbles and jeers someone mutters quite clearly: 'Little prick, I'll have him, jacket or no.'

There is a lull while the mate swigs from his mug. Luke has emptied his long ago.

Now he is thirsty again, but needs to piss even worse. But he cannot leave. He needs a jacket. Down here it is grown warm enough, with all five dozen or so men crammed in together like growing chicks, and god knows how many dozens more packed in on every other deck. He can feel the heat storing up under his shirt like wadding; sweat, even, between his toes. But he thinks of the darkness up on deck, the swaying ropes that stretch up into the emptiness, the cold stars twinkling out of reach, and the winter wind that gusts out of nowhere, and shudders.

'Come, lads,' says the bosun's mate. He's beyond weary. 'Let us throw for this jacket.'

The next mess along jump to their feet to protest: don't let them nab the last jacket, for what use is the waistcoat in foul weather? The mate barely glances round. He points to each of Luke's mess in turn: 'One, two, three, four, five, six.' Luke, sandwiched between William Winn and Tobias Fleet, is three. The mate shakes the die and lets it spill. 'One.'

Nick grins. Until the mate holds out the jacket. He could barely fit one shoulder inside it, let alone two. A loud shout of laughter escapes the red-headed fellow in the next mess and Nick turns quickly to look.

'What!' Nick blusters. 'Are your tailors mice, that they sew garments this very small?'

'Do you want it or no?'

Nick receives it with a mocking bow, his eyes flicking back to the laughing red-headed man. 'Aye, sir, and I'll present it to my very own mouse. Might have been sewn to order.'

As Nick pulls him to his feet, Luke sees Burton and Little exchange glances, for it would fit either of them, if rather more snug. 'Here, a fine grey coat for ye. You have your own tail?' and he gooses Luke's arse yet again. Nick's fingers dig deep into his right buttock and hold there. Luke grows hot, with the pain and humiliation. But what can he do?

He puts the jacket on. It is very loose and roomy about the shoulders, and missing two of its three buttons. It has the smell of the grave. But despite everything he is very glad to have it. He fastens the one button across his chest. Perhaps he will get through this. He might take Nick's ribbing, the grabbing and goosing — all the excruciating attentions that leave him sore and sorry — even Nick's damn thieving, he thinks, if he might help him get by. Daddy's boy.

'Who will throw for the waistcoat?' yells the mate.

'Yah,' yells one of the men. 'And who will bring me some hot dinner!'

'A hot bint!' returns Nick.

'A fat hot whore with a well-greased ring!'

'You rattling shag bags, I'll don the thing myself,' says the mate, and flaunts it to and fro above his head. Half the buttons are missing. But now they see it they all want it, now it is all there is left to covet. The mate yells that he will do this fair: he will throw for them again, for the whole deck this time. The men rub their hands, and quiet down. At least there is sport in this. Some take bets. And it is their fates played out in miniature. Their chances are slim, but they must take what they can get.

Now I must slip away, thinks Luke, now I have my jacket, for I must find a place to piss. Everyone is below, and it will be dark above deck. With one eye on Nick, he starts to make his way to the aisle. But as the bosun's mate throws the dice again and again, the men grow more than restless, it's getting ugly. Luke starts to panic that he will never get away, that he must piss his pants again. His nose is hard against another's back, and he clutches at a sleeve as the bodies press and sway.

'Five!' yells the mate, and then he must have handed the waistcoat over for there is a great roar of disappointment, a volley of whistles. The mate raises his voice again. 'Leave it lads, leave it! I am for the main deck and some clean air.' He elbows his way past Luke and is gone in a moment.

Luke struggles to follow in his wake. He spies him again on the upper deck by the carpenter's bay. It's empty: the benches and lathes attended only by shifting tumbrels of wood shavings. The men on this deck are all in their messes too, curtained off by sheets of canvas hung from the beams.

'Sir, please sir,' he calls in desperation, just as the mate puts his foot on the ladder. 'Where is there a pot, or a closet?'

The mate peers down. He sees the grey jacket first, then he recognises the Northumbrian's little lad, lost inside it. Green as fresh peas, not a damned clue. He should just let him learn the hard way. Then something in him relents. He spits, cocks his head towards the bows.

'Beakhead's through there, daddy's boy.'

Chill air bathes Luke's face as he shuts the low door behind him. He finds himself at the very prow of the ship, slowly moving up and down with the swell of the ocean. The sky is a deep inky blue. Hazy shapes dot the sea about, the rest of the fleet floating like giant birds, all speckled with lantern light. He looks up to where a pair of marine walk up and down a massive wooden grating that runs out above his head, their red coats flaring. Both carry muskets, bayonets fixed. For a single flashing moment he sees himself leap over the netting and away into the darkness. He can hear the splash he makes, feel the shock of the water as it closes over his head.

By the time they turn and walk away he has control again. Breathing as shallow as he can, he ducks under a thick slanting beam. There he unbuckles his belt and, holding the pouch of coin safe in one hand, squats down. He presses the back of his head against the timber to steady himself. Where it hits the grating the hot piss sprays back on to his ankles and thighs.

Almost immediately the door bangs open and two or three men barge through, their voices raised and quarrelsome. Before they can stumble upon him Luke scrabbles to raise his trowsers, splattering his hands. He's belting his trowsers in the shadows as they unbelt theirs; he's slipping back inside as they piss out into the darkness.

Chapter Twelve

It didn't take long, did it? How quick you undid all my sore-learnt prudence. Dairy Lou winced when you dipped your finger in the new-bought cream Hester left on the kitchen table, and broke its crust. Dutiful Miss Fletcher hurried to close the kitchen door after you, to save the heat every time you flung it open to see if the snowdrops were through. My toes clenched as I watched your kitten, little black Neptune, claw at the lace on your cuff while you talked on and on regardless. And every night I took your mending to the kitchen and sat there while Skeggs ogled Nels, making every stitch as perfect as it could be. Soon I had your wardrobe in order, the clean folded piles as pleasing to me as my pats of fresh butter had been.

But then, as I gathered up your discarded linen day after day, not daring to look up at you as you changed your dress yet again, I

came to love the sag of it in my hands, all
warmed and softened and filled with intimate airs. I grew used to being shut up in
that dishevelled house, with the candles flaring and the fires stoked while all outside
was grey and damp and chill. I did not miss
the clean green air of the fields, the milky
breath of the cattle. I began to think of my
dear old dairy as a dull and empty place, a
church with nothing to worship.

You were my new idol. You were as startling and inspiring as the church of St
Nick's we attended every Sunday, its high
arches and soaring pillars festooned with
red and blue and yellow painted angels. Our
old country church certainly seemed a squat
little tub beside that, with its evil-smelling
patches of green damp.

Your room was my new sanctuary, and the
long hours we spent there were my worship-
ping. You breakfasted on chocolate, and I
learnt to wait until Nels was called away
before I scraped off a great mass of sugar
and heated it all together and brought it up
to you. You took yours with cream, which
Hester thought childish. Perhaps it was
more the fashion that way. I did not know. I
did not care. For when you shared a pot
with me, as we huddled before your fire,
and I felt that thick liquid spreading its

warmth inside me, the intense sweetness and subtle agitation of the spirits it induced, I could not resist.

Oh the ladylike delights you introduced me to. You decoyed Hannah by having her make up a fire in the parlour while you sneaked the key to the caddie and taught me how to serve a dish of tea. And as Hester scolded her for profligacy we shrieked and giggled and hushed each other like little girls, trying so hard to be grown genteel. I was thrilled through and through. Thought I had found myself a new sister.

I marvelled at Hester's forbearance but, with the Captain away three weeks in every four, she had his business and that of the household to manage and was often from home or shut up in the parlour. Nels would sigh and shake her head, but what could she say? It was easy to see that you did not charm her as you did me, but she could not rouse herself to object. Even when the accounting was out for such as the sugar she would not suffer more than the inconvenience, for Hester knew very well who was to blame.

Hannah's watchful eye missed nothing. Every night she and I undressed for bed and talked of nothing much more than whether Skeggs's nose was growing more like a plum or less, and would Nels ever manage to make a raised pie stand up by itself. But one day she stopped me on the stair by the coloured window, as I struggled up with two pails of fresh water I had heated in the copper. I had never known anyone for bathing like you, you had me move the dresser and fill the bath before the fire in your room most every week. You had no idea how many pails of water that took. It was all the steam that left your precious almanacs limp and wrinkled but I doubt you even noticed.

'She took a bath last Monday too. How's I supposed to finish the wash?'

'I can always pump more,' I replied coldly.

'Nor you can't, Louise Fletcher. Our rainwater tank may be the biggest in Harwich but it ain't that big,' she said. 'Don't you know the water here's no good? It may as well be brine for pickling. That tank is low already and it will run quite dry if you fill her damned bath today. Tell her she can't have it. She don't know half the upset she causes.'

But I was quite the loyal little miss, wasn't I? You were my mistress and what you wanted it was my business to provide.

'You do your job, and I'll do mine,' I said to her as I took up the pails again, and that night there was no little chat before she blew out the candle.

If Hannah had hoped to check my devotion she chose the wrong complaint. I had never bathed anyone before you, see, bar washing the teats before milking, or dabbing at my mother's blistered fingers. I had never sat on a low stool by the side of a high bath with a foreign sponge light as a puffball in my hand, while the steam rose all around like a washhouse and the fire sparked and chuckled.

I remember the first time I took up the warm water with the sponge and pressed it against your shoulder so it ran down in quick sparkling rivulets. I could hardly breathe. You asked me to pour in the last pail I had set by the fire to keep warm and I watched the force of it dimple your skin. After a while, when I scooped a lock of your hair back up into your cap, you said quietly, 'You do look after me, Dairy Lou. No one ever looked after me so.'

When the day of Mrs Fressing's masquerade finally came, towards the end of March, you sent me out first thing to Mr Townsend's counter. Furious, you were, because the hair dressing you had ordered from London had come with no ties or fastenings. 'What does the man expect me to do? Carry them in my mouth like a bird?' By then, I knew what was expected of me. I sat you down and patted your cheek and clucked over you. I cast about for a dish of sugared almonds and fed them to you, one by one, until you stopped twisting about and sat with a rueful look in your eye. Now I could leave you. I packed the wax berries carefully back in their box and set off at a pace to fetch ribbon to match.

Lordy look at me, I thought, as I hitched up my skirts to cut through Hopkins Lane and walk briskly straight past the Three Squirrels with my head high, something I would never have dared do even three weeks before. Miss Louise Fletcher, dairymaid no more, but the trusted maid of a prominent family, what knows her way about the town. I had taken up your old rabbit muff to keep my hands warm, for after days of rain the sky was high and blue and the still air cold as iron. Yes, I looked the part all right. I had your cut-down striped callimane gown and a set of old stays you'd never worn, and over that the black silk cape. It kept out the cold no better than a cobweb but it was fine and it was yours and did I feel like a lady as I hurried past the taverns with my eyes fixed dead ahead.

Only as I passed the Swan further down

Church Street a hand grabbed my elbow and I bleated like a sheep.

'Let me alone.' The muff slipped right off my hands.

'Hush, hush now, little Louise. Don't say you forgot me?'

He was redder in the face and swaying like a poppy but I knew old Joe.

'What do you want?' I snapped, and I could hear something Handley in my own voice for the first time.

'Well now's, I was on my way to West Street to fetch you but a fellow here wanted my advice, you know how it is. It's your mother, Louise, she's fetched up poorly.' I stopped wiping at the muff. 'What it is I don't rightly know, but —'

'Am I to come home?' I broke in, and as I said it I knew in my heart the farm was home still, and this fine old life with you wasn't to last. I'd be tending my poor mother from now on. I knew it were my duty. But to leave now?

'She's took bad, my girl, and they said to send for you sharpish.'

'Are you headed back today?' I asked.

He nodded. By the look of him he'd be headed straight into the salt marsh if he took up the reins now. But I had to go with him.

'I'll come find you, Joe. Wait here for me, won't you?'

CHAPTER THIRTEEN

He makes his way back to the mess, hoping he will not have missed supper. The fug of boiling pease is everywhere now, a bell is ringing and hurting his head. He is desperate for feeding. He tries not to meet the eyes of the men he passes, rackety and restless. They are all desperate for feeding. He wonders if Nick won the waistcoat after all, wonders if Nick always wins everything. He can feel the bruises coming up, on his cheek, his sides, his buttocks. Oh, he well knows he needs Nick if he is to survive, but he has his pride. By god must he stand up to him. Once he has food in his belly.

Nearing the mess, though, he senses something is wrong. All the men stand rigid, with their backs to him. They are alert, like dogs who've caught a whiff of fox. If they had fur they'd be bristling. Quiet as he can, he slips through to the eighth gun. The press of watching men is too thick for Luke to pass, so he ducks round to the gun hatch but Winn bars his way.

Where their mess table hung between the great guns stands instead the red-haired man from the next mess. He is shirtless and panting hard. Outlandish blue-black tattoos snake across his hairless chest to his navel. His bushy whiskers crackle and glint like hot wires. But his eyes are the palest blue, girlish and soft, the skin about creased with amusement.

Facing him, only inches away, is Nick, stripped to the waist and his head thrust forward level with his powerful shoulders, like a dog straining on a leash. He rocks slowly on his heels. His back is to the lantern and Luke can't see his face.

Blood splatters the ginger whiskers before Luke has even registered Nick's blow. The two men close upon each other. Nick has his face buried deep in the other's shoulder, his cheek half closing his right eye. The light from the swaying lanterns washes over every bulge and ripple of their torsos. Luke watches their feet stamp and slide, like horses in a winter huddle, until Nick breaks away with a roar and kicks out. But the man twists and jabs, jabs again and again, so that Nick must cover his face, then his belly. Little bubbles of spit spurt from his mouth

170

with each blow. Eventually, sucking his belly in, Nick roars again, grabs him round the throat and lands them both on the deck and he's pummelling the man's face back and forth while a sort of spray rises.

Nick doubles up with a yell. The other man is come out from beneath him and has his long legs clamped over Nick's, he's fighting to sit up and jabs his elbow at Nick's neck. They have each other by the throat now, are struggling to their feet and stand braced together, their fingers pressing deep into each other's necks, their heads forced back. Luke sees clearly the compass tattooed on the man's right elbow, its points stretched hard. Then he slips, his head is forced against the roof timbers, as Nick's greater bulk pushes against him. But he does not fall back, he is braced like a deck post himself. His thumbs dig deep pockets in Nick's red throat.

Just when Luke thinks they will choke each other to their deaths, both men drop to their knees. Their hands fall away. Each takes great, tearing gulps of air. Nick's opponent puts one hand to his bleeding nose, feels about blindly for support with the other. Nick's face is stained a deep purple. His chest is heaving, like he's broken from the depths of the ocean.

Nick sits back on his haunches and scrubs his hands over his face, smearing the blood, shaking his head. The other man is on his knees, eyes closed, hands braced on his thighs.

'God damn,' says Nick, his voice thick. 'God damn it, Charlie, mate,' he says to his opponent. 'Lend us a hand now.' And he holds his hand out, still smeared with blood.

Luke stares in disbelief as the man called Charlie pulls Nick to him. They hug each other, long and close. Then Charlie shoves him away so hard they both sway on their knees, and laugh. Nick nods to Bramley, who throws the waistcoat down between them with a curse.

'You're a cocky bastard, Stav, so you are,' says Charlie. He swipes the waistcoat to him and hawks a mouthful of blood.

A file of musketeers breaks through the ranks of the men with their sticks and butts. Officers and mates come clattering down the hatchways. Ugly things are said. Bramley is up and talking into the enraged face of a blustering officer as the sturdy lads line up behind him, shielding Nick and Charlie from view. The officer strikes Bramley across the face with his stick. Then Powell comes from nowhere, forces his way between them, baring his teeth, and bears the brunt of the officers' fury.

The word goes out: there has been trouble on every deck. Fighting among the men will not be tolerated. The newly pressed men must know what naval discipline means. One man from each deck is to be given fifty lashes as an example to the rest. And there will be no supper for the men tonight. The scaldings will be fed to the pigs.

The place erupts. There are howls, jeers, men smash their cans into the sides of the ship and hot flip sprays and splatters their shirts. They are on their feet, climbing over each other, but the marine mount their bayonets and stand steady. One by one the men drop their arms, and turn to look at one another. Their eyes say it all. Luke sees Nick suddenly sit down again and rub at his thighs, interlace his fingers across the back of his neck and stare at the floor.

When all the fight is gone out of them, they are ordered up above deck. They move in small sullen groups, watched warily by the officers. The night air is dizzying. Luke is light-headed with hunger. He staggers as a flopping weight of canvas is tossed into his arms, heavy as a dead dog. It is his hammock. He copies the others and heaves it over his shoulder, the wooden tag banging against his thigh.

They are told to sling their hammocks where they will. Going below again he sticks close by his mess mates, for he has no idea what to do. They all follow Nick down to the lower deck but once there he turns his back on them, lashing his hammock up first, then climbing in silently, mindless of his injuries.

It's William Winn who takes pity on Luke. 'Ignore them,' he says, and pats Luke's shoulder, when Burton and Little offer to show Luke how to tie a noose to hang himself. Winn helps Fleet too, who is so downhearted and tired out that he is crying for his mother. 'I needs my vittles,' he says, again and again. 'What's the navy for, 'cept regular vittles?'

'Milksop,' says Bramley, as he wraps his blanket about him like a tube. 'What I needs is a good shagging. Oh yes. Just one more good deep rutting before we brave the briney —'

'Shut your face,' retorts Nick suddenly, from the depths of his hammock, 'or I'll give you one.'

Luke's legs cast long shadows across the wide empty boards. He is one of the last few left standing on the whole of the lower deck. The rest have flitted up into their roosts like birds. Dozens of them, hung in parallel rows, disappearing off into the darkness. The hammocks are slung so close together Luke has to wait for the ship to roll level before a space clears for him. He grips hold of the ropes, and after three attempts he manages to slip inside.

Nick, bulging in the hammock at his side, is silent and still; but from the dark come the mutters and curses of all the other men, dozens and dozens of them. The snores begin, like some hellish farmyard. An outbreak of coughing spreads. He hears hawking, and spittle landing like birdshit.

He knows he is crying and stuffs his fist in his mouth, bites down. For this is when he cannot help but think of her. Lying close by his side, her warm flesh spilling over his.

Nick swings against him hard, deliberately it seems. And again. Luke can be silent, but he cannot stop his shuddering. Then Nick starts to sing, low and ragged. His words are muffled by the cloth but the slow, lilting rhythm is clear. He turns about to face Luke.

'I'm bound away, me lassie,' he sings quietly, as though for Luke's ears alone.

'For the sake of you, me lassie.'

Luke feels Nick's broad ribs press against him as he draws breath, then sings on.

'So dry your tears and have no sorrow,

175

'*I'm bound away.*'

The next breath they take together.

'*For the sake of you,*' whispers Luke, '*for the sake of you.*'

Then he jumps as a voice rings out, 'Oi shut it, you collier bastard!' Nick struggles upright in his hammock, yells back, more angry voices answer.

Luke draws the blanket up over his ears, feeling the canvas squeeze him like a cloth pudding. But his stomach swings light as a bird. He can smell the hot fresh lamb only the officers are eating. And their words ring in his ears: there will be discipline, at all costs. For they must sail, and soon.

The *Essex* does sail, the very next day. She is packed with men now, they swarm out of the hatches like ants. Beaten out of their hammocks to the call of a piercing whistle and shoved up the ladders to be mustered on the dark, cold deck. The floggings must wait until they are underway.

Luke is shown his station, a larboard pin on the main deck. He stands in line, shivering even in his jacket. He listens to the bellowed orders, but he does not understand a word. He puzzles at the thick ropes that snake about the pin, cranes his neck to see where they might lead. It is so dark still he cannot see the rest of the fleet. There is a sound of hammering, and he catches a whiff of woodsmoke, and frying onion, smells so homely that his stomach spasms. The bell rings again, he is set to lift and carry, for the decks are still not clear enough to be cleaned, and when the bell rings again, they stow their hammocks and are piped below to breakfast.

Three decks means three men to be flogged. Each mess waits to see which of their number is to be lashed. Luke is trying his damnedest not to vomit. Nick urges spoonfuls of burgoo on him, some hot purl. 'Drink it, laddie. Will steady that lubber's stomach of yours.'

He shakes his head. The gruel thickens and cools. The sips of purl he has already taken burn in the pit of his stomach. He stares at the grain of the mess board, while his ears ring and the voices come and go.

Tobias Fleet fiddles with his mug, spinning it round and about like a top. He looks like he's about to cry.

Henry Little's face is stiff as a poker. 'Nick,' he hisses. 'Nick, won't they least tell us where are we bound?'

Nick shrugs and leans back, putting his arm roughly about Luke, who shudders as his gorge rises again. 'Bastard captain don't never tell a bugger, do he?'

'I hear 'tis Spain,' says Burton.

'More like the Indes,' puts in Bramley. 'Chasing Admiral Vernon, ain't we? We'll be out for months. Didn't we stow enough barrels of briny pig to sink us?'

A figure swings down the aft hatchway and the din quiets immediately. The men hunch over their tables as the officer looks them over. There is a cough or two, the scraping of mugs. When he moves on they straighten and meet each other's eyes again. Reprieved, for now.

The autumn sun is clear and harsh. Where it catches ropes and spars it slashes sharp shadows across flesh and wood alike. The sea is a flashing tumbling silver platter, and cannot be looked at for long. Luke looks for land instead, casting desperately around for sight of even a sliver, but there is nothing. Finally, when he is ordered over larboard to help clear the deck, he finds it: the long sloping rise of land to where the chimneys smoke and the spire rises. But before he can fix it in his mind he is ordered below.

The roar of the water grows deeper, and louder. It's like being inside a water mill and hearing the wheel start to turn. Luke is on the lower deck, both arms straining under the weight of a sodden rope as thick as his waist, one of a long snaking line of men holding the great dripping anchor cable. With his knees braced and his lungs bursting in the thick air, he shuffles to and fro, trying not to let his feet slip into the gaps in the planking. Every time the barrels below shift, they release another belch of bilge water, fouler than any muddy marsh. The anchor is already raised, men must already be aloft unfurling the sails. But Luke and the others can see nothing, hear nothing. They must stand there still, arms trembling and shoulders singing out with pain, as the rope grows heavier and heavier; there is a hitch somewhere, perhaps they will have to recoil the whole length.

Now the ship's sides groan like a barn in a storm. The lanterns shiver and the roar of the water so close outside grows still louder. The ship sways, a dancer balancing on one toe. And then Luke can feel it, though his feet are firmly planted on the solid timbers; he knows they are moving, she is surging forwards, carrying him away like a reluctant child.

Six bells, and she is well underway. No land to be seen now, not a whisker. Only the blue ocean, surging wide and deep, and the clean rim of the horizon. The ship seems quite out of control, she pitches and rolls and bucks and strains so. The ropes creak, the very timbers creak, and above his head the huge white canvases crack and shudder like a storm cloud. Luke is terrified: never before has he known all his world to shift and slide so.

Most all the company is assembled on deck, and the rest hang overhead in the swaying rigging. A man vomits on to an officer's shoe and is thrashed for it. The first two men are brought up for punishment. One is lashed to the grating. Luke sees the white flesh of his fingers swollen and grimed. Dead man's fingers.

Tremmel brings the third and final man up. He curses and twists but Tremmel cuffs him about the head with his stick, and prods him in the small of the back, to walk the rest of the length of the deck. The men watch. Luke scans their set faces. Not one cries out or protests, or shows their own relief. They refuse to shame the man with their pity.

The man passes before Luke. With a start Luke sees that it is Powell, the butcher from Colchester who disputed with the bounty man. He holds his head high, biting on his full red lips. His torso is broad as Nick's but he's all blubber. His tight new shirt is already split under one arm. Then he stumbles, he is sobbing shamelessly. Luke's chest tightens, and he casts about for Nick and Charlie. They cannot let this man take their punishment? But there they stand, side by side, heads bent, impassive.

The marine give out the first drum roll. It is ragged, almost comic, like a cat skittering across a roof, for the drummer boy is blushing new. Luke raises his eyes to the highest yards and rigging. All are empty now, the sails tightly swagged like rows of little cocoons. He waits. When he can hear it has begun, he chooses a rope, the highest he can see, and traces the line of it from one end to the other. He does this again and again, to the rhythm of the waves, blocking out all other sounds, until his neck aches. He searches for the angels he saw up there that first day, the wings that sprouted from their backs as they perched on the rigging.

As Tremmel pushes Powell on to the grating, Luke is squeezed back into a corner, he can see nothing of it now even had he wanted to. The stairway to Luke's right is crowded with men. They sit all along the ledge behind him too, their bare feet dangling above his head. Some are weeping with him. Luke feels like a fly who has wandered into the spider's web and become hopelessly entangled.

The final drum roll sounds, the boy has the hang of it now. It's only when the crowds part and the surgeons take the three men below that Luke dares look. Powell's naked torso is bloodied all over. Luke sees his back is scored across many times, like pig rind for roasting. But he is walking. The other two have to be carried.

Luke gets his head over the round hole before he vomits. The bare wooden bench is fouled and damp. He ducks down beneath the huge timber to check, but no man sits there neither. And there is no one on the grating above. Alone. He stands and looks up to check if he can be seen, just as the marine steps out. He crouches down again, heart pounding. How he has craved even a minute's privacy, the need for it claws at his heart. He waits until the marine turn back to the deck. He has seen, squeezed in the corner between the curve of the bow and at the platform's edge, another privy, a low and elegantly curved seat. Less chance of being seen there, under the heavy tackle and swinging ropes. It strikes him as very strange, that this stinking place should be done up so like a parlour, all carved and ornamented with yellow arches and columns. There is even a little roundhouse, with three arches and a round window and a shiny blue door, which he does not dare enter.

He sits down on the curved seat, painted shiny black. Fit for a fine lady, were it not already stained and dirtied. From here he can see the length of the massive bowsprit stretching out and away in front of him, not a soul upon it. Great curving timbers splay out from it to form a sort of cage, a massive ribcage. The high black bulwark rises up behind him. Orders are being shouted behind him, heavy boots thump on the decks. But he is here, alone.

Already some of the gulls' heads are white as ghosts. Winter is coming. The sky beyond, the sea too, both are blue and huge and empty. Air and water, water and air, they fill his eyes. He breathes lungfuls of the chill salt-filled air.

And for a moment, for one crucial, dangerous moment, his mask slips. He feels his face softening, his eyes spill, his jaw grow slack. He huddles his knees together, grasps his elbows. But nothing will hold it back. Out of nowhere, the bitter emptiness he has kept clenched in the pit of his belly comes howling up and out and he has to open his mouth wide. He finds himself keening, rocking, unable to stop. Drool spills over his lips, helplessly he watches it drip down on to the grating.

He calls her name. Once, softly, but now he has heard his own voice say it, she is so real to him again he must say it again and again, calling to her across the water. Never before has he called out with such naked longing, not even when he was taken. Only now, now when it is too late.

And now he remembers something of it. The hand on his shoulder, gripping. The song dying away. The sudden widening space about him, a cooling of the air. Is he in the street now, or still inside? He can't see clearly, his head is spinning. He jerks forward but stumbles. Someone cries out and then there is nothing but spreading, sickening pain and blackness.

Something, somewhere inside him, must have kept alert, for even over the shrieks of the gulls, the creak of the rigging and his own sobs, he hears the scuff of the shiny blue roundhouse door opening. In one swift movement he wipes his hot face with his cuff, blinks hard and stands with his hands ready by his sides, to face whoever comes. Back inside it all goes. He must lock her away. There is no choice.

His eyes are still blurred, and it takes him a moment to recognise the man. His blue coat, his breeches and stockings are those of any officer. But when Luke summons up the courage to meet that steady, dark gaze he knows him to be de Clare.

De Clare's face is concerned, troubled. He clears his throat and says gently: 'So, Fletcher, is it your head again? May I?' And he moves to take Luke's cap.

'No,' Luke backs away. 'No, no.' He fumbles at the panel under a yellow arch. But it is a blind, the door is in the next arch along. He wrenches it open and disappears inside.

CHAPTER FOURTEEN

I hoped with all my heart the ribbon was to your liking, for if it weren't I hadn't a hope of getting away. As you fingered it I watched your face, as was my habit. I liked particular to see you glance down, your lashes lay the softest fringe across your cheeks, so dark and fine.

You let the ribbon fall and pushed the box away. It would do.

'Now, was the *Mavis* in?'

Henry's ship was expected in April, but word had come that it might arrive sooner and so every day that week you had sent me to the quay to check. For it would be glorious were he to escort you to the masquerade, you said. You wanted to show him off to the local gentry, and for him to see you the finest of the county. Know what a catch he had made. And then he would be more than eager to sit down with the Captain and make the final arrangements before he sailed again. You'd be a married woman by Christmas. And I, I would be a lady's maid up in town. What could be finer? What indeed?

'Lou?' you asked again, frowning. 'Come now. Did you see the *Mavis*?'

'I did not,' I said. After meeting Joe I had quite forgot to go on to the quay.

You pulled a face then, but I knew I had to risk it. 'Miss, I did see Joe, old Joe.'

'Who?'

'From your uncle's farm. He says my mother is taken ill.' I waited.

'Badly?'

'Yes, I think so.'

You could always surprise me. For straight off your whole face softened and you leant over to rub my forearms soothingly. 'Ah, you poor girl. I'm so sorry,' you said with a frown. I realised then, of course, you could not but be remembering your own mother.

'Of course you must go,' you said firmly.

I let out my breath. 'Thank you, miss.'

'Tell Joe to come fetch you.'

I dropped a curtsey I was so grateful. I had not expected it to be so easy. 'Thank you, miss, thank you,' I said. I could hear my voice shake.

All at once I was back there up in the wide fields, and full of resolve. I had no good news of Luke, at least not yet, with which to ease my mother's mind, but I could try to give her hope. I could keep her indoors and clean and tend her. Yes, I could treat her like a lady, now I knew how. And if Hester would advance me my first month's wages, due next week, then Harwich had apothecaries, their windows hung with snake skins and peacock feathers, and every remedy you could wish for. I knew it would be her lungs that troubled her, certainly she would need something to ease her bones. Was Mary dosing her? I wondered. And my heart leapt sudden at the thought of seeing Mary. I had not realised I had missed them both so, felt guilty then for not thinking of them, thinking only of you.

An hour or two later I came to your door, found you before the mirror still. 'I'm packed up, miss,' I said.

'What?' you said, in such a tone that I stopped dead. You stood up and the ribbon spooled from your lap. 'You mean to go *now*?'

I nodded.

You gave an incredulous laugh. 'Certainly not.' Swiftly then, you came over and guided me to sit beside you on the bed. You snaked your arm about my waist. 'Lou, dearest, Lou, my love, surely you did not think to leave me now?' And you turned my chin to you, so all I could see were your clear brown eyes, so close and bright. 'Goodness, Lou, don't I need you? Tonight most of all. To dress me, to do my hair, remember that page from the almanac? And those dear little mulberries, you chose the perfect ribbon, and who else could place them right?'

Taking up both my hands, you pressed them to your bosom, jiggling your feet impatiently. 'Oh Lou, do not turn sour on me. I promise, you shall go tomorrow. Forget old Joe and his cart, much better I see you on to the morning stage myself. And then you can stay home with your dear mother as long as she needs you.'

I could not speak. Had there ever been a time I had not done your bidding? How well you had trained me. And how much I wished to please you, always.

'Mary will be tending your mother well, I'm sure.' You smiled. 'Fair drowning her in cordial, no doubt.' I'd talked much about Mary: far more, I realised, than about my mother.

'Lou, dear.' You had that tone in your voice now and I knew to be still. 'This is what I've been trying to teach you all these weeks, after all. It's the reason you're here. You want me to appear well before the society, don't you? You want Henry to see me at my best?'

I nodded. I did, at least I thought I did.

'And for him to want me, more than ever? Well, that is your task, Lou, remember. To make me a gentlewoman, worthy of such a catch. And Lou, when he marries me, just think of the life we will have up in London. And he will marry me, if you do your duty well. Lou, remember that.'

Your tone was light but I could not miss what you implied. Your welfare was now my main, my only, concern. You were my mistress, after all. Then you smiled at me and as you did you tucked the end of a ringlet into the corner of your mouth and closed your teeth on it. It was a habit of yours and it always distracted me. I wanted to curl my little finger about the ringlet and slip it out, all stiff and wetted.

'Oh, my dear little milkmaid, you have come on so fast!' you were chiding me. 'Who else could do as well? Imagine Hannah, pressing smuts all over my bodice. Imagine Hester's great fingers squishing those lovely mulberries!'

You held my gaze and I had to smile. You knew you had won then. You always did.

'Yes, yes, you see,' you said in triumph. 'Now you can make me so fine he'll want to marry me within the week and we'll be in London before May Day!'

And so it was agreed that I should visit my mother after the masquerade. No need to find Old Joe and tell him I would not be coming. I felt uneasy still, but I told myself there was nothing to be done. I reminded myself that my mother's health had often failed at the end of winter and come right again with warmer weather. I would not fret, I would put her from my mind. And so we plunged into the whole business of dressing you.

I took down the lilac silk made up as an Égyptienne dress that Mrs Birch had sent only the day before and gasped again at its splendour. You thought the sleeves a tad too skimped, but agreed it rather good 'for a provincial maker'. Since Henry's long looked-for ship had not yet arrived, it was agreed that Hester was to accompany you to the masquerade in his place. You went down to see about her gown, leaving me to press your best chemise, brush and sprinkle the new jessamy gloves and shut them away again in their bag. By dinner time I had done most of what was left to do.

While the Captain was away, Hester had got into the habit of dining with us in the kitchen, for you were so often out or still abed, and she did not see the sense of dirtying a fresh cloth. But when I went down to dine she was not there.

Hannah pushed over last night's ham. 'They're shut in the parlour still, Miss Hester and Miss Rebecca both. What's it about now?'

'Opened door,' said Skeggs, chewing hard, 'this morning, I did. To a fellow' — he swallowed — 'With his hands full of bills. Ha.' He forked another slice.

Nels sighed. 'Here we go again. Sooner she's married off the better — 'scuse me Louise, but it's true. Hester's a fine young woman and she don't need this.'

Then we all jumped, for we heard the parlour door wrenched open and footsteps in the hallway. And then your voice, fierce and outraged. 'I will not hear this. You treat me like a child!'

Hester must have followed, for her voice was just as loud. 'Enough, Rebecca, I have had enough. Once you are married — if you are married — you will have to run Henry's household as I run ours. You say he expects to find you a gentlewoman, well you must know a gentlewoman keeps her own inventories and accounts, she regulates —'

'Oh yes, dear sister!' Your voice was harsh and mocking as I'd never heard it. 'Oh yes, for she must order the coal, she must ruffle his shirts, she must keep up the damned preserves!'

'Rebecca, listen to me. If you marry Henry he will be away at sea for months at a time, longer than ever Dadda is away. How will you manage? Do you even know how to number linen? How much of the Canary wine is left? What will get the stain out of that cambric you ruined last week? I have tried, truly I have. Perhaps our mother could have done better. But as you are, you would not make him a wife.' She took a breath. 'You are not qualified to make him more than a mistress!'

There was a horrible pause, and we all looked at each other. I held my breath.

Then you spoke firmly, and a little quieter. But still we heard every word. 'You never did think I would amount to much, did you? Well, do not worry about me. Of course, an old maid must concern herself with such things. No, wait, you do not understand. At least one of us knows how to fish for a fine catch. I have caught myself a specimen. Remember Henry and I are to live in town, he has promised me that. I shall not need to put up butter or mess about with fowl and swine and country morals. When he is ashore we shall entertain the fashion, and when he is away I shall buy in what I need. But for now you must cut me some slack, until I have reeled him in. Let me but catch him, and I need never worry you again.'

I picked at a dried bit of dough on the table. I was ashamed on your behalf, that they should all hear you talk so. But still my heart beat faster. I was a little proud, you see, proud that it was I who was to come with you, away from all this. Already Hester's prudence had come to seem a trifle dull, her scruples overstated. Skeggs no longer alarmed me but merely irritated. Billy was a pain, Nels was of no consequence, Hannah a sort of wearying cipher. No, I did not care one whit about any soul in the Handley household. Bar you.

We heard one of you go up the stair and the other come to the kitchen door. I looked up and it was you, with one hand on your hip and the other fussing at the back of your hair. Your cheeks were flushed and your eyes glittered. You took a breath and your voice was perfectly composed once more.

'Sadly, my dear people, my sister is indisposed and shall not be able to come masquerading tonight. No doubt she will be much missed. But, rather than waste the full five shilling her ticket has cost — for economy is the greatest virtue, I have heard

— I shall take another as my companion.'

You stared hard at Nels and then Hannah, daring them to make reply. Skeggs fiddled with his pipe. My heart was hammering in my chest.

'Lou, what do you say?'

Now you looked at me. And of course I nodded and smiled, then grinned, and clasped my hands together, for I could not think of anything finer, had not dreamt of anything more wonderful, than walking through the doors of the Assembly Rooms at your side.

CHAPTER FIFTEEN

Luke is learning fast, but every encounter with Nick or his like leaves him gasping still. Now they are at sea he moves as one with the rest of the ship's company, in constant motion: copying, watching, following. But he feels very much like a child once more, a mutinous, helpless, terrified child.

When he curls up in his hammock he dreams the ship has come to life, and in a fit of wickedness has taken him up and carried him off and all the kicking and howling in the world can't get her to set him down. He clutches at her ropes in desperation and hatred. He downs every mug of beer or purl or flip he can get his hands on. Some days his feet seem to skate above the slanting, bucking decks and an invisible cushion softens the pain whenever he knocks his head on some beam or other, which he does a dozen times a day.

Other times it's as though all the fear that

coursed through his veins and flooded his brain has set like a kind of jelly. He wakes in his hammock, squeezed like a newborn calf and so fuddled with bad air that his mouth tastes of old pennies. He tumbles out in a daze and never quite shakes it off.

Bramley laughs at him. 'Sorry little milksop.' He takes advantage. Burton would sneak Luke's biscuit the moment he sets it down by his platter. But as Luke has little or no appetite he rarely protests. He keeps his head down. Barely speaks. Bramley and the sturdy lads turn their attention to Fleet, who squeals every time they knock his elbow from the board.

Only Nick looks out for Luke. He grins when he spies him. He calls Luke 'my fresh lad', says he is sweet as river water, has him sit beside him at the mess table. He seems to be always on hand. 'Snap to it, laddie!' he tells Luke as he fumbles to fold away his hammock. Then he shows him how to tug it tight enough to pass through the bosun's ring and so saves him a beating. No call for gratitude: quick now, Luke must run up on deck to stow his hammock with the bosun's pipe screeching in his ears. He won't look at the great tossing grey waters around them now, won't look at no one. Just squats down to tug the canvas tight over the netted hammocks, and make the knots slowly and surely, as Nick has taught him.

This is his world now, he can pace it from side to side in the time it takes him to draw breath. He gets the knack of matching his step on to the hatchways with the sway of the deck. He always watches for the heads to empty, half opens the door to make sure, before he dares visit. He moves where he is told, never meeting a man's eye if he can help it. Some childish part of him believes that if he won't look at them they can't see him. There are fights still, every day, and floggings too.

Every job he is given he carries out to the letter. Three strokes with the holystone, dip and move on. Hold the rope and brace, look only at the back of the man in front of you. It works, for a while. He has seen what happens to men like Powell, who dispute and resist. Powell is out of sick bay now, working under close supervision on the quarter-deck with the other troublemakers. The stoop-shouldered officer Tremmel has it in for him, never lets him alone.

Luke is grateful for his lubberly station, manning a larboard pin on the main deck. That first day at sea most of the pressed men ordered aloft baulked even at stepping up on the sides. They climbed two or three rungs of the shrouds and then clung on and refused to move, until the mates closed in with their starting sticks. He saw one man swing round to the other side of the shrouds to escape the blows and when a gust came it lifted him clear away, like a curled leaf torn from a branch. The warning cries died away in an instant for the man was blown overboard and there was only the wind loud in Luke's ears.

All he has to do is run to that larboard pin and tug on the rope whenever he is yelled at. He looks for de Clare, but in all the hordes of men who move about the ship, too many to count or know, he never sees him. He sees Dominique, though, the loblolly boy, who stands before the foremast every morning, banging a wooden pestle against a mortar and calling for the sick and injured in a fluting, hesitant tone. One by one, men collect about him, men who nurse explosive coughs or crushed fingers thick and black with blood, who limp painfully or stagger with fever. But most days the officers strike them away. The ship is sailing badly, she lurches about like a mad dog, not a hand can be spared lest she overturn altogether.

'Thank the lord — for men like you, Stavenger,' Tremmel tells Nick. He's so drunk he can barely get his words out. 'You able men — you show the bastards — it's done all right! Have our backsides rammed all the —' he screws his forefinger into Nick's shoulder, and licks his lips '— all the way up Ipswich dock — weren't for you.'

Nick, mustered an able seaman and assigned to the mizen top, has proved himself the most able of all the pressed men, almost despite himself. He has a talent for it, never puts a foot wrong. And he's fast, so fast, carrying that great bulk of his up and into the air like the wind itself is lifting him. Nick makes a face for the boys when Tremmel lurches away, but Luke sees how bright his eyes have become.

He too is grateful to Nick, for the harsh words that save him from beatings or worse. Bramley says Nick is Luke's sea daddy, but not in Nick's hearing. 'It's a lucky lad, Fletch,' Winn tells him solemnly, 'that has such a right proper seaman to see him straight.' Nick proves a generous soul indeed. He shares all he knows with Luke. Never make a knot you can't loosen, he tells him. Shows him how to make a cunt splice, how to form an eye, even how to angle the holystone so as not to tire too easy. Names the parts of the ship for him, her sails, her rig, her very timbers, as a dame teaches her charges by recitation. Luke cannot recall his land daddy treating him so well. He never shared out his meat, when they had any, nor bought him an extra blanket, let alone gave him a woollen jacket. No man has ever treated him so well.

But then Luke thinks of the fifth coin, that Nick still has, and his heart starts to thump with anger and resentment. His prick of baccy. The errands he must run and the slops he must empty. He sees, also, how Nick and the red-headed Charlie glance over at him when they talk, for they are thick as anything since their fight, always conferring over the seventh gun. Charlie is the top-man of the main and Nick can't keep away. They both know they are the best of the rest, but who is the best of them?

Despite all Luke's efforts to lie low, Nick draws him into their rivalry. Damn that lubberly station, he will get his fresh laddie aloft, make a top-man of him. He'll have a word with Tremmel and trounce that Charlie, he'll have Luke raising the mizenmain with him in six minutes. Whenever there's an idle moment, he has his arm clamped firmly about Luke's shoulders, has Luke craning his neck so he can point out the intricacies of the mizen rig, and how the canvas moves, and touching his palm to his cheek so he feels the winds. Charlie watches them, smoothing his whiskers and smiling, always smiling. Luke can think of almost nothing more terrifying than going aloft, with either of them. But what can he do? When Nick claps his arm about his shoulders, squeezes his neck between his fingers, Luke winces and smiles, and submits.

And the wind must have changed again, for the holler goes out: away aloft! In an instant Nick and Charlie are gone from his side, racing for their shrouds. Charlie reaches his first, Nick has a little farther to skit past the longboats and dodge a couple of dozing marine. Luke watches him swing up by one hand, jacking his feet straight on to the third ratline and he's off and up on the windward side.

'Come on lads!' he roars as his men clamber up after him, six, seven, eight of them. The mates are there, lashing out at their feet to get them to climb. The men cluster around the lower ratlines to escape the blows. The mates yell and curse at them, the last man to reach his station will always be whipped. They start to edge their way up. Nick climbs steadily and rapidly away from them, up and out of sight behind the billowing mizen sail.

Standing by his larboard pin, Luke takes

the rope as it's paid out to him and steadies his stance. He has worked hard to copy every move the other men at his station make. He stands now with his knees slightly bent, holding the rope lightly. While he waits he scans the mainmast shrouds for Charlie. He spots him already well above the main fighting top. 'Eyes on the job, lubber!' The mate's stick lands on his upper arm and he drops his rope. Down comes the stick on his arse as he bends to pick it up. 'Damn your useless hide, Fletcher.'

But soon as he can, Luke is watching the top-men again. They seem to him to have a sort of awesome freedom, moving about up there in the billowing canvas clouds, or perched on the rig like birds, the wind fluttering their bright kerchiefs. Luke longs to be alone, he is never alone, and there is so much air up there, so much space. But he could never join them, the very thought of the climb makes him dizzy. When he sees them swing about up there he knows very well why Nick has named him mouse: he is a timid, scurrying creature, looking for his hole.

Nick appears high on the mizen yard. He lets go of the mast and steps out on to the yard. Luke gasps. Nick is running along the top of it, like a child across a plank bridge, his shirt flagging out behind him. He is so high, maybe one hundred feet in the air, higher than the tip of the spire at Harwich. Then, after only a few paces and without even slowing, he drops down abruptly behind the yard, both arms outstretched above his head. Luke's heart plummets too and he shuts his eyes. He remembers the man who was blown into the sea that first day.

But Nick is still there, he can see his head and shoulders steady above the yard, and his yellow kerchief. He watches him edge out along the foot-rope as the other men come out from the mast, lined up like gulls along a roof ridge.

Luke's main-topsail tumbles down above his head with a sound like falling rocks, and he flinches for fear he will be crushed. The ropes creak and grumble as they all strain to tie her in. He looks up and round just in time to see the mizentop unfurl at the tips, a butterfly spreading its wings, and there is Nick sat above it, straddling the larboard yard-arm, king of his world.

Chapter Sixteen

We were horrible late for that masque, remember? I blamed myself, never having done that sort of fancy work before — curling your hair near singed off my fingers. This was my biggest test so far, and oh how I wanted to please you and to be proud of you, my own handiwork. Everything took so long. But you never were one to be hurried. You acted quite patient and encouraging, and how grateful I was. Gay voices and footsteps sounded in the street below, but we stood one minute longer before the dressing-table mirror.

I hoped to heaven you were pleased with what you saw. The figure I saw reflected in the middle panel might have walked through the mists of time, to my mind you were indeed the finest queen the Égyptiennes could have ever known. Your fine bosom, that you had not let me whiten with powder, spilled over the outlandish bodice, your skin creamier than ever against the shimmering violet silk. I had curled your hair hard and high, and it drew up your face somehow, gave you an imperiousness that struck me as the spit of a Pharaoh's queen. The wax berries, that I had nestled and tied over your left ear, looked ever so real in the candle-light. They were quite as succulent as your lips that you had rouged yourself, using paste from a tiny pot hidden in a drawer. Finally, you'd handed me a heavy chain of red and sea-green stones, that had been your mother's. 'What Hester don't know won't hurt her,' you'd said, and dipped your head for me to clasp it about your neck. When you looked up again you smiled at me like a child on her birthday. I'd never seen you look lovelier, Becca. Never forgotten how you looked that night.

But there too, squeezed into the smaller pane of mirror to the left, was my reflection, and looking at it then I did not know whether to feel cross or forlorn. For it had struck you as the most amusing jape to dress me for the masquerade as the milkmaid I had been all my life.

'Come now,' you'd chided me, 'it is in the very spirit of the thing, do you know nothing? There will be sailors there and other milkmaids too no doubt, and none of them real. You shall play your part so well, Lou, they will think Hester the finest actress of her age.' You had decided, in the spirit of devilry that masquerading required, that we were not to let slip that Hester had refused to attend despite Henry's continuing absence, and you were taking your maid in her place.

Reluctantly, I'd retrieved my old work clothes from my box. It was only a matter of weeks since I'd swapped them for your silks and muslins, but they seemed from another lifetime. The woollen bodice itched my neck, felt bulky and oh so staid. There were snags I had not noticed before in the heavy frieze skirt and I was sure it still stank something rancid. I stood rigid with humiliation as you tugged a huge mob cap low over my eyes and teased out my hair either side into a windblown thatch, giggling all the while. Most ridiculous of all, I was to clutch a tiny tin pail, dressed with butter muslin and filled with almond sweetmeats shaped as butter pats. Nels had not thought the extra work these gave her amusing in the slightest.

'Miss, they will think me a right fool,' I had said when you dangled it before me. 'They will know me for what I am, it is too shaming.'

But you'd overcome all my objections. 'Do you not know how to have fun? This is the art of it, don't you see? Here, take your mask.'

You handed me the ribbon-bound stick and I put the black felt half-mask to my eyes. It was like pressing a blackbird's wing to my face. I felt myself inside a dark tunnel, the world narrowed so all I could see was you. I wanted it that way. I resolved to keep it tight to my face, I would be as a carriage horse in blinkers.

You laughed. 'Now see yourself? You look ever so amusing, I swear you shall be the sensation of the evening, not I!'

You squeezed my hand and we turned to go. And just then I happened to glance at the mirror's other panel, the small pane to the right. All it reflected was your bed, the yellow counterpane rucked where we had sat upon it, and strewn with almanacs, hair rags and the London papers. But of a sudden I seemed to see a figure there, that of a gentleman I had never seen, but knew to be tall and fine. I forgot all my qualms about my dress and the silly little pail. For I fancied I saw Henry, your husband to be, standing by your side. He filled the frame, and he drowned out all other thoughts, for he reminded me of what I had quite forgotten: that I had dressed you so very well for the man you said you loved and were to marry.

Most of all I had not expected the sound of it. The glaring lights, yes, that dazzled like the setting sun. They blurred the frames of the upstairs windows and cast down great pools of illumination on the street and gardens as we walked there, hand in hand. The swarms of society, yes, those too I had anticipated, buzzing ever more loudly as we threaded through George Street. The way was blocked with carriages, each with its flaring lamp and jiggling harness, a miniature ship coming into anchor, with all the same shouts to make way and halt and curses aplenty.

My jaw trembled despite all my efforts to be calm, my cheeks were hot despite the night air and the chill off the water. I gripped your hand ever tighter as you nodded to the gentlemen in livery. We mounted the soft-carpeted shallow treads up to the first floor and I bit my lip with worry that I might stumble or drop the stupid little pail. I felt myself the hen to your partridge, smaller, duller, but devoted still. And it was then that it came: the most extraordinary tide of sound, flowing down over me. It was a sort of a shimmering din, that increased with every step we took, and it brought me out in goose bumps all over.

By the time we emerged into that vast panelled room, filled with people standing about and sitting in clusters below gilt mirrors and burning candelabras, each holding a mask to their face, it had become an all-engulfing roar. One after another, folk turned to see us, and you let my hand drop and stood slightly aside, to show yourself off. Cast loose, I swayed a little, even shut my eyes a moment behind my mask. It was then I began to make out all the various elements of that magical sound. The shuffling slippers and grating boots on a polished floor, the press and rustle of silk and taffetty against velvet chairs, the tingle of glass and silverware, and over all that the boom and surge and trill of dozens, hundreds of voices.

Here were all the gentlefolk of the town and beyond, that Hester and you had turned over so often in your talk. Tall Mr Richards, garbed in red, marching from group to group like a wooden soldier, his shoulders stiff and his face like a skull. Young women with narrow shoulders and twisting fingers, blushing and awkward; a girl dressed all in pink muslin, her face pale and her eyelashes pale as a piglet's. Was that a daughter of Sir Philip Parker, our Member for Parliament no less, come over from Erwarton?

The men were mostly clustered together about a long table laid with three punch bowls and quantities of cut glasses. The women reclined on sofas and low chairs, craning their necks about to see who was there and whether anyone might bring them refreshment. Yes, the place was crowded beyond belief, and unbelievable hot. As fast as a candle blew out, a footman was there to relight it. And the ceaseless talking, all the bared teeth and fluttering fans and sudden laughs. It went right through me, that sound, like I was a plucked string. I took up your hand again and you squeezed my fingers, whispering from behind your mask: 'Now, let us launch ourselves.'

You nodded to a fat old lady bedecked with green feathers, who pointed her fan at me and shrieked with amusement. A tall pallid gentleman removed his mask altogether to wink. You acknowledged them both, and the rest, dipping one elegant curtsey after another.

'Come, we will not stop, let us see the room,' you whispered again.

I followed in your wake through the clusters of spindly chairs arranged on a

Turkey rug by the fireplace. On the way you took up two cups of sherbet from a tray and handed me one, and then we were across the carpet and the room that I had thought so large revealed another wing to the right, lengthening maybe forty feet away to where a band of players sat beneath the hugest sash window I had ever seen. They had laid down their instruments and the dancing floor before them was empty and vast.

Taking a sip of the sweet, foaming sherbet, I looked about, at the many-hued flotsam of harlequins and sailors, balladiers and blackamoors, fools and columbines washed up around the corners. I could scarce believe these people were real, ordinary citizens. Some sat at small tables playing cards, others stood about spooning jellies into their mouths or nibbling at pastries. All were dressed lavishly and quite disguised behind their masks. They were fantastical, yet none so exotic as you. And there indeed was another milkmaid, though her gown was the softest creamy lawn and bedecked with blue ribbons, and she carried a small hairless dog instead of a pail.

'Oh, what a disappointment!' you said, in a peevish tone.

I turned to you in surprise. 'What do you mean? It's wonderful, miss, wonderful.'

'Just look at them all. Why, there is Betty Thornton. She's been telling the whole world she would come as an angel. And old Mr Wilkinson, who didn't know he liked to dress as a wench. Damn me, Lou, I could tell you who everyone is here, and where's the excitement in that? And now,' you said, downing your cup, 'here approaches Mrs Fressing, our lady directress and the outright ruler of her band of governors. What a little queen she is. Watch her run at the men, with that frisk and jump she has, like a gambolling lamb.'

Indeed even I could see she cut a rather undignified figure. She wore her hair à-la-blowze, her hoops were huge, and her skirt billowed before and aft, fit to trip her at any moment or, at the least, to reveal more of her nether regions than was seemly. As she approached us she stretched out her neck and rolled her eyes.

'Rebecca, my dear, you are magnificent, as ever, as ever.'

Her skirts had sailed ahead of her, and she quelled them just in time.

'You make a very fine orientelle, Rebecca.'

You merely nodded and smiled.

Mrs Fressing eyed me blandly. 'And who is this most convincing milkmaid?'

'Why, Nessie, she is a milkmaid,' you said

solemnly.

A nervous titter burst from Mrs Fressing's lips, then she looked at me again. She knew Rebecca was playing her, but she could not let herself be bettered.

'Goodness, Hester, I am so sorry,' she said, taking my hand, 'you look so small, so convincing common.' She blanched. 'I mean to say —' Her hand stilled, she had felt the size of my hands, their roughness, and I wished you had found me gloves to fit. 'My dear, what did you —'

'Nessie, let me put you out of your misery, this is not Hester at all, but a young milk-maid come a-visiting from the country.'

So I was not to pretend to be Hester after all. You had changed your game again, and I did not quite know if I enjoyed it, although it did amuse me to see this silly woman squirm so.

Mrs Fressing looked hard at each of us in turn, obviously confused and not a little put out, despite her fixed smile. 'Well, I see that, but —'

'You see that you do not know everyone, Nessie. Ain't that something? And I shall not even introduce you for she is to be our secret, at least for now. Promise me you will not tell? Good. And now, what of Henry? I am so impatient for news. What does Mr

Fressing say?'

Mrs Fressing launched on a long account of everything that she had gleaned from her husband regarding the movement of the ships in the harbour that week. Partway through you set down your empty cup and beckoned over a man to serve us all with wine. The gist of it all was that the *Mavis* had in fact been spied in the outer roads, and that Henry might very possibly be here tonight, at some point, but of that she could not be sure, what with the winds and the tides being something she never understood.

And then the band struck up with a squawk of pipes and scrape of strings, for the dancing was begun. You and Mrs Fressing were soon surrounded, for which I was most grateful, and I backed away with my wine to find myself a seat.

For a while I had nothing to do but watch, and sip at my wine, and as liveried men came by so often to fill my glass I lost track of what I'd drunk. I was more used to beer than wine. The dancing figures moved before me, flashing blue and yellow and pink and dun, and I amused myself by attempting to identify the stuffs and working out whom their wearers thought they might be. I imagined how, when we got to London, I might attend more such occasions with you. But then, was it really done for ladies to take their maids out with them? Hester had not seemed to approve at all, though I had put that down to pique. I had not seen anyone else here who looked like they might be a servant, whatever their costume. It was all in the bearing, I thought, and I sat a little straighter, watched how the seated ladies set out their toes before them, so's they peeped out from beneath their skirts. I sat so a while, but then felt all eyes upon me, grew dreadful conscious of how slight my bosom yet was, how large my feet must seem, and shrank to conceal them.

And always, I kept an eye out for a fine young man with a seagoing air. Of course Henry might already be here, fully costumed as lord knew what. But whenever I saw a naval-looking fellow in coat and breeches, my chest tightened a little.

The dancing went on, and my cup was refilled, and still I did not seem to see him. I searched for you, watched you move from group to group, but saw you greet only other women and old men. In the end I grew, though I would not admit it to myself, rather bored. Slowly I realised that rather than dreading Henry's arrival I should be worrying about my mother. I should be with my mother. Yet here I was. And so I forced myself to listen to the conversation of my neighbours: a plump young girl who had slumped down alongside what looked like her mother, both quite out of breath and fanning themselves vigorously.

'Would you look at that girl?' the mother was saying.

'Her there?'

'No, there, hanging on the neck of our Member for Parliament, no less. Yes, in the spotted pink.'

'What there?' The girl pointed her finger and her mother slapped her hand down with her fan. She giggled. 'Goodness, Mother, what a sight!'

I looked across the room, following their gaze, and saw the very last person I was expecting to see there. My own sister Susie.

I knew her by her waist, her tight tied little waist, and by the way she moved her hips. She had unhanded the old MP, who stood swaying and nodding foolishly some feet away, and had taken up the hand of a burly man dressed as a tar, in wide canvas trowsers and a full checked shirt. Neither of them held masks. He grinned at her stupidly and was obviously quite drunk. She wore a flimsy skirt spotted pink, over another yellow one, with a spotted pink bodice and a thin muslin apron pinned up high. She had a pink mob cap tied tight about her chin, with lashings of pink ribbon two inches wide. Her hair was all ringleted and kinked close about her eyes. Her cheeks were rouged and her lips were reddened. And she was singing, I could hear her rough voice quite clearly over the fiddles and the pipes and the hubbub.

'Don't you see the ships a-coming, don't you see them in full sail,' she sang, slapping the tar's chest with every line.

I knew this air, I had heard it sung by the gangs of women who strode down to the dock in gangs of six or seven every time a new ship came in. They dressed just as brightly, moved their hips so, shouting and singing and blocking the street and followed by shouts and lewd whistles.

The mother beside me patted my arm. 'Shocking, ain't it? I did say to Mrs Fressing, I told her myself quite some time ago, it was a mistake.'

'What was?' I asked dully. I could not take my eyes off Susie. What was she doing here? I saw others look over at her, toss their heads and laugh, and I burnt with shame. I had to go to her, find out why she was dressed so, and take her away. Did she even know our mother was ill?

The woman talked on. 'Why, the admis-

sion, of course. Told her straight, you're setting it too low. Never attended any assembly
at Bury, even Colchester, that weren't a
sight more. But she would insist. It's our
very first masquerade, we must be sure of a
good attendance. Some would say she don't
know what she's about. But she won't be
told, no, not that Mrs Fressing.'

On and on she ran, her daughter clucking
and nodding beside her in a relish of delicious indignation. Then 'oh!' said the daughter suddenly, and stopped fidgeting. The tar
had turned his back and, leaning heavily on
Susie's shoulder, was pissing into the fireplace.

'Didn't I tell you?' said the mother with
satisfaction. 'Now didn't I? Five shilling
indeed!'

The footmen had noticed too, and in a
moment Susie and her tar were being
escorted to the stair. I ran after Susie,
caught up with her just as the doormen un-
barred the double doors. Her cap was half
off her head and she was trying to wrench
the ribbons straight while they wrestled with
her companion.

'Susie? Susie!' I took her by the shoulders.
'What are you doing here? Who is this man?
Why are you —'

She looked me up and down. 'Well fuck

me into next week. If it ain't mutton dressed as mutton.' She was terrible drunk. 'That lady of yourn turned you out already? Look at the state of yer.'

I was furious, beside myself with shame and rage. 'Look at yourself, Susie. How did you get in here?'

'Same ways I hopes you did, darling. Kind gent paid for me, didn't you, Todger?' The tar had given up resisting and stood like a horse in harness. 'Done well for himself, this boy has.' She patted the heavy sack of coin hung about his neck, then turned back to me. 'What you think? I'm a respectable girl I am. No sneaking up the back stair for me. He got me a mask too, though I can't seem to place it. Waste of time, though, eh. Had a sight more fun down the Swan.'

'Who is this man? What about Jem?'

'What about bloody any of them?'

I swallowed. 'Are you living here in Harwich now, Susie? Do you not know —'

An attendant took a hold of her arm. 'Oi, hang about now!' she yelled at him. 'Can't you see I'm holding a conversation?'

They had the doors open now, the cold night air streaming in. A crowd was gathering in the street to watch. Before I knew it they'd thrown the pair of them out in the street. The tar staggered hard but kept to his feet. Susie, though, toppled full length and lay in the dirt, quite winded, her skirts up about her thighs.

I made a move down the steps but one of the gents in wigs barred my way. 'You may'nt come back in, miss, if you leave now.' And even in all my distress I knew I could not leave you. I knew too, that if I stepped over that threshold I would be back out there with the tars and the whores and no way back in, just another country girl come to town to try her luck.

So I watched from the lighted doorway as the tar helped Susie to her feet quite tenderly. Kissed her cheek, brushed at her skirts and fiddled hopelessly with her ruined cap. Then they set off down the street.

CHAPTER SEVENTEEN

Nick takes the poker and brings its red hot tip within an inch of singeing his whiskers. The fiery light glints off his eyes. He grins at them all.

'Get on with it, Stav,' mutters Charlie. Charlie's flaunting that waistcoat, new bone buttons shining jaunty bright under a yellow belcher kerchief furled and pointed as wide as his red moustache. Charlie has beaten Burton and Bramley at cards, again, and is restless, looking around for another game. His left leg, braced against Nick's sea chest, does not stop jiggling, like a rope quivering in the wind.

'The cans, laddie, come on,' says Nick, with an eye to Charlie.

Luke takes up the black jack he has filled with beer and starts to pour.

'Not so much,' says Nick. 'You know now.'

Luke sets the first mug before him and Nick lowers the poker's glowing tip into it as though to douse it. But a bright white foam surges up and the beer splutters with a noise like hail on a windowpane. Nick sighs with pleasure and breathes in the taffy fumes.

'God damn give it here.' Charlie snatches the mug and downs the hot flip in one, drenching his whiskers.

Nick jabs his poker into can after can. 'Come on lads! Drink down and here's to Nicholas Stavenger, newly master of the mizentop!'

Yes, he's as full of it as a penned-up billy goat, is Nick. Before this latest triumph he told them many times of how he cozened the lieutenant into signing him up as an able seaman that first day, drawing an able seaman's pay, but without any papers to prove himself. Burton and Little moon over their cans as he tells it all again to Charlie.

'I told him, boys, your gangers snatched me from out the Billy. Pulled me straight out the smacking cunt of my dear little bint. No room in my goddamn throbbing breeches for my papers or aught else, was there? Then I told him good, I was in collier brigs up and down this coast all my life, except for two voyages to the Indian, and rated able from the first day I stept aboard. I knows my rigging and my sails. I can handle a gun as well as a woman, and my drink too. Damn it, I'd been with Captain Fawcett in the *John O'Keery* out of Staithes for three seasons, was due to cast off with him for Berwick that same day. Oh, yes, I faced that fellow fair and square — not quarrelsome. He liked my spirit, he did, after all the sad lubberly bastards he'd had through weeping for their wives and children. Prove yourself lively, lad, and I'll rate you, he said.

'Oh, I more than proved myself, lads. And it was after that squall in the dog watch yesterday, when we got her reefed faster than a fly lands on shit, that the Captain himself came to me. Good man, he says, good man!'

Coming from any other man, Nick's talk would have riled long ago. But there is something unarguable about his bristling bulk, his braying good humour. Luke is not immune and nor are the rest of the mess. Messing with him is like supping up close to a roaring bonfire: uncomfortable sometimes, but irresistible when all about is cold and dark and damp.

The squall is still blowing strong up there, but down here on a Saturday night, huddled on the end of Nick's sea chest, with his belly full of beef and biscuit and his eyes watering with the vapours off the flip, Luke is warmer than he has been in a week. His chilblains itch like fury, but Nick's good salve has eased his rope-rubbed palms. He takes up Nick's blue checked shirt and starts on the shoulder.

This is Luke's new role, tailor to the mess. Nick likes his neat ways, he's got the nod from Charlie too, after he fixed up his waistcoat. 'Nimble pair of hands on him, I'll grant you,' Charlie told Nick when he first saw him pleach out the blood from Nick's trowser leg. 'Send him over to plait my cue!' The men of other messes started to come to Luke with socks and shirts to mend in exchange for an extra ration or two, but Nick put a stop to that. Luke's his boy, his nimble tailor mouse. After Nick had the carpenters make him a sea chest — noticeably larger and nobler than Charlie's — he offered Luke's coin safe keeping there. But the nimble tailor mouse has sewn a pocket into his trowsers, sewn it tight shut, and he's keeping it there. He's trusting no one. He dreads the day Nick persuades Tremmel to send him aloft. Falling to his death may yet be his only way off this ship, he can still see no other. But he's holding on to that money nevertheless. It's all he has.

Charlie's gazing at the lantern now, his

pale eyes unfocused, the cards slack in his hand. Luke's been watching Charlie's game: the man thinks he is better than he is. I'll play Charlie one day soon, he vows. Maybe in a week or so. Start growing those coin of mine. And then, when I gets back, if I gets back. Something crunches in the seam under the pressure of his fingers. He pokes it out on the end of his needle.

Charlie takes up the poker to make more flip and starts up the one they call 'Spanish Ladies', but Nick cuts in, booming out:

'There once was a maiden gay
'Who wished to sail
'Who wished to sail.'

A tall figure staggers into the mess with the lurch of the deck and sets the lantern swinging. He is shirtless and Luke can see his large belly sway, and the mat of criss-crossed scars crusting on his back. The sweet stickiness of ointment wafts from him, as he puts his hands on Nick's shoulders to steady himself.

'Woah there!' Nick hates to be touched by anyone, even Charlie. He shoulders him away and Powell sprawls back against the gun.

'I'll tell you what, mister pizzen mop,' Powell says, wiping his mouth, quite unperturbed. He is very drunk indeed.

'What, you great barrel of slush?' asks Burton, sniggering and looking sideways at Nick. Nick rolls his eyes and the sturdy lads both grin.

'I'll drink to Stan Ellena,' pronounces Powell. 'On the morrow! Yes indeed.'

Nick screws up his face incredulously.

'You dozy bastard,' says Charlie.

Luke looks to Nick. 'Why's that?' he asks. 'What's he saying?'

'He thinks we're off St Helena.'

'Where's that?'

'Where's that? Long way from here, laddie. Way way south out in the Atlantic. No, dim bullock means St Helens.'

'St Helens?' Burton's face brightens and he tugs at Nick's sleeve. 'That's the sweetest water. Keeps longer than all bar London river water.'

Nick keeps a straight face. 'Oh aye?' he says.

'Then we must be in for a long voyage indeed,' says Burton earnestly. The whole mess knows the lad's ambitious, that he wants only a chance to prove himself. This may be it. They sail against the Spanish, and their galleons of gold, he keeps reminding them all, we'll take prizes aplenty. Huzza, boys, huzza.

Powell wags his finger in Burton's face.

'No, no, I must correct you. I distinct—'

Nick and Charlie exchange contemptuous glances and drown him out:

'She showed the captain
'Her passage fair
'And he fucked her
'Then and there.'

'St Helens,' Nick says with relish, fixing Luke with a baleful, billy-goat gaze. 'By god, I've filled some casks at St Helens, and I've relieved myself of a load too.' He pats his crotch contentedly. 'Need to keep bugger sweet too, it's going to be a long voyage. Let's hope a couple of heavy-laden bum-boats come rowing out to relieve us poor boys, eh? Not a pair of tits on the ship even to look at, the bastard woman-hating captain.'

'The lad don't need to hear that sort of talk,' says Powell, affronted. 'And some of us have wives ashore, d'you hear?'

Nick grins, and beats the poker to and fro inside his empty can as if it were a bell clapper:

'The men had her too
'All night long
'When morning came
'Her cunt was gone.'

'Nick,' says Charlie, shaking his head. 'You can do better than that.'

'It's not right,' says Powell. 'That's a good Christian lad there.' He sweeps out an arm in Luke's direction. 'Look at those fine eyes. There's a mother somewhere worried sick, am I right?'

'This lad don't need his mammy, what he needs is a good seeing to, don't you, mouse? Put some colour in those cheeks.'

Charlie's smile spreads as Nick puts his arm about Luke and squeezes. A wave of panic hits Luke, and when Nick releases him he jumps up, dropping his bobbin. He finds it and sits back down across from Nick. But Charlie watches him still.

Powell is talking on, his face forlorn and desperate. 'How can you live like this, boys, with only a locking box for all your possessions? This is not a life, this is not a home. It is a prison, a floating prison and the sentence unending. For shame, Stavenger. When I think of my young Samuel. He will not know me, if I ever come home at all.'

Luke's fingers tighten about his needle. He can feel Powell's longing, his love, as strong as his own. So can the others.

'Gad, give it a rest, you old lubber, we've barely been out a week,' says Burton in disgust. 'We're not even in the Bay. St Helens, you pisspot, it's the Isle of Wight, we've only made it to the Isle of Wight, damn contrary winds.'

Powell sits down beside Burton as if struck and clutches at his arm. 'The Isle of Wight? Why, I have a cousin at Ryde.' He laughs helplessly.

Charlie and Nick exchange glances.

'Thinking of doing something you oughtn't?' asks Bramley. Powell stops laughing.

Nick sits back, pokes out that lizard tongue. 'We'll be all day rowing those barrels, Powell. Coming and going, ever so hard to keep track.'

'Easy for an officer to get distracted, I'd say,' adds Charlie. His leg has stopped jiggling. He sits still as a cat, watching Powell's face. 'Easier still if he had a little something to distract him.'

Powell looks from Nick to Charlie: hopeful, puzzled, desperate.

'That bastard Tremmel would be glad to see the back of you,' says Nick. 'If only he had a little something to keep him sweet. Me and Charlie here, we could have a word.'

Nick sighs. 'Shame, isn't it, old butcherbones,' he says, 'that you refused that bounty. Nowt to help you on your way, so to speak.' He watches as Powell grinds his knuckles into his palms. 'How are you to put your hands on some coin, I wonders?'

Then Charlie claps his hands together. 'Come, Powell, you're a clever fellow, that's plain to see.' He takes up the cards, turning the pack round and about between his fingers. 'Let me play you.'

'I thank you,' adds Powell, getting to his feet. 'But I say farewell, boys.' He makes a grand gesture. 'I shall take my chances.' His eyes are wet, his red mouth working.

Luke stabs his needle into the collar of Nick's shirt and speaks up, his heart pounding. 'You want a game, Charlie? I shall play you.'

Charlie swings round, his eyes crinkling with amusement. Then he turns back to Powell. 'See there? Our little lad would play, and you would not. Shame on you.' He waits.

Charlie shrugs and sings out with glee: 'He has no stake, he will not play, he cannot go, he will not stay. Nick my boy, what do you reckon his chances are?'

Nick sucks in his breath. 'Not worth a damn, I'd say. Not worth a damn.'

'You got nothing to stake, Powell? Not a damned thing?'

Powell looks wildly from one to the other. Like a pig with a knife to its neck, thinks Luke.

'I'll play you,' Luke says again.

'Luke will play too,' repeats Nick. 'Least-ways he's in funds, I'll vouch.'

Charlie looks to Luke and nods. 'Then we'll both play ye, Powell.' He smiles his most reassuring smile. 'What's your stake?'

Luke sets aside the shirt, his fingers trembling. Nick fills the empty mug, and rams the still warm poker in it. He holds the mug, gently steaming, under Powell's nose.

CHAPTER EIGHTEEN

I hardly knew what to think as, shaking with anger and dismay, I made my way back up the stairs to the masquerade. Of course I understood what had become of Susie, though I could not have admitted it just then. But anger overwhelmed any shame or pity I might have felt. At that moment I wanted nothing more to do with any of my family. I cursed my father and brother for shirking scoundrels, who abandoned us to poverty and disgrace. I despised my mother for her lack of resource and my sister for her weakness. And I gave thanks for the Captain's summons that day, for you were my only hope, it seemed, the only person in my life with any ambition, and pride. Yes, I thought, I will go away with you to London, and together we shall make a life worth living, one that's clean and warm and safe and respectable.

I was back in the midst of the crowd, all

chattering at once. Word of the antics of the tar and the whore had clearly spread in a wave across the room. I must find you, I thought, before you hear of it. Persuade you to come home. Everything will be all right when I am alone with you again. At last I saw you by the fire, sitting in a low velvet chair as you did at home, with your feet stretched out and your slippers off. I watched from several feet away as you reached down for your cup and scooped it up elegantly between your fingers. Beside your splendour the other girls seemed to me gawky and unformed, the older women faded and gaunt. You lifted your face to listen to one of your young friends who rested her elbows on the back of your chair.

'Yes,' you were saying, 'for Henry has an uncle of great influence who will see he makes his way in the service.'

'Rebecca is a clever girl,' said your friend, addressing herself to the various women and girls seated about. 'She soon established that while Henry had a future he had no family to disapprove, no watchful mother —'

'You know very well, Hatty, it was not like that at all. When we met it was at just such an assembly, when they had just opened the Navy Hall, don't you remember? He was the most charming and delightful fellow I had ever met, that was all there was to it. And I simply cannot wait until we are married.'

'Well *I* simply cannot imagine it,' replied Hatty with a neutral laugh. 'Our Rebecca, a naval bride.'

'Do not doubt it,' you said evenly. 'And I shall make him an amiable and accomplished wife.'

At this Hatty and the others giggled and spluttered. You sat up and cast about a bright confident smile.

'I will, I will! An amiable and —'

'Rebecca,' retorted another laughing, 'you do not read, or play, or do any work of any kind!'

'I will, Lucy, I say, just watch me.' You sat demurely now, your head inclined. 'I will offer him eye service. And when he is away, as I fear he must be only too often, I will be a lady sufficient unto myself, brave and enduring —'

'Yes, until his ship is lost and you have to endure his pension alone,' retorted Lucy.

'Hush, do not talk so!' You looked about in mock indignation and spread your hands pleadingly. You saw me then, but you did not smile or bid me come closer. You only slid your eyes away and shifted your seat slightly.

'Really, Lucy —' you continued, and then you all spoke at once like chattering jays. All your animation was play acting, I could tell. You did not look at me again. I knew on the instant you were displeased with me. I turned cold — had you seen me run after Susie? Guessed that she was my sister? I took myself away and after some minutes you detached yourself from the group and came over. I stood before you, trembling.

'Where have you been, Lou?' you asked. The pantomimed outrage that you had shown your friend was gone and your voice was only mildly petulant. 'I wanted to show you to Mr Fellowes but he is gone now.'

Had you really missed the scene Susie had made? I realised the hall was so crowded that it was quite possible. And in my relief I did not care that you were so cool with me, did not mind that I could not confide in you, as I longed to. I was glad simply to be with you, to breathe your scent.

'And look, Lou, you need to fix these.' You touched your fingers to the wax mulberries, that hung precariously over your ear, and your fingertips came away stained red. 'Uggh.'

'Here, let me.' I snatched your hand away

before you did more damage. 'Come away from the fire, they're melting.'

You pulled me towards a tall door that was all window. 'Open it up!' you ordered the footman who stood to attention beside it. And when he continued to gaze impassively over our heads: 'Open it up before I smash the damned windowpanes.'

The window gave on to a long and narrow balcony, and we slipped ahead of the press of people at our backs to gain hand hold on the railing. The western end of the quay seemed a matter of yards away and the night air that flowed over us was damp and smelt of weed and tar and mud. It seemed we might leap across and grasp the masts of the ships moored there, for we stood almost level with their yard-arms. Most all the ships were dark, save for lights shining from their crow's nests, and lanterns at bow and stern. But still there came an ebb and flow of fiddle and drums and men singing. It was very late now and all else was silent, no splash of oars, no traffic from ship to shore.

When I had finished with your hairdressing, you closed your eyes and bathed your face in the damp cool air. 'He's not coming,' you said.

I had to think who you meant. Henry? He

was the reason for your coolness? Oh never mind him, I thought.

'We should leave then,' I said. 'It's grown very late.' All I wanted was to be home with you, undressing you, settling you safe in your bed again.

You turned to lean against the rail and face me, as though you had made up your mind about something. 'No,' you said firmly. 'We may as well enjoy ourselves, now all the old stoats have gone.'

So we stayed on. I watched you sport with the young men of the town who remained, while Mrs Fressing and her ladies remonstrated in a huddle at the top of the stairs. Then you took command of the gathering by the buffet, demanded the last of the beef, reaching over to carve for the both of us. You shouted down the table for more tarts and custards, had them fill our cups again and again. The men competed to tell their stories. One greasy-faced fop found my pail that I had set down when I saw Susie, and slammed it down on the table before us, wagging his hands over his ears and making strange donkey noises. You tossed the butterpat sweetmeats at him like he were a dog and he snuffled for them on the floor. 'Asses' milk! Asses' milk!' he spluttered at me, laughing fit to burst, and neither of us knew what he was about.

But when you tired of him and you sent him a look he crawled away. I saw the other young ladies watch you from behind their masks, and exchange glances, and I thought I could read jealousy in their tight faces. Their nice little ways made them as dull as wrens. You were radiant. And seated beside you, despite the ungainly garments you had clothed me in, I felt that I glowed too.

Then the band struck up again but so many people had left that the sound echoed about the vast emptied space. The long windows had been left open and the candle flames shivered in the draught. Only the young people remained and the atmosphere was quite overexcited. The girls giggled as they took the men's arms. Suddenly you made me a mock bow, took my hand and led me out to dance. I saw the girls laughing behind their hands as you lifted my skirts to show me where to place my feet, and wanted to melt with shame.

I tried to protest. 'No, please, miss, you know I cannot —' But your face was right there before me, smiling, encouraging, and you had your arm round my waist. 'Everyone will see.'

'What's to see? And who is here to see us? I swear I would happily be snubbed by every

239

one of these dullards. Come on, before I am a married lady weighed down with her household belt. Come on.' And you whirled me about, so my heavy skirts slapped against my legs. 'Come on!'

The young men stamped their feet and whistled and I tugged hard on your hand to steady myself, pulling you up against me. Your face was flushed and you'd lost all your haughtiness. I tugged at you again, felt the flesh of your arm yield beneath my fingers. Our eyes were level and I saw your mouth quiver. I took a step, and then another, and you came with me. And then we were dancing together, not one of the country dances that were the only dances I knew, nor the genteel one you were trying to teach me, but some combination of the two, another dance, all our own.

I awoke not in my bed but in yours, my cheek deep in your feather pillow. No familiar rustle of straw under my ear. Only a smooth silence, solid and soft. I opened my eyes. There, cast against the door, lay the wreck of your lilac dress, a rumpled hulk in the shadows.

I shut my eyes again. And there you were with me. I could hear you breathing, slow and deep and warm at my back. My heart thudded hard. I put my hands cautiously to my breast and found I still wore the milk-maiding costume, with just a corner of your blanket thrown across my waist.

All these weeks that I had slept in my narrow bunk in the attic, I thought myself grown used to being alone, for I had never before slept without my mother at my side. But here, now — so close to the warmth of you, breathing you in — I did not know how I had borne the loneliness.

I turned, slowly, and I watched you, and watched you, as my eyes adjusted to the little light that came under the door. I looked long at your high forehead, your straight nose, your still lips, your dark, dark lashes. I found a tiny mark on your left temple that I had never seen before. Eventually I reached out to touch it with my fingertip. It came off in a sticky crust. And, in the moment before I realised it was but a smear of melted wax from those ruined mulberries, I felt almost winded by the notion that you might have been hurt and wounded in some way, and I had not known.

Then I must have slept again, for a brisk knock at the door roused me sudden. I sat up. Hannah stuck her head round the door in a flood of daylight. You groaned and stirred. I blinked in panic. Then, without acknowledging my presence, without even seeming to see that I lay there beside my mistress, Hannah announced to the shadows at large: 'Tell her Mr Wilmington's here. Hester's entertaining him but get her dressed sharpish, she's expected in the parlour.'

I saw you together for the first time, as I passed through the hall with my bundle. Nels had called me back into the kitchen to press a twist of salt gargle on me, as a gift to my mother, and I saw him: standing in the parlour before a fire that burnt as brightly as any Hannah ever managed before or since.

He was slighter than I had expected, and terribly well dressed in a trim white wig, dark blue coat and very clean breeches. His shoulders were very broad indeed, but I thought his legs puny, and rather bandy, like those of a calf. I only saw him in profile, noted that his chin was firm but his head small and his complexion high and rough and blotchy. He stood slightly bowed, his body stiff in a show of civility, gesturing with his dish of tea, and as I passed the door he turned slightly, but did not catch my eye.

You did not turn. You sat by the table, one

hand poised over the tea kettle, gazing up at him. Your face was as fresh as ever, all the creases gone, your wrecked ringlets mostly concealed by a gauzy morning cap. And your eyes were fixed on his face, serious, alert, with that look I knew so well. That look that said, you are my whole world, come to me, tell me everything.

Then I heard you laugh, a bubbly, birdlike laugh, and he turned instantly back to you, intent as a hunting dog. You took the end of a ringlet into your mouth and smiled.

Skeggs stood in the hall with the street door wide open, I could smell all the freshness of the day. The stage would not wait on me. My mother was sick. I had to go.

Yes, I know it now: that was the moment.

But what I said to myself was: Hold up, Lou, what about that flowered skirt, hadn't she often said it was Henry's favourite? Must just make sure it's pressed ready to walk out in.

I turned away from Skeggs and the open door, from the fresh day and the waiting stage and my sick mother, turned my back on my old life entire and hurried back up the stairs to your room. I set down my bundle. Only one shutter was open, the fire was quite out and in the half light I could see all much as I had left it. Hannah had

243

made the bed in our absence but that was all. There was powder all over the dressing table and half a dozen skirts tried on and thrown over the screen. And a deep sweet smell in the stale air, as of overripe apple. I breathed it in, found your scent and your sweat and your skin that always gave off the warm bitterness of cloves.

But — and now I could stand still no longer but must whirl about setting all to rights — you were not there with me. You were down in the parlour with that insufferable man. Nonsense, he was a very fine man, a very good catch indeed, that was plain to see. I had the blessed skirt in my hand, was about to bring it down when I heard the front door slam. I went to the window and opened the shutter and saw you walking up West Street towards the marketplace, with Hester on the one side and Henry on the other. I saw him take your arm, and I saw you turn towards him, the ribbons all a-flutter in your cap.

In a flood of envy I knew the three of you to be walking out, Hester your chaperone, out on to the gentle slopes of grass up about the Ramsey light house where you and I had walked so many times. I knew that there you and he would turn, and together admire the fine prospect over the great harbour and

Suffolk beyond. And then perhaps the London stage I should have caught would rattle right past you, splattering mud as you strolled in the sunshine, for the weather had turned and the ground had softened. Everywhere in the wet earth there would be slender green grass poking out, the sea would be fresh sparkling and the sky wide and soft and blue.

I should be glad, I told myself as I stood alone in that stuffed-up little room, glad that he is here, for the sooner you are married the better and we shall be off to London. But, as I moved rapidly about your room, picking up and folding and tidying, I found I could not feel happy at all.

Now, Henry was not here to oblige me, was he? He was here to woo you, to wait on your father's return, and that's what he did. He stayed in town a good four or five days more. You took tea with him and Hester in the parlour, and each time all the finest stuff was brought out: the silver kettle on its silver tray and the newest tea pot, the best tea dishes, a full bowl of sugar lumps and tongs to take them up with. Nels had iced a rich plum cake, and as you handed him a slice its flanks glistened moistly in the thick afternoon sunshine. 'Someone pull those blinds or I shall be forever screwing up my

245

face,' you ordered.

It was I who drew down the blinds, who walked behind you on Beacon Hill with a parasol, who ran back to fetch your sketching materials, and who broke the sticks of charcoal to make them appear well used, for you had never opened the box. My mother waited for me in vain. I was there at your bedside each morning and evening with your most demure gowns, as you asked, fresh-pressed and sweet-smelling. I worked over your mending every morning while you paid calls, dined in the kitchen while you and Hester entertained Henry and your other guests. When you returned late from your walks with Henry I dressed you with speed and skill, and when you went out I took great pains over your fine linen and stockings, often sitting by the fire long after Nels retired, for I always waited up for you and brought you your hot water whether you wanted it or not.

You did not notice any of this. Henry was your game now. You were as intent on taking him as he was on taking you. You took me for granted. I consoled myself that this was how it should be. I should be no more than your shadow.

I stayed on at West Street. I buried my guilt and I stayed on. I thought once or twice of seeking out Susie as I went on my errands, of asking her to go to my mother in my place, but I never saw her. I never saw Joe neither. When word finally came from Mary that my mother was on the mend and I wasn't to worry or hurry back, I told myself that it had all been for the best, and no harm done.

I even accustomed myself to Henry. I no longer started when I heard his deep, halting voice rise up the stair and I knew he was in the house. He was always in the house. I grew used to the way he rubbed at the hairs in his nose after taking snuff, knew to stand back when he tugged for his handkerchief. A great sneeze is much to be admired, you stated, unflinching. When prompted, I complimented what you called his easy manner, and his graceful attitude. I observed how your face softened when he was about, how your posture grew more upright. Saw how he came to Hester's rescue when her harpsichord playing faltered, for she never had much time to practise, saying such as 'Forgive me but I have been struck sudden by an idea, perhaps you might both accompany me to the assizes tomorrow?'

And you would turn away from the window and smile at them both and shake your head, 'You are too kind, Mr Wilmington, yet we must decline, since I hear they are to try not one but three murderers.' For he was not to know that after the fashion plates your favourite reading was the court reports and the more shocking the crime the better.

'How I appreciate Henry's conversation,' you said. 'He knows so much of the world and I discover I can share all my finer thoughts with him.'

I found myself a new position, no longer seated by your side but standing slightly behind and to one side, as the flank bird flies in a migrating flock. But often, when I saw how he stared wetly at you, pawed at your hand, held his smile as you talked, showing all his sharp little teeth, I thought what a booby he was. Lord, he even gathered you fresh nosegays of violets and snowdrops, to add to those pinned and withering above your fire.

And there one day, filling the doorway, swooping in like a great black bird, was your father. Henry rose neatly at his entrance. I could not read the look the Captain gave him, his eyes were watering still with the wind. But he nigh trampled the man in his eagerness to get to you, to hand over the spoils of his latest voyage, to woo you in his turn.

'Aye, now, Wilmington,' he boomed, fit to rattle the tea dishes, 'and you don't see none of this finery aboard that damned navy frigate, now do you, sir?' Hester reached out silently to steady the tea table as the Captain strode over to set down a dripping box of oysters, then a casket of good tea, and a box of Spanish ribbon taken as a prize and bought for a song from a man in Antwerp. 'No prizes yourself yet, Wilmington? No? Well now, early days.' Henry valiantly muttered his admiration, but you cooed and smiled over the last present of all: a shivering little black monkey on a silver chain, that hopped straight on to Henry's shoulders and had to be coaxed onto your lap, where Hester quickly tucked a napkin under its bony rear. Henry smiled thinly on.

'He's something fine, but so late? Dadda, you knew I wanted him for the masquerade,' you said, pouting and playing with its ears. 'You missed the masquerading, both of you, you tardy creatures!'

You glanced at me then. I saw only the mock disappointment in your eyes, saw nothing in them for me: no memory of what we had shared that night, how we had danced and laughed and danced until they came around to put out the lights. How I had helped you down the assembly room stair for both our heads were spinning and I must have helped you from your dress and to your bed too, but all I remembered was how I had lain by your side as you slept late into the day and listened to you breathe. I looked away, looked at anything but you.

'No matter now, Dadda. Henry, do not look so crestfallen. Have you the London papers?'

The Captain lifted his empty hands. And there Henry took his advantage again, announcing that he had taken the liberty of writing to the Cocoa-Tree in Cheapside that they send you what papers and journals they thought suitable. And he offered the Captain his snuff box. Despite prompting looks from both his daughters, the Captain declined and lit up his belching pipe instead; would not even sit to smoke it, but strode about the room as about his cabin. Then Hester stood, and you rose also, clutching the monkey to your breast, and I followed, for we were to leave the men to make the final arrangements before Henry sailed for the new war.

CHAPTER NINETEEN

'If Powell wants to get home more'n he wants that fine Dedham sausage so be it. Not a spot of green anywhere. Do us all proud.' Nick belches and pours a half bucket of sea water over his own head. He cleans his ears with his cuffs. It's an hour or so after midnight and the two of them are new up on deck again. Luke has lain awake half the watch listening to Powell's sobbing prayers.

'And Charlie will really fix it like he said?'

Nick cuffs him impatiently. 'Ah, never mind all that, laddie. Think on lassies in those bumboats. Forget Powell. You're well in funds now, aren't you, my canny lad? Say farewell to that tub of lard, and hello sweet titties. Up she rises one more time I say.' He clutches his crotch, and grins. 'Happen twice.'

In the event the Captain holds the bumboats off when they come. When they refuse

251

to turn around, he orders the marine to fire in the water. Nick watches the waving, screeching women disappear into the mist and spits on the deck in disgust.

'It's a Sunday morning, Stav, and he's a preachy bastard,' Charlie tells him.

Bramley adds: 'There's always the loblolly boy.'

'Stick your yard up his tight little fundament,' sniggers Hogmarsh.

The whole crew is mustered on deck while the Captain reads aloud. Then the chaplain calls them together in worship. Luke shuts his eyes, feels the weak sun on his face, as Burton whispers of the time he tied a slow charge to the tail of the ship's cat, and let it loose in the military officers' mess at meal time.

Three boats are lowered, crammed with empty barrels. But Luke is set to scrubbing the forecastle and when he manages to look over the side Powell is not in any of them. The sun is well up and the mist has cleared by the time they are back, fully laden with casks and low in the water. Luke hangs desperately on the end of one of the pulley ropes, his feet dragging across the deck. Then he sees Powell across the deck: Tremmel ordering him to heave a barrel on to his back and Tremmel watching scornfully as he staggers, almost falls.

As eight bells sounds and the watch troops below, Luke manages to catch Powell at the hatchway. He snatches at his sleeve.

'Is it done?' he asks in a whisper. 'Tremmel?' But from the set of Powell's face, he knows. When was Charlie ever to be trusted? Luke tugs Powell out of the flow of men and stares at him. 'But without Tremmel? You've no chance.'

Powell stares dully back. Luke recognises the look on his face. The man is as desperate as he is. Then Burton and Little catch Powell up by the arms and carry him away below.

Several bells into the next watch the coxswain points his stick at Luke. 'Oi, you lad! Over here. And you.' He gestures to Nick. Luke looks around for Powell but he's nowhere to be seen. Luke and Nick stand back to let a marine pass, then another, before they can step over the side and climb down into the boat. As Luke sits down, he spots Powell seated at the outer end of the row in front. His thick mass of dark hair is streaked with grey. Tremmel is nowhere to be seen.

Luke takes up his oar. The great wasp-striped hulk of the *Essex* slowly recedes ahead of him. Already it is stained and the paint flaking. 'How far to St Helens?' he asks Nick.

Nick only grunts. Luke turns to look but cannot see beyond the shoulders of those before him. He pulls and pulls, his palms stinging and sore already. And before he knows it he hears shouts and the wet grind of the bow cresting into shingle. The shore smells, of weed and mud and woodsmoke, brings a lump to his throat. He looks round, catches a glimpse of warehouses, nets and cranes. There's a sudden shout and when he looks back Powell is gone.

Luke's oar clatters in its eyehole. There is Powell, heading across the beach, staggering in the shelving sand. Everyone is watching. Luke stands up.

'Back to the boat!' yells one of the officers, his voice cracking. 'Back to the boat!'

All the men in the boat have turned. All strain to watch Powell run, gamble everything for freedom. Luke cannot watch. He takes hold of the side of the boat with both hands. He looks down at the surging foam, the churned-up sand only yards away — it seems he can see every grain, every broken shell — then back at Powell, running for his life. Then, swift as he can, he lowers himself over the side.

'Shoot him! Shoot!'

Before the surf can wet Luke's feet, his upper arms are gripped fierce and for a moment he is suspended between boat and shore. He struggles wildly but he is held fast.

A flash of red cloth and glinting metal high on the shore. Powell falls before the sound of the shot echoes back from the warehouses. His body sprawls and kicks on the shingle.

Luke feels himself dragged roughly back into the boat. As the marine close on Powell and heave his limp body up by the shoulders, Luke gives a great cry, a bellow of anger and despair. Nick claps his hand over Luke's mouth and holds him tight.

Nick makes room for Luke to sit beside him at the mess board.

'Come on, laddie,' he says briskly. 'Everything all right up there?' he asks Charlie.

'Aye, aye, wind set fair, fore tops at the ready.'

Nick rubs his hands together. 'Come now, and will you all take a drink?'

With their crisp clean kerchiefs, pressed by Luke to stick out like yard-arms, with their gleaming white trowsers tight about their bulging thighs, their eyes bright and caps set just so, Nick and Charlie are as dandy as mantel ornaments. Bramley and Burton and Little grin at each other: it's quite a coup to have two such able top-men messing with the likes of them tonight. Hogmarsh overfills two mugs and thrusts them at Nick and Charlie, the beer spilling out on to their laps.

'Where's that fine piece of Dedham belly I was promised, boys?' Charlie asks, bestowing his smile on them each in turn.

'Fancy some flip?' says Nick.

'Yes indeed,' answers Charlie.

'Luke, go fetch the poker.'

Luke doesn't move.

'Luke, the poker!'

'Fancy some flip, mousey?' says Charlie.

'No. No, I don't.' Luke raises his chin, stares Charlie full in the face.

'Go on, you'll have some. How about you, Burton?'

'Yes, indeed.'

'Come on, laddie,' says Charlie.

Winn sets down a steaming barrel of scaldings and a platter of sausage beside it. 'Here's your Dedham dainties, boys, now who wants some?'

'Luke, turn your back,' orders Nick.

It's not Luke's turn, but he swivels slowly round on the bench.

'You want some flip, mouse?'

'No, I don't.'

'Who's it to be, Luke?' says Winn, holding the first piece of sausage where Luke can't see it.

Luke closes his eyes anyway. 'Hogmarsh.'

'Hah, hog for the hog,' laughs Little.

'Damn my boots!' says Nick brightly. 'That smells good.'

'Next,' says Winn.

When they are all served, Luke turns back and watches them all tear into the sausage, scoop up the peas, tap and dip their biscuit.

'How can you do that?' he says, his voice cracking.

'What?' says Nick, his mouth full.

'Eat that.'

Nick sniffs it. 'What's the matter with it?'

'It was his.'

Nick shoves in another mouthful. 'What do you want me to do? Bury it at sea?'

'Don't you realise he's dead?'

Nick looks puzzled. 'Who's dead?' he says.

'Aye,' echoes Bramley. 'Who's dead?'

'Powell.'

'Powell?' replies Nick with a frown.

'Who's Powell?' says Charlie.

Nick lays down his knife and looks about blankly. 'Anybody know a Powell?'

Luke stares at him. 'This time last night. You drank with him and tricked him and took all he had from him —'

First Nick, then Charlie, then Bramley, Burton and all the rest of them break into song, a great slow swinging obscene shanty about their mothers.

Luke turns over his platter and makes for the aisle.

Before he has gone two yards Nick is up on his feet and has grabbed him by the elbow. 'Wait, you little fool.'

Luke kicks out at his shins. Beats his fists into that solid chest. Tugs at the dangling disk and tries to rip it from his neck.

Nick fends him off, like a bear batting at a squirrel. 'God damn, stop it.'

'How can you, when that man is —'

'Dear Christ,' Nick says evenly, straightening Luke's collar. 'I know he's dead. He's dead and gone and weeping like a leaky pump won't make him any less dead.'

Luke feels everything collapse inside him. 'Why?' he cries out bitterly. 'Why didn't you let me go?' he cries. 'I wish I were dead, I wish —'

'Hush now,' Nick says softly. 'Hush. He's dead and you're alive.' He gives his arm a squeeze. 'Get yourself up on deck and stay there, laddie, stay there till you have a hold of yourself.'

Now there is nothing but ocean. Luke knows they are travelling, on and away, always. The ship never stops its shifting and heaving. The wind always blows. Loud and howling across wastes of deck. Shouldering its way through hatches, licking in snickery whispers through cracks and under collars. The clouds shift and stack and move on. The rain comes down and sheets across and drops shimmer in the air like jewels. The bell rings, the pipes call and the watches troop up and down like the sun, round the clock. Yes, everything is moving, all the time, he does not stop, there is no rest.

But at the same time he feels nothing is changing at all. Powell is gone, but here he is, with Nick and Charlie and the rest of them, every day is different and every day is the same. His world has shrunk to this. He knows the decks well now, hardly stumbles at all when it's dark. He knows the pipe calls, the meaning of the yelled orders from the shape of the sound, before he even hears the word. Sometimes he knows precisely when the half-hour bell will ring and there it comes, it almost makes him smile. The cold worms in the biscuit still make him gag, but the spirit he drinks to numb the taste seems to clear his head. He can sleep bundled like a dead rabbit, and his hands are hardened to the ropes. Sometimes he strokes the yellow callouses and thinks maybe that is it, his soul is callousing over. Because he can change nothing, because there seems to be no hope, he has stopped himself feeling.

So he watches himself as he goes about his business, as a gaoler might watch his own prisoner. Keeps an eye out for him, because it's his job, not because he cares a damn. Knows he's better off than most. Better off than Powell for sure. He has his place now. He's Nick's boy. If he needs anything, Nick can help him out. More thread, his own small bag of salt. What he really wants is a knife. Nick has kept him safe so far, but all the same. He has heard what can happen on the orlop deck when the steward is pissed and the purser looking the other way.

He takes one last look at the blackness beyond but there's nothing there, just the roar and hiss of the sea and the buffeting wind. He turns his back and goes down below. He'll drink like Nick drinks, drink himself blind, drink himself senseless.

CHAPTER TWENTY

'Lord Cathcart is to take full one fourth of the entire Navy. What opportunity for advancement there will be. How many ships is that? No, for all their riches and armament, the Spanish have no chance against men such as Henry. I shall not listen to my so-called friends, for he shall triumph, he may even take a prize. No, no, he shall take a prize, I am sure of it. Why on his last voyage, do you not recall, if it had not been for that cowardly second lieutenant — Lou, keep up, will you?' You turned on me: a dozen paces ahead, hands on hips, skirts soaked a full six inches with dew.

I had never known you rise so early. Last night we had waved Henry off as he was taken out to his new vessel. But you had not slept a wink, you said, and bade me accompany you to the top of Beacon Hill — for simply to spy his frigate in the outer lanes might bring you some comfort. And so here we were, halfway up in the long grass, our breath fogging a little still despite the hazy sunshine. There were blackbirds digging for worms, and fresh rabbit droppings. The breeze off the sea was soft and quenching, the sea itself a brilliant glittering expanse. And there you were: cheeks burnished, eyes bright, holding out your hand to me.

'Let's go back,' I said flatly.

'What?'

'Look at your skirts.'

'Oh don't nag, Lou. Come on.'

'It's too far,' I said to your back.

The flies were rising and I lashed out at a bluebottle drilling straight for my cheek. Slowly you came back down, holding your skirts high in a deliberately mincing fashion. I would not smile.

'Oh so solemn,' you said, pulling a clowning, foolish, mournful face. 'Just like the whey-faced dairymaid of old. Something must be troubling you? Tell me.' You stroked my cheek, sought my eyes with your softest, steadiest gaze. 'We have no secrets, do we?'

I could not have told you the truth then, for I did not know it myself.

'You have seen his ship now,' I said stiffly. 'Let's go back.'

'But it's a beautiful morning. I could walk

to Walton and back.'

You, who would send me up and down the stairs on the slightest whim, a forgotten glove, a jar of salve. But who never left her chair, her bed, unless fashion demanded, or some appetite prompted.

'I have so much to do. We have so much to do now.'

'Spare me the nuptial nonsense, please. Hester is bad enough. What *is* the matter?'

I could not answer you. My thoughts were spinning about so in my head I could not utter any of them. But back again and again came one unsought notion, stinging fresh. Here was I trailing up a dew-sodden slope for a mere glimpse of your fiancé's damned ship, when I had not gone to see my own mother when she might have been mortal ill, and all on your account. It was a bitter thought, an angry thought. Yes, I had stayed away, for you. Stayed to watch you woo him, no, to help you woo him and how well it had been done. Look how happy you were now. Your future was assured. A great hopelessness overcame me. I could have sunk down in the dew and sobbed. At that moment, it seemed I had given everything for you, and it had all been for nothing.

And then, then I clutched at another whirling thought before all the rest, because

I could not bear to hear one word more on Henry, to think on you and he another minute. It was all quite simple. Quite clear. I was miserable now because I had misplaced my duty. I had put you before my own mother, my own blood, who for all I knew was a-bed once more and coughing, her bones too sore to work, and pining for her long-lost child.

'Lou! What is it?'

Your tone demanded an answer. So I gave you one.

'When does your father sail again?' I asked.

'Later today, I think, it depends. Yes, look.'

You gestured to the channel, where all the little vessels swung laxly on their painters, and two even threatened to cave each other's bows, so ill-judged close had they been anchored. I saw that it was slackwater, that strange pause between one tide and the next, that you had pointed out to me on one of our earliest walks. It always amused you, you said, to see the giddy aimless movements the singly moored vessels made, without the tide to tug them into line.

I left you there, wondering. Hurried down on to the strand by the light house and took the sandy path along the embankment, passing a couple of sad stunted orchards. I remember the fish guts there, the shrieking gulls, and the yards of nets, little bits of gill and shrivelled stuff stuck in them. My feet slipped in the chill shingle. The wind reached up under my skirts, and fingered my neck nastily. There was such space above and around me. I had not realised until then how safe I had come to feel within the town walls.

In the lee of a humped-up boat sat three fishermen, their salt-stiffened beards thick as barnacles. They stared and muttered in my wake. I held my head high, as you always did. You never paid no attention to men's 'nonsense', common or not. 'Such simple creatures, men,' you'd said carelessly, as you waved Henry off. 'I just had to flutter and sigh, and there he was in my hand.' As though the capture of a coming naval officer by a provincial packet captain's daughter — an achievement that was your triumph, and the envy of all your friends — was nothing very much at all.

A gang of molls swung past on their way into town, three-abreast, arms linked. 'Out early!' someone shouted. 'In late!' replied one. She wore a high black hat like a stove pipe, and two thick feathers tipped with pink. Another's yellow and blue shawl slipped from her shoulder to reveal a rouged nipple, puckering in the breeze. The third had a double row of yellow beads wrapped tight about her neck. None of them was Susie.

I cut through Church Street, down the back of the Bell. On one side the great tarred warehouses and drying sheds, on the other the ranks of ships at anchor. Masts and rigging scored the skies. Soon I reached the King's Yard. Many ships were to be built here for the new wars. The hammering and shouting and sawing, the hot tar and the fresh-sawn wood, pervaded the Handley house as soon as we opened the doors in the morning and went on till dark, so's I scarce noticed any more. Here was the first in dry dock, a yellow-boned carcass already high as your house, propped up by rows of treeposts. I passed piles of tree trunks, men sawing at trestles and carts disappearing through high double doors. And more men at work everywhere, swarms of them, gripping their axes and calling to each other from atop stacks of barrels.

The packet pier stood gusty and cold in the shadow of the King's great storehouse. The *Dolphin* was the only packet in, bucking and jostling in the choppy water, its red and white flag tugged hard by the breeze. The Captain was easy to spot. Taller than them all, always bundled in his greatcoat, his black beard wagging against the blue sky.

As I walked out on to the pier the planks gave unnervingly under my feet. When I looked through the chinks I could see the waves flowing under me, one after another after another. It made me a little dizzy. I went all the way up to the foot of the gangway, where a man stood by his trunk. I paused to steel myself: I would step past him on to the gangway, hail the Captain, curtsey, smile and ask him for —

But I could not do it. I could not step off the solid pier into that floating world of men. Some instinct of self-preservation told me I should have no business there. And even as I fought my reluctance, a still worse prospect presented itself. For how was I to address myself to the Captain? Demand that if he had information on a certain sailor boy I required it of him directly, sir, for my humble mother? Was I, his daughter's maid, to whom he had barely spoke all these months, to come aboard his ship uninvited, to disrupt his work, merely to ask about her private business? What impertinence. He owed me no favours.

No. I flushed up. It had been a foolish impulse. I could not imagine what had possessed me. I stepped away, and just then I caught the movement of his arm against the sky. His booming call stayed me, and I stood motionless as he made his way to the top of the gangway.

'What is it, Louise?' he asked. His eyes twinkled and there was a twitch about his mouth. 'More cakes?'

I flinched with embarrassment. He chuckled and said, almost tenderly: 'What has my girl sent you for now?'

'Nothing, sir,' I said, remembering finally to curtsey a little.

'What then? Had enough?' He set his arms akimbo. Oh he was in a playful mood; cheered, no doubt, by the success of his negotiations with Henry. 'You do not wish to run away to sea I hope? 'Tis no life for a girl.'

I shook my head. But he had given me my opening. I attempted a laugh also. 'Not myself, sir, no indeed. Please you, sir, I would ask you about one who did take to the sea, that was my brother, sir.'

I dared look up at him now but the morning sun was behind him. Hurried, I went on, 'I have been meaning to ask you, my mother would know, if you please, she has been much ill. Well now, she is better.' I stopped.

He cleared his throat. 'I am glad,' he said, finally.

'We have not had word of him since he came to Harwich to seek work on the sea. Certain 'tis a long time now but she would have me ask if there's any word in the town about what became of him.'

There, I had said it. The longest address I had ever made him, and the most impertinent.

'You have not told me the boy's name.'

'Luke,' I said. 'Luke Fletcher.'

The Captain stared at me long and hard, until I wished I could slip from sight through those chinks in the pier. I fumbled with my skirts, looked anywhere but at him. Finally he shook his head.

'No, Louise,' he said. 'You must tell your mother I regret — I very much regret I cannot help her.'

I stared. I had not expected such certainty. 'Then perhaps your men might know something of him?' I said. 'You might ask —'

'No, Louise,' he cut in. 'I have seen many men go to sea from here. So many never return. She must give him up.' Then he said, more gently: 'Tell her I am very sorry, but she must give him up.'

I curtseyed deep to hide my distress. He had turned his back already, was striding back to the bows. The passenger behind me cleared his throat loudly and hoisted up his trunk so swift that it struck my thigh and sent a jabbing pain through me. I scurried back to the safety of the shore and tried to calm myself.

At first, despite my beating heart, all I felt was a queer sort of flatness. So that was that. The Captain had been my one hope. Where could I turn now? I had not thought I cared for my brother, had I carried out my mother's request out of duty and goodness. But just then I felt her loss as keenly as if it were my own. And I knew I could not go to her now after all, with nothing to comfort her.

You were just where I had left you, only you were sitting down now, as though weary, in a patch of short turf that was full in the sun. I watched you pluck deliberately with your fingers at strands of grass and toss them aside. When you finally looked up your eyes were so liquid I could have sworn you were about to cry, had I not known by then that you did not cry.

You wrapped your arms about your waist as though you were chilled, and you spoke slowly. 'You must never,' you said, '*never* go off like that again. Do you hear me? Never, Lou, never.'

I was mortified beyond endurance. To have walked off without permission, to have left her mistress all alone out there like that, was quite unforgivable in any servant. I knew it well, and yet I had done it deliberate, and without a second thought. I dropped down beside you and took your hands in mine. I begged you to forgive me, swore I would never leave you, swore on my mother's grave that I would serve you better than ever if only you would let me stay by your side.

You came round, in the end, after much coaxing and stroking. I had at least learnt that much, I realised, how to bring you round. And by the time we made our way back down, the sun-struck sea all aglint and flashing in our eyes, I quite trembled with relief. Well that was that, I thought. I had made a fool of myself before the pair of you, but no matter. We had agreed that I would indeed go to see my mother that very Sunday. I would tell her that I had tried my best, had an answer from the Captain himself. I would tell her she must mourn for Luke now, but know that while he and my father might be lost and gone she had her faithful girl with her still. And then I would tend to her just as well as I had to you, for did she not deserve it? I had been saving back some of my wages to buy for you a trifle from Mr Hammick's warehouse. Well, that coin I would give now to my mother to keep for hard times and I would grow her a pile of coin each time I visited. And when we went to London I would earn more and I would send her more.

When we went to London. I smiled then. For I would set my mind to preparing you for the wedding, as I had for the masquerade. And I would think only of you, my dear, the future Mrs Wilmington, and of the comfortable life that awaited us both in Wapping.

But then, within weeks I think, just before Easter, all my hopes and plans meant nothing at all.

CHAPTER TWENTY-ONE

The more Nick drinks the more cheer he spreads. The officers love their Northumbrian tar; they love Charlie too, both singing out strong and true up there, way above their heads. When the pair of them are holding court high on the crow's nests, their laughter filters down like pieces of sunlight.

Even when the weather worsens in the Bay, as expected, Nick and Charlie's magic holds. The men all cling to it, as to a rope: the seventh larboard mess, the mizen boys, the mainmast lads, all of them. Because by god is it bad. First the slow leaching of the light as the banks of cloud build and build. The solid lead of the swell buckling up. The wind, high and keening at first, then forcing itself on them, tearing at their clothes and roaring in their ears. Even in the day the sea is vicious black, the sky bruised and the only relief from it all the flaring splatters of spray and the white churning wake. Luke clings to his larboard rope as he slides across the deck and watches with horror as the sea rears up before him like a mountain of slate, sending the *Essex* crashing to the bottom of the valley.

Everything that can move is lashed down, but the men must still crawl about, cling shivering to the flexing shrouds. Luke sees a man out on the bowsprit disappear beneath the foam as she crests and when the deck tilts up again he is quite gone. The main gun deck is often awash but down on the middle deck little of it reaches the seventh larboard mess. They keep the ports closed as much as they can but they are stifling, the stink of the stirred-up bilge is everywhere, the vomit and the soil, and they must have some air. Nick and Charlie laugh and leap aside when the foaming sea pours in through the opened ports, sending pots skidding and the cat into a frenzy.

The fresh water has gone turbid and the sea water has leaked into it. They say the barrels were dirty when it was put in, but Nick does not care. 'Come now,' he says, 'we have a gallon of ale a day, lads! There's fresh tatties and salted pork and banyan day only twice a week. We're all still here, damn it: none of us washed overboard or missing parts.'

Hogmarsh pokes his swollen gums and tries to smile. He has been at the pumps every day and the blisters on his fingers look like bladderwrack. Bramley's pale and silent, he has a scaly, ulcerous rash across his cheeks, but as the pipe shrills Nick takes him up by the arm. 'The gales'll blow the rottenness out youse.'

One night a sprit is carried away, and the *Essex* hoves to for repairs, her rigging sagged and frayed. 'Will take us forty days to reach Madeira, when we could do it in twelve,' spits Tremmel, wiping at his mouth with a damp and soiled kerchief. 'Damn it all. Damn it all.'

Then they're off again, fighting their way through the waves and there's no time for card games now, or dominos, for grooming or mending. The stove cannot be lit but they all gulp at their cold scotch coffee as though it were flip. Charlie twists at his whiskers, that are as bedraggled as a drowned cat's. Grimly, he and Nick swap tall tales, as always. Once, off the coast of Greenland, Nick tells Charlie, I fell from the yard and didn't stop till I caught hold of an icicle hung off the lower yard. When I was a lad, Charlie tells Nick, I fell all the way down to the staysail and bounced right back up to the mizentop. Bramley makes the effort to laugh but it's Luke who Charlie and Nick glance to. Now there's no scope for flourishes aloft, now the two of them are cooped up below, their rivalry has turned all its focus on to Luke. He has seen them confer and look towards him. Noticed how Charlie's eyes linger on his face when he thinks he's not looking, just as Nick's do.

Luke knows now that to them he is something special. He still has that freshwater quality, it has not been quite washed away. His skin is clear and smooth, his limbs slender. The muscle he is building only makes his rig hang better and his movements more buoyant. The wind and the weather have burnished his skin so it seems to glow, deepened the blue of his eyes. His work is neat and good, he does not speak out of turn, there is nothing foolish or sullen about him. Nothing brutish. No, there is no one like him in the whole vessel and he fascinates them both, he can tell. Perhaps he reminds them of the young lads they both once were: blithe and, yes, beautiful. They both want a piece of him.

Come on up with us, they say to him, winking, like it's an honour, a privilege. And in the world of the *Essex* it is, everyone knows, that to win the favour of either man bodes well. But when Luke looks up at the tossing masts with their ravaged sails, imagines himself high up there and clinging on to a sodden piece of rigging as soft as chewed baccy, he grows dizzy with fear.

'Come on lad, prove yourself,' says Charlie one day and he's off, saying he'll have a word with Tremmel. Nick watches him go. Nothing comes of it that day, or the next. But every day that passes more hands are down, with broken bones or crushed limbs, with sickness or scurvy or simple malaise. The men are winnowed from the masts like grain. Luke knows his day must come.

Until then, he must strike a balance between them. His loyalty is to Nick, but he knows better than to cross Charlie. One night, when there is a lull in the storming, Charlie sees Luke mending Nick's shirt. He gives him the waistcoat the next morning, with special instructions for the stitching of a torn pocket. Luke does it swiftly, hands it to him when Nick's back is turned, but Charlie must call Nick across to admire the stitching, and smile as Nick nods briefly and goes away without comment. Nick comes across Charlie laying out his Chinese dominos for Luke. And he must stagger into them, as if with the swell of the ship, so that the game is scattered.

The next day the storm is back. Luke

watches them both swing up into the rigging and set to work. The wind is fiercer than ever but up they must go. Nick moves steadily, Charlie is nimble and unhesitating. Luke finds himself hating them both, for their skill, their bravery, and praying that god might brush them from the masts and blow them away.

In the end it's numbers that decide the matter: god's dealing the hands, implacable as ever. The mizen is three more men down: two in sick bay and one missing in the night and feared washed overboard.

'Right,' says Nick. 'Enough talk. That boy's coming up with me,' and he takes him by the hand to the quarterdeck. 'He's got it in him,' shouts Nick over the wind. 'Any fool can see that!'

Tremmel nods distractedly, he has enough to do keeping his hat from flying away. No one asks Luke if he wants to go. They need all the hands they can get.

'It's a piece of piss, laddie, you'll fly up there!' Nick shoves him in the small of his back. 'Get on wi'ye, don't let me down now.' Then swings himself up and ahead.

And in the end it's not even because it's Nick up there, waiting. It's not because of the hard stares of Charlie and Burton and the rest of them, if he dallies on the deck any longer. They will glance at each other and spit and that will be the beginning of the end. Not for fear of the bosun's starting stick neither. He's felt that a fair few times now and can take it well enough. It's not even because it is his duty, because the lower mizen sail must be furled without delay.

'Up you come, laddie!'

In the end it's because somehow he has always known he must go up there one day, and today is the day. Nick calls out again, so all can hear. Follow him up and sharpish. There is nowhere to hide.

Luke takes one last look up at Nick's dark bulk hanging there. Then he puts his foot to the side, reaches up for the lower rungs of the Jacob's ladder and heaves himself up. He feels the weakness in his fingers and wrists immediately. He has never climbed so much as a tree before, cannot imagine how he will haul himself up twenty, thirty, more like forty feet. He balances on the wide plank, the wind whipping at his shirt and lifting his trowser legs.

A hollowness spreads in his chest as he turns to the ropes and settles to climb the ladder. The great wide expanse of sea pulls at his back. Nick disappeared as soon as he made a move. He don't dare look up. Feet on the flats, hands on the straights, the hairy rope fibres rasping his soles and palms. His heart pounds heavy, like a pestle in a mortar. Don't look down, don't look down. Climb like a man now, with vigour, with economy, with pumping thighs and loose shoulders. Level with the bottom of the sail now. He glances at it as the wind whistles between the canvas and its whipping rope. The great pocked mass of it breathes above him. That clean yellow canvas, now riven with saltwater stains and splashes of tar.

Steady, steady now. The ladder bounces and he feels the wind catch him, ream out a space between him and the ladder. Gripping harder, he inches up into the great sky shimmering above. Nothing is solid or graspable but the ropes, he looks only at the ropes.

Above the dinning in his ears comes a voice. Nick, calling. He dares a rapid look up and sees him leaning over the first platform, grinning. But Luke cannot make his own face move in response. His hands are clenched fists. And he realises, with an intense terror, that to clear the platform he will have to let go of the rope, lean back and out three or four feet to grasp the platform edge. He looks about, desperate for a rope that might help him.

Now he has stopped climbing, he feels the heaviness of his limbs and the hopelessness of his getting on to that platform. I've seen the men dodge over it dozens of times, he thinks. But how did they do it? Did they let go with their hands or their feet first? What had they reached for?

'Over here, Luke, over here.' Nick's face appears. He gestures to a fat rope hanging straight down. Luke swings his right hand out and up above the platform to grasp at it. Then he loses his grip with his left. With all his weight wrenching at his right hand he feels his feet begin to slip too and for one terrifying moment he is hanging in empty space, his ears pounding, before he catches at the edge of the platform, his feet scrabbling for purchase like a cat's.

Now he is clutched tight around the platform, breathing hard. He has to move up or slip off. Tensing his shoulders he grabs higher up the rope with one hand, pushes hard on the platform with the other to pull his ribs up and on to the wood. He wriggles there, a landed fish, until Nick swipes for his hand and drags him upright, his knees and shins scraping the platform. Nick's face is fierce.

I'm embarrassing him, Luke thinks. I'm embarrassing myself. Another man is coming up behind now. He can see his fingers grasping at the platform. There is not room for them all. Strung out along the outer end of the yard-arm, two men wait. Luke can see their faces screwed up and watching. Nick calls out to them and runs along the top of the yard to the middle. Then in one slippery movement he crouches and lowers his feet on to the foot-rope. As he does the men bob about, like gulls on a wave.

Luke clutches his arms tight around the yard, that is broad as the flank of a horse, and feels with his bare feet for the foot-rope.

'Call first, damn you!' yells Nick. 'Call out before you step!'

Luke calls, a tight strangulated cry that the wind takes instantly, but the men have braced themselves, flexing their knees and watching him. He steps out.

There is nothing below him now, only the foot-ropes, nothing to hold on to but the hand-lines and the yard. He inches along, the yard rough against his chin. As he reaches the centre, where Nick stands, the line he stands on suddenly dips down so far with their combined weight he can barely see over the yard. A final man joins, the rope jounces about and Luke clutches for a hold. But then the rope seems to level out and he feels himself rise.

Nick is right by his side. He shouts into the wind. 'Reach for the seam, Luke!'

He must let go of the stirrups and lean right over the yard. Only the weight of his body stops him from falling back and away with the wind. He copies the others, plucking up a fold by the seams that run like puckering scars across the canvas. Up and over the yard they lunge, reach down, hoist up and over. Foolishly, he thinks of folding sheets tugged straight from the apple trees. What flimsy things they had been. This sail is heavy as a sack of grain, and largest and heaviest here at the centre. Now he understands why the middle of the yard is prime position, why Nick takes such pride in it and such pains to retain it. Together they beat the folds into a bag before them, as if batting down a giant petticoat. Luke is sweating hard now. He hears himself grunt and wail, and cry out, but the others do too, with each hoist and heft, and he joins them.

The common cry brings the sail up far easier. From nowhere he finds a rhythm, as the folds pile up before him. Held between them, shoulder to shoulder, moving as one many-handed creature, he feels a thrill of kinship with these men, whom he does not even know by name. There is comfort in it. Gratitude. And more, he feels solid, truly present for the first time since he came aboard. He has forgotten all about the precariousness of his perch, how swift and certain his death were he to fall. The wind is thick in his ears, muffling everything else.

Nick pauses to wipe his brow. Then he lunges forward over the yard. Luke cries out, reaches for Nick's belt. Nick bends double, reaching for the last section of sail. Luke hoists himself up, stretches down too, but it is beyond his reach. Then Nick calls up, 'Grab the edge!' and calls again, louder and to all: 'Hoi!' Together, they make a grab and up in Luke's hands comes the very bottom of the sail he had climbed by so long ago. He grips the whipped rope with a sort of wonder.

'And hitch her!'

Swiftly he copies how Nick wraps the ratline around the rope that runs across the yard and tugs it tight. A clove hitch, he's seen him do it on deck, it's one of the things Nick has taught him without seeming to. Luke's fingers have a life of their own.

'Bend her, boys. Make fast.'

And it is done. They all hang there a moment, catching their breath, and now Luke can see the deck below. The tarry stripes between the planks seem narrow as anything, but the shouts come up clear and distinct. He watches a man in a red cap walk across the deck directly beneath. I could hang here for ever, Luke thinks, knock that bastard's cap off with my toes. Something of Nick's swagger swells up inside him.

But Nick is gesturing for him to move along, back to the tilting platform. When he gets there, Nick grabs for his arm and holds him tight as the others swing over and down without a word. Before he knows it, they are alone.

'Nick!' says Luke, his arms and legs and voice trembling with excitement. 'Damn it!' and he makes to fling his arms about Nick's shoulders. But Nick only tightens his grip on Luke's arm. He grins hugely at Luke, then casts his gaze upwards, to where the wind rages and the upper mast sways like a reed.

'Let's see how you do's,' he says.

Luke looks up, then back to Nick, aghast.

If he had not already stepped out on the yard and furled that mizenmain he would not have gone on up, whatever Nick might have said or done to him, what man would? But something of that swagger holds, that euphoria floods his muscles and has clamped hold of his brain. He steps out on to the ropes. Starts to climb.

The shrouds narrow and catch at the sides

of his feet. The next platform looks even smaller than the first. The wind fills his ears and the shouts from below fade away. With each step he feels the roll of the ship increase, and he grips tight as the mast leans heavily larboard and back.

Heaving himself up on to the next platform, he sees an older man crouching there, small and wiry, with a blue kerchief muffling his mouth against the biting wind. They stare at each other a moment before Luke sets off up again.

His hands and feet move of their own accord now, climbing those shrouds as steady as any staircase. Yes, he'll climb right on up and kiss the bloody angels. Before he knows it, he has grasped the upper yard, its sail tight furled. There is nothing but wind here, a chill, fierce stream that buoys up his jacket and fingers his armpits. It coaxes tears from his narrowed eyelids. Yes, he says to himself, blinking hard, oh yes. Over the yard he goes and on up the shrouds, the wind filling his lungs like sails, driving him on, until he has his left foot atop the upper top sling.

And now he is standing atop it, all alone, with only the weaving mast and the bristling ropes and the raging wind for company. The long tail of the pennant whips away behind him. He looks around, at all that space and air and freedom. Everything below, and everything behind, is gone. He feels the peace of it, the emptiness all about him; he feels the wind press against his chest, wrap itself about him, and he flings one arm out wide to welcome it.

That night is a Saturday night. Nick is more than ready to celebrate. He sits Luke by his side like a new bride and sets to recounting and toasting his talents. 'God love you, laddie, didn't you go? Like a mouse up a bell pull with the church cat after ye!' His eyes are bright and moist. Flagons of rum are set about his feet. All know Nick has a secret stash, smuggled aboard somehow, but none have yet discovered it. As long as he's so generous with it, though, they'll not look too hard. Most Saturday nights end with Nick blind drunk and picking a fight with some fellow fallen from favour or simply passing through. They come off worse than badly, but no one interferes with Old Nick. Even the officers turn a blind eye now.

Charlie paces past and casts a sly smile Luke's way. Burton and Little stare openly. Didn't know mousey had it in him. Hogmarsh sniggers, while William Winn quietly refills Luke's can for him.

And Luke rubs at his blisters, picks at the

tar stuck to his arms. The trembling has stopped but he can feel every muscle in his body, hot and tight. The elation has subsided also, to a sort of constant thrum. Like fast-flowing water under a bridge, it threatens to tug him away from all this. For in his head he is up there still. Until now, his only escape has been to think of her. But that hurts too much. Now, though, he thinks, I will have this too, to sustain me. He knows he must go up there again, and soon. Closing his eyes, he downs his flip in one, matching Hogmarsh can for can.

'To the *Essex*!' he calls out suddenly, in a hoarse voice still chilled from the heights, and Burton and Little fall about laughing.

'To our Essex laddie!' roars Nick, and he starts up a quick little ditty about the juice of a Colchester native. Hogmarsh stumbles to his feet and away they go, him and Burton and Little, arms locked about each other's shoulders, dancing and stamping round and about in the space between their sea chests and the gun. The tails of their shirts whip round and sting Luke's cheek. But he is so full of new sensation already he hardly feels it.

'God, Luke, I'm minded of meself I am, when I first went out aboard the *Starling*.' Nick has told them many stories of his early days on the collier brigs. His first time out he was ten years old, taking the place of his cousin who'd been smashed against the rocks of Staithes three day before. Wind in those parts is so strong there's folk been blown off the town ramparts, never mind those out at sea. But Nick wasn't daunted. No, Old Nick was never daunted. He took the sea by her throat and shook her. 'I was a little lad like you, though you'd never guess it would you? But look at our hands, now, look at our feet.'

Luke holds out his hand as Nick splays his fingers beside him. The back of Nick's hand is wide and brown as a paddle, and coated with reddish hair, as riddled with blue vein as the biscuit is with maggot. His fingers are thick and gnarled with scars now but they're long and strong. He lays Luke's hand atop his. Luke's fingers are almost as long, but his bones are fine and straight, and his skin looks like the finest grained leather. Then Nick places his bare foot beside Luke's. Nick's toes buckle where Luke's lie straight, but they're matched in length, narrow as punts.

'You're like me, laddie.'

Luke shakes his head.

'Oh, yes, I can see the sea in you all right. You're no freshwater creature.' Nick nudges him. 'Look after those hands, mind. Sailor's no good without his hands.'

Luke stares at their hands and feet, that are like those of father and son. Luke sees that his skin is no longer pale as milk, has lost its translucence. He knows his hide is tanning, his rind is hardening, his muscle swelling. When did that happen? He has slipped his mooring, can scarce remember what it is to feel anchored. Even as he presses his hand down, and Nick's thick fingers twist to grasp his, he is moving on currents, tugged away. She has him now, the sea.

The flip got the better of him. He lies slumped against Nick's belly, his head spinning. When he opens his eyes the lanterns swing gently over a mess empty of bodies. Charlie has gone back to the seventh gun to play cards, he can hear his slow chuckle and the others' groans. Nick's voice is in his ear still, agreeing with him solemnly about women, but Luke does not recall what he might have said.

'God, a man needs a little comfort, so he does. Damn right, laddie.' Nick is kneading at Luke's shoulder, digging his fingers deep into the bone. Luke doesn't protest. The probing feels good in his aching muscle. He leans into Nick, breathing the warm fuggy airless atmosphere of the mess like a cushioning in his lungs. His bones remember the chill up there. By god, he was glad of his jacket. It has a nasty rip at the left armhole now, doesn't recall how it happened. He'll have to mend it, later.

'You know, I once had a boy like you,' Nick continues, his voice low and slurred.

You did? Luke wants to ask, but he cannot summon up any words.

'I did. A fine boy he would have been. Like you. I would have taught him too. Seen him right. She should have known that.'

Luke waits, but Nick says nothing more. Who is this she? Nick has talked about so many women he cannot be sure. What does it matter? He just wants to lie here, in Nick's arms.

Nick wraps both arms about Luke's shoulders to squeeze him tight. 'Ah, you don't want to know, lad. No, you don't want to know.'

Luke lets Nick hold him. He wants the warmth. Nick's bonfire heat. He snuffs at his sweat, strong and acrid, and lets himself imagine he is Nick's own boy. It's too much, the smell, the smothering heat, but he does not draw away.

'Nick?' he says, feeling the hairs on Nick's

chest brush his upper lip.

'Hmm.'

'My coin. My winnings. Can I stow them in your chest like you said?'

'Hmm,' says Nick. He slips a finger under Luke's cap and, tugging it down a little, starts on with his singing. This time, it's just for Luke.

CHAPTER TWENTY-TWO

I was peeling off your glove. You'd come in from the garden, where a heavy rain lashed at the new buds. That was a fine new glove, one you should have been saving for your trousseau. The wet must have shrunk it, or your arm grown yet plumper. 'Stand still,' I said. 'Miss, please!' Last thing I wanted was to stretch or rip it. Finally your creased and reddened palm emerged, with a red spot at its centre and without a thought I smoothed and rubbed at it to encourage the congested blood away.

You flexed your wrists while I tugged both gloves straight, and now I could see that the spot had not gone and that there were more, about both hands and wrists. You saw me looking and stretched your arms before you.

They seemed to appear before our eyes: angry red circles, one after another, the size of split peas. I looked you full in the face. Now they were about your jaw and cheeks, seeming to buzz like angry bees. You bent to the glass, put your hands to your face.

'Send for my sister,' you said in a small, frightened voice. 'At once, fetch Hester.'

I was bidden out to the sodden garden to collect herbs. While Hester put you to bed I wandered in exile up and down the paths, reciting their names to fix them in my mind, to push away the name of what I had seen flaring on your skin. I found little more than pale shoots or black stalks but I folded what I could in my apron. Still I searched, rain trickling down my face, until the blueish grey light of early evening came over the garden. The haze of early apple blossom had spread like a mould and there was no bird-song.

The Captain stood at the kitchen table, his tankard at his side. He tore and pounded what scraps I had brought and mixed them with the contents of small stoppered bottles and pungent pinches of dried stuff he tipped from greasy pouches. He had Nels melt a scoop of fresh butter and pour it into a heated glass.

Then we all followed him upstairs, Hester and Nels and Hannah and Skeggs and Billy and I. None of us spoke. I think we all believed that, if we did not give it a name, it would not be happening. We would not have to think about who might have brought it to the house, or what it might mean for you, for all of us.

We watched from the door as he crossed to the hearth and lit a taper from the roaring fire there. The shutters had been locked in place, the curtains drawn and he had but one candle to see by. What light there was flickered red and yellow, the shadows crowded in.

And now my heart beat harder as I watched more closely what he was about. He took a tin plate and turned it to the candle so its polished surface caught the light. And he dipped a narrow brush into his ink bottle and wrote upon the inside of the dish words that could have been English or Latin or some heathen signage for I could not make them out. Then he set down the brush, unstoppered a tall glass bottle and poured a quantity of dark liquid into the dish. This he swilled around several times and decanted into a wide-mouthed tankard. When he laid down the dish the words had disappeared.

To me it all appeared a form of witchcraft. But I held faith with your father, I did, right up until the moment he put the tankard to your lips. You had laid limp throughout his preparations, your eyes closed. Then Hester drew her fingers across your forehead to rouse you and slipped a supporting hand behind your shoulder. Your eyes opened, glassy with fever already. He bent to you, whispered softly. But when he tried to tip the liquid into your mouth you grew sudden fierce and batted his arm away. Hester gasped as liquid slopped on to the sheets.

'Come, come, girl, you must take it.' He spoke gruffly now, as he would to Skeggs or any of us. 'You must.'

Hester stuffed pillows behind your head, and he tried again. But now you grew fierce, you sat up, and hissed back, 'No, No!' You looked about the room wildly, searching.

I could not stand by the door a moment longer.

'Stop, sir, stop,' I cried. 'She does not want this.' I rushed to your side and plucked the tankard from his hands. It smelt evil. He snatched it back without a word. You sank back down, breathing heavily.

'Stop him, miss,' I pleaded. 'You can see it will do no good.'

Hester looked at me coldly. She took the tankard from him and I thought then that it would all be over. But she turned to him and said: 'Try the other.'

So he took up the glass of liquid butter

which he had set by the hearth to keep warm and held it to your lips. Only you dashed it from his hand and sent it splattering across the room. Then you spat at him, full in the face.

At this he caught hold of your arms and crossed them over your chest, pinning you down. Now your eyes were quite wild and you twisted to and fro as he reached for the tankard again.

'No,' I cried, 'No!' and Hester took me by the shoulders and shoved me back to the doorway and went to help her father. Hannah sat with me in the kitchen while I wept. Skeggs had his arms about Nels. 'Remember her mother, Skeggs,' she was saying over and over as he squeezed her. 'Remember her poor dear mother?' We could hear your cries upstairs, the Captain's rumbles, Hester's soothing.

I must help you, I thought, I must. For without you I have nothing. If you were to die — And all I could see was a blackness. I could not imagine life without you.

The Captain shut himself in the parlour. Hester went to him but he would not call a doctor, said he would continue to dose you and she must nurse you alone. The whole household was closed up: no one came to call, none of us went out, and the marketing was left inside the garden gate. When the knock came I watched Skeggs totter down the path and bend his ear to the closed gate, listen, nod.

'There's a fierce number down in town and no mistake,' he said grimly, setting the baskets down on the kitchen table. 'And a dozen dead of it out on the *Bideford* already.' Nels gave out a little cry. 'Weren't they under quarantine, already?' she asked. 'Was it Gunnell came to the gate? Did he speak of the Checketts?' The Checketts were her great friends, who ran bumboats out to the Navy vessels. 'Did anyone have news of my brother at Castlegate?' Hannah asked. And I bit my lip and thought of Susie.

For three days we sat and waited, lit all the candles we dared for the rain did not stop and it was dark as winter inside and out. But you only grew worse. We listened to Hester shout at your father. The boards creaked above our heads as he walked to and fro, to and fro.

Hester took me out to the still room early on the fourth morning to prepare some waters. I could see from her drawn face that you were no better. She talked to me of stoppers and extra cloths but I could not bear it.

'Why will he not listen?' I blurted. 'What if —'

'Do not say it!' she said, her voice fierce. 'Do not.'

'But Miss Handley,' I took her hand now, squeezed it. Nothing mattered but you. 'Miss, we cannot let her —'

'I know, Lou, I know.'

'Then what can we do? Why does he persist?'

'Because of our mother,' she said shortly.

You had neither of you spoken to me of how your mother died, but I recalled Nels's words that first week. 'Because he let that evil man physick her?'

She rubbed at her pale cheek. 'No, Lou, no. Because he would not.'

I stared at her. 'But Nels said —'

'Oh, what does Nels know!' she said vehemently, and I could see the tears in her eyes. She pulled the door to and leant back against the wall, cradling an empty jar in her arms.

'Nels knows nothing. She was not with us then. That man Peter was our friend — he was Father's manservant from Africky, a long time back, for as long as I could remember he was there. Peter swore he could cure her, that she would recover if he could use his people's medicine. My father had relied on him many times before, his medicines had cured many on their voyages together. Peter treated us, as children, he gave me black beans to chew when I had the flux once. But we were arrived in Harwich by then, and my father forbade Peter come near her, for he would be respectable ashore, go to the Christian doctors.'

Hester put the jar down on the shelf with great care, wiped at its lid with the side of her hand.

'She died, Lou. And Peter would not stay with us after that. And look what my father does now.'

She pulled out from her pocket several tiny papers.

'He kept some of Peter's herbs, and his receipts. I took these from his desk, thinking to make him stop but he has them by heart. Do you see? He does for Becca what Peter would have done for our mother. And if it is a sort of witchcraft, he does not care.'

'But do you not care? Miss?' I was frantic. No wonder you were not improving. It was as I had thought, he was killing you with heathen potions.

'What are we to do?' I asked her. 'Your sister has the small pox. Likely she will die.'

I had said it. She stared at me, her eyes filling with tears.

'You must do something.'

Finally Hester sat down and wrote to a Doctor Winchcombe and a Doctor Fairhall. She wrote to Henry too. I saw the letters, brown with vinegar, as she handed them to a boy through the half-open door.

Doctor Winchcombe recommended we expose you to the elements. A night on Beacon Hill, well wrapped about the kidneys but your arms and breast exposed. Doctor Fairhall prescribed a series of cold baths, alternating salt and fresh, to be carried out daily until a cure were effected. The Captain refused to contemplate either. Hester wept.

He kept to his parlour and she nursed you now. Would not let the Captain near. Left Nels to manage the household and kept me running up and down with pressed muslins and herb waters. I saw you only through the half-open door as I passed them to her, your face horrible swollen, and I ached to be with you, to comfort you.

A whole week went by, and nothing changed. We heard the bells ringing for Easter, day after day, but none of us ventured to St Nick's. Doctor Winchcombe came to the door once. The Captain would not admit him. I heard the doctor shout to the closed door: 'Some damned foreign captain has broken quarantine, that's what.

We've not had this cursed disease here for months.'

Skeggs turned away stony-faced. But as we ate our dinner silently in the kitchen that day, I thought back to the week of the masquerade. How Henry had been delayed, and missed the entertainment. But had come visiting the very next day. And the Captain too. How many days later? Had Henry disembarked without permission? Had the Captain? I could not but wonder.

I never told you that, did I? Did you ever suspect it? To this day I do not know for sure that either was to blame. But that day, the resentment and fear and, yes, hatred for the pair of them that had been building in my heart would not let me be still any more. Yet when I came to do it, I felt exceedingly calm, quite at rest in my mind. I went to your room and knocked on the door. Hester came to open it and I drew her out to stand by the window. I wanted her to see my face, that I was serious and would not be diverted. My hands were trembling but I lowered my chin and spoke as firmly as I could.

'She is no better, is she?'

Hester could not look at me. 'Perhaps, in a day or two, if we all pray —'

'With no doctor? Nothing but lavender

water and kind words? Listen to me, please. At home, they say that if you be well, and you share the bed of one with the small pox, it can be that you draw off some of the disease, lessen it some. My mother told me her aunt lay with a cousin at Lawford and it did work, it were not witchcraft. The cousin lived.'

'And your aunt?' Hester asked. 'Did your aunt live?'

When I did not answer she drew breath sharply and looked away.

'All the same,' she said after a long moment, 'we must try it.'

But when I saw what was in her mind I almost laughed.

'No!' I said. 'No. Not you.'

I closed the door behind me and went to your bed. Hannah had built up the fire and tight drawn the shutters and curtains, just like my mother had told me. The sweat pricked my lip and forehead. The air was thicker than it had ever been, but sour now. I knew you were watching me, your eyes were open wide. It was so dark I could not see the marks upon your face. But I feared them, how I feared them. I looked to the door in panic: it was shut tight. I was sealed in now with the illness, with you. Slowly I

pulled my cap from my head and laid it on
the arm of your blue velvet chair. I untied
my bodice and stepped out of my slippers. I
dropped my apron and skirt. When I rolled
down my stockings the fire scorched at my
legs, the hot air billowing my chemise about
my waist. And swiftly now, so that I could
not think what I was doing, I lifted up the
heavy bedclothes and slipped in beside you.

'You are a fool.'

I felt the tears start behind my closed
eyelids.

'A foolish country mouse.'

I found your hand and squeezed it. It was
hot, swollen.

'Go away,' you said. But your voice was
clogged and feeble.

I let go your hand and turned on my side
towards you, tucking up my knees behind
yours and curving my body about you like
spoons in a drawer. Your shift was limp, your
flesh hot and slick.

'No, miss,' I said. 'No. I will not leave you.'

How to describe those days and nights? It
was like being buried alive, buried deep in
sweated bed linen and the awful, fatal sense
of responsibility for your life. All outside
sound was muffled, I could hear but our
own breathing, the swell and heave of the
bedclothes as we shifted, the tickle of the

pillow stuffing, the thud of our blood beating.

At first you kept your back turned, denying my presence, let alone what it might mean, for both of us. Much as this pained me, I would not withdraw. Such disregard you had shown for my feelings, over many weeks; why, could I not match you? I did not woo you with words, but I did persist. Whether you liked it or no, I would save you if I could.

But then, as the fever mounted, though you still did not speak or turn towards me, I could feel your sinew slacken. The heat began to radiate, then flow from you in waves, until you lay pooled in your own sweat. Your breast rose and fell with each increasingly ragged breath. A shivering set in, and progressed, with a terrible relentlessness, from a tremble to a jerking and a tossing that brought forth moan after moan.

Now you let me take your hands to comfort you, and I found them embossed all over with small round studs of pox, like grains of rice quilted into the skin. I ran my hands over them — slowly, lightly, torn between a fervent wish to soothe and a dull horror of my beloved's new pebbled flesh.

Now you let me take hold of you, you were beyond protesting, beyond caring.

Without hesitation I wrapped my arms about you, plucked the dampened hair from your brow and breathed the softest imprecations into your hot ear.

I tended you as I had never tended any living thing before. The cream and the butter I had watched carefully, my maiding I had laboured at diligently. But now, now I squeezed my whole soul to attempt a cure. I strained my eyes in the half light to detect the smallest change in colour of the pox, hoping not to see them turn black or ooze blood, which meant certain death. With an effort of will that left me exhausted I attempted to draw off your distress, absorb your exhalations. I held my body against yours, absorbing your heated humours, letting your sweat settle and encrust itself upon me. We came together like the kissing crust, where loaves rise and fuse together in the heat of the oven.

Then came the moment when the inflamed poxes could swell no more and they began to burst, and ooze a foul-smelling pus. The layers of skin flaked like the crust on a pie. Caught up in your own agony you pulled away; I too backed away into the shelter of the bedclothes, I could not help it. You cried out now, as though your body was being flayed, and clutched at me in a frenzy.

'Hush, miss, hush, dear miss,' I answered every cry, hour after hour. But I knew you did not hear me.

We were both smeared with pus and sweat and flakes of skin, our hair was meshed together, our shifts clumped as one. I knew not whether I had taken the pox from you and would be destroyed by it myself and had not time to care, so taken up was I in keeping you from tearing at your face and arms and neck and drawing the fatal blood from the sores.

Hester came to the door often, day and night. I would hear it open, sense her standing there. Sometimes she would whisper with another, I would hear the Captain's low rumble, Nels weeping. Then she would call out: 'What would you have?' Often I was too taken up with tending you to answer, other times I had been desperate for her to appear. 'Bring us water to drink,' I would call out then, and shock myself with my cracked, unfamiliar voice. The door would close, and a little while later there would be a flask of water on the table, clean damp cloths. I wept when I lifted the linen on a platter and found a half dozen of Nels's little cakes, still warm and fragrant.

I would jerk awake from a heavy slumber to hear your moans rising and rising before I could summon reassurance from my thick throat. Sleep would drown me again while you were still far from settled. A heavy despair began to spread through me. At least, I thought, if you are to die we will be together. Then I imagined how it would be if only I survived and I turned my back, stared into the darkest corners of the room and tried not to let you feel my sobs.

One day I surfaced to find you lying curled on your side with your face towards me, hidden deep beneath your tumbled hair. I lay very still. Your breathing seemed impossible light. All was quiet. No gulls, or rumble of carts, or movement in the house. Was it early morning or late evening? I could not tell.

Carefully I drew a hank of hair away from your face and touched the back of my hand to your forehead. Still hot, but not slick with sweat. And when I fingered a pox on your cheek, its lid slid away dry on my fingertip, a harmless, empty crust.

How I wanted to hug you tight then, to squeeze you to me, to share my joy. To stroke your cheek, to soothe you, for you were to be well again, I had not lost you. But you were sleeping still. Slowly, I raised myself on one elbow. A hazy light came from under the door. The pox was so thick still there was not an inch of your cheek I could stroke without catching the crust of one sore or another. My tears dripped on to your scarred and swollen forehead. Then you opened your eyes. They are the same as ever, I thought, your stern dark eyes. You are still my Becca.

I knew what your eyes were asking me, and all I had to do was smile. And then I kissed your cheek anyway, light as a butterfly. You pulled me to you and I buried my face in your neck, in your hair, and even as you winced you put your arms about my shoulders and held me tight.

CHAPTER TWENTY-THREE

It may be Luke's arms that hug the yards, his feet that curl about the ropes, their rasping as familiar as a slipper, but in truth it is Nick who buoys him up, keeps him safe.

Below as well as aloft. Burton and Little hang on Nick's every word, Bramley sniggers at his every jest, Hogmarsh moons about in his wake. But now that his lad has proved himself out on the yards, Nick only has eyes for Luke. Luke can feel the resentment in the mess. Knows Charlie's pique too, however much the fellow smiles and strokes his whiskers. He would feel such hurt himself, if he were to see Nick favour another so.

Yes, Luke is more than a little dazzled by his sea daddy now, he's just like all the rest of the company. Whenever he sees Nick's colossal bulk approach, Luke's muscle slacks with relief, with gratitude; his life consists in watching Nick's every move, his skill, his infinite resource. He can scarcely recall how he used to wish Nick dead and gone, to wish his attentions away.

The *Essex* seems to have made an accommodation of her own also. They're past Madeira and well out in the ocean, the weather is set fair, the winds all favourable and she covers many leagues each day. The number of men in the sick bay swells a little every day too, like the growing litter of some perversely breeding creature, but the men left standing work together well enough.

And as he sways there aloft, alone in the middle of the wide, wide ocean, nothing about him but sea and sky, Luke is suspended. He thinks of her but the tears no longer come. This is all there is. He has no sense of how far there is to go, how long it will take for him to find her again. But his longing for her grows every day, filling all the wide space about him to the very edges.

Nick is no fool. He sees more than homesickness in Luke's eyes, up there, scanning the horizon day after day. Nick may have scoffed at Powell's pining for his wife, cannot even speak of a woman without leering, but he knows a lovelorn lad when he sees one. One warm night, as they ride up there on the mizen cross, ride easy on a lulling swell with new and strange stars bristling about their ears, Nick pops another wodge of baccy in his mouth and nudges Luke.

'Betty,' he says thickly, suggestively. After a moment, 'Tess?' Then, 'Nance.'

There is dancing down on the forecastle and a constant scraping of fiddles from the poop. Up here in the silent dusk the din resounds loud as a ball. Luke can easy pretend he has not heard, let alone understood what Nick is asking. But while Nick is everything to him here — all that sustains him — the very thought of her eclipses Nick in an instant. He swallows, and turns to face Nick.

He says her name slowly, feeling his scurfed lips meet and then peel part. He says it again, because he can. And now the tears prick, for he realises his mistake. It is just her name on his lips, a breath in the night. He has released her to the vapour, and she remains as intangible as ever.

Nick nods, and chews.

Luke struggles to bring her back. 'She was promised to another,' he says, 'but we, but now —' His head is filled sudden with the vision he had, of their cottage and their patch of green pasture. 'She did love me, she said.' But does she still? How long must she wait for him?

Nick sucks in his breath, raises himself on

his elbow. Luke knows what's coming. Nice! Nick will exclaim. How'd you catch her, runt like you? What you got in your trowsers, eh? But Nick says none of these things.

'Oh she'll wait,' is all he says, and he pats Luke's arm heavily. 'Fine lad like you. Lucky lad like you.'

Luke tugs at a knot. Then he asks: 'And you? Do you not —'

Nick shakes his head violent. He sniffs and slaps the yard. 'Got a damn fierce mistress here, ain't I? Must ride her hard, eh?'

They never talk of her again. But after that night Luke begins to see a changed Nick. Only with him, mind, never with the others at mess or together in the heat of the work — only at moments when they are relative alone, strung out on the yard waiting on the call, or safe below, swinging close in their hammocks. All hunched up on the main one day, splicing rope, he notices Nick's eyes suspicious bright. There's a tremble in his hands when he cuts at his baccy. When Nick croons *I'm away, me lassie* as he swings in his hammock after eight bells there's something in his tone that makes Luke keep his eyes wide open till he winds to the end. Nick drinks harder, too, is for ever slipping away for a tot. That grey, dishcloth look persists until the dog watches some days.

Aloft and alone together, Nick will tell Luke snippets of his life, show him glimpses of the tall, reedy, red-cheeked young man he once was, back in Berwick, walking the ramparts, soft-hearted and yearning for women. God, young Nick loved women, the sea had nothing on women.

One blowy day, as they slip back down the ratlines from a long and testy session aloft, he tells Luke he had a missus back in Berwick. He tells Luke her name. Elizabeth. A real-spliced missus. Now that is a surprise. First a son, now a wife. Luke knows not to ask now, he waits. For late one Saturday night, when Nick will prop himself up on one elbow, pull him close and pour them both another.

A violent lurch wakes Luke and sends him sprawling out of his hammock, headfirst towards the gun carriage. He clutches for Nick but the hammock is empty. He must crouch motionless for a long moment, his head still spinning with drink. The sea rushes heavy against the hull. What bell is it? He can scarcely have slept an hour. All around him men slip from their hammocks, cursing and staggering as the deck tilts to port beneath their feet. Shouts and footsteps thunder above his head. A lantern flares at the stair, a man yelling hoarse for assistance on deck.

Even before he reaches his post he knows something is wrong. Trembling and still half asleep, he takes up the rope and breathes in the quicksilver night air. The deck has righted itself. The wind is strong but steady and the stars are clear and sharp: this is no storm. He scans the seas, but no enemy has been sighted: no one is yelling from the crow's nests, no officers clustering to peer through their scopes. But there is shock and dismay in the air. He can hear a man groaning over by the helm, several voices raised in pain. The master is calling on god to witness his trials and that's de Clare's smooth voice, begging calm. Luke stands on tiptoe to see him, the white cravat gleaming as he bends with a lantern over a man doubled up by the bulwark.

'What happened?' Luke asks the man by his side.

'Christ knows. They say that's Furniss there.'

The man looks in a bad way.

'Say he fell.'

'But he's a waster, man,' exclaims another. 'What's he doing up aloft?'

'Fell from the mizen cross.'

The mizen topgallant hangs high above,

wide and full as a drum, its yard empty. But half a dozen men straddle each end of the main mizen yard, grappling to rein in its bunt, which has blown up obscenely into a swollen creaking canvas belly that obscures the mast.

'Poor bastard.'

'Is he sore injured?'

'Worse,' says a man coming through with a lantern. 'Fell on the crossjack, he did, slid down the great yard.' He calls back over his shoulder. 'Fell a dead man, right under the nose of the helmsman.'

A dead man. The shouts and screams of pain come from another man, then, Luke can see him now, cursing and rolling about on the deck. Angry shouts come from every direction, from out on the yards and in the rigging and the officers all yelling back. Luke can't make out any of it. Another voice in the darkness says: 'Tis why she yawed about. Helmsman took fright, he did.'

Luke hears de Clare call for stout men. After a while the crowd parts to let them through with their burden. Four men hold the body, averting their eyes from its lolling head and dripping, mangled shape. Furniss. Luke stares and stares, at the twisted angle the legs make, the canvas trowsers soaked in blood. The others have bowed their heads and he copies them, pulling off his cap and kneading it in his hands.

Then comes another man, young and skinny, his shirt torn, clutching at his misshapen shoulder, helped along by two others. A third totters along behind, his contorted face a sheet of tears and mucus and his hands held out as if in supplication. His forearms and palms are raw and bleeding. Luke's gorge rises as he smells the rope-burnt flesh. All around him men cross themselves as they watch the sorry procession go below. Luke does the same.

'The pity,' intones a voice, 'the pity of it.'

'Make way!' comes a call from behind. 'Make way now!'

De Clare's face is rigid, his eyes glittering. He walks upright, trailing one arm, as though leading an animal. About him the murmur of shock and speculation has been replaced by a sullen grumbling. Following in his wake is a lumbering, swaying figure. It hangs its head, clutching stiffly with both arms at its ribs. Luke struggles to see who it is. The man's face is hidden. Then he recognises the swell of the shoulders, and the shell, glinting on its thong about his neck.

And he sees now how angry the men are. They press up behind Nick with raised chins and clenched fists. They say nothing but they look ready to knock him down. The officers glance urgently at one another but do nothing. Luke does not understand. Clearly Nick has been hurt too. But to hound him so? No man on the ship would have dared do such a thing before tonight. Nick would have snapped them in half. Now they poke at him like a bear in a pit. And he does nothing.

'Nick!' he yells out, his voice thick. 'Nick, over here!'

Nick looks about him, his eyes blood-red and maddened. When they fasten on his face, Luke can't help flinching. Nick's jaw works furiously.

Then de Clare tugs on Nick's arm, guiding him down the hatchway. A low muttering breaks out in the great press of men behind Luke. Luke does not stop to hear what they say, but hurries down the hatchway after Nick and de Clare.

He opens the door of the dispensary to see the stove burning away furiously and a number of iron pots steaming before it. The place is in order now, shelf after shelf of bottles and jars and packets, and bunches of herbs in paper bags hung from the beams, pungent and powdery. But there is no one here.

He turns away from the door. The long lump that is the body of Furniss is already wrapped in a hammock and wedged up against a wall. A marine stands guard. And there is de Clare, winding a bandage around the sobbing man's hand. Before Luke can speak, de Clare nods: 'Over there. Tell him I'll be with him shortly.'

Luke finds Nick hunched in a dark corner, clutching at his ribs. He crouches beside him to touch his shoulder.

'It's Luke,' he says.

Slowly, Nick inclines his head until his stubbled cheek just touches Luke's forehead. He stays like that a moment. Then he makes a small hollow noise, like air shaken from a sack, and crumples into Luke, pinning him down.

'Nick, hush, Nick,' says Luke, panicked. Instinct tells him to put his arms about Nick, to comfort him, but it feels all wrong. People see weakness in a woman, they want to help. See weakness in a man, they want to stamp it out. He knows that now, and hates it. He pushes Nick away and gets to his feet.

'What happened up there?' he asks.

Nick quivers, sniffs, makes ugly noises. He does not look up. 'Lord pity me, pity me,' he says over and over. 'I made her go back out there with me. Wanted to see for meself.'

Luke folds his arms and frowns. Has the man lost his wits?

Nick turns an angry, anguished face up at him. 'Tell me, what sort of mother lets a lad on ramparts in such weather?'

Luke claps his hands together. 'Damn it, Nick. What happened?'

But Nick has hold of Luke and drags him down, hissing urgently in his ear. 'She grabbed me about the neck, like. I'm trying to get her off me, trying to get to where it happened, to see where my boy fell.' Then he roars out. 'Christ this woman wears a lot of garment! Get off of me!' And he pushes Luke so hard he lands sprawling on the floor. Nick reaches out for him on the instant, sobbing. 'I'm sorry, Lisbeth, I'm so sorry.'

Luke pulls away and stares at Nick's twisted face, his wet, working mouth. Now he is sobbing. 'I waited such a long time. I called down to you, Lisbeth. But lass, oh my lass, you never moved.' Did Nick fall too? Has it smashed his wits in?

'Fletcher?'

Luke tenses. De Clare stands beside him. He has removed his blue coat and rolled up his shirtsleeves to reveal strong, pale forearms. His perfect cravat hangs loose and smeared with blood. Luke has seen his figure move about the ship but never again, since those first days aboard, looked full into his face, as now. He has forgotten how afraid de Clare makes him feel. He gets to his feet.

'I don't know what happened, sir,' he says quickly. 'I've been asking him but — he needs a drink, sir. He's raving. I'll fetch the man a drink.'

He makes to move past but de Clare touches his arm lightly and Luke feels the hairs there rise in alarm.

'Perhaps,' says de Clare quietly, 'you might ask Dominique to bring a pan of hot water?'

But Luke can hear his watch being called. He turns away without replying, hurries up and away to his station. Now Nick is not there drooling on him, Luke feels a great wave of pity for the man. He does not know where he is, nor what he says. Those boys should show him more respect! Remember who he is, by god.

He's jabbed hard in the shoulder. He turns to find a full-bearded man glaring at him.

'Does he live, the bastard?'

'Who?'

The man stares, mouth half open in

mockery. His breath is foul.

'Your man Stav.'

'De Clare is seeing to him.'

'De Clare is seeing to him,' minces the man, and Luke sees his spilling teeth and the red, erupting gums. 'Tell your daddy we'll see to him all right.' Luke stares after him, rubbing at his shoulder.

Winn stands braced behind Luke, as they wait to take in more sail. The spray splatters over their heads and the wind takes half his words. But Luke pieces it together. How the wind brewed up fast so extra hands were called on deck to make sail. Winn had not even thought to kick Nick and Luke awake, though — pissed as porpoises they were, lolling half out their hammocks.

Next thing, Nick had come up anyway, roaring drunk. He bellowed out in the dark, 'She's blowing hard? I'm your man. Who's with me?' Bosun's mate cheered, said she made such poor headway she needed all the hands she could get. Nick collared two young lubbers: Furniss and a carpenter's boy. Come with me lads, Nick'd said, I can loose a sail and turn a lubber able faster than any man alive. He kicked them both up the shrouds.

'They were all out on the yard,' Winn says slowly. 'Looked like they'd loosened the gaskets already. But then the bunt blows out first, sudden as anything. Knocked off a lad at the larboard yard-arm. Furniss, I reckon. Fell on the crossjack. He was done for right off.'

Luke's heart is thumping. That could have been him up there, any one of them, their fate his.

'I saw a lad,' says Winn, 'clinging to the ratlines, halfway down the sail. They got him back on the yard but he'd pulled his shoulder out.'

Luke swallows hard.

'And Thompson. He was nearer the bunt when it blew out. It flung him right back on the shrouds, nigh burnt his hands off afore he could get a grip.'

A fury comes over Luke now, a bitter raging. He is suddenly not at all sure he wants to hear more. But he has to ask. 'And Nick?'

'Bunt was pulling all over, he just sat tight behind it, out of sight. Stayed until they said they'd come and get him. But then, I don't know, Luke, he just fell. I saw him drop from the lower shrouds, a dozen feet or more.'

Luke knows now, but he wants to hear Winn say it. 'Nick was at the centre of the yard. He loosed the bunt too early.'

Winn nods sadly. 'We've three men down,

one of them dead, thanks to him. Nick's done for, Luke.'

Luke goes right down to the orlop deck, a place he usually avoids, before he finds Charlie. He stands in a knot of men by the empty purser's office. The tight-furled points of his yellow kerchief wag in the light from the lantern at their feet. Luke sees him squat forward on his haunches and hiss curses into the snarling jaws of a solid white dog. Its owner has it tight about the collar but still it twists and thrusts to get at its tormentor's face, only inches away. Charlie purses up his lips and blows a kiss at the dog, all the while glaring bleakly into its eyes. At Luke's approach he smiles broadly.

'Little Luke. What can I do for you, my unlucky lad?' The dog's owner tugs on its collar as it rushes forward, barking furiously.

'You must come.'

'Must I now?'

Luke is well used to Charlie's arch ways. He sets his shoulders. 'Nick fell, he is hurt bad.'

The men about take their hands from their pockets. Charlie just shrugs. 'Indeed,' he says evenly.

Luke stares. He has not expected this. Charlie is Nick's best mate, the man to rouse up some rum and a wad of his best baccy and be down there in a trice, with perhaps a blanket to wedge behind his mate's back. And Hogmarsh and the rest of the mess, rallying round. Where are they all? The dog snarls and twists at his feet. He can feel his anger rising.

'Nick's in sick bay.'

Charlie smiles on, inscrutable as ever.

'Charlie, why don't you —'

Charlie takes his arm, and steps into a dark corner.

'Listen, Luke. You know our boy Nick. Good lad and all that. But he's not the steadiest hand on the tiller, now, is he? You know what I mean. Bit of an unpredictable bastard.'

What of it? Luke wants to ask. He's your mate, Charlie. You look after him when he's in trouble. But he knows as well as anyone what Nick can be like. He remembers the boy Nick beat up on the tender. The lad didn't last long after that. He thinks of all the times then and since that Nick has pulled rank, got thundering drunk, picked a fight out of nothing. Only last Saturday he cracked a lad's head against a post, he ended in sick bay. The whole mess laughed then. Not now. No, Luke has been safe, at the eye of the storm, but Nick has ruffled a lot of tempers.

'So?' he says. But he can feel Charlie tense, and lose patience.

'You're not stupid, Luke.' Charlie fingers Luke's kerchief, gives it a little tug. 'He's on his own now. Leave it, all right?' He walks away, back to the men and the whimpering white dog.

Luke watches him go. That was Charlie trying to help him, he realises. Charlie knows how it goes. And so he's dropped Nick like a hot coal. The thought makes him sick. That damned Nick's all I've got in the world, he realises. That drunken, vicious collier bastard.

He finds Nick alone, slumped against a wall of the sick bay, his ribs bandaged from top to bottom. He helps him back down to the lower deck, slings his hammock for him in the usual place and holds it steady, has to heave him in. Then he sits down to wait while he settles.

At supper Luke watches as Winn silently distributes the biscuit and beer. No portion for Nick. No mention of Nick. No one looks at Luke, or speaks to him. One by one, the others leave, until he's alone at the board. He wraps half his uneaten biscuit in his kerchief and tucks it into Nick's fingers for when he wakes.

When they are all roused out at midnight, the bosun's mate jabs at Nick's hammock with his stick like he's flushing out a rat.

'Out or down,' he snarls, holding his knife to the ropes. 'Out or down.'

And Nick curls up and takes it, tips gingerly out of his hammock to crouch wheezing and wincing while the man screams at him to get to his station. The others are long gone. But Luke helps him to the hatchway. Nick still hasn't spoken to him, or looked at him. Luke wants to weep. This is Nick, who was up and away to the shrouds before a man could draw breath, who boasted he could get men to furl a main-sail in less time than it took to take a piss. Nick, who had a ditty for every occasion. Nick, the joker of the pack, king of the yard.

Up on deck, a space clears around Nick as he comes through. Luke follows some feet behind. Nick looks like he might fall at any moment. Now he stands swaying by the mizen shrouds, his arms about his ribs. The men block his way. They fold their arms, stare him out. An officer comes up to Nick and orders him away aft. Nick reaches out to grasp the shrouds. The officer yells again, and bats his hands away with his stick. But Nick stands there still, hanging his head.

■ ■ ■ ■

The court notice is nailed to the main mast that evening, as the marine beat a roll of drums. Able top-man Nicholas Stavenger, master of the mizen top, is found guilty of High Treason, since during hostilities he has aided the Spanish by endangering the ship and destroying a subject of the armed forces of the Crown. The penalty is Death.

Luke traces a trembling finger under the freshly inked words. He cannot take it in, he must read it through once more, but the crowd about the mast eases him away. He leans on the bulwarks, his stomach heaving. Then he goes below.

When he reaches the middle deck, de Clare stops him with a hand to the chest.

'Where do they have him?' Luke asks, his panic and anger getting the better of his naval manners. He is close to tears. 'They cannot do this. Any man might make such a mistake.' But Nick does not make mistakes. Everyone knows that.

'Any man can kill another. That is why we have such courts. So you men will learn their first commandment: thou shalt only kill thy enemy, not thy fellow.'

Luke stares at de Clare, baffled by his riddling talk. He remembers well how de Clare helped him: dressed his wound, found him his station. De Clare was his last hope. But his skin pricks with unease. De Clare is not vicious, like so many of the officers. He does not threaten or fight or leer or cajole, like Nick. He merely watches, and smiles. But that is enough. Luke would not owe anything, to anyone, especially not to this man. But without Nick he has no one. So he must beg.

'Sir?' he asks. 'Might you do something? Speak to the Captain, perhaps of Mr Stavenger's good character? I would be most grateful —'

De Clare's gaze penetrates him yet again. He dredges up all the fine phrases he knows. 'I plead with you, sir, I throw myself on your mercy. If you would only oblige me in this, I would be entirely in your debt —'

He realises he is grasping the man's sleeve, his grimy fingers have hold of de Clare's lace cuff. He looks up in alarm at de Clare's parted lips, his lustrous eyes that are pools of blackness.

De Clare brushes off his cuff, then steps back smartly, and gestures for Luke to follow. As he lifts back the canvas screening of the sick bay, an acrid reek sears Luke's throat, all pus and flux and bile.

De Clare laughs briefly. 'See how popular I have become?' Luke stares at the close-packed cots, the men who lie tumbled and groaning on the deck. 'And to think, we have not yet engaged the enemy.'

De Clare sighs gently and clasps his hands. '*Bien,* you must know, since the ship is so short of hands already the court must be merciful, whether it likes to or not. No, your able seaman friend is too valuable, however foolish he has been. He will be demoted, of course. But they will not execute him.'

De Clare takes him by the shoulders and guides him towards the hatchway. There de Clare continues evenly: 'Of course, he will be punished still.' Luke holds his breath. 'Only a hundred lashes.' He observes Luke's reaction. Then he reaches out, rests his hand against Luke's paled cheek. 'I'm afraid our Doctor Roberts will see he takes his full punishment.' His fingers move to Luke's chin, as though to prop his head up. 'But do not worry. I shall be there.'

Luke is watching this time, as the lash spins through the air and the spine bones are laid bare, sudden stripped of flesh and glistening in the fresh air like the nibs of new teeth. Later a rib, a strip of white like a piano key among all the dark inch-thick gashes, and Luke remembers Powell the butcher and the work he did every day to keep his young family, wielding his cleaver, letting it fall again and again and he sees him falling on the beach, the blood-red roses exploding on his back. This time, when he can watch no more and looks to the heavens, hearing the whistle and cut of the lash, the jeers of the men, there are no angels. Luke longs to be aloft again, more than ever. Even without Nick. For he cannot let himself imagine what life will be like without Nick at his side. Life in the mess, about the ship. He watches Bramley's face, Burton and Little. Charlie. The pocked man. They all know him to be Nick's boy.

Chapter Twenty-Four

Once the crusts had begun to slide, you fingered them silently. You explored your arms, your shoulders, and when your hands moved towards your face, I could hear your breath come faster. I trapped your hands between my own.

'Hush, Becca, hush,' I said, as I had said so many times before, and kissed your knuckles, hard. Once more I put myself between you and this fresh torment.

When Hester came to the door I told her the good news but would not let her or your father near the bed. Fetch Miss Rebecca's cold cream pomatum, I told her, every jar, and saffron too, all that was in the house. Then, with the shutters still part pulled-to, for the light hurt your eyes, I scooped all the cream into a copper bowl and pounded in the saffron until the mixture turned a soft buttery yellow. I had to sit on the window seat to do it, I was too dizzy to stand. Hannah brought in fresh bedding and took the old away to be burnt. Your new counterpane was blue.

I peeled off your reeking shift and laid you naked on your back on the fresh cool sheeting. I stroked the ointment I had made over your skin, taking care not to pick off crusts that were not ready to move. I did this slowly, again and again, coming to know the smallest of craters as well as the freckles on my own hands. I felt no trepidation. It was as though you and your flesh had become mine.

I saw how you looked at me now. I thought you might ask me why I had done it, risked all to save you. But if you wondered, you did not ask. I believed you knew, perhaps had always known, and now you had proof. I felt your eyes upon me often, and when I turned to you the expression on your face was solemn, as it had never been. But being Becca, you did not tell what was in your heart.

We rose from the bed as from the grave, light-headed and insubstantial as air. I hugged you close, and felt your new frailty, your diminished shoulders, the jut of your chin. We did not speak much. You were still weak. And I could not trust myself. Even before I unfolded a clean chemise for you, I took care to hang a sheet over the dressing table mirror.

I did not leave you alone. I did not leave your room. Nor even a week or so later, when you were able to converse, laugh and take sustenance. And you would not be parted from me. When I dressed you, did up your hair, we stood and moved as one. When we talked it was in a murmur. We sat close together, our hands entwined. Tucked each other's hair away, adjusted each other's caps. It was as though I were your talisman of wellness, as though you would be yet again exposed if you did not keep me with you at all times.

No. Neither of us quite returned to the world and the roles we had previously inhabited. The household saw us bound together by gratitude and relief — but that was not all. We had discovered a secret pleasure in this intimacy.

In those first weeks, the cooling, softening pomatum brought you sweet relief, such that you cried out in gladness and begged me not to halt. I tended eagerly to your face, then your hands, your wrists, your neck. You lay with your eyes closed, and had me go on, seek out the creases of your elbow, the hollow of your armpit, the fold between your breasts, all the heated secret places that had given you so much torment.

It was through these ministrations that I discovered the greater delights I could procure you. One day you lay so beautiful still I thought you slept. I took up yet more ointment and traced a slicked finger over your lips. You smiled but did not speak. Your face and neck glistened in the half light. I took a line along your collar bone. Then down, and down, over your nipple, and around its brown anchorage. You caught your breath. I bobbed your nipple in and out like a buoy in water, and you giggled. It was a game of sorts, an amusement to us both: that hellish nightmare was over and we were girls together again.

Thus encouraged, I warmed the pot in my hands and took it below. I grew heady on your musk. Under cover of the bedding, I lifted your still-heavy breasts and played my fingers lightly across your ribcage. More giggling. I rested my head in the hollow of your stomach and nuzzled your belly button until you protested and pushed me away.

We both grew solemn then, somehow. I leant my head on your thigh. After a while, I dared to toy with your private hair. When you shifted on to your side I found the swell of your buttocks and a hint of hip bone, to be polished in my palm like a rounded chair back. You wriggled, clamped my hands between your thighs so that my knuckles cracked and I begged to be released. Then there was a knock at the door and Hannah was there with a can of water.

We played so, like puppies, on and off for some days. I fancied you to revive a little more with each maul, nip and nuzzle. Then one warm evening, with the shutters propped open for air and rising up through them the sounds of the street where we never yet ventured, and the sky a hazy pink above the rooftops, one night as we squirmed together, our chemises rucked up and I slid the side of my bare thigh between your legs. I met there a shocking wetness and warmth that quite dizzied me. After a moment you answered with your thigh: nudged open my legs so that I slipped forward full on to you. Your hip found a sodden warmth between my legs also. I felt there a throbbing and a violent heat. We lay wedged thus a moment, silent, and heard each other's hearts beat like fools. With each breath our bodies shifted some, hefting up and down, up and down. Tears sprang to my eyes. I heaved up on my elbows and, without a thought in my head, kissed you hard on the lips.

Then I shrank down in shock at what I

had done and found I lay pillowed on your breasts. The movement had redoubled all that I felt. It was a torment to remain still, and so I struck across and about you until some sort of rhythm came to us, and then I was lost.

Sixteen days we had lain in darkness while the pox ran its course, and ten days more we stayed abed together. And soon, too soon, the household bade us join them. Spring had come and Hester and Hannah had been hard at work, but silently, for though each morning we woke to a barrage of birdsong we had not heard a squeak of their labours.

We floated down the stair, that was now strangely wide and cleared of all encumbrances. All the grates were bare, the curtains took down, and there was a lightness and an airiness to the house: the expanses of uncurtained window, polished floorboard and clean-swept carpet seemed vast and bright and hurt my eyes. I had to move swiftly to shield the landing mirror from your view. As we came to the kitchen I saw with alarm that Hannah had scrubbed the pan bottoms till they shone, and I was glad when Nels distracted you with titbits: a fresh curd cheese, which she had wrapped in sage leaves, warm beer she had sweetened with honey.

Your father and Hester were waiting in the garden. He smiled and held out his arm to help you down the steps. When you came out into the clear sunlight I watched his face. His beard wagged as he swallowed hard. Hester came forward rapidly in his place and reached for your other hand, her eyes wide and unblinking. I willed them not to show you what I did not have the courage to let you know. Behind you Nels wiped a tear and Hannah clutched her elbows, pursing her lips.

Hester led you down the path, into the bright fresh air drifting with apple blossom, to the seat at the bottom of the garden, there to be wrapped in blankets and shawls. Then she sat herself down cosily beside you and left me standing.

'To think!' she exclaimed, not looking up at me but unpacking her basket full of fresh and tempting foodstuffs, tiny early strawberries, even asparagus. 'To think, Lou! Remember, I had you sign that paper swearing you would leave our employ if the pox were to strike you down. Heavens strike me now if there is not a sweet irony in the workings of fate!' And she reached out to squeeze my hand tight.

Why, in her eyes I was almost family. The pox had left me quite untouched, no pits and scars and blotches marred my skin. I did not need to look in any mirror, I could feel it, I knew, I was clean as ever. And newly respected too. The Captain came to me with a purse of money, pressed it upon me with trembling hands, and said how blest had he been to have found me. He would drag Hester and the rest all off to St Nick's to give thanks, which place I knew he never entered from one year to the next.

You rose up suddenly, the blankets slipping from your lap. Hester broke off from her smiling and clucking and your father rushed to take your elbow. I wanted to weep as I saw you shield your face, as if from the sun, and flee back into the house.

You sat at the dressing table with your back turned. The sheet I had hung over the mirror lay pooled behind you. You had your face in your hands and you were crying, great, shuddering sobs that shocked me so I could not move.

'Do you think me a fool?' you said, your voice almost a squeal behind your hands. I took a step forward.

'Becca, they have not had time —'

'I saw their faces. What were you thinking?' You kept your face between your hands, your fingers clutching at your hair. And your muffled voice went on and on. 'That you would hide me away, that no one would ever see? That I would never see what —' your voice broke.

You pushed your hair brutally from your face and leant forward to the mirror. Your eyes were red and swollen, your mouth fixed in a wet, ugly grimace. And all over your cheeks, your forehead and chin, standing out redder than ever, were the pits and scars, some purplish like bruises, some shiny and hard, others soft and wet and disgustingly, nakedly pink. That smooth sugary skin, that glowed evenly, that never reddened or even creased, was gone for ever, splattered like dust by rain with craters and marks and hardly a finger's breadth between them. For the first time I saw you as you saw yourself, as others did and would see you. I could hardly bear to look.

'You came into my bed to cure me.' Your voice was pitiful now. 'You said you had cured me. What sort of cure is this? Look at me. Go on, look at me.'

I looked, and you looked back at me, I saw your eyes that were still you.

'Becca, you are beautiful to me,' I said. It was the truth. I went to you and hugged your shoulders. Perhaps only I could see

340

how much the ointments had already done to improve matters. The scars were raised now as much by your distress as anything, I told you. They will fade, you will grow used to them, in the end no one will even notice them. You will be beautiful again. How could you not be? You were the most beautiful thing I ever saw.

But you heard none of it. 'Were! How much worse is that? I would not care half so much if I had been an old sow like Hester.'

There was a sob from the door and we both turned to see Hester herself standing there. You hid your face again as she came towards us and stood by, uncertain. Then you wiped your eyes and turned angrily to face her.

'You wrote to Henry, didn't you, when I was ill? And you have not heard from him, have you? No! Of course not. He will not come to see me. And if he does I will not receive him. Who will have me now? I will have to take an old sea dog who will spend his life at sea so's not to have to look at me, and satisfy himself elsewhere.'

Hester put her arms about you and together you sobbed. I sat back on the bed. I had not thought of Henry until that moment. I was surprised even to hear his name. I could not understand why you even cared what he might think. I wanted to shake you. He does not matter. Forget him.

'You shall hear from Henry, I promise you,' Hester was saying. 'And if there are difficulties then there are others, goodness, so many others —' And when you flung yourself into her arms she took you into her room and left me alone in yours.

In the end all I could think to do was to lift up the mirror and fold it flat. I took it down to the kitchen and from there to the cellar, wrapped it in sacking and stowed it on top of a barrel in the dry cellar at the back. Then I cleaned off the dust from the top of your table, took a cloth to your bottles and cleaned your brushes. And then I pulled the shutters to again, for the afternoon sun was coming in strong and hard, and making my eyes water. I sat down on the bed and all I could see was dust, everywhere, swirling crazily in the yellowed air.

Hester put you to bed herself when the evening grew cool and ordered me to fetch a warm brick for your feet. As I lifted the bedclothes I sneaked a glance at your face and found you laid back on your pillows, watching me. Your face was very pale, and in the twilight, so far from the window, it looked almost smooth again.

'Poor Lou,' you said softly.

I came to stand beside you.

'You knew it might kill you too. But you came into my bed to cure me.'

I could only nod.

'Come here,' you said, with the saddest smile I could imagine. My heart gave a great leap. I lifted the counterpane so it would not pull at you and sat down on the edge of the bed. You put both hands to your mouth, as though to hold the words back.

'I did not want you there, Lou. It was horrible to me, to be touched, to be held. I wanted to die.' You began to cry. 'But you would not go, would you? Stubborn Lou.' You wiped at your eyes roughly. Turning towards me, you laid your hand upon mine and looked at me as though you had never truly seen me before.

I do not think, Becca, you left my side after that. Not once. No more rising and rushing away without a glance, expecting me to follow. No, you waited on my consent, would not move without me. Now, when you coaxed me, it was not to prove your power but out of need.

Many, many nights I have squeezed my eyelids shut to recall each moment of that time. What pleasure came first, then what followed, and how their progression went. And always those moments have come to me, as much a torment as a comfort. But now I cannot order them, too fleeting are they: a mere series of pictures and sensations. Only, when I heft up a sheet over my head so that the light changes, or watch a pennant ripple and tug at its leash, I think of those afternoons in your bed. Hear women laugh inside a house and see the open window through which none spied us. Brush a patch of crusted salt spray from my skin and recall how our slick dried to a crazed and brittle film. And when I watch the young girls huddle on each other's laps to giggle and shriek, I smile to recall our giddiness. But rarely, only rarely do I snuff a scent quite as heady and salted and honeyed as was ours. Then I cross and clench my thighs and hold tight to my memories.

How wanton we grew, how quickly. No more blushing Lou. Heavens no! I was taken beyond blushing. I thought of you every moment, listened for your step every minute I was not with you, as alert to your presence as to a hot coal fallen on the carpet. When overcome by our pinches and fondlings under cover of the heavy blossom in the garden, we ran breathless and hand in hand past a staring Hannah and swept the bedroom door shut behind us, giggling. Yes, you were mine at last.

And the household smiled at our fondness, was gladdened by your returning colour and animation. The Captain whistled and sang his way about the house. He charged through doors and thundered up and down the stair like a boy. Hester's relief was almost ridiculous. We would see her sitting over her accounts with her pen poised and idle for minutes at a time, only coming to when Nels nudged Hannah and Hannah giggled. I sat next to you in the parlour now, when we dined, held your hand under the table, and saw your father watching you across the table, memorising your every feature, every gesture, for before long he set sail again.

This time there was no question of your coming down to the quay to see him off; come June he hugged you hard at the foot of the stair. You turned your back even before the door was shut. That summer we were a houseful of women, under a watchful Hester who barred and shuttered the house with extra care for the navy boys were pouring into port, their departure for the war expected almost every day. Billy had been dismissed and while a gardener came in the day to assist Skeggs, now no man but he slept in the house and how did my heart lighten. Your convalescence went on and on. And so did my joy, for never had I imagined such pleasures as we had.

Every morning that I woke to the sound of screeching gulls and the frantic hammering from the yards and found myself in your bed, my heart thudded loud with excitement. The house and the garden were our playground, both filled with blossom and the brightest of green leaves, for Hester brought in sprays to fill the empty grates. I lay in your arms, watching the gulls soar and circle above the rooftops, and felt quite giddy with happiness. We were like a boat cut adrift, floating far out on the currents of our own passion, invisible to those on the shore.

CHAPTER TWENTY-FIVE

As the dew dries men swab the deck, they clog the rigging to strip and mend the frayed lines and worn blocks. The lower shrouds vibrate to the ceaseless sound of hammering. The sky above is cloudless, huge and bare. Nick lies deep in the belly of the ship, oblivious to it all, flat on his chest in a cot in the sick bay. Doctor Roberts has seen to it that the flogging took most of the flesh off his back.

Luke holds his hand for long minutes, and cries silently into his own sleeve. Nick is senseless, his blood loaded with de Clare's good brandy, but his body jerks occasionally like a landed fish.

'You must leave,' de Clare tells Luke. 'Know that Mr Stavenger has been expelled from the company. No man will converse with him now. I advise you to leave him be, or they will do the same to you.'

Luke shakes his head fiercely.

347

De Clare tries again. 'They will smother him in his cot or shove him overboard if they can.'

'Can you not shelter him? I have coin —'

De Clare tuts, pats Luke's shoulder rapidly as he straightens up. 'I do not care to, *mon petit.* I have always thought the man had the face of a murderer.'

When the mess dines at noon, Luke sets down his can, takes a deep breath. He has thought long and hard but can see no other way.

'Boys, 'tis a tragedy Furniss is dead,' he begins, 'of course it is.' He looks from one to the other. Bramley, Burton, Little, Hogmarsh. Their mouths are ugly, their eyes hostile. 'But you all know our Nick,' he continues. 'Captain made him master of the mizen top within the week, remember. When did he ever let us down? Remember how proud you all was to mess with him? Listen now. The man made an honest mistake. He's taken his punishment.'

They say nothing.

'He may yet die,' Luke says desperately.

'Bastard killed Furniss,' says Hogmarsh with cold obstinacy. Now Luke remembers, one fresh morning, Hogmarsh playing with the shavings from the carpenter's bench.

He and Furniss throwing them up in the air so they shimmered, released their resin like incense.

'He murdered Furniss,' echoes Burton, 'and nigh murdered the others too. Any man tells me I owe Nick should look out for himself.' He glares at Luke. Even Winn sits silent, hangs his head.

They're just as lost without him as I am, Luke thinks. They want Nick dead now because he disappointed them, proved not worthy of such worship. They have hated me because he showed me the favour he never did them. Now it's too late. And so they take their grief and anger out on me. He understands, but it makes him no less scared.

Bramley kicks Luke's leg. 'We've all seen you tripping down to sick bay, Fletch, playing the pretty nursemaid to him, your tongue up his arse.'

Luke sits tight.

'You leave him to drown in his own murderer's blood, all right, we're warning you.'

Bramley reaches over for Luke's portion and tips it on to Hogmarsh's plate. He pours Luke's beer into his own can. No one makes a move to stop him.

'Yes,' he says judiciously. 'You let Nick alone. And we'll let you alone.'

Luke sits by Nick's cot, oiling his wounds as de Clare has shown him. He listens but Nick doesn't speak, does not even groan. When the pot is finished and he thinks Nick insensible, he searches Nick's pockets for his knife. Forgive me, he pleads silently, as his hands lift and part the layers of cloth. When he cannot find the knife he falls forward on to Nick's chest. You bastard, he hisses through clenched teeth. You collier bastard. Then, just as Luke gets to his feet, Nick speaks.

'What was that?' Luke asks.

'Not her fault, mine' is what he said. 'Not her fault, mine.' And as Luke crouches by his side he says it again and again, his mouth a dark gash against the canvas, his eyes running with tears until de Clare appears, shaking his head, and gently takes Luke away.

They come at him while he is still closing up Nick's sea chest, in the darkest part of the orlop deck, forward, between the empty purser's office and the cheese store. He hears a scuffle of feet to his right and a boy's voice, high and reedy: 'Missed your way to the sick bay, have you?'

It could be Hogmarsh, but he's not sure. Slowly, Luke lowers the lid of Nick's sea chest. His arms and shoulders feel weak as water.

'Let me be, boys,' he says quietly. 'Let me be and I shall be away.'

'Aye, back to daddy-o,' says another voice, deeper, slower. He can't see them. He has not thought to bring a light. He has found Nick's best knife, though, has it folded neatly in his palm. It is six inches long and scratched into its ivory handle is a strange sprouting tree, the trunk scored into diamonds. The sheathed blade is thin and well worn and terrifyingly sharp.

I would rather they pushed me overboard, thinks Luke, take my chances in the sea, than end my days down here. Charlie told him once this is where the dirty French stow their dead bodies, idle bastards bury them in the bilge and let them rot. No, I will show them the knife, get up and away, try my luck up on deck.

But they're on him, coming like rats out of the darkness, and before he knows it he's rolling on the boards, his sides and his face blossoming with pain. His head's held fast against the deck and he hears the blood pounding in his ears, the barrels in the ballast below grinding away, as the kicks hump his body nearer and nearer to the edge of the planking, where it falls away into the absolute blackness of the bilges. He grasps about desperately for the edge, a post, anything to hold to, to haul himself up. His fingers close on the knife, and he doubles up over it, fumbling at the hinge. A kick to his groin sends him sprawling but he has the blade out and swinging in a great arc. A cry of pain, another, and he staggers to his feet, swinging and jabbing about wildly again and again for he cannot see them, only hear the tearing noises of their throats and their bare feet shuffling.

'Leave me be!' he shouts but it comes out a ragged whisper. 'Leave me be.'

CHAPTER TWENTY-SIX

One warm morning we were fooling in the parlour, thinking ourselves quite alone in the house. We danced about the room, snatching for each other's hand or skirt. You had on your new shoes with the high heels, that had been ordered for your trousseau, and your skirted rump wagged in the most provoking fashion.

I think we were playing at the hot press, which had recently arrived in the town. The gangers had set up quarters at the Bell Inn, rounding up volunteers for the expedition against the Spanish. Little did we care, if drunken seamen fell foul of the navy boys and were carried back off to sea without so much as a by your leave. But the Lieutenant in charge, a tall dark fellow with a long curling wig, came to dine with the Captain once and he'd quite taken your fancy.

Laughing, you let down your hair in imitation, and we took turns at playing the imperious Lieutenant and the struggling sotten seaman. I staggered around the table as slow as anything, you must catch me quick, I was thinking, for I longed for you to take me. And you came at me, so sudden that you knocked me forward on to the table's rounded corner. The unexpected pressure through my skirts made me gasp, and my knees buckled with the sudden, flooding pleasure of it. Close behind me you came, caught me up about the chest and leant against my back. I felt your breath hot and ragged in my ear while you dipped your hand inside my chemise, caught at my breast, shifted your hip to rub my parts against the smooth wood. I grew desperate to touch you, must reach behind to ruck up your skirts. The blood rushed to my head and I was biting my lip not to cry out when the door opened and in walked Hester with her marketing basket.

You drew your hand from my bodice immediately and stepped back, pushing at your skirts to order them. I bent my head low over the table, not trusting to show my flushed face. I could see my fingers, glistening still, I could smell them even.

Hester said nothing, but set down her basket, cleared her throat. I think perhaps that was the first time I even asked myself what we were about. My god, I thought, looking at her pale face, her puzzled eyes, what does she see? What have we been doing?

You gathered yourself sooner than I. 'Sister,' you cried, 'see here our poor Lou. Feel how her heart flutters.' And you thrust me forward. 'Look you,' you continued in a high fluting tone, 'how she droops!'

Hester clasped tight the handle of her basket. 'She needs air, perhaps?'

You clapped your hands. 'That's it! Poor country Lou has been pent up inside too long. A turn up Beacon Hill, perhaps?'

Before Hester could speak, you had me stumbling past her out into the hall. 'Come, Lou,' you called out loudly, 'let us fetch our hats!'

But once we reached the turn of the stair you put your hand to my breast and squeezed. The yearning flooded back. By the time you pulled me into your room all I wanted to do was push up your skirts again and bury myself in you. I slammed the door and pushed you against it, too impatient even to reach the bed.

That night, when you went to lock the bedroom door behind us as usual, you uttered a small cry and stood very still, your hand upon the doorknob.

'It's gone,' you said.

'What?' said I, who was standing at the window, watching the swifts shimmer against the high summer twilight, feeling my heart soar with them, for this was always the best time: together and unobserved at last.

'The key, you fool.'

I went to your side. The keyhole was indeed empty. You opened the door and peered about on the landing.

'Perhaps it's fallen out,' I said. 'Or in your pocket, perhaps?' and I slipped my hand in playfully. But you pulled away.

'Her pocket,' you said grimly. I only had to look at your face to know who you meant.

'But why?' I said foolishly, for I knew very well.

'Damn her,' you said, with feeling. You walked slowly to the bed and sat down, tugging at your fingers. When you looked up your face was quite stricken. 'Where is he, Lou?' you asked. 'Where is Henry?'

At first I was confused. What had Henry to do with the key to your door? But then I realised. It was already late June. There, in the chest between the windows, your trousseau sat slowly creasing. For since your illness Henry had neither broken off the engagement, nor confirmed it. Your Aunt

Tabitha had certain knowledge that he had been at Portsmouth staying with his uncle: letters had been sent for him there. But no reply came. The wedding date had long passed. But the matter was never spoken of, it was as if it had never been proposed.

I had been glad of it. I had thought you were too. But now, as I stared at you, I came to understand. For we could have been gone up to Wapping already, together. And once there, you would be mistress of your own key-belt at last, every room in his house your own, our own. Dull old Henry would have sailed away to the war, perhaps never to come back. I stroked your cheek, drew my finger over the pocks there still, the familiar shallow hollows dampened by your tears. 'Hush,' I said, 'please, Becca, my love.'

You kissed me then, hard. 'All is not lost, Lou, all is not lost.'

A warm wave of stale air, heavy with dust, made it hard to breathe. As you closed the narrow door behind us and the draught moved on, I understood that the space we entered was so large, so long, that the air moved in it even as in the street, it had its own currents. The loft made up the attic not just of the Handley house, but that of the whole terrace, our house and half a dozen others. Dusty Dutch windows gave a thick-moted light, as though into a church aisle. Bare tiles clung to battens, and the rough boards were spattered with white-wash. Broken furniture and dusty trunks lay all about, and the dry husks of flies, moths and spiders. In one place the plastered wall was eaten away and I recall seeing there the fresh pink bodies of baby mice, curled in their nest.

You beckoned me into your arms. But I refused, pointing to the gaps in the shrunken floorboards. 'Not here,' I said, with a half-laugh. For I had caught a glimpse of red blanket, and a pair of clay pipes. We stood directly above Skeggs's room.

I had never paid any attention to the narrow deal door directly across from where the secret stair divided in two, one branch curving up to the men's attic, the other to mine and Hannah's. I had thought it concealed only some sort of closet. I had never guessed, until you opened it that day, that it might hide a third stair. This stair had been wider, for we had climbed it abreast, and steeper, and had led us straight up and past our servants' rooms, that were in the rear wing above the kitchen, to this higher attic giving on to the main run of the terrace.

'He won't be there now.'

'Even so,' I said, a little stiffly. I was more nervous than I would admit. But wary as I was, I could not resist exploring this new space. I stepped under a rafter and pulled you after me. We crossed the Handley attic, that was quite as crowded as the rest of your house. This neighbouring area was almost empty, containing only a few folded lengths of canvas and coiled rope. It was darker too, with no windows. You paused.

'Come on,' I said.

We passed across two, maybe three more houses — I couldn't be sure — and only stopped when we reached the far end. It was a brick wall, the unfinished mortar seeping like frozen water between the bricks. One small window looked to the east but cast little light. And there, under the dim western eaves, lay a great wide folded wad of creamy sail canvas that glowed like a moonlit pool.

And so, that very night, as Nels and Hannah sat out talking in the twilit garden long after supper, and Hester stepped out to an assembly, I took the squirrel stair as quiet as I could, slipped through that new door and climbed to the attic. As I eased open the door the light inside was grey and everything indistinct, but I felt the warm air on my face, close and heated by the day's sun. I stood a moment to tuck my hair under my cap with trembling hands, then moved along to where the sloping roofs disappeared either side into cobwebs and darkness. There was candlelight far ahead, flickering up and across the brickwork.

And there you were, as you had promised. You had spread a soft dark counterpane atop the pile of canvas. You had brought wine, and two glasses, a blanket or two, even a dish of weeping figs. As you looked up at me, you put your hands to the ribbon of your chemise.

I had the strangest feeling just then. That in my passing through that long dark attic, from one house to another, I was no longer Lou but become someone else. My heart beat so hard I thought it this new person knocking to get out. I felt a surge of energy. I strode over and had my arms about you in an instant. Falling back on to the counterpane I hauled you into my lap. You kicked your heels in delight.

'Becca, my Becca,' I breathed, and taking your chin in my fingers I put your lips to mine.

But as we kissed I began to hear sounds: muffled shouts, and music, the scrape of chair legs, feet slapping on a stair. Not in the loft, or even immediately below us, but near enough. I pulled away, nervous all over again.

You exploded into giggles. 'We must be above a tavern. You may fetch me a drink when I grow thirsty.'

There in the rear wall, I saw a door, tiny and narrow, that must lead to a stair.

'Becca, look there. What if someone comes up?'

You widened your eyes. 'Goodness, what sort of mouse are you? The latch is broken but I've pushed something up against the door. Go on. Go and see.'

Wedged against the foot of the door was a low wooden box, its hasp bound up with a length of hemp.

'Closer, Lou.'

The box was not large, formed from one fat section of tree trunk as long as my arm, and it was cracked and battered, flattened on one side and bound about with metal hasps. Dust had settled in its grooves and knots, and the edges were rounded and blackened with wear. It looked to have carried its owner's treasures safely in ships halfway round the world, a wooden world within a wooden world. What long-lost man had sunk to the bottom of the oceans but yet his sea chest had surfaced in this attic? I could find no initials carved nor trace of paint. There were four small holes set in a square near the clasp: perhaps a name plate had been attached, now long gone.

Such a trunk, my mother had told me, had my father with him when he boarded the *Sprite*. But he had never returned, and nor had his trunk. Such too must my long-lost brother have acquired somewhere along his way. Might still have.

'Go on, Lou, open it!'

The clasp was not locked: only the length of hemp held it. I looked to you and you gestured impatiently. I untangled the hemp. Then I took hold of the lid with both hands and lifted it. One of the leather hinges had perished and the lid slid back so that the other nearly tore.

Out came a waft of the briny sea itself: the tarry, bracing odour of seamen's garments. There were no long-lost treasures. Just a small flattened wig, looking like the skin of a dead decayed rabbit. And folded beneath it, a set of sailor's slops.

You did not speak or move but I could see your eyes shining. This time I did not hesitate. I took the wig between two fingers and set it aside. Then I shook out the short jacket, of blue kersey wool. It was double-breasted, unlined and buttonless, rough made but barely worn. Beneath was a yellowing shirt in blue-and-white-checked linen and drawers to match. Folded so stiff that I had trouble to unfold them were a pair of wide-kneed canvas trowsers. And at the very bottom a curled leather belt and a soft, worn, Monmouth cap.

I could just hear voices from the tavern but they were far below. And so, slipping off my apron and skirt, my bodice and chemise, I pulled on the drawers and shirt over my bare flesh. I struggled into the trowsers, wrapped their stiff tops about my waist. When I set the blue jacket about my shoulders the trowsers slipped to my knees: I fastened the belt heavy on my hipbones. Finally I tugged the cap over mine own and scooped my hair inside. I looked down at myself.

My girl's body had disappeared within the figure of a common tar. Yet within such coarse wrapping my flesh felt very soft and frail still. I felt my heart expand within my loosened chest and waist, and my nipples bob against the linen. The rough canvas rubbed between my thighs in a most unaccountable fashion. I felt the sweat prickle in my armpits and above my lip.

'Oh, Lou,' you said, staring.

I saw how your cheeks had reddened. How your breath came quickly.

'Look at you,' you breathed again. And held out your arms.

That night I was a different creature indeed. A common seaman made his way across the dipping floorboards to his mistress's bedside and surprised her there, small hands tucked safe in his pockets, his cap dipping over his eye. A slight, pale creature he was to be sure, one who did not seem to have the strength to raise a sail. But though he said little, he was eager to give satisfaction and his handiwork was nifty all the same.

You seemed to like this forward youth mightily and stroked his long narrow fingers, lowered your bosom against his flat chest. I made to unbuckle the heavy leather belt but you stayed my hand, said it gave you great pleasure, just where it was. And, if I made certain adjustments, I found it served me well too. The cap came free though, was dashed away, and our hair fell together in damp coils about our necks.

As the summer went on that hot little room grew hotter still, and the seaman stripped to the waist to perform his tasks, kneeling, just as you liked it. You ran your hands over my smooth shoulders, my small breasts. Come, boy, you would say, come now.

We came to the attic as often as we could. You presented me with a sailor's bright red kerchief, that I kept inside my chemise and knotted about my neck as soon as I had closed the attic door behind me. Now, when we had taken our pleasures, I would lie back with an arm draped around my girl's sloping shoulders, as though assuming possession. I would smooth out the ends of the kerchief, tug the knot jauntily to the side. I took the pipe from your lips and pulled on it myself. Once or twice I tapped it out so hard on the brick wall that it snapped and I tossed the useless reed into the corner with a soft 'damn it'. I fingered the hair on your forehead and gazed greedily at the vessel of my love, appraising the width and length of you, rising and falling like creamy hills into the waves and rumples of canvas.

More and more, when you closed your eyes and drifted into sleep, all the while close harboured in my arms, I did not find myself struck down by sleep, or at least if I did it was only for a moment. It seemed the more I laboured the less I wearied. It stoked a fire inside me that would not be sated. Afterwards, there were often pains in my belly, and a feeling of being sluiced out, reamed by love, expanding to contain the whole world within me, like a whale. Gingerly, I fingered the nub, at the centre of my parts, that was the spring of all my pleasures. It would be swollen and hard and I wondered often how much larger it might grow. I felt my sinews tremble, then, my legs arc, my heart thud louder and harder until I must jump up and pace about.

And then I found myself declaiming to you, mindless of whether you would hear me or no, all the fine words I had heard Henry use in praise of your beauty, and more.

'My dearest girl, my fine mistress, oh miracle of loveliness, when I behold your enchanted bosom heave so, what a trance of joy am I flung into, that I cannot but contain myself, I am brought unto the brink of bliss —'

And striding to the bed I would raise your chin and seek your mouth and run my hands over your body until I roused you again.

You smiled at my fine words, said they came queerly to a young mouth, that was made for hard kissing. At this I blushed, and cried hotly in a rush of feeling:

'Then, madam, see you like this?'

And I straddled you with my thighs and took you up tight.

'Or perhaps this?'

And turned you swiftly on your front and fell upon your back, lifting your hair from your ear to whisper:

'I'll see you right, miss, I swear I will, for I can serve you better than most, I swear.'

'Swear then,' you said, quite still, your eye shining and your mouth a-quiver.

'I swear.'

'I swear by god.'

'Damn it I swear by god and the devil I shall, I shall. You must think no more on that fine fellow Henry for you are mine —'

At this you hushed me.

'Yes, I am yours, my lily-white fellow. Henry? His name means nothing, my dear.'

And you stroked my arms, kissed my trembling hands and gently tugged me to you.

All made sense to me now. Everything I had felt for you, from the very beginning, when you stood in the dark hallway by the banked-down grate and asked me who I was. How I had watched you, and longed for you, all these months, how I had felt when you came close, how I had wept for you when you were ill, and kissed you when you recovered. And now, in this sailor's rig, I knew ours was a game, a mere dance, no longer. All awkwardness was gone, these clothes fitted me like no other.

I had felt myself as rudderless as a boat at slackwater, casting about in the channel for direction, lax at its anchorage. But from the moment I had picked up that rig I had felt a current tug at me, my sinews tauten, all my senses stand alert. I was intoxicated, helpless. Now when I was with you, I watched myself from afar, as I had watched the seamen. Each remembered move and gesture worked itself out of me and as you seemed to respond I added more. When I pressed myself against you, I grunted as I had heard them do. I rubbed the back of my neck to soothe the crick, slowly, and firmly, as I had seen them do. I held your head, fingers deep in your hair, and bared my neck as you kissed my chest.

About in the streets, back in my everyday garb, I found myself watching the young men of the port as they walked and worked and fondled their wives. I remembered how ugly they had seemed when I first came to the town, when I had rounded a corner and found them lounging in the street with their dogs, or coming towards me bowed under the weight of barrels, their faces distorted with the effort. Now I saw how their muscled bodies seemed to spring open and shut, so agile and practised in movement were they. How their garments laid lightly on their frames, would shrug up to reveal a torso or calf. How they ran their fingers through their hair not thinking how it might be disturbed, used their whole face and posture with which to speak. The drawing power of their long, sea-trained gaze. And how they looked at the women. As I looked at you.

Queuing at the fish stall one day, I stood behind a seaman with a fresh prick of tobacco dangling from a string over his shoulder. The yellow rope that bound it looked fresh and the rum that soaked the tobacco inside smelt sweet and dark. The length was right, and the girth, at the tip at least.

And so the boy made his first outing in public, one hot, windless evening while the family dined with friends and the household disported on Beacon Hill. I made some excuse to return to the house, dressed myself in my rig and left by the garden gate. I could not meet the man's eye, merely nodded to the pricks of tobacco hanging from a nail and handed over my coin. I did not yet trust myself to speak. I slung it over my shoulder as I had seen them do, stuck my hands sailor-like in my pockets and with my heart pounding whistled my way back to the gate unseen.

The next night, before passing through the attic, I raided the large jar of pomatum in the Captain's room and stroked a quantity on to the prick, softening the rope fibres until they were slippery and perfumed. Then I wrapped it carefully in my kerchief and tucked it beneath my belt.

Climbing the stairs I felt the weight of it, nestled against my thigh. I advanced upon you and guided you against the wall, kissing you hotly. Then I guided your hand to my parts. At first you were most surprised, puzzled even. But then you smiled, and made free and taught me much.

CHAPTER TWENTY-SEVEN

De Clare catches him up under the arms. Pulls him into the dispensary and sits him by the stove. Has warm water readied, fresh cloths. He prises the bloodied knife from Luke's fingers, smooths the hair back from his forehead, speaks softly to him in his own language that Luke does not understand.

Luke cannot be held. He breaks away, paces from stove to table and back again, for something within him is stirred and will not be quelled: he must fight them all for if he does not he will be lost. He presses up against the door, cries out 'let me at them'. But he cannot even manage the latch.

De Clare waits patiently by the stove and when he sees Luke crumple and the tears come he guides him back and sits him down again on the three-legged stool.

Much later, Luke will come to understand that de Clare must have waited for him there, at the fore hatchway on the middle deck. Yes, it is only afterwards that he realises how de Clare must have watched him. And waited, oh so patiently. Taken most pleasure, perhaps, in the anticipation. But all this Luke realises too late. Luke thought he was clever. And he is, cleverer than most. He has made it so far. But now de Clare proves cleverer still. For what could the poor wounded boy possibly suspect, as the kind surgeon dabs expertly at the cut upon his left temple, one hand cupping the back of his head as you might hold a baby's skull. All the while de Clare talks to him, distracts him.

'Tiens,' he says, frowning. 'So close to the eye, why, what is left of your brow here is less than nothing. But we will do what we can. Then I will see to your lip, and that poor foot.'

Just as de Clare is pouring a dose of opium into a large spoon, the door bangs open. Luke freezes when he sees Bramley in the doorway, nursing a bloodied hand. But de Clare does not miss a drop. He tips the spoon into Luke's open mouth, and in one step is at the door, closing it behind him.

When de Clare returns, he is alone. 'I would ask that you go to my quarters,' he tells Luke, wiping at Bramley's blood where it has dripped on the threshold. 'Quickly, if you please. Dominique will light your way. And give him this, for the purser.' He scratches out some words on a scrap of paper.

Luke is already on his feet. De Clare smiles. 'You understand me, I think.'

Luke nods. 'Where's Bramley?'

'Anderson is seeing him,' replies de Clare. 'And the others.' He smiles wryly. 'It seems there has been yet another *fracas.*'

Luke watches de Clare's face closely, but he cannot tell what the man might know.

'If you would excuse me, for the moment,' says de Clare. 'I must assist in the treatment of our friend, or he may lose a finger at least.'

When Dominique enters, holding a rushlight, Luke is shocked. The boy is even more feeble, if that were possible. Face thin as a deer's, eyes hollow and haunted. He looks at Luke sideways, seems about to speak. And then he holds the door open silently, and leads Luke down the aft hatchway, all the way down to the orlop.

Luke's heart pounds hard to find himself here again, so soon. It is all he can do to wait outside the purser's office, and not to flee. He looks over his shoulder, again and again. Then Dominique is slipping his thin fingers through Luke's, and leading him aft into the foul and terrifying blackness where they came for him. Through drifts of coal, tumbled from the fuel store: resinous stacks of firewood and slumped sacks that give off a harsh grating odour.

De Clare's promised sanctuary turns out to be no more than a dank and airless six-foot-square aft of the mizen mast, walled with sheets of raw canvas nailed to the beams, and set about with chests and sacks. Three wrapped hammocks swing from their hooks.

Dominique leaves without a word. Luke watches the light go with him. He is as alone here, near the very foot of the mizen, as he was at its cross tree. The surgeons' cockpit is well below the waterline. He listens, but can hear nothing but the regular creaking of the ship's timbers and the intermittent shift and scuffle of vermin below and footsteps above. The air is foul. He curls awkwardly atop a chest, his limbs stiffening and his torso sore beyond enduring. But soon he is overtaken by the dose, and a spreading velvety softness in his head and limbs. The rough wood becomes a pillow of feathers. He dreams.

He opens his eyes to the flare of a lantern, that makes of the canvas walls a glowing oasis. An eating board has been fixed to the mizen, and laid with a linen cloth, two steaming bowls of pea soup, a flagon of brandy and two tumblers. And there is de Clare, his legs crossed neatly, sleeves rolled back down, a fresh wig, cuffs and necktie immaculate again.

'Always this trouble,' he is saying. 'I do not see the cause for it.'

Luke struggles to sit up.

'Don't you men all know the penalties for fighting? But then, I must ask, why flog a man when another has already wounded him? I do not consider this a treasonable thought. Perhaps it is merely selfish. I have enough company in my work as it is.'

He looks enquiringly at Luke. 'Ah, excuse me, please. Here.' And he proffers one of the bowls with a flourish.

Luke watches de Clare as he sups his soup, inhaling the savoury pea fug as it rises. He leaves his bowl untouched. To swallow anything seems impossible.

De Clare holds out a tumbler brimming with brandy. 'To us, my dear fellow.'

Luke knows he must say something, must learn what de Clare might intend with him, but he can manage no more than 'I thank you, sir.' He gulps clumsily at the brandy.

'Sir!' De Clare flaps one hand dismissively and laughs, showing all his good, strong teeth. 'You must call me Gilles, I think, my friend. We are friends now, are we not?'

Luke swallows a second dose. He knows he must not anger the man. 'A better friend to me than my mess mates,' he says bravely.

De Clare laughs. Then he leans forward and puts both hands on Luke's knees. 'Now,' he says in a serious tone. 'I must say to you, once more, do not concern yourself any longer with Stavenger. You can do him no good now.'

Luke's mouth works. 'What will become of him?'

De Clare shrugs. 'He will not go aloft again, that is for sure. They will work him on the quarterdeck, under close supervision.'

'But Tremmel and the others —'

'No, indeed they will not treat him well there. But it is for the best. And I believe it would be for the best also if you were to remain here a while now, at least until you are a little recovered. What do you say?'

'We are to be mess mates?' says Luke, with a crooked smile.

'If you like.' He smiles. 'Consider yourself under my protection from now on.'

'Thank you, sir, but —'

'Please, *mon ami,* call me Gilles.' The tiny lines at the corners of de Clare's eyes crease with amusement, but his mouth is set hard, pouting even, no longer smiling.

Luke swallows his drink in one and shuts his eyes, so there is nothing but the brandy scorching his throat, flooding his veins. Then a sudden stinging pain in his split lip makes him cry out.

De Clare stares a moment at Luke's reddening mouth, at the hot fresh blood spilling from his gashed lip. Then he slaps his knee, and sets down his tumbler. 'What am I about? I must yet dress these injuries.' He opens up a round leather case and plucks out small bundles of linen, a brown stoppered vial. He hands Luke a clean cloth.

'Hold that to your lip. How are your ribs?'

Luke cannot reply, he feels he may faint.

'I should inspect. Lift your shirt, if you would.'

When Luke does not move, de Clare leans forward. 'Please, let me.'

It is no use. De Clare need not be anything less than civilised. Time, that had been running too fast again, stops now, for Luke. He has no future, no past. Slowly, as slowly as he can, he turns his back to de Clare, bends his chest to his knees. He imagines himself fled: flees, in fact, inside himself, where he cannot be touched; where he can be Luke always, no matter what.

De Clare runs his small hot hands closely, evenly, over Luke's shoulders. Then he slips them inside the back of his shirt and reaches up and under, up to his armpits. He strokes slowly down the flesh and the muscle either side of Luke's spine, down his back to his waist, and there they rest, spanning his lower back. Luke's heart is thumping. Is that all? Slowly, he starts to edge away, praying for de Clare's hands to release him. But then he feels the man rest his head against his lower back, press his hot face into the flare of his buttocks. His hands remain where they are, resting on his hips. As slowly as he can manage, Luke moves first one foot then the other, hearing the boards creak startling loud.

And de Clare lets him go. Luke turns around, quite bewildered. De Clare breathes deeply, his chest heaves visibly, but the look upon his face is professionally abstracted, quite unreadable. De Clare clears his throat, says only: 'And now your foot. The left, was it not?'

Luke puts his hands behind his left knee to raise his foot on to the chest. He can see his leg tremble. He tugs the shirt about his legs as best he can, clasping his hands at his groin. Once more, de Clare lays his warm, soft hands on him. The foot is grazed and swollen like an overripe fruit where they stamped upon it. De Clare applies a dark, sticky ointment and binds it up with linen strips. Luke looks over his head, at the narrow gap in the canvas hangings, tries to penetrate the darkness beyond. He is disappearing.

De Clare clears his throat once more and proffers a tiny open tin of cloves. Luke fumbles one between his fingers and when de Clare cracks a clove between his teeth Luke does the same, letting its clean aromatic heat sear his mouth, numb his lips.

His ministrations complete, de Clare sits back, smiles. Luke is hardly able to breathe.

'Very good' is all de Clare says. 'So, now we are done. More brandy?'

Luke stares him full in the face, uncomprehending. What is the man saying? De Clare is smiling at him fondly. Ah, Luke realises dully, de Clare is a gentleman after all. Of course, he will take him to the Captain for punishment, only for now he would help him prepare himself.

Luke takes dose after dose. It burns brightly in his chest, floods his veins, makes his knees swim. One more dose, and he will be ready. He will stand in a minute. Only for now, just for now — he cannot look at de Clare, cannot speak.

De Clare has pushed two chests together and set a mattress atop to make a bed for Luke. He doses him again from the opium spoon. 'Now I must work,' he says. 'Sleep.'

Luke struggles to sit up. He is not ready, but he can bear it no longer. 'The Captain?'

'What about him?'

'You will tell him —'

'About your little *fracas*? With Bramley?'

Luke lets out a sob.

'Shh,' says de Clare. 'Shh. It is nothing to bother the Captain with.'

Luke finds he is clutching at de Clare's hand once more, squeezing it, desperate. 'You will not tell?'

'I will not tell, young *monsieur Luc.*' He smiles.

And despite everything, Luke is unconscious within moments.

CHAPTER TWENTY-EIGHT

I didn't know what I was about. How could
I? I was so young, so naive. My passion led
the way and I followed. My love for you had
clenched and hardened and formed itself
into this boy, who had come unbidden.
When we lay together I felt him harden and
grow slick, and knew he was awake. No, not
only then. Even when I looked at you, over
breakfast, ahead of me in a crowd, dozing
on a chair, he was awake.

From that very first day he came all
seemed right, and made sense. He took
over. I had no hand in any of it, it seemed.
He was powerful and strong and passionate
and what he did made you happy. I was
happy, too, to carry him in me. When I sat
beside you in church, when I stood by Nels
waiting for the iron to heat, even when I
was jostled on the street, or leered at from a
dark doorway, I knew I had him locked
away inside me, like treasure in a chest. I

kept him safe of course. I dared not flaunt him on the streets. He existed only for you. Both of us, living only for you.

Thus we continued for some weeks. I funnelled all my new being into that attic room. All my life was there. Indeed, about the house we found we became quite demure again. I slept every night again in my own bunk, though it was torture to know you slept below alone, and our attic nest empty. Though we never again found that key, Hester seemed quite to have forgotten whatever she might have seen. I carried out my duties to the letter, and more, while you worked your charms on your stern old sister: cheered her with plans to venture to Colchester for the assizes, brought her to smile sometimes, and even laugh at Nels's meandering tales again. So our idyll continued.

July passed, and the Captain came home one week with a host of gifts for you, even a pretty yellow parrot in place of that bony little monkey that had pined away while you were sick. Your fond father sat you upon his knee and sang to you and I swear I saw a tear in his eye. But I never heard him make mention of your looks, or Henry, and soon enough he went away again and we returned eagerly to our secret room, that we kept entirely to ourselves. There was still no word from Henry himself. I knew you sat in conference with Hester on the subject late into the night but I did not care to overhear, or even to ask you what you said or what you felt; in my mind he was gone for good. In any case there was no more talk of betrothal, and neither I nor Hannah was summoned to work on the trousseau.

August dragged on long and hot; a thin grey dust rose up from the streets and the morning breeze only brought a stink from the crusted marshes. Hester complained that the endless clanging in the yards gave her sick headaches, and since her room was unbearable stuffy she closed herself in the parlour, hanging dampened cloths over the sashes and drawing the shutters. Nels set down to do her work on the kitchen steps, where there was a little air and she could catch Skeggs dipping into the beer barrel.

I found myself standing on tiptoe by the window, longing for the farm again, where there was always a breeze from the open fields, and for the cool and quiet of the dairy. My thoughts turned to my mother then, who I knew would be up before dawn and out there sweating in the sharp stubble, her labour unceasing. But she seemed a distant figure to me, a speck in the fields. I found I could not summon much feeling for her at all. Perhaps, I thought, now we were both out in the world, she had forgotten her daughters too. For though I had sent for news of Susie — without telling, of course, anything of the masquerade — I had had not one word from her all these months since.

And so I buried myself in you once more, in our heated secret life. Late in the evening, when I opened the tiny casement to let some air into our hot little room, and it filled with putrid odours from the waste heap in the back yard of the tavern, you lay bare and sweating on the stripped bed and I buried my face in your flesh, nuzzling into your musk.

The heat didn't touch you, didn't drain you pale and weak, or stoke you red and irritable. Your flesh was always the same, tawny, solid, unmelting. And how delighted I was to see how, on our long solitary walks up and over Beacon Hill, the wind and the sun had worked on your scarred and pitted skin, smoothing and polishing it as well as my ointments had soothed it. You always tied your bonnet firmly back on, though, before we passed back into town and would not look up whoever hailed you in the street.

This made me sad, to see you so sudden

shy. But — and I am ashamed to admit it — I felt a thrill too, that I had you to myself, and myself alone. For while Hester went out and about perhaps more than ever, bought herself new caps and dresses, seemed to blossom now you kept to the shadows, there were no more dinners and entertainments for you. You never asked after the gossip of the town, or returned any calls. Henry's London papers stopped arriving and you did not even seem to notice.

Our passion seemed to steady. Just as the restless heaving and jostling of the mass of vessels in the harbour stilled in the endless calm. We had found our rhythm: we rose cheerful and respectful with each other in the morning, spent the day together with an intimacy and gentle consideration that was no longer remarked upon. And when the sky grew hazy and the dry old beams of the house creaked and ticked, yearning for the cool of the night, we made our excuses and retired up the stair to our room. Hester wrote her letters and kept up her household books at a certain hour and did not like to be disturbed. Nels and Hannah sat out as much as they could in the evenings, or chatted at the back gate, and Skeggs was like a tom cat, on the prowl till late. And how thankful I was then for that narrow, squirrel stair that spiralled so steeply up the core of the house, to the attic, to our room, to our bed. How swiftly I raced up it, my fingers barely skimming the walls.

You know how sometimes the summer sun can seem to make everything possible, stretching the days so long that time seems to stop, yet there are hours enough for everything? That's how it was then. There seemed time enough. I thought those days would never end. It never occurred to me that I might not be the only one with a secret to hide.

But I am getting ahead of myself. There was something else stirring in those long hot weeks, something I was glad then I never told you. Now, of course, now I know that if I had, all might have been different. You might have kept me for your own. Or might it have made no difference? Perhaps I would not be stopped. He would not be stoppered, now he was out.

At the end of that same month the town filled with crowds to see off the *Centaur,* for she was launched with much ceremony. We went to see the spectacle — the first I ever saw. For all the frantic activity there had been in the navyard all spring and summer long, she was the first of the new-built vessels to be finished. She had sat in dry dock for many months, towering above the houses, even over the church. You polished the dust off the attic window one day, as we were dressing, and pointed out the gilt paint at the stern. 'Look at the quantities of gingerbread! She is painted up and will be away within the week!'

Hester procured us a view from the first-floor window of the Spinnells' house and from there we looked down on the massed soldiers and seamen, hawkers and drabs, lame old sea dogs and excited children pressing towards the shore. I looked for Susie, as I always did. But there were so many women of the town crushed below, all bright dressed and furbelowed up, and I could not find her figure anywhere.

Then, as I gazed down, I saw among the crowds, leaning up against the heavy timbers of the treadmill crane and oblivious to all, a young sailor in wide trowsers, straddling his girl. One arm was about her waist, the other stretched to the wood above her head as though to support himself — or hem her in, I could not be sure. All I could see was her drooping hand and a mass of dishevelled hair. But I felt a dull pain deep in my belly, like the echo of a hunger.

I tore my gaze from them and looked about, saw how the holidaying seamen made free with their women — watched them walk about the town, hand in hand, or arm in arm, and hug and fondle without a mind to who saw them. And now, for the first time, I thought how would it be to walk thus with you. Not hand in hand as sisters, or good friends, or mistress and faithful maid, but as lovers, as sweethearts. The great ship was afloat afore I had mind to notice her, only Hester bellowing patriotic huzzahs at my ear woke me from my reverie.

On the way home I watched them still, the tars disporting about the town, watched with a sort of dull longing and envy. I lingered behind the party, let my gaze roam over one muscled young man after another. And I fell to wondering in earnest about my brother Luke.

Had he been one of these men, whom I looked at with such — I could not name the feeling. Was he still? I was only a girl when he left: I had not known him at all. Why he had gone, what he had sought, why he had not returned? Had he had his own love? What had took him away? I wondered for the first time: what had he felt, inside? Was it this, this stirring, this restlessness, this constant agitation of the senses?

By the time I climbed the five steps in your wake my course was determined. I must know what had become of my only brother. Not now to soothe my mother's worries, but to satisfy myself, this ignorance and longing. If I could find him, I might divine what would become of me. It seemed there was no one else could tell me.

I thought, briefly, of wandering the streets in my sailor's rig, of mingling with the men and asking those I met for news of him. But no, that I could not conceive, I simply dared not do. As I lay in my own narrow bunk and stared out between the roofs at the wedge of blue sea that had become as familiar to me as the sconce above my mother's bed, I even imagined fleetingly how I might take myself down to the Three Squirrels and sit there, until I caught wind of something, anything.

For I was beginning, in some obscure way, despite all our happiness, to feel a little alone.

CHAPTER TWENTY-NINE

Luke wakes under heavy blankets that smell of limes, with only the distant watch bells and the fluting pipes to mark the passing of time. De Clare returns with another man to sling their hammocks for the night. Luke can barely open his eyes. This, de Clare tells him, is Anderson, the third surgeon's mate, and newly billeted to his mess.

Anderson is a tall cadaverous man with a shelving brow and, when he removes his wig, a huge, gleaming scalp. He nods to Luke. 'Very good,' he says tersely, as though to himself, 'very good.' Before he turns in, he fixes a small rushlight to a beam by his head and reads for a while, from a small book with a thick glinting strap about it.

Once Anderson's wheezing breaths have settled to a steady, sleeping rhythm, de Clare puts out his light also and steps into his hammock, that swings an arm's length above Luke's mattress. The third hammock,

390

that Luke had thought Dominique's, remains furled and empty. Luke lies wide awake, his eyes open now, all his senses alert.

De Clare begins to speak. Quietly, elegantly and at length, with an intimacy long foreign to Luke. De Clare's words affect him in ways he cannot account for. He finds himself lulled, transported. Perhaps the drug works upon him still.

First de Clare tells him how he came to ship aboard the *Essex*. 'A series of misfortunes, you could say, not unlike yourself, I would imagine.'

He was born a man of some quality in the Channel Isles, and had gone to Paris to seek a wife, only to be cheated at the tables out of all his family could afford him. 'Eventually I found myself utterly unable to subsist. I made application to the surgeon of a merchant's ship bound to Guinea. I am not immodest when I claim to have proven myself of worth. And I found something stirring about the marine life, for all its discomforts. You see all life aboard a merchant ship, I can tell you.'

Then he tells Luke of his admiration for the men of the east, their mysterious ways and gratifying arts. 'I was quite seduced. But time passes, and a man must build himself a career.' After some years he made his way back, and put into Dartford, where he was lucky enough to make the acquaintance of a certain admiral. This admiral spoke of the sudden death of the proposed second surgeon's mate on a naval vessel, ready after many delays and about to embark for the new war in the Indies. The admiral was only too delighted to sponsor his new acquaintance.

'*Et bien,* here we are. On the godforsaken *Essex.* I fancy His Majesty's Navy agrees with you as little as it does with myself, or poor Dominique. My poor child spends tonight in the sick bay, alas. But I must admit myself more concerned with you. You are quite the young gentleman. I have often wondered, how did you find yourself in your peculiar situation, here among such men? We have some kinship in this matter, do you not think? Tomorrow, I must hear your story.'

Luke dresses himself. Dominique has brought him a set of cleaned, pressed garments. De Clare commanded it. When he has buttoned up the waistcoat, and belted the breeches about his waist, he finds Nick's knife, folded away deep in one of the leather pockets. He flicks open the blade, it is clean and dry.

He is resolved. He must thank the surgeon for his care and return to his work station. He must conceal his injuries as best he can. He must prove he can work as well as ever. For he knows he cannot spend another night with de Clare. He will not be able to evade him long.

'A very good morning to you, *mon petit ami.*' De Clare twists in his seat at the dispensary desk, smiling broadly as he looks him up and down. 'A fine new rig indeed. And a jaunty kerchief to match, I see. Your own colour is much better too. Much livelier. Here.' And he breaks off a lump of biscuit and holds it out to Luke, catching the crumbs in a cloth. 'Now close the door. Sit with me.' He indicates the three-legged stool by his desk.

Luke nibbles at the biscuit. He swallows. 'I thank you,' he pauses, and smiles deliberately. 'I thank you, sir.' He will not call the man Gilles. 'I thank you for all your kindnesses, with all my heart. I shall not forget. But I am due on deck, my watch has started and I shall be missed.'

'Ah,' de Clare takes a sip from his tumbler. 'Come, sit by me a moment.' Then he passes to the door and fixes a wedge through the latch. When they are both seated, de

Clare drapes his arm about Luke's shoulder, letting his hand lie against the smooth cloth of the waistcoat. His nails are not short, but very clean.

'Very good, very good. Now, *mon petit,* I have a proposition for you. You need not return to your station. I do not think you will find it very congenial just for the present.' His voice is low, almost whispering, in Luke's ear. As he speaks his fingers play on the top button of the waistcoat. 'How would you like to stay here with me, and work here in the sick bay? I think you will find it a far safer berth.' De Clare unfastens the button, then the next, then the next, each slips from its hole easier than the last as he gets the knack of it. With his other hand he brushes the hair from Luke's ear, so his pungent breath falls hot on Luke's neck.

Luke sits very still. 'You have one boy already,' he says carefully.

De Clare sighs theatrically in his ear. 'Ah, but poor Dominique, he has not been well for some time. You have seen yourself how he looks. I purged him well yesterday, but today he has lain down and will not rise, despite all my urging. I simply cannot manage without him. I have told the Captain he must be relieved. Your Lieutenant agrees.

You are to replace him as my loblolly boy.'
De Clare's fingers have slipped beneath the
waistcoat. 'I shall be in your debt.'

Luke holds his breath, pulls in his ribs.

'Sling your hammock alongside Anderson
and me, work with us in the sick bay. We
lead quite the most secluded life. You will
not have to stand watches, or mess with the
men. Make perilous journeys up the mast,
or down to the orlop alone.'

De Clare speaks as lightly as ever but
Luke can hear the man's heart booming
deep inside his chest, a raging sea pent up
in a cave.

'What do you say, Luke?'

De Clare's hand presses softly against his
chest. Now Luke cries out. De Clare pulls
away, his chair scrapes hard and knocks
against the desk. His face is stormy. He tugs
at his necktie, breathing heavily, straightens
the chair, composes himself.

Without taking his eyes off de Clare, Luke
rapidly rebuttons his waistcoat. Blood seeps
from his split lip and trickles to his chin. He
will not lick it away. He does not want de
Clare to see his tongue.

'Good,' says de Clare. 'Very good.' He
steps to a small mirror hung by the narrow
window that overlooks the heads and peers
into it, makes adjustments to his necktie,

his wig. '*Bien.* It is agreed. But first, we must neaten you a little.'

De Clare wipes the blood from Luke's chin. He combs out Luke's hair again — in the interests of hygiene, he says — so that it hangs close about his cheeks. De Clare gathers it up in his hands and stands a moment, looking at him. Then he plaits it back tightly and sets a leather cap square on Luke's head. And then — always in the interests of hygiene — he hands Luke several pieces of clove to chew before sending him up on deck with the pestle and mortar.

The warm wind seems to knock Luke about the head. The sunlight on the wide empty ocean is dazzling. He has been below for ever and a day. But it is only mid-morning. The ship runs smoothly ahead, the sea a deep, deep blue as far as he can see. They are in the tropics now, and Luke has never known heat like this, thick and solid, even in the middle of the ocean.

He limps forrad of the foremast, to Dominique's post, and looks around. All about him the company have stripped to the waist and their bodies, all shades of red and tan and scurfing peel, glisten with sweat. A dozen men unload hammocks from the bulwark nets to be washed in three large, low tubs. The soaking shirts and yellowing underbreeches emit the piercing scent of chamberlye.

He beats the pestle in the mortar, he cries out Dominique's rhyming call to the sick and injured. And all the time he is looking for those who came at him on the orlop. For his mess mates Bramley, Burton and the rest. For Charlie. He scans the length of the ship, up in the rigging, watches the hatches. He examines the figures strung out on the mainyard. There is a flash of copper-red hair. But he hangs too high for Luke to know if it is Charlie or not.

Here's Bramley, though, limping to the water butt at the main mast. Luke's heart thuds. He watches Bramley lift the dipper, sees his bandaged finger. He drinks once, twice, and then his eyes meet Luke's. Luke's grip loosens on the pestle. Bramley hears the knocking falter and he cocks his head and grins at Luke so insolently that he is quickened to defiance. He slams the pestle again and again so hard against the mortar he almost drops them both. Bramley drops the dipper and swings confidently away and down the hatch.

Luke stands at the foremast for the space of two bells, tensed and ready. He sees Hogmarsh conferring with Winn, he sees Burton and Little at their pin, their backs to him all the while. But none of them comes near him.

And none of the men who do answer his call seems to know him, or even note that he is not Dominique. There are so many in this company, he thinks, or perhaps it is the fresh costume: they cannot tell me now for Nick's boy. And how he longs for Nick of a sudden. For his familiar coarseness, his straightforward brutality. For Nick to grab him by the collar and bully him up the mast, to bellow and curse at him and keep him sane.

He gathers six men in all. One needs a dressing replaced on an ulcerous cut. The second sinks down at his feet, complaining of the bloody flux. Another crushed his toe when he dropped a cannon ball he was cleaning. A tiny grey-bearded man nurses rheumatic hands, and two young men lean on each other trembling and dejected, they can support the scurvy no more. The master's mate cuffs these last two upright, and sends them back to their stations.

After Luke delivers the remaining four to the sick bay he must take a bell down the aft hatches and ring it on all decks, come back up the fore. No one accosts him, even so much as speaks to him. When he returns to the sick bay with another batch trailing behind him he finds Anderson attending to the first. Somewhere in among the cots there must be young Dominique. Anderson sets Luke to airing the sick bay with pans of charcoal washed with vinegar. Then he thrusts his wig in his pocket, strips to his waistcoat and creeps on all fours underneath the rows of cots to dose the sick. They are packed so close Anderson must force his way up with his bald pate, keep the cots asunder with his shoulder. Luke follows to take up the dirtied dressings. Nick must be up on the quarterdeck already, under the eye of the officers.

Anderson curses: he has discovered another man cold and unmoving. He takes out his knife and starts to saw at the ropes of the cot. Luke collects the chamber pots to be emptied at the heads. And as he finishes up, a clutch of pots in each hand, he catches sight of de Clare at the dispensary window, watching him.

All afternoon, Luke must crouch by the stove to feed it with fuel. His breeches and waistcoat are stifling hot and itchy. But he will not remove them as Dominique did. He watches de Clare constantly, as he scratches in his papers and cuts and mixes powders, watches him as he would watch an ember that threatens to fall from the stove. One of the men who knocks at the door looks him up and down and asks, 'Where's pretty Dom?' Luke hands him his dose without a word.

Too soon, though, the long night comes; and it is long, for the surgeons do not work the watches. De Clare has Luke sling the three hammocks. Luke lies in Dominique's, next to de Clare, with Anderson the other side. At midnight, as the feet of the larboard watch slap up the gangways above their head, as Anderson snores, de Clare shifts on to his side and stretches out a hand. He strokes Luke's forearm, makes a bracelet of his fingers about Luke's wrist. Luke feels himself manacled. De Clare asks him again for his story. But Luke will not speak. De Clare sighs. Then he tells of his thoughts, when he saw Luke that first day aboard the *Essex*.

Quite a vision, Luke was, among all those evil-smelling fellows. A slender boy, not tall for his age, pale and trembling with grey hurt eyes. A child yet, perhaps. But a set to the chin, a way of setting the hips, with one foot turned out before the other, that drew the eye. That rig worn so lightly, as though it barely touched the flesh. Shoulders lost inside that shirt but the hands, the feet, they were something. Long, and strong, and capable they looked. Subtle. Those hunted eyes, though, and that cap drawn down so close over the ears: how could a man not be intrigued?

De Clare shifts on to his side. Luke can feel his breath on his face.

And when Luke finally stood close before him at the muster, it was the boy's skin he admired most. Translucent and gleaming as a fish's underbelly. Not a wisp of hair upon his cheek, his chin as smooth as a baby's.

De Clare lays a hand upon Luke's cheek. The scent of limes comes from his very pores. 'Look at you now, my boy. *Tiens,* you are changing. Feel the muscle here, about your shoulders. The cords of your neck, thicker. And the skin of your face, feel. It is the sun, the wind. And, I fancy, the beginnings of a beard.'

He makes a small sound of regret. Nick, Charlie, they too looked at him thus, with something of this longing. De Clare mourns the disappearing of the freshwater boy and, perhaps, his own routed magic, his own disappearing grace.

'These eyebrows, see, quite bleached. The wound there will heal. But your poor lips, that were like peaches, so cracked and dry.

A great pity. You no more belong on this vessel than I, my young friend. Your hands too, callouses here, and here.' De Clare's hands move constantly, land here and there like birds. His voice goes on and on.

CHAPTER THIRTY

I was so deep preoccupied, I did not immediately notice how Hannah's attitude might have changed to me. I had always taken great care not to wake her when I crept back to the room we shared at night: though the stair and the door and the floor all conspired with their creaks and squeaks against me. But I had never worried overmuch. She and I had no great intimacy to preserve, no confidence to betray. And, now that I loved you, her friendship was as appealing as plain water is to a man who has a taste for strong liquor. We rarely even spoke, moved about each other so blind we might have been strangers in the street. So when Skeggs came by the yard one still afternoon, where I was helping Nels shake down ripe mulberries into a net spread beneath the tree, and harrumphed at me: 'Back soon enough, ain't you?' I did not know what he meant.

'Did she not tell you, girl?'

'Talking in riddles again, Skeggs,' said Nels, picking a stray berry from her bosom before it stained and popping it in her mouth.

'Hannah. I met her coming up Church Street not a hour gone. Told her to fetch you down there herself as I had to attend the Captain.' He set down his barrowload. 'Blood and thunder, did Hannah not fetch you?'

I shook my head.

'Then you'd better hurry, girl. For I met a fellow this dinnertime name of Toby Melcher. Says he knows something of your brother Luke.'

I have never forgot what I felt when Skeggs told me that. A sort of dull euphoria, a dizziness, a thumping in the ears as when I hung upside down off a gate too long as a girl. At last. An answering tug. A strand of hope.

'Where is he,' I asked, 'this Toby Melcher?'

'Why, down the Three Squirrels of course.'

Of course. Somehow I already knew it.

'Could you not have told him to come to the gate?' Nels said.

'Fellow said he would not come to Handley's house.'

'You know our Lou can't be seen in there.'

Skeggs stamped his foot like a child. 'You thinks I's just a useless old goat, Nels, don't you deny it. Well, here I is, attempting to assist.' He took up his barrow again. 'I's told you now, ain't I?'

Even as he reached the back gate there was Hannah herself coming in, opening up the back gate and casting a cool look at the three of us. I stepped right through the mass of fallen mulberries in my bare feet, almost slipped as I came up close.

'Hannah? Have you not something to tell me?'

'Tell you?' she said, airily, her gaze flitting to Skeggs's face. 'Oh, that old fellow?' Her small dark eyes met mine. And for the first time I could see not just indifference in them, but naked hostility. She laughed. 'You don't want to rush down there, Lou. Ain't you got better things to do with your time?'

She smirked at Nels, who folded her arms, closed her wide frank face, would not look me in the eye. And for the first time I felt them both against me. What had been said, I wondered briefly, what whisperings behind my back, while I gazed at you and lay with you? I felt strangely calm, though, calm like river water that yet conceals a tugging current. For while there was a chance I could catch this Toby Melcher and hear what he

405

had to say, I could not dwell on any of it. I did not pause even to wipe my feet and put on my slippers, was out the gate before Nels relented a little and cried out to stop me.

An old woman was mopping out the doorway as I approached. Her slops reeked of vinegar and vomit. All the windows lolled wide and a blare of sun shone harshly on the sticky tables and broken clay pipes and scuffed stools. I stepped past her and peered back into the gloom. The place seemed deserted. It was an hour or so off noon.

I went into the darkness, holding my hands out before me, though afraid of what I might touch. Low voices came through the floorboards from above, the thud and scrape of boots, a woman's repeated, muffled calls. I ducked round a partition and there, in the light of the open back door, were three figures sitting at a table. I knew them for tars on the instant. One was slumped forward across the table, the other was leaning back with his long shoreside pipe in his mouth. The third sat with his back to the light, his Monmouth cap askew.

'Is any of you Toby Melcher?' I asked, reluctant to approach nearer.

The man with the pipe grunted. 'Who wants to know?'

'Lou. Miss Louise Fletcher.'

406

I moved into the light of the open door so he could see my face.

He grunted again. 'Leave me, boys,' he said shortly. 'I'll join ye again.'

Toby Melcher was an ugly little man. He was old, maybe forty; red-faced, hunched and solid as a lump of worn brick. His face barely moved as he spoke. But I sat determinedly down across from him in his friend's still-warm chair, leant forward in eager anticipation of every drawn-out word. I knew it was impossible for me to stay long here, certain I must not be seen leaving such a place. I felt a great urgency: for I must know all I could of my brother now the chance was come, and quickly.

Don't I pity her now, that young girl Lou. So innocent, so keen, so desperate for some sort of key to unlock — what? How could she have known?

'Skeggs says you can tell me of my brother Luke.'

'Aye.' Toby fiddled with his pipe, did not seem keen to talk at all now.

'Fletcher,' I said impatiently. 'Luke Fletcher.'

'Aye, that were him,' said Toby confidently.

I looked at him hard. The man had spent his life in his cups. How could he possibly remember? 'Indeed? What did he look like, your Luke Fletcher?'

He reached out swiftly to nip at my chin, and chuckled when I recoiled. 'Why, right like you, girl. Knew you for a Fletcher right off I did. He weren't much older than you then an'all. A muddy little lad, thin as an eel, just like you. Big hands, see. Bigger feet.'

I drew my bare feet in sharply under my skirts. So it was true then. It was Susie who took after my mother in looks, but they all had seen Luke in my wan narrow face, my shadowed watery eyes. I could not see him. All I remembered was how his firm long hands had cupped my armpits as he swung me above his head.

'Believe me, love, I knew your brother all right. Remember the day he started on the packets. Your own mother brought him down.'

I shook my head at that, and began to doubt him all over again. How many times had my mother told me Luke went off in the night with all her savings from the pot behind the brick by the bressumer? I tried to remember waking to find him gone, but I could not. I did remember, before we left the house on the shore, her pulling out the brick, and showing me the emptied pot that was never refilled, and cursing them both, father and son.

'Captain took him on straight ways,' said Toby. 'Trade was building up fine then.'

No, he was mistaken. My mother had never once said Luke worked on the packets. Nor had the Captain. Didn't I know Skeggs for a sot and a fool? This fellow had spun him a tale and he'd swallowed it whole.

'Which captain?' I asked then, for I hoped to catch him out. There were only five of them working the packets and I knew them all by name.

He sucked hard on his pipe then. 'You don't know?'

I shook my head.

'Why, your very own Captain Handley, my girl, when he'd just come to town, bought into the *Dolphin*.'

I stared. 'But I have asked the Captain myself. He didn't know my brother, never met him.'

'Aye, girl, aye.' Toby cradled the bowl of his pipe, shifted in his seat. I waited. 'Well, there you are,' he said. 'And you working in his house now. It's a shame.'

'What is?' I said, gripping the table as my puzzlement turned to anger. 'Tell me? What do you know?'

Toby cleared his throat and cradled the bowl of his pipe in his hand. 'Did ever so well, ever so fast, didn't he, your Captain?

Best house in Harwich, so they say. And what a catch his daughter's made on the back of it all. Don't tell me you don't know what he's been up to?'

I replied hotly: 'The Handleys are the finest —'

'The Handleys,' broke in Toby loudly. He shut his mouth abruptly, and scuffed at his red knob of a nose as he watched my face. Then he said with feeling: 'Folks like the Handleys don't get rich without someone paying for it.'

I wasn't sure now I wanted to hear any more. But I had to know. 'Tell me what you mean.'

He raised his eyebrows at the sharpness in my tone, but as I continued to stare at him and he saw my entire ignorance he shrugged. 'Your Handleys, miss, is the finest family of smugglers Harwich ever saw!'

'I don't believe you.'

But straight away I knew he was right. Hadn't I even suspected it myself, hadn't Hannah hinted as much, in those early days before my mind filled only with thoughts of you? Those huge cellars, always full of goods, the stairs practically a storehouse for an ever-changing array of strange parcels. The tunnels Hannah spoke of so knowingly. Skeggs and Billy, coming and going at all hours, dragging and heaving. And Billy dismissed. I had never known for what precisely. The Captain's endless presents for you: why, he'd once presented you with a diamond ring, told you he'd retrieved it from the gullet of a cormorant lady of France, what had swallowed hard at the sudden approach of the customs man. You'd laughed — had you known well enough how he'd got it? And yes, the *Dolphin*'s long absences, when everyone knew the packet schedule pasted to the wall of the Three Cups showed sailing for the Low Countries on Tuesdays and Sundays regular. I had only ever welcomed the Captain's absences, never for a moment considered where he went or why.

Yes, what Melcher said made sense of many things. But in that moment none of it mattered as much to me as what he might have to say of Luke.

'What has any of this to do with my brother?' I asked him.

'He turned your lad over, didn't he?'

Still I did not understand. 'Captain Handley did?'

He shook his head sadly. 'Someone had his eye on your brother: he'd proved himself a proper little seaman. There was another war on then, perhaps you was too young to recall. Navy boys had their eye on your brother. And Handley knows what's in his best interests, always did. He weren't going to stand in their way.'

It was as though someone had closed their hands over my ears. For I knew well what this meant. I could feel the blood pounding in my temples. I stared at Toby's silent, moving mouth. He waved his pipe in a wide arc across the table between us, and back again.

'When Luke found out, he had to cut out and quick, didn't he? And that was farewell, my Lukey boy. Whole world out there,' he said, tucking the stem back tight between his teeth. 'Man can get lost.'

Now I began to understand what my mother had said when the Captain came for me. 'I suppose he thinks he's doing right by us.' For by taking Dairy Lou as his daughter's maid — when he knew very well you wanted a practised girl — that must have been the Captain's idea of making amends to the Fletchers, of quenching his guilt for stealing their only son and selling him on to save his own skin.

'Letter of exemption!' said Toby bitterly, and spat so hard I could hear the spittle hit the boards. 'Join the packets and you think you're safe.'

Then he looked at me, and his hard

mottled face seemed to soften. 'He was a good lad, your brother. He would never have left you and your mother so. But he would not be pressed.'

After a long moment I nodded. 'Thank you,' I said dully. I turned to leave.

'Whoa, girl!' said Toby, reaching after me and staggering into the table. 'I'm not done yet. Sit down, sit down. Listen to this, girl, what I've been trying to tell you.'

He clasped his hard red hands about mine and I let my fingers go limp, sat very, very still. He will tell me Luke is dead now, I said to myself, was quite sure of it. And that will be the fine news I bring our eager mother at long last. I could not look at him.

'I came in off the *Bideford* myself, last night, bound from Turkey. Now listen, we was docked in Gibraltar and I met a fellow who served with your brother, five month or more after he took off, set to sail round the Horn they were. Only Luke jumped ship, he said, took his chances around the Windward Islands. Now, this fellow last heard of Luke aboard the *Archant* off the Cape some months ago. And hear this. Which blessed vessel did we pass coming up the Channel? And is due in on the tide this very day? Yes indeed, the *Archant*!'

He rapped the table with his pipe so loud

I jumped. Then he smiled, squeezed my hand so hard I thought my bones would bend. 'Old Toby shall be here tonight for sure, for young Luke and I have plenty to yarn over. But won't he be glad to greet you, my dear, his blessed sister?'

Chapter Thirty-One

On Saturday nights Anderson dines with the warrant officers. De Clare spreads the eating cloth and lights his two candles as always, attempting, as he says, a civilised repast. Luke keeps his eyes down as he eats. De Clare presents him with finer meals than he has yet tasted aboard, but he has no appetite. He eats only to keep his strength from failing. When they are finished, there is silence. There are some men trying for a quiet kip several yards away, beyond the coal store. They do not stir. Drawing out a cloth-wrapped bundle from a bag of waxed canvas, de Clare opens it up to reveal a couple of small leather-bound books.

'Do you read?' he asks Luke.

Luke nods. He does, a little, his mother insisted.

'But not French, I think? No matter. Perhaps this one will interest you in any case.' He hands him the smaller of the two books. It is scarcely bigger than his hand. There are pooled stains on the greasy leather, the ribbed gilding is flaked and dull. As Luke touches the soft, almost feathery pages, the book falls open with supple ease.

At first he does not know what he sees. A pair of engravings, one larger than the other. He bends over the book, presses the pages flat. Then he makes out, amid the slanting, curling patterns, the figures, two of them, one bent over the other. He looks away rapidly.

'Not to your taste?' says de Clare, taking the book from him, and opening it at another page. 'Now this I like.'

Luke hears boots skitter towards them over the fallen coal. Anderson pokes his bony head through the canvas flap. His face is blotchy with drink. He looks from de Clare to Luke and smiles thinly. When Luke turns to de Clare again the books are back in the bag.

Every night de Clare's intimacies extend a little further, but only a little. Luke does not understand his circumspection, except that even in the dead of night there is no guarantee of privacy for anyone, officer or crew. Dominique may still be among the sick, unable to protest his replacement, but Anderson hangs there at their side every night: a heavy, silent chaperone. Luke understands very well now, why de Clare has taken him in, why he has not gone to the Captain. The figures from the pages of de Clare's foreign book dance in his mind. So this is what he wants, needs. Another boy of his own to play with, a fresh, clean boy. And so Luke must play his part; and as he does he shuts his eyes, remembering his times up the mast. He's climbing, one foot then another, hand over hand, always climbing, up and away. One rung at a time. And he wonders what he will find when he finally reaches the top, when there is no more rope to cling to.

One night, de Clare takes Luke's hand and lays it flat on his own stomach. There's little flesh there, the sheets of muscle are tight and hard, trembling. He guides Luke's hand lower, to where the tip of his member pokes hot and wet. Luke wills his fingers lax, and numb, unfeeling. But in the end he clasps on and de Clare sighs.

As Luke's hand works, de Clare reaches out suddenly to grab him behind the neck and pull his head down into his hammock, into his crotch. Luke has to hold hard to the sides of his hammock not to fall out. Both hammocks swing wildly. De Clare pushes Luke's head deeper. Luke cries out but de Clare holds him there. Choking, Luke twists away, as far as he can get.

'Leave me be!' he hisses at de Clare, weeping. 'I will go to the Captain!'

De Clare breathes heavily, regains possession of himself. Then he laughs. 'The Captain indeed?' Anderson stirs deliberately in his hammock, coughs, and is still.

'Plenty of us aboard this ship, *mon petit,*' says de Clare quietly. 'But only one of you.'

The next day Luke goes looking for Dominique. He is no longer in the sick bay. He cannot see him about the ship. Finally, he steels himself to approach Anderson, who gives him a queer, sideways look. 'Overboard, my boy, did you not know?'

Luke shakes his head. He feels sick.

'Day or so ago. Jumped, too. Sorry little kinchin.'

Luke does not know whether to believe him or not and it shows in his face.

'Best place for him,' says Anderson harshly. 'Poxed to the hilt.'

Chapter Thirty-Two

I did not care a damn who saw me leave the Three Squirrels. I did not notice who jostled me, nor where I walked. For he lived still, my sea-stolen brother. Not only that, but he was returned, by god, would be here in this very town before nightfall. And I would see him again. I put my hand to my mouth, felt my lips numb, my whole face a tremble. I took your red kerchief from my bodice and wadded it tight in my fingers.

There was so much I longed to know. It might seem idle stuff — did my brother have such a kerchief? A sea chest of his own? A girl, even, to clasp about the waist and pull to him? But there was so much else I could ask him, so much I must tell him, what I longed to tell but could tell no other. He was my own kin, he would understand. And perhaps I would feel less alone. Standing there in Church Street with a dog snuffling at my skirts and the stench of stale piss rising about me, I realised I would not try and get word to my mother straight ways. I would tell no one what Toby had said, not even you. I would go back to the Squirrels tonight and see Luke alone. My sea brother. And then I would know what to do.

I went back through the gate. The yard was empty and the tree stripped bare of mulberries, their purple juice on the path already crusting. I had quite composed my face by the time they saw me through the kitchen window. I made sure to meet their curious, hostile eyes. 'Nels, Hannah,' I said, as I tied on an apron and took up one of the preserving jars, 'see these smears. Let me wash you these bottles once more before you heat them.'

Later that same afternoon Hester came to the kitchen to ask me to fetch a pair of scissors from her room, and while I was looking through her workbox I heard the street bell go. I went to the window and peered down, for we had so few visitors now. When I heard Skeggs bid someone enter and Hester call down from the parlour, I reasoned this must be a visitor for her. I would take the scissors to her in the parlour, then, before they came up and swiftly too, to have my errand over with the sooner, so that I might rejoin you out on the rug you had spread under trees. There were yet hours and hours before I could see my brother. You were always my best distraction: I could be with you and never think of anything else. I took the squirrel stair for speed. I fairly sailed down it, facing to the treads, as sailors do.

Out popped I on to the landing, only feet from the parlour door, and right up against the back of a straight male figure, his shoulders broad in a blue coat. I recoiled, cupping my hand swiftly over the point of the scissors. The man turned in surprise but his arms were still clasped about Hester's shoulders and hers were frozen about his waist. His skin was dark tanned and his spotless white wig askew but I recognised that bony chin, that startled watery eye. Henry.

'Well!' he exclaimed, straightening his wig and brushing down the skirts of his coat as though he had bumped up against something dirty. Hester flushed and clasped her hands together.

'My goodness, Louise!' she said, her tone flustered and girlish as I had never heard her.

I looked from one to the other, unable to believe my eyes. Hester recovered herself somewhat, and laid her hand casually upon

Henry's arm.

'Certainly,' she said with a smile, 'none of us expected to see our dear friend Mr Wilmington again so soon, now did we?'

I looked at the pair of them. I would not play her genteel game. Hester might not have known straight off what she had seen that day she discovered us in the parlour, but any fool might see what these two were about. I made sense of her buoyant mood these past weeks, her great sociability and her careful dress, those long hours of letter writing. You and I might have concealed what we had been at, for weeks and weeks, and felt not a moment's guilt, but we had not dreamt dull Hester had any secrets from us.

Hester and Henry, together. You might have thought me thrilled, perhaps, to know you rejected by him at last, and entirely. But all I could think was: how could he spurn you now? For your own sister, and without a word to you? This man, on whom we had showered such attentions, now proved as fickle as any other. And so I grew angry.

'How long?' I asked coldly.

Henry cleared his throat and seemed about to speak but, caught between two glaring females, thought better of it.

'Goodness,' Hester began, quite on her dignity. 'Louise Fletcher, you will not take such a tone —'

'How long?' I demanded again, my voice louder.

Henry squared up to me. 'Young girl, your mistress and I are engaged,' he began in his best naval manner, 'not that it is any business of yours —'

I stepped up close. I felt the boy burn inside me, his sinew tighten. 'When?' I shouted in his face. 'When were you going to tell her?'

'Tell who?' I whipped about at the sound of your voice to see you mounting the stair from the hall. And when I saw the shock on your face, your uncertain expression and wavering glance, and knew I had not been able to shield you from this, I wanted to weep.

You reached out for the banister. 'Mr Wilmington,' you said quietly.

He bowed to you stiffly. 'Miss Handley,' he replied. But he could not look you in the eye.

I knew you could not but think of your ruined face and I trembled with pity and indignation.

Hester stepped in front of him. 'Becca, darling —'

But the expression on your face silenced her completely. There was a moment when no one moved. And you did not look at me, not once.

'Sister,' you said finally, in your most condescending tones. 'You are welcome to him.'

Back down the stair you went and we heard the street door slam behind you.

Out in West Street the air was heavy and the sky almost yellow, not a breath of air came down from the quay. I could hear shouts and shrieks and frantic music from the marketplace. The harvest fair was on, there would be dancing and singing and stalls lit up well into the night. The odour of roasting meat and burnt sugar. You would not have fled there.

I jumped back as a waggon loaded with hay rattled past. Looking after it as it trundled on its way towards the towering masts, an idea came to me. Perhaps you had gone down to the packet pier, for news of your father. Had he known what was afoot? I was grieved now, as well as angered. Did none of them love you, care for you at all?

Even before I stepped out on to the quay I could see the *Marlborough* and the *Eagle* there, their white and red postboy pennants hanging limp, but not the *Dolphin*. The air was fresher out here and I breathed in great gulps. Where now? You must feel just as stifled, I thought, trapped and desperate in this place — and suddenly I knew absolutely that you were fled up Beacon Hill, where we had walked so often. Of course, you would be waiting for me to find you there.

As I turned, though, I caught sight of a woman sitting hunched on a bollard. You had your back to the town, facing the water and the *Dolphin*'s empty mooring.

I ran to you and crouched at your side. You would not look at me at first, even when I took your hand and kissed your wet cheek. Then you spoke. 'I always knew him for a fine man of business. God, he could fleece those passengers, when the seas were rough, but he could see they were desperate to sail. Rubbed his hands twice over when he saw a Scotsman.'

I put my arms about you and pulled you into the shelter of a side doorway in Bradley's warehouse. There you sank to the ground, quite careless of the silted rubbish, your skirts bunched up before you.

'I was Dadda's prize commodity, wasn't I?' you continued, as though we had not moved. 'I even found my own husband, a far better prospect than he could ever have imagined. Only, once I was damaged goods, he had to make the best of a bad deal. Lucky he had his second-best daughter in reserve, eh? I'm no good to any one now, am I? I'm lucky he does not tip me over the side at dead of night like rotten fish, or a bolt of mildewed cloth.'

And though I now despised your father more than any man alive I could not bear to hear the bitterness in your voice. 'Your father loves you, Becca, he would not abandon you.' I said, 'It is Henry who has wronged you. He has gone behind your back —'

I was ready to rush back and stab him through the heart, as he had you, with the scissors I had so recently held in my hand. I only wished I had thought to do it when I first saw him there on the landing.

'Henry never saw me until today. He took her word for it, that I was disfigured, worthless. My god, what poison did she drip? Oh this must give her the greatest satisfaction. To humiliate me like this, at last, after all those years as my foil. I always thought she set me off to the greatest advantage.' You laughed bitterly. 'No longer.' You twisted to face me. 'Tell me I have some prospects left. My looks are not entirely gone?'

The shadow of the doorway fell half across

your face. The rest was exposed to the harsh afternoon sun. I could be quite truthful. 'No, no, of course not. The scars are much improved.'

'I don't give a damn for much improved. Can you see them or not?'

I stroked your cheek, as gentle as I could.

You took hold of my hand and then you began to weep in earnest. 'Of course you can see them. Who cares what she wrote to him. Let her have him.' But your face crumpled anew.

I hugged you to me. 'They don't matter, Becca, none of them, you know they don't. Don't cry, please don't cry.'

You could not stop.

'I love you, Becca,' I said desperately. 'You know I love you.'

But at that you struggled to your feet and fled the shelter of the doorway. And then you whirled about, your hands on your hips like a fishwife.

'What good is that?' you shouted back at me, your face fierce. 'What damned good is that?'

This time I was quicker. I caught up with you right outside the Bell, on the corner. I grabbed you by the arm and tugged you to a halt. You struggled and cried out but I did not care. The street might have been empty for all I knew. I held you firm, my fingers digging deep into your wrist. I wanted to hurt you.

'What good is that?' I echoed viciously. 'What good is that?'

I had you by the shoulders now, shaking you till your hair fell down from your cap. I could not stop myself.

'Remember this?' I said, and thrust my knee hard between your skirts. 'And this?' and I pressed my face against your bosom and nipped at your flesh. I took you by the hair and pulled your face close to mine. It was quite pale, your mouth fallen open.

'This is good, isn't it?' I said, my breath coming in great gasps. And I kissed you hard on your open mouth, took your lips in mine, drove my tongue deep inside you.

I forgot I was wearing my skirts still, my lace cap with the long lilac ribbons, my satin slippers. All I could hear was the blood rushing in my ears. All I could feel was your warmth and wetness. Stars rushed in the blackness behind my closed eyelids. I clung to you and clung to you. You could not say this was nothing. This was everything. This was all I had. I could not let you go.

And then it came, a sudden deluge, shockingly cold, drenching my head and shoulders, the force of it plastering my hair over my face, seizing up my shoulders, pouring down my neck in rivulets. My whole body convulsed and I pulled away, spun around wiping at my eyes for I could see nothing but a blur. The smell was thick and bitter and yeasty, filling my nostrils, making me gag. I wiped my eyes again and looked for you.

You stood a foot or so from me, your eyes wide with shock. You too were drenched, your hair flattened to your skull, your bodice dark with liquid, trails of it straggling down your skirt. You were sobbing, your hands held up in horror.

Then I heard them. Laughing, jeering. 'Got you!' they called. 'Better get us some more ale in, ain't you?' There were half a dozen of them, several steps away from us, standing with their backs to the tavern. Country boys, their chests bare and their smocks tied about their waists. Come for the fair, to sample the Harwich life, to see the sights. They raised their emptied tankards in a mocking toast.

'Here, I nose a stink, let's have at your notch,' shouted one.

'Aye, and we'll wear out your muffs, you moon-eyed hens.'

A handful of girls peeked out the doorway, their faces by turns worried, amused, sullen. Help us, I pleaded silently. Help us. But I knew they could not.

Then one of the men lurched for you. I moved to stop him but he elbowed me to the ground. I looked up to see you pull away, but too late, he had you tight about the waist. Poking out a thick tongue, he licked your neck, in one long slow stroke from your collarbone to your chin. Then he turned to his audience and smacked his lips. They fell about laughing.

I clenched my fists, but they were empty. You stood there alone, shaking, in the middle of the street. And I curled my knees up beneath my skirts, with my face in the sodden dust, and wept.

CHAPTER THIRTY-THREE

Luke watches de Clare write his letters. The man has a fancy writing box, so's the ink bottle will not slide away, with clips to hold the paper straight. And he studies de Clare's face. It has long lost that polished tombstone gravity. More often than not these days the man's cheeks are flushed, his mouth puckered, he bites his lip and his eyes dart here and there. These are the symptoms of a man unsatisfied, Luke thinks. A man who would have more, if he could. Who must have more.

'Who do you write to?'

De Clare looks up surprised. Luke has never asked him anything.

'Do you write to your wife?'

De Clare shakes his head warily. 'No.'

'Who then?'

De Clare leans back, sets down his pen. 'Tonight I write to my sister.'

'Where is she?'

'So many questions!' De Clare picks up his half-written letter and blows on it. But he cannot resist his interest, Luke notes. He must respond. 'She lives in Paris.'

'But then why do you write? How will your letter reach her?'

De Clare looks at him as if he were an idiot. 'Well, *mon petit,* we near the Windward Islands. From there my letter may return with a supply ship. His Majesty's Service would see that my letters are delivered, at least so I would hope. I have not had word from Brigitte for many months now. I believe she may not even know I am embarked upon the *Essex.*'

'When do we make land?'

'Heavens, how should I know that? But we must take on fresh water soon, this has been a damned long unseasonable voyage. And I would prefer we get the worst of the sick ashore: in such heat they shall become most insanitary. I have hopes we may drop anchor within the week. And so, you see,' he turns back to his writing case. 'I make good use of my time.'

That night, it is Luke who reaches out, who lays his hand upon de Clare. 'Gilles,' he calls him at last, 'my Gilles,' and the man's eagerness would break another's heart. Luke will not let him kiss him upon the mouth, nor venture between his legs. He will allow him to knead and squeeze his flesh, though; fondle his buttocks, smooth his thighs, caress his shoulders and neck. De Clare gives a gasping sob. 'Gilles,' Luke whispers again, 'my Gilles,' hushing him. Anderson does not stir in his hammock, breathes on evenly, as though fast asleep. But then Anderson can always be counted on never to rouse, or speak.

The next night, as he promised himself he would, Luke leans over, holding to one side of his hammock for balance, and takes de Clare's sex in his fist like a length of hot rope. De Clare groans, entwines his fingers in Luke's hair, whispers to himself in his own language. Anderson sleeps on. Then a party of midshipmen thunder down and set themselves down only yards away. They make such a racket, stamping up and down and singing to high heaven, that the canvas walls flap and gap and before long de Clare curses, and pushes Luke back into his hammock.

The night after that, Luke does his best, grows almost reckless in his teasing, for he is desperate now also, despite all the dangers, for a resolution of a different kind. He puts his mouth to de Clare's prick. De Clare arches his back, braces one foot against the beam. He grows suddenly silent. Then Anderson moans, and tumbles out of his hammock to retch into a pot, again and again. He spits and coughs, and curses, sits hunched over the pot a long while.

De Clare grinds his teeth with frustration. His hot, damp fingers stroke Luke's neck, grasp at his ear. '*Mon dieu,* give me the first surgeon's cabin,' sighs de Clare in his ear, 'starboard of the butt of the after mast.'

'What do you mean?' asks Luke carefully, when Anderson has clambered back into his hammock and snores again.

'Jesus, for privacy!' says de Clare, 'I'd give my eye teeth for the privacy.'

Luke lies still a while. He wipes at his mouth, waits for his breathing to settle. Then he says slowly: 'We might satisfy ourselves fully, Gilles,' he says, 'if we were to have privacy.'

CHAPTER THIRTY-FOUR

I don't know how we made our way to the attic. Leastways no one stopped us. When I locked the door behind us, my fingers were trembling so hard I dropped the key with a clatter. Gone was the sturdy boy who had taken great strides across the boards and flung you upon the canvas bed, who had coaxed you and played with you and watched your face with a sort of triumph. He had deserted me, when I most needed him. Or rather, I had forgot he was still contained within, for never had I felt myself more small and female and defenceless.

You walked ahead of me the length of the attic, almost to our nest. You took a few more steps then stopped. I swallowed hard. Moving by habit alone, I lifted your hair over your shoulder to unhook your bodice and skirt.

'We must get you out of these,' I said stupidly.

You were shuddering. I stroked my hand over your shoulders, felt the goose pimples rising among the scars. I wanted you shut up, safe and warm and clean in my arms again, and I was so sorry for what I had done I could not bear it. Tears pricked at my eyes.

'Becca, you are chilled through.'

Our nest was as we had left it last: the sheets rumpled, the pillows askew, the counterpane dragging half on the floor. You never would let me tidy it. 'Who's to know?' you'd say. 'You're not my maid here.' And I'd reply, 'Indeed, mistress,' and we'd both giggle.

I hugged you to me then, your shift clammy and wrinkled, felt the whole length of your body against mine. But it was no use. You stood rigid, looking at nothing.

Rapidly I tugged the bed to rights and folded you within, like a precious relic, tucking the covers tight about your chill limbs. I shed my clothes in a pool, struggling with the sodden laces and heavy cloth. And I snuck in beside you, just as before, when you were ill, when I saved you.

Only everything had changed.

When the shivering finally stopped, when we felt the heat come back to our bodies, filling the space between us, when I felt you slacken a little, I spoke first.

'Forgive me, Becca. I should not have been so rough there in the street.' My anger had turned to dismay. 'How could you not care for my love, Becca? I would do anything for you, you know that.'

I told you how sorry I was, told you again and again. How I had wanted to protect you, to fight them, kill them even. I loved you, and I could do nothing for you.

But you kissed me and hushed me and begged me to listen.

'That's it, don't you see? What did you think would happen? It could have been worse, far worse. We cannot risk that again, Lou.'

Your voice was dull, indifferent. I felt such shame then, such grief for what I had ruined that I grew angry all over again. How dare you bid me be quiet, who had thrilled so to my forwardness?

'You don't understand anything, do you, Lou?' you said finally, plucking the damp hair from my forehead. 'I know you love me, I am so glad you love me I cannot tell. But think, Lou, what future is there for us?'

I lay very still then.

'I don't care about Henry, truly I don't. He's a footling ninny and Hester's welcome to him. I should have guessed. I knew his ship was in at Portsmouth weeks ago, he and Hester must have written to each other many times. I would not see it, that's all. I cannot even blame him: he has his own career to think of.

'But he was my main chance. He was my way out of Harwich. I knew my hand was not the best but if I played it right I'd be away from here. Christ, Lou, I'm a Handley. Yes, we're richer than most but we're not fine folk, not by a long chalk. I begged my father for a proper lady's maid, someone trained up at Sudbury or Cambridge, who could show me how. He brought me a dairymaid. I was disappointed, I can't deny it. I confess I even thought it a joke. But then — well, you know don't you? How I came to feel about you? And then I was more desperate than ever then, to marry dull old Henry, to have my own household at last, so that when he would be off at sea again, I could be alone with you, just you. I couldn't wait.'

Slowly, I took this in.

'You never said,' I burst out. 'Damn it, Becca, I was so jealous of him, every time you looked at him —'

But you hushed me again. 'And then, when I was ill, and you did what you did, how could I not love you then, Lou, even if

438

I had not before?'

I could scarcely breathe. You had given me your body so many times, and that had been enough, more than enough, but you had never spoken like this before. It roused me to new hope. But your face was despairing.

'What can we do, Lou? Who will have me now? I will have to scratch about for a local man. And if I find one, there'd be no call for me to have a lady's maid. No, I'll be bartering for a pig and chickens to make his purse go further and that pathetic masque ball will have been the high point of my social career. Nels said Mr Deering's been sniffing about.'

The very thought horrified me. Mr Deering, with his pudding face and dirty nails. 'You need not marry him, Becca. You need not marry anyone.'

You grew angry now. 'Oh! Don't you see it still? If I don't find a husband, and Hester goes off to Wapping with Henry, then she will be the one with the lady's maid. I shall have to take her place. I shall be shut up at West Street, running the place on a shoe-string, with only silly Nels and mean-faced Hannah and sorry Harwich society for company. Cards with Mrs Fressing, the Higham races.'

'I will stay with you. You will still have me, Becca. I will not leave you.'

'Lou,' you gave a little, bitter laugh. 'I will have no need for a lady's maid at all. It would be utter pretension in a provincial spinster. If Hester will not take you to London with her, my father must let you go back to the farm, or to another lady, a real lady.'

I could not believe you were talking like this. 'Becca, listen to yourself. You speak as though everything were hopeless. But it's not. Don't we have each other? Why can't that be enough? Becca, look at me.'

Your eyes were brimming over with tears and I kissed each in turn, trying to staunch the flow. I covered your wet face in kisses as you tried to twist away. My mouth slipped on to yours and fastened there, would not let go. And then, as we clung together, as our breath quickened, as you put your arms about me, it came to me.

I broke away and wiped my mouth with the back of my hand. I sat up on my haunches, then flung away the covers and strode over to the corner behind the door, where the old sailor's chest sat. I flipped its lid open with my foot and bent to grab its contents.

I stuck my legs into his trowsers, hopped

about, hopeless, ridiculous, desperate, all at once. I shrugged on his shirt, pushed the cap so far down over my eyes it blinded me and I had to push it back up my forehead. I wiped my eyes and felt the trowsers slipping, grabbed for his belt where it had skittered away. And then I searched out your red kerchief, shook it out and tied it, tight and proud, about his neck.

My heart was pounding. I saw you watching me, saw how awkward I must look. I felt a fool, then, a foolish girl with wild, impossible notions. But I also saw how alone you were, there in the bed, as vulnerable and alone as you had been when you were ill.

I grew sombre again. To save you from the pox all I had needed was courage. To save us both now, I needed to convince you. If you did not agree, then all was lost.

I adjusted the belt, and stood with my feet a little apart. Then I clasped my hands before me, as though in church, and lowered my shoulders.

'Here he is,' I said. 'Here is your true husband.'

You stared. I felt your gaze travel over me, grew conscious all over again of my narrow shoulders, my high breasts, my soft limbs. I set my chin firmly, and stared back at you. I could not read your eyes at all.

'Turn around,' you said softly.

I faced the brick wall, raised my fingertips to its hardened swells of mortar. Then I heard you push back the covers and your feet come across the boards. You slipped your arms lightly about my waist and before your fingers met I tugged at your wrists, clutched them together, pressing your fists into my groin.

'Why not, Becca?' I said desperately. 'Why not?'

But you only stood there. I could feel your warm breasts move against my back with each breath you took. We stood like that a long, long moment.

Then you leant your cheek into my shoulder and rested it there. I let out a ragged breath. There was a chance. I must not let it slip away. And so I spoke rapidly, not knowing what I would say before the words came out of me.

'We can do it, Becca. We must go away. As far as to Walton maybe, or to the hiring fair at Colchester. I will say I am come back from sea and I will find work in the fields, there must be plenty about. My mother could do it, so may a sturdy young lad.'

I turned to face you but you buried your face again in my shirt. I stroked your hair away, lifting it, searching for a smile, a look of hope.

'Perhaps we will have to sleep under hedges a day or so,' I went on, 'but no matter, the weather is so fair. I will work hard, we'll find ourselves a cottage perhaps. We might have pigs. A cow.' I stopped, for you had taken your hands from about my waist.

'A cow?' you said slowly, pushing back your hair. Your expression was incredulous. 'A cottage?' You took a step back. 'You would have us live like labourers?'

'For a while. I work hard, you know that, we could do better, by and by.'

'Yes, and perhaps I could take in washing?'

When I heard that familiar mocking tone in your voice I felt a terrible falling sensation in my belly, as though all the sap in me were draining away. I had uttered my most secret, private hope, that I had hardly dared dream, even to myself. The look on your face said it all. Pitying, denying, scornful. But I would not let you go.

'I must be with you.'

'How, Lou, how? Living as a common labourer and his wife? If we do not die of hunger, we will be found out.'

'Then we must go further away, to Kent, perhaps?'

'Kent? We may as well go to the Low

Countries! Yes, let us go there instead. I cannot wait to introduce you to my mother's family!'

'The Low Countries, then, why not? I do not care.' I was desperate. I did not mind what I said, as long as you did not say no.

'Across the channel indeed, where you do not speak the language, and know no one.'

'All the better then, you can hide me away. I shall be your mumbling, silent husband. You speak for me. I will find work, we will find a way to live.'

I looked up. You were pacing about by the window, your arms folded about your breasts, shaking your head. I wanted to weep. What would convince you? What did I have to give you?

Nothing, but myself.

And before I knew it he was upon you. He kissed you so hard you staggered and he held you tight, clutching at your hair to support your head, cradling your shoulders and guiding you blindly back to the bed, his eyes closed tight and his mouth hard upon yours.

CHAPTER THIRTY-FIVE

The island is all Luke has eyes for now. To his mind, land has always been a flat thing, low and endless. Islands little more than mounds or shelving ridges, places about which the sea laps but has not yet soaked through. He has not imagined land such as this: erupted from the sea in a series of high mountains, rising steep and straight as sugar cones. An island such as this: lush with green, slashed by crevices thick with mist, awash with bright blooms that are orange and cream and scarlet. How sweet must they smell.

But he will not let himself stare, like the men who mob the rigging above his head. Who yearn hopelessly for soft sand beneath their feet, for sweet water, fresh meat, real women. The ship's company are tied to the ship, they are her workings, and as likely to set foot ashore as the halyards are to walk. No, Luke will not curse, or fight, or mutiny, not now, when he is so close.

'See the waterfalls? The caves?' asks Gilles. 'Dozens of caves. One, they say, leads to Hades.'

'To where?'

'The land of pleasure, *mon petit,*' says Gilles, letting his arm drop, his hand cup Luke's buttock as the deck rolls. And only Nick, labouring close by on the quarterdeck, sees Luke let him do it.

Luke does not move away. He cannot lose his nerve now. He has used all his powers of persuasion, powers he did not know he possessed. He has played Gilles as best he can, but kept his thighs close-clamped. As Luke is careful to remind him, there is no privacy on the ship. They cannot risk a full abandonment.

'Dear Gilles, perhaps if you spoke to the first surgeon,' Luke had sighed longingly, 'about his cabin starboard of the butt of the after mast?' For he well knew that suggestion was too forward, and would provoke Gilles, who is sensitive about his lack of advancement; he watched Gilles sulk, realise that they must find another way. Then Luke had to soothe him and coax him anew.

He waited until long after Anderson slept before he first spoke of his plan. Gilles could not suppress a barking laugh, and whispered vehemently: 'If we were to be caught I would lose my position on the instant. You would be flogged.'

'Then we must not be caught.'

Gilles was silent. 'My child, I thank you. But it is impossible.'

'Gilles,' Luke said firmly then. 'You want me, don't you?' God, the words come easy, he thinks, when you want something bad enough. 'Take me. I am impatient, as you are. Take me ashore with you, Gilles. We will find a place where we can be alone. And I will be yours, Gilles, completely.'

And then, just as Luke was beginning to worry that Gilles would shut them both up in the starboard cabin and to hell with the first surgeon, land was sighted. Not the mainland he had hoped and prayed for, only this string of islands, appearing like mossy stumps in the violet dusk, but he does not care now. He wants so desperately to be ashore again, to drop to the steady ground and lie still, and safe, and free, and alone again. He is not entirely clear where this island is, knows it is a world away from home, and from her. But he must make land again, and be away from this ship.

The side of a ship at anchor is a very public place; marine patrol the deck as the long boats are lowered and the officers depart in their shore-going best, the shore boats come out and the people of the ship crane their necks and spit in the sea and curse, the pressed men sullen beyond endurance, so crazed are they to be near land and forbidden all its pleasures.

Those officers favoured with shore leave do not conceal their glee. The first surgeon is accorded the privilege of accompanying the sickest ashore to set up camp before the fort. But Gilles and Anderson must remain aboard. When the first batch are despatched, Gilles watches the first surgeon step into the boat with them and cannot restrain a curse.

After a day or two Gilles manages to obtain permission to go ashore for honey. These islanders speak French in the main, he explains, he will have no difficulty finding direction. Luke stands demurely in the presence of the Captain for the very first time. What a small man the Captain is, so short and erect under his large hat, he would not have thought it. Yes, the Captain is nodding sagely, the island is renowned for its honey. It does miracles, cures fevers, mends wounds, smooths out the pox. Mind you save me a pot.

Herbs, too, interjects Gilles, here are rare plants he would be lucky to find again. 'Of course, sir,' Gilles shrugs, gesturing elegantly at his faithful loblolly boy, 'I will need help in carrying such bounty.' The Captain laughs. 'Out of the question. While you dally ashore, my dear doctor, your sorry charges shall only need young Fletcher the more.'

Three more days go by. The Captain is well established ashore, and those lieutenants left aboard flex their new-found authority in vexing ways. Unseen and ignored by all, Nick sees how his old protégé and his new master watch the boats come and go. The deck fills with barrels of red and yellow fruits the size of a baby's head. Luke snuffs for the sweetness of land; it is starting to madden him too. Early one morning, while the white sea mist still clings to the lower shrouds, Gilles summons a shore boat and begins negotiations, but a hand falls on his shoulder. The steward has reserved this vessel.

The next morning Gilles and Luke are there again at dawn, listening for the plash of oars. They are glad of the white mist that cradles the ship and quiets all sound, like a pile of feathers. They have a number of clean sacks with them, a small barrel for the honey. Gilles hands it all down the side to the men on the boat and then sits astride the bulwark, one eye on the marine who stands to attention only feet away, bayonet fixed. Luke comes to stand by his side; they bend their heads together and pretend to confer.

The boat men whistle impatiently. But Gilles warns Luke with his eyes. Not now. There are too many men about the deck. First the bosun stops by, he has something he must tell to Gilles, then a boy comes up beside them to empty slops. Already the air is heating, it bathes Luke's face with damp promise. The sixth watch will be up soon, almost every man in the ship up on deck at once to see them. They must go before then.

Gilles's face remains grave, immobile. But when the boy empties the slops with a splash, he jumps, and fumbles at his cuffs. There's eight bells sounding, the bosun's pipe. Luke takes a step towards Gilles. Now, before all the people are up. The shrouds at Gilles's shoulder start to jounce and creak. The starboard watch is descending. Gilles's composure quite deserts him. 'Stay,' he whispers abruptly, looking up. *'Pas possible.'*

Now the sixth watch pours out of the hatches, their faces dark and weary in the thin blueish light. And then, as Luke is jostled by the flow of hands, up the hatch with them comes Nick, so fast Luke has to press his hand against the man's bristling chest to stay upright. The man's breath is sweet with stale rum.

Nick staggers. Then he steadies himself and looks at Luke there before him, one hand on the bulwarks. He looks to Gilles poised by the ropes, dressed for the shore, sees the careful distance between them, their tense faces and the island beyond.

'Whoa!' Nick says thickly. 'Whoa there!'

And before either of them can react he rolls away and swings heavily up and back into his element, up on to the long-forbidden mizen shrouds; but not before the jeering begins and the starting stick lands several times on his shoulders and buttocks. Has he gone mad? wonders Luke. Would he invite yet more punishment?

Never mind Nick. They must go. But Gilles has stepped back down from the bulwark, turned his back on the longboat. Luke shakes his head at Gilles fiercely, willing him not to give up. He is about to call out to him when a voice booms out behind him.

'I'm bound away me lassie.'

It's Nick, singing out from the shrouds. His voice, so long unheard, is startling strong. His song fills the deck, echoing off the mist as if in church.

'For across the sea, me lassie, I'm going to fight for you,

'Think on me each day, me lassie, I'm bound away —'

The quartermaster, beside himself with fury, yells at him to stop. 'No singing there, no singing on duty!'

Luke cannot understand. Stop, Nick, please stop, he thinks. Do you wish to die here? For they will shoot you. But on and on Nick goes, hanging there only six or so feet up the shroud, singing his broken heart out while the other hands look at him queerly, cough, keep their heads down and out of trouble.

'For the sake of you, me lassie, I'm bound away —'

He sings with his eyes tight shut. He does not stop.

'Christ I will have you hanged,' screams the quartermaster, climbing up to slash at Nick's leg. He cannot have discipline already ragged begin to fray. The marine turns to watch, shoulders his rifle, another runs to his side, fumbling with his powder.

Now Nick opens his eyes and plays to the crowd, a joker to the last. He bows theatrically, and gestures with one arm, serenading the quartermaster in a lovelorn fashion, his eyes popping with the effort, and for a moment, with the Captain gone and the men so resentful and despondent, a ripple of laughter passes through the company.

'For the sake of you, me lassie, I'm bound away —'

Nick holds the note, a long, long note, and as he sings he turns his eyes on Luke, wide and unblinking. Luke cannot look away. For Nick is singing the chantey he sang into his ear that first night in the hammocks; he's singing solace and escape as best he can. Luke could not tell why Nick sang then, but now, as he stares up at him helplessly, now he knows.

And so he holds Nick's gaze as long as he can, tries to fix his figure in his mind. Tries to reconcile the great burly man he once knew, that pale ox, with this crazy apparition, deep-tanned and scarred, shrunk and weary, who clings on to the rig, who sings to save him. Yes, Nick is his sea daddy still, looking out for his Luke, saving him if he can. This is Nick's penance, Luke realises suddenly, for the boys he knocked down, the son he lost, the wife he let fall to her death. He would save me, at least.

Luke looks about him, at the whole company craning their necks up at old Nick, to see him singing out in the shrouds where such song is strictly forbidden, and marvelling at their old entertainer returned once more. He sees the cursing officers and the marine levelling their rifles. And he sees all men's backs are turned to the shore, to the bobbing boat, to him and to Gilles, poised to flee.

Now Luke feels his own voice swell inside him, his thickened throat opening to sing out, to shout his gratitude, and his pity, as he has never once done.

But there is no time. Gilles is already over the side. He tugs at Luke's leg. Luke holds Nick's gaze one reckless moment longer. I'll think on you each day, he promises. Thank you, Nick, each and every day. Then he is down the ropes and under the sacking, just as Nick's song is cut off mid-flow.

Chapter Thirty-Six

Becca slept on, but the boy was parched, the root of his tongue sore and his lips swollen. The darkened attic was hot and airless still and the familiar sounds from below louder than usual, echoing out through opened windows. He lay motionless on his stomach and stared at the sea chest in front of the door. The lid was open as he had left it, and he saw the painting on its underside as for the first time.

He saw women naked on small islands of sand, each with its own banana tree. He traced the curve of their breasts as they strained upwards to grasp the fruit. One or two figures were bent double, dipping their fruits between the crude white waves as if to wash them, and their buttocks appeared huge and bulbous. He thought of all the sailing men in the world, the women they had lain with, and all the pleasures they had taken for their own. And he wondered where they all were now, all these far-flung men. Marooned, sailing hard or safe harboured.

And then they came back to him, old Toby's words. His own brother here in Harwich again, newly landed, and to be met at the Three Squirrels this very night. How could he have forgot? He pulled his shirt urgently over his shoulders, then turned to look at his mistress. Still she slept, the curve of her cheek glistening with sweat. All the frailty of her illness had vanished, she was as soft and rounded again as a kitten.

But he could not sit and watch her sleep, as he loved to do. He must go. It would be too hard not to see his own brother, to let this chance slip through his fingers now when he most needed him. He could be back within the hour: she need not know he was gone. How many hours he had spent in this attic. Fairly dozens now. Yet never had he ventured below.

He retied the kerchief about his neck: that none had laundered but he, nor even seen, and was as fresh as the day she had bought it for him. Then he knelt by her side to stroke her hair. And smiled to see her dash his hand away as though it were a fly. He could see their future now. He had made them a plan. Had turned it over and over as she slept, like a pebble in his pocket, till it was smooth and perfect. He would execute it soon, before it wore a hole and slipped out and away from him. But first he must go seek out his sea brother, if only to look into his face, to see what he could find there. A sort of compass perhaps.

And then he would return, and she would be persuaded, and they would embark together. Tonight. He knew how cross she was when wakened. Then he must bring her back some drink: would not a mouthful of cool wine quench her irritation?

He put his foot to the sea trunk and pushed it from the doorway. Then he put his ear to the door to listen. There were footfalls and creaking below. His heart began to pound. He shook out and donned his jacket, trowsers and cap. He retied his mistress's purse and hung it about his neck as the sailors do, so as not to lose it when in drink. Slung the prick of tobacco also, why not, but under his shirt for he has seen so many swiped in the street. Before he pulled his Monmouth close down over his ears, he separated his hair into three hemps and plaited them fast together and sealed the end with candlewax. Tugged out a little hair in front of his ears to hide his naked cheeks.

He felt he might be approaching his true

self and he wished for a mirror.

Then something of what he was about came to him, a dim bell sounded. But in his intoxication he could see no other way, would look no further than the moment he would greet his long-lost brother, and he would be whole again. He lifted the latch. He felt his way down one flight of the stair, then another. There he paused to put his eye to the gaps in the wall panels that gave on to the upper rooms of the tavern. The place was crowded with seamen and shore women, their eyeballs rolling in drink and scarce capable of seeing each other, let alone him for what he was. For sure, he recalled, the expedition was to sail soon and all were squeezing what pleasure they could from their last hours on shore. No time to waste.

He felt his way to the very bottom of the stair and along a narrow unlit passage to the back of the building. Here he fumbled until he found a door, through to another passage and then a final door that creaked open on to a small, dark deserted yard. He stood behind a barrel for a moment or two before he saw a tapster step in, empty a basin down the drain and disappear again. After a minute, he took a breath and followed him out into the street.

CHAPTER THIRTY-SEVEN

Luke does not look back. Cocks are crowing from the shore, loud and shrill, long before the houses appear, hovering above a misted beach. He smells woodsmoke, singed bread, goat dung. There's a fierce chattering of birds in the dark bushes and strange trees strung out under the cliff. Land, plants, houses, animals: he should recognise these things, has longed for them so, but they are no longer familiar to him. The houses seem to be all roof. They sit on stilts. The crabs are huge, and the tiny birds flash an exotic yellow.

The boat crests into the shingle and this time no one prevents his escape. He stands up and steps out. So simple. His heels thump awkwardly on the packed grey shingle that cracks but refuses to sway. He waits for the shouted order, the crack of the musket. But none come.

And so he breathes in the humid breath

of land, of damp dust and loam and green growing things, to steady himself. Instead he grows dizzy on the warm, rich smell of this strange land; he never knew it so strong, so heady. He closes his eyes a moment. If he did not know better he would think her here by his side, for it is her smell: sweet and cloying. He wants to sink down in this spot and never move again. Be still. Nuzzle her neck. Breathe her in. He almost forgets why he is here, what he has promised to do, what he must do.

Gilles is talking rapidly with the boat men. His sudden nervous laugh echoes back from the red cliff. He tips them heavily and asks where he can find the wild bees. No, no, he shakes his head and draws back, they have misunderstood. We must gather the herbs before the sun is high. They point up the cliff, draw lines in the shingle. '*Évitez les singes,*' they are told, as they leave. Avoid the monkeys. One of the men pantomimes biting his own hand.

Gilles and Luke set off up a red-earth path towards the underhang of the cliff. Soon they are out of sight of the village. The light dims and the heat thickens as the sounds of the forest issue around them. To Luke they are hellish: long shrieks and rapid clicks, deep hollow clunks that chill his bones. The canopy closes above their heads, huge mast-like trunks hung about with a looping disorder of fibrous hawsers and cables. Luke sees Nick hanging there still, clinging on.

Gilles takes firm hold of his hand. They walk like this until they are above the mist and can glimpse the sea lightening, the curve of the horizon about the *Essex*. Luke remembers seeing his own home at just such an unaccustomed distance, as just such a floating prison. But he is not free yet. Gilles tugs him along, walking fast. Though they have left the heavy barrel at the base of the cliff, there are roots and creepers everywhere, they must watch their step. They have left the sea breeze behind too; Luke feels he might smother in his own sweat. Now they are on rockier land, among scrubby thick-leaved trees. Luke reaches out to touch the grey and white-veined rock at his side, slick with moisture. It bulges overhead, huge as a main sail solid with wind. If it fell it would crush him completely. He checks Nick's knife is still deep in his pocket.

When Gilles releases his hand and strides ahead and out of sight, Luke is taken by surprise. He is alone. Properly alone at last. Sheer rock rises to the left of the path, to the right flowering bushes and ferns and then a long drop to the sea. He looks back down the path and thinks about doubling back now, hiding in the undergrowth. But the path is too steep, the leaves too thick, Gilles would find him easy, and if he runs all the way back to the beach he will be seen. Gilles is calling.

Luke rounds a turn in the path and Gilles is there, waiting, his hands full of grubbed-up dewy herbs, their roots dropping wet earth. Luke walks up the path towards him.

Now he sees Gilles is standing at the entrance to a cave. The uprooted herbs lie abandoned at his feet. This is the one, he says. Luke looks at it. The rising sun streams straight in, warming the pocket of rock. He looks at Gilles again, standing in full sunlight, the heat of the day coming up fast. Gilles beckons to him impatiently, takes him by both wrists this time. Luke can see every pore, every hair on his cheek, the mole above his left eyebrow. But those dark eyes have lost none of their power.

He should have fled the minute they were ashore. Gilles can read him now just as he did at the muster. Luke may be stronger than he was, but not strong enough. Gilles has his hands fast. Luke cannot reach for his knife. Even if he manages to, now the moment is here, could he use it, could he really kill the man? Inside, he decides, when Gilles is less vigilant, he will make his escape. In the dark. His mind feels quite clear. He is resolved to it. It will mean nothing. He will be free. This is his moment.

He rises up on his toes, kisses Gilles lightly on the mouth.

CHAPTER THIRTY-EIGHT

The moon was low still and the flaring lights at every street corner dazzled his eye. But the crowds grew and the shouting and soon he knew he had his way. Swagger through, boy. And his legs moved swift and fluid though his mouth was dry. He breathed fresh vomit, tobacco smoke and sweat and the tang of beer. The faces came on and on at him until he felt his resolve melt a little, wished to slip away into an alley. He knew himself to be safer among the crowds if only he would keep his head down, and so he forged on. Snatches of song blurted at him. He repeated them under his breath. *'Way, haul away, we'll haul away Joe.'* And: *' 'Tis home, dearie home, aye, 'tis home I want to be.'*

His legs moved in rhythm and then there it was, up ahead, where the crowds clotted the street to a standstill. The Three Squirrels. Entering the ground floor of the tavern at its darkest extremity, he slipped into a mass of bodies shuffling and swaying about in waves of heat and noise. He stumbled against a bench, was jostled and buffeted by a huge oily-skinned porpoise of a seaman, causing him to near sit in the lap of a wench. She yelped and pushed him away without even looking up.

He thrust forward his hip so, stuck his fingers down his belt. He saw many men about the age of his brother, who had the look of the sea, but he could not see his brother in any. Luke would come, he felt sure, he would come.

He went to the counter and gestured with his coin as he had seen others do, found it snatched from his fingers and a jar of Canary set afore him. This he raised to his lip and took a mouthful of the sweet juice. So sweet and slacking was it that he took another and another and when he set it down it was refilled. The girl looked him straight in the eye as she poured, held her bosom before her like an offering.

Flushed with his success he squared his shoulders and turned to look about once more but was clasped about the waist by a veritable saltwater emperor who started up a tune in a booming voice.

'*It was one morning,*

'In the spring —'

All about him swayed to the yearning, circling chantey. Held tight against the man's sweaty flanks, he swayed too and thought it wise to raise his voice for the chorus, thinking to drown his high tones in the general hubbub.

'Oh gad curse gold,
'And silver too —'

As he sang out he looked into all their faces. He saw the full jowls and small eyes of the Dutchmen, the dark bearded chins of the southerners, the sharp cheeks of the Norwegians. He saw a broad-shouldered youth who turned to face him and he saw the terrible scar about his mouth. He studied one lad who stood and sang with his hands clasped at his back, his wet red mouth working, eyes tight shut. Now there was a right proper tar. No beard to speak of, cheeks like apples still, yet he tossed his hair from his eyes over and over, did not miss a beat.

At the song's tail there was a general huzzah and he too raised his fist. Something roared through him. He downed a can of flip, and struck up another. Now he stood shoulder to shoulder with a crew, found himself nodding furious agreement with one and sundry that a sailor should stick with

466

his sweetheart when once he had found one true. His heart burst with goodwill for his unlooked-for comrades, brothers all. But he worried still that he would miss his true brother, and that she might soon be awake and wondering. His head was swimming. He would wind his way to the end of this tune, take one more turn about the place, and then be gone. And then he saw Toby Melcher. Across by the open window, plain as day, his head a-roll on a taller tar's shoulder as they both sang out.

The boy shouldered his way over, stood swaying before his oracle. Toby looked up and the boy saw he had tears in his eyes.

'Where is he?' he asked Toby right off, and he could hardly hear it was his own voice. 'Luke Fletcher, is he come?'

Toby wiped his eye and reached out for the boy's cuff. He tugged it once, twice. 'I am very sorry, my lad. We are all very sorry I'm sure.' Then he shook his head.

The taller man looked from one to the other. When he saw Melcher would not speak more, he cleared his throat and spoke for him. 'We met a terrible range off Walton, see. When she went down there were plenty about but Fletch never got picked up.' He rested his hand gently on the boy's shoulder. 'I am sorry, lad. Did you ever sail with our Luke?'

And now it is happening, here on the sacks spread on the dust and the animal droppings. His waistcoat undone, his breeches tugged asunder, the rock hard against the back of his head and the weight of Gilles upon him, pressing the air from his lungs so he cannot cry out, cannot move, cannot breathe. Gilles finds his mouth and presses his lips, his teeth, his tongue against him. He feels Gilles's prick, round and hard against his belly like a length of pipe, an extra limb.

But then Gilles pulls open Luke's shirt to spread his hands upon his chest. He pulls back, he cries out his astonishment. Luke comes up on his elbows, now he must free himself. Gilles forces him down on his back again, fiercer than ever. He leans one forearm heavily across Luke's shoulders. He grasps feverishly at Luke's breasts.

'Your name,' he hisses into his neck. 'Tell me your name.'

He cannot say it, even now.

Gilles puts one hand about his throat and squeezes.

Toby Melcher is cursing hard and loud as the tar wraps his thick arms about him, blaming Captain Handley for Luke's fate,

468

cursing him for a smuggling thief and the sea for a treacherous whore. The boy stares and backs away. Another tune strikes up, more plangent than the last, the crowd is so solid he cannot see his way to the door. And so he sinks back obscured in a corner, fuddled and floating, drinks down some gin too fast and scorches his parched-again throat.

His brother lost to the ocean, now joined with his father and all those other dead men, sinking down to the darkened depths. His compass gone. Now the tears come, hot through his tight closed lids, for he does not know what he is to do.

'I am Luke,' he murmurs, 'I am Luke.'

Even as his lips move, Gilles has found the vacancy between his legs. Now he draws back once more, panting, amazed, uncertain.

But Luke has closed his eyes. He is frozen, and all alone. No, he moans, closing him off, shutting down, denying all of it. No, no, no.

Gilles takes a breath, a great shuddering breath. He pulls Luke's knees up and wide. He heaves into him. He speaks into Luke's ear, a warm scented blast of triumph. 'Ah, I have you now,' he says. 'I know you now.'

He hides his face in her kerchief, for none

must see his tears. And there swims up before him such a clear and comforting vision. Of he and his love together, making a home in a cottage inland, with a cow and patch of land and all the good stuff his hands could work for her, so much that she would forget all the fancy draws of town and society and live quietly with him and him alone.

A fury takes hold of Luke. He tugs one arm free, then the other, letting Gilles's full weight fall upon him, and casts about, his fingers scrabbling for his breeches, for the knife in the pocket. One hand closes on its hasp but he cannot unsheath it. Gilles has found his rhythm, pressing his face into Luke's neck. Luke waits, waits, and then he puts the knife to his mouth and unhasps it with his teeth. As he raises it Gilles lifts his head and strikes out with his elbow and the knife goes flying.

Yes, they must leave the shore for good. And once he's swapped his seaman's attire for that of a country lad he reckons he will manage pretty good. For Becca likes him very well as a boy. Yes she does. And with her money they could get themselves a cottage, and if he could pass as a labouring man outdoors too he could earn them a living — not a fine one for sure, but quiet and good. Why, he can smell the sweet grass, feel the soft breeze on his face, the clasp of her fingers in his.

He struggles to his feet again, holding his jug close against his chest and sings out with all his heart.

Luke falls back, winded. Without losing his stroke, Gilles pins both arms back above his head and holds them fast. Luke cries out but closes his eyes, bides his time, tries to breathe in the intervals between thrusts. As Gilles's movements quicken, as the hand that pins Luke's hands slackens, as Gilles draws it away to brace himself against the ground at his side, Luke's fingers close about a large rock by his head. It is wide and flat on the top, flat and smooth as a holystone. He grasps it with both hands. Surely it will be too heavy for him to lift. But he finds he can raise it a little way off the ground with ease.

He lets it drop back, breathes, waits.

Even with his eyes shut he feels the tavern empty about him, the sudden cooling as the door bursts open. But he is no longer there. He sings on above the shouting, has his eyes shut still when they grab him and push him to the floor and the jug flies out of his hands. His cheek grinds against soaked sand. 'Leave me be!' he cries angrily. Leave me my dream. But they hoist him up by the collar and shout in his face and drag him outside, they are dragging them all outside.

Luke draws a deep, deep breath. The muscles in his arms, in his shoulders, in his back, remember how he climbed the shrouds, the reach and pull and surge of it, how they heaved the weight of him up on to the yards, right up there with the angels and they save him now as they did then, give up all their new-found strength to smash the rock squarely into Gilles's skull.

He is outside in the flaring street now and there is the tall Lieutenant, the tall dark fellow with the curling wig, his sword drawn and pistol ready, smiling at them all. That one, yes, and him there. He cries out again and struggles to free his wrists, to twist away and flee down the alley but someone puts out a foot to trip him and then comes the blossoming pain at the back of his neck.

CHAPTER THIRTY-NINE

There is the light changing, grown suddenly dimmer. A figure blocking the cave entrance. Squatting short and wide, hair standing out all about his head. A strange chuntering noise as he skits about on his haunches and sets down his paws. The monkey bares its teeth. Screeches. It has no tail.

Now he must stand up, but the cave roof is lower even than the orlop. His head thumps into the rock. He sits down again. His hand sinks into a slick of something thick and gritty.

Out on the path, he breathes the wet scents of the fleshy plants. Drags loose branches in front of the cave mouth. There are not enough. Chest heaving, he wipes his fingers again and again, wraps the shirt about them and squeezes, squeezes. Nails rimmed with blood, deep in the pores. Shirt pink with it. He pulls it off, throws it away.

It snags on a bush like some huge obscene flower.

Now there is darkness again, and he's kneeling, tugging at the body. But what grates out from beneath it is one of the sacks. He tries again, looks away as the legs slump sideways at the knee. He feels about for the waistcoat, finds a jacket. His fingers close on the cold brass buttons. He curls up, hugs his knees. Oh god. Oh god.

Outside again. He piles up the branches. There is rain now, heavy and warm and wetting. He pulls on the breeches, buttons up the jacket to the throat. Pain between the legs, and deep in the belly. He is shivering hard, teeth knocking. Crying, crying. Bloodied shirt, stuffed out of sight, inside the jacket. He searches deep in both pockets for Nick's knife. A long moment, a long, long moment to understand it is gone, that it is too late. He looks at the mouth of the cave, unable to move.

A scuffle as of feet on the path below, branches crack and sway. And he is crashing up through wet undergrowth, snarled in creeper and stinging leaves. A narrow and muddy terrace. A low shelter built against the cliff. Panting, with the tearing taste of iron in his mouth, he crawls inside. He holds his breath, listening. The rustle of small creatures in the long grass outside, a bird landing on a branch. Far, far away, the tinkle of a bell. The wind soughing in the bushes.

The sky violet and roosting birds overhead. He is very thirsty now. The path is steeper, and wetter, large pebbles clatter down. The trees are taller, closing overhead. Dusk comes down fast here, faster still among the trees. He sees lights dance ahead, the lanterns of the men and he crashes off the path into the undergrowth. But it is too thick. Sobbing, he runs back again. Fireflies. The lanterns are fireflies.

The foot of a deep valley. The path crosses a muddy river bed and forks in two. He takes the left fork, over mossy boulders. Under a huge bulge of rock, he sees a smooth plastered doorway and an iron-railed gate.

Inside are steps and a white wall glowing in the base of the rock, with one narrow window and a wooden door, half open. More fireflies inside. No, three long-lit candles, a wooden cross on the opposite wall. Rock hollowed out to form a small bowl. He dips his fingers in the holy water again and again, making the sign of the cross. God forgive me. God forgive me.

Morning. He stands at the gate. Stilted

houses high on the far side of the ravine, lit up by sunlight. Smoke rising. Faint voices. Singing. He follows the river bed down in the hope of finding water. A low field, a fuller stream and a washing area, smooth flat rocks in a wide square.

He kneels by the river, cupping mouthful after mouthful of water. He pulls off breeches and jacket and takes the stiff crumpled shirt into the fast-flowing water. The cold is nothing, the thrust of the current nothing. Crouching down, ducking under, he watches the shirt stream away, shed colour like waving weed. He surfaces, bundles it up; squeezes and beats and slaps it against a rock, smearing the moss until the shirt runs green as well as red.

Eventually, hands stiff and calves numb, he climbs out. Dark splatters and pools of blood stain the breeches still, butcher's tang on the jacket. Now her kerchief. The knot is hard to undo. He kneels on rock and holds it by the corners. Watches until the water runs clear.

Singing. Women singing. Women down from the village. He snatches up the shirt and runs up the other bank of the river to hide. Their faces and arms and feet shining black. Their clothes red and white and yellow and blue, bright as the birds. Their heads tied about with cloth, as jaunty as a sailor's kerchief. Four women, three old and broad, one young and narrow, let down their bundles by the washing place and tuck up their skirts.

He listens greedily to their voices, their high, hesitant, lilting, screeching voices, drinking down every drop of sound. How long since he heard one woman call out to another? Laugh? Tell a long rambling story looking from face to face, lift the back of her hand to her face, dissolve into giggles? Turn strict, hectoring, even, or hunch her shoulders, grow mulish and sullen? He looks and looks, shivering naked in his den in the branches and feeling like a monster in the darkness, an underworld creature who would terrify them if he were to reveal himself now, as he has become, as he truly is. An unnatural creature, who has killed a man. He cannot make himself clean again, he will never be pure now.

Stillness of noon. Garments spread to dry on the grass and rocks and bushes and the women labouring back up the path. Silence. He stands up to ford the river, to stare. And stare. Three white petticoats, one trimmed with blue stitching. Chemises, with broad sleeves and intricate ruching. Bonnets big and small, ties flickering up like pennants as they dry. Splayed out there, weighted down with stones and with the breeze rippling over them, they look like apparitions, like ghosts. Effigies, of women long gone and never to return. He walks up to a chemise drying on the long rock nearest to him, lifts its sleeve. The linen is rough and slubbed, but long worn soft and yellow about the cuffs. He glances about him, considers briefly, what it would be to put it on. What disguise that would be.

He pulls on his shirt, and sets off down the river bank. He has his waistcoat in one hand and the chemise in the other.

The sea. A tiny spoonful between two steep hillsides. And a small stone shelter with a store of fibrous roots. He sucks at the green and yellow fruits from the trees. Craves bread now, and warmth, and meat. There are fishing vessels out there, he can see their white sails bob. One or two dwellings ahead and a cluster of them by the bay. He squints up at the sun, trying to judge how far the village may be from the bay where he landed.

Alone on the hot hillside, he finds a small square house with smoke scragging from its roof, he sees the penned goat, the roosting hens. He waits: no one comes in or out. Dogs bark, but they are far down the valley.

A thin white cat arches at his feet as he steps on to the threshold. Inside is choked with smoke. A couple of chairs, a fire smouldering in a high stone hearth, a paved courtyard beyond. When his eyes have adjusted, he feels about the shelves and recesses, pulls out a loaf end and some sort of dried fruit, soft and brown. A musty sweep of fabric brushes his forehead: a skirt hanging high above the mantel-stone. It is a sign. Another sign.

He unhooks the skirt, a dark, heavy thing, looks about for a bodice. He has to climb into the sleeping loft before he finds one. He bundles everything up in the skirt, slides down the ladder and runs for it.

Disguise, he thinks as he dresses behind a low mossy wall, where the field meets the forest. Disguise, deceit, deception. I will cheat them all as I have before; I will save my life; I will get back to you. His heart is pounding fit to burst. He drops the chemise over his shoulders. He hoists up the skirt, ties its tapes. He shrugs the bodice on and tugs at the laces, twisting his wrist just so to tauten the tapes, without even thinking about it. Pull them straight, let them run loose through the eyelets and then snug across, that's better. He feels the weight of the skirt shift on his hips, the tightness about his ribs, his breasts pressing up against the bodice, the loose airy darkness about his thighs, and his hands stop. The ends he is about to knot together fall apart.

I come back to myself then.

In that moment, all that Luke is, all that he has seen, all that he has done, I see for myself, clear as if I were his own mother. For the whole of my time aboard the *Essex* I had moved as him, spoken as him, thought as him. He had no longer been contained within me, it was he who hid me, and I buried myself so deep that I had forgot myself.

But no more. I am here now, standing alone on this hillside of a distant island, dressed in another woman's clothes. Common women's dress: home-spun linen and worsted. The plain, everyday working clothes I wore all my young life without a second thought. Only it's his hardened hands and arms that show at the sleeves. His sinewy muscle that broadens my chest and thickens my neck, swells my calves. His wind-scuffed face and salt-thickened hair. And his scarred and deep-tanned hands, that have a man's blood on them.

I weep for him. For what he has become.

Because he cannot go back, or undo what he has done. My young Luke Fletcher is a deserter now; worse, he is a killer. He will hang if ever they catch him.

Yet I should be proud of the boy, like a true mother would be, for how he has protected me, hidden me and let me escape. I should wrap my skirts about him, bend my bosom to his head, shield him well when they come for him. But he has lain with a man, and killed a man.

And he has carried me across the sea and stranded me here, alone with no coin, friendless, and far, far from you. You will have thought I ran away, that my courage failed me in the end. You will have searched and waited and hoped and finally given me up for lost. And you will weep over me no more, for I showed myself wanting, proved another faithless and inconstant lover.

Yes, he betrayed us both, that boy Luke. The sea took him all right. I trusted to his strength — I had no choice — and he did not fail me; I have survived, but at what cost? I grow so angry with him I wish to beat him with my fists, tear his hair, scratch his damned face.

Because now I am truly alone. He cannot help me now. And I deny him absolutely, with all my heart. My Luke is a murderer: if he is found he will have me hanged. And I cannot die without seeing you again. I must get back to you, somehow. Prove I did not leave you, that I do love you, that I will do anything to be with you again.

I stow his rig behind the wall. I tug that bodice tight and tie it well. And then I un-pick it and tie it again with care, for I have made a ship's knot. I let out his cue, and I fold over a corner of your kerchief and tie it low over my head, to hide his scrubby hair. I soften my shoulders, let my arms fall lightly to my sides; my elbows neat, my fingers loose. I lower my chin, and try to widen my eyes, narrowed by so many months of wind and caution.

I set off down towards the village. I feel my shoulders come forward, tensed and leading, and try to walk from my hips instead, first letting one forward, then the other. I watch the rhythm come back to my skirts, see them sway and billow, let my rump bob and roll like a ship. I suck in my waist, draw my step together when it threat-ens to straddle and I take neat little steps. I almost fall over in my efforts to mimic what I lost so naturally. I feel like a fraud, a fool. But I walk on.

I have not been walking long when I hear

them behind me. I am on the river bank again, where the grass is springy and damp and easier underfoot than the hard, uneven road. That's how I can hear their heavy, crunching tread, the scattering stones that make the birds fly up out of the trees. I turn my head but they are hidden by the bushes where the road curves. They are on the road I have just walked along. I passed a cross-roads some way back, they must have come from the other road. Several of them, walking in unison. They could almost be marching. I walk faster, break into a run. Hitch up my skirts and jump over a narrow stone-lined gully, up the bank to where the road rises into a low bridge over the river. The bridge is too low to hide under, the water too deep to ford. But if I can get to the other side of it, crouch down in its shadow.

They spot me just as I run across the bridge, only my skirts hidden by the parapet. Their shouts burst out of them, abrupt and loud as gunshot. Fowl scatter across the river, beating the water with their wings. I scramble to the wall and crouch down but it is useless. I hear their boots break into a scuffling run, hear metal clinking and snorting laughter.

Why did I run? Why did I show my guilt so clearly? I have made myself a victim, I realise. They will have me now. Can they have already found Gilles? It is not impossible. He told the natives on the beach where we were headed, they gave us direction. There was only one path up that hillside.

No, no. For if they are looking for anyone they will be looking for Luke: loblolly boy, murderer, deserter. Not some lone female wandering the hillsides. They cannot know what this girl has done, however wild she looks: how could they? Steady as I can, I stand up straight, dust off my skirts and turn to them.

I gasp like a girl. I cannot help it. For they are men whom I most feared to see: British marine. Five of them. They look road-weary and ready for diversion. Their red coats are open and dusty, their shirts rumpled, but two of them have their rifles cocked and levelled. I almost run again; instead I gulp for air, raise my chin, stare them out.

They take in my kerchiefed head, my tight bodice and bare feet. They stare at my bare brown arms, my scarred and weathered face. I see how I puzzle them. I am no lily-faced lady, nor a nigger girl neither. I am some kind of woman they never yet saw.

And the fear I feel is not the fear a woman always has before men, born of their bodies, their strength. It is too late for that. I am no longer afraid for my body, but for my soul: of what they might see in it, what they might tell of it.

Uncertain now, they lower their rifles and crowd around, all meat and smoke and sweat.

'Pitch me in the ditch,' says one to another, and it is a shock to hear the plain English tongue in this place. 'What a piece of old scrag.'

He bends to look at me and I turn my head from his long black whiskers and slanting blue eyes. There were fair dozens of marine aboard the *Essex,* was he among them? Might he recognise me, even now?

'Young scrag,' says another. They swap insults, as though I cannot understand. They call me filthy, unnatural.

I must find my voice, my girl's voice, that was light and young and innocent and would mean no harm. I must plead winningly, evade them neatly, as I have seen good girls do at home, though I never got the knack.

'Now you leave me be, sirs,' I begin.

The one with the whiskers frowns, offended, for now he knows me to be English, and to understand them. Or is it the roughness I myself can hear in my tone, the sea-learnt challenge and block, how unseemly it is? I try again for the girlish.

'If I may walk on,' I say, and smile this time, and hold out my empty hands. 'I have nothing for you.' I grow conscious of the unaccustomed tightness of the bodice, that makes my poor breasts swell obscene and dangerous.

'Hee hee, we may have something for you,' says another, carbuncle-faced and sweating hard. 'You got nothing, you fancy a little reward.'

Another cuts in: 'You don't want to be walking about on your sweet chick-a-biddy there's a murdering cull a wander on this island.'

'Indeed?' I say, and clasp my hands over my bodice, which serves only to draw their eye. Cool, yet careful to appear shocked, a little afraid now.

'We's out to do him,' says the whiskered one, stepping forward importantly. 'A British tar he is too. A pressed man. Bastard jumped ship, then he dinged an officer. Traitor. Dodgy little cock, he'll be.'

I wring my hands together and shake my head in dismay. I do not trust myself to speak.

The whiskered fellow clears his throat and takes my arm. 'Better come in with us, my lovely. Provide you escort back to — where is it you belong, you dirty puzzle?'

'Aye, and we'll watch your apple dumplins.'

I pat his arm and smile as I extract myself. 'I thank you very well, sirs. I am to my sister in the next town, she and her husband expect me.'

I make to slip past them but it is too late.

'What town is that then?'

I cannot answer, and they see it. 'If I do not come soon they will look for me,' I say desperately.

Another man pushes to the front. He wears the same coat but his hat is cocked. He has mean little eyes and a wide greasy smile. He speaks rapidly to the first soldier, who jabs him in the chest with a finger. I take my chance. Squaring my shoulders, I make to walk past them all, head held high.

One of them, I don't see who, reaches out and snatches the kerchief from my head with a shout and dangles it high in the air. A tall yellow-faced fellow makes to toss it in the river but as it flies out his hand I snatch it back. And then it all comes: I square my shoulders and clench my fists and curse them all, loud and long, with every foul phrase I have learnt aboard the *Essex* and some more besides.

When I am done I am a-tremble from fingers to toes. They stand about stiff as masts and twice as speechless. Swiftly I tie up my hair in the kerchief and walk away, my back rigid, willing them not to follow me. I feel them watching me as I walk, watching my waist, my hips, my ankles. When I am some way gone, and am beginning to think myself safe, they set off to follow me with dragging steps. But though they mutter, and laugh, and holler their bawdy songs at me, they do not close on me.

The sun is high, the sweat trickles down my neck. We meet no one on the road. As I reach the first house one of them whistles long and low. Then they walk on along the road.

Only once they are out of sight do I see my mistake. I have reached the village on the shore. Here beneath the unnatural stilted houses are nets and upturned boats, and at the end of the wide red dusty street the grey shingle slopes down to the sea and all the small boats. What better place for His Majesty's marine to land, for His Majesty's officers to resort, to find a wanted tar?

I shrink back into the shade of the nearest house and scan the hills behind me. The fort I had seen from aboard the *Essex* stood above a narrow beach, with a sizeable town beyond. But to left and right of this bay there is only tangled forest, thick and green, and a strip of falling white water in a mossy cleft high up. The mist has all gone, the high hills stand out hard against a deep blue sky. Perhaps the fort sits at the next bay along, around that headland. Perhaps the island is small, and it is just the other side of these hills. And the *Essex* too.

I make my way under the stilted house, where fat chickens roost in the deep shade, to squint out at the dazzling waters of the lagoon. My heart sinks. For beyond the small boats there is no mistaking a large ship, moored out a way, a three-master.

It may not be the *Essex,* I tell myself. I cannot make out her flags. There were many other three-masters in the squadron. For one wild moment I imagine that she has already sailed. Sailed away with my ballast of guilt and left me free to live out my days alone. But then I remember the numerous sick encamped ashore, the Captain bent on gathering resource for his exhausted vessel. We were told quantities of slowing weed were to be scraped from her hull. No, the *Essex* will not sail for days, with or without her full complement of surgeons. The marine will be searching a while.

I may be ashore, I may be free of that ship, that man, but I am not safe yet. Not free yet. I try to remind myself who I must be.

When I have wiped my face well on my skirt, I step out into the full sun and walk down the street. There are black men squatting in the shade under the stilted houses and they all turn to watch as they suck on their pipes: a strange white woman, alone and abroad in the heat of the day, walking down from the forest. The women of the village, clustered about their children, nudge each other and point, step out into the sun to look after me, hands on hips. Now they are calling out loudly, their voices thick as though their mouths are full of fruit. I will ignore them, they are nothing, it is only the white men I must fear. Then I glimpse two white ladies in wide straw bonnets peering down at me from a flower-decked balcony, skirts pale as ghosts. They whisper behind their fans, half rise from their seats to crane after me.

It is all I can do not to run to the sea and drown myself in it. This is no disguise. What I am cannot be hidden thus. I am not one thing nor another. For I see now that only the nigger women wear skirts like this. But they have their heads heavy turbaned, the cloth tied in high peaks. Bright patterned cloth wound about their shoulders, revealing their breasts. And none wears a worn red kerchief about her head, tied low at the neck. I feel like a street cur, a whore in church. All they do is stare, and talk; but I begin to wonder if they can all see what I am, what I have done. Is it written in my face for ever? My cheeks burn but I carry on walking, without a clue as to what I'm going to do. I cannot appeal to these fierce, frowning blacks, nor call up to the pale ladies. What would I say? Use the words I learnt from him — *mon cher, mon petit, je bande pour toi.*

I reach the shore and sit down, among the crabs and scuttling things, the washed-up dregs. No one comes near me, save a couple of raw-ribbed dogs that circle and bark. I must be as outcast as they. I sit there a long time, until the sky floods with a terrifying crimson light, and the orange sun hangs heavy and huge over the sea, and the water turns red as blood.

My stomach grinds with hunger. I watch the gulls dive over the boats as they come in, and the men pulling up their nets. I hold out my hand as they come up the shore with their dripping baskets and eventually an old nigger man tosses a fish to me. I weigh it in my two hands. It is solid and glistening, bloodless.

There are windows lit behind me now and a warm wind coming off the water. I stand up, and follow the sound of pipes and a drum to a tavern. The smell of night flowers and grilling meat makes my mouth water. But there are the men again, crowding the door, pulling on their pipes and disputing furiously. Most are niggers, but now I spy some striped canvas trews, a Monmouth: here are tars too. I take my fish back to the beach and see there that a fire has been lit, away under the cliff.

The dark figures fall silent as I approach. I hold out my fish before me. *S'il vous plaît,* I say, please.

Only when they turn their faces up in surprise do I see who they are. They have removed their cocked hats, their swords and sashes. But as I shrink away one of the five reaches out and grabs me about the wrist, wrestles me down beside him.

'Ha!' he says, ' 'tis the nasty boar cat back again. Watch her claws, boys.'

He is very drunk, they all are. They clap each other's backs and laugh at me. But I'm not half so strange as everything else on this island. We understand each other. They gut my fish and spear it on a stick and hand it to me to hold over the fire. They offer me their rum. It is sweet and thick and I drink it down fast.

Even when I have eaten I am still dizzy, find it hard to make out what they mean to say to me. They ask me who I am, what I do here alone. I know this is dangerous, that I must pay more attention or try and leave, but my mind is frozen again, just as it was that first day on the *Essex*, when I had to decide. Decide who to be. I ask them if they have found their man yet. They shake their heads, say they are directed to search these villages and then the town. They point south. It's where they would go if they were him, and they laugh. I nod, drink deep, hoping to hear why.

After a time they fall silent. One pokes at the embers. There is a new tension in the air. I struggle to sit up. They have decided something. One of them leads me away under the cliff, away from the others and presses a coin in my hand. He gestures back at the group and I know what he means. Lie with him, or stay with them, all of them. His hands are warm about my waist, his breath quick. Everywhere I look is black now, sea and sky and land, black as a cave.

I take the coin, hold out my hand for another.

■ ■ ■ ■

The next morning, before it is light, I am walking north along the beach, away from the village and away from the town too, two coin in the pocket of my skirt. It is hard going. I am so bruised about that I must straddle my legs again, just like a tar. The thought makes me laugh and then I bite my lip so I do not sob.

I had thought myself numbed. By god I had drank enough. I had thought myself so filled with the blackness no more could hurt me, I had sinned so bad that I could sink no lower. But as the first one lowered himself on to me in the sand I was there in the cave again, in the darkness. I had told myself that having done it once I would be able to accustom myself to it. Women do, after all. But as I close my fingers about the coin to hush their grating I know I can never do this again. I would rather die.

I walk until the sun is up and suddenly the mist is gone so sudden as if it were never there, and the heat swells and swells. I walk past turtles and huge rounded shells, a-glisten in cradles of grey sand. I walk until I reach a line of jagged rock that plunges straight into the sea, cutting off the beach.

Lifting my skirts, I make to wade out a way, but the sand shelves away as steep as the rock falls. And I cannot swim. So I tuck up my skirts and head up the beach to the edge of the forest. I push through the under-growth and into the trees and up a steepen-ing slope. Before I know it I am climbing again. I take hold of roots and vines as though they are the mountain's rig, curl my sea-hardened feet about them and hoist myself up. Monkeys dance about my head. My chattering shipmates. I find I am glad to use my strength again. To have to exert myself, so that I cannot let my mind loose, so that I do not miss my footing and fall.

Before long I am high in the dark sweat-ing forest, among tree trunks buttressed like church towers. I can hear rain splattering above, heavy drops land here and there like falling fruit. I find a path, low and narrow as though made by animals, and funnel myself into it. After a while it peters out and I must push through bushes to find another. I follow this for a while until it begins to head down again. I retrace my steps, take another path that ends after only a few yards in a small space, the plants trod-den down as though by deer. The green air is so close and humid I cannot breathe. I sink down, curl my legs under me, wonder what to do. My coin, my dress, are no damn use to me here. I think perhaps to climb up the vines that loop half a dozen thick from tree to tree, and find a lookout, but the canopy is solid and high as a church roof. I sit until I feel I will take root in the warm damp loam, grow green shoots of my own. Well, girl, they will not find you here, I say to myself. You might be at the bottom of a well. And I have to laugh, for I know I am lost indeed.

I get up again, of course, after a time. I go on, until my skirt is torn to pennants and my skin welted with bites and my thirst so great I would have drunken seawater if I could have found it. And after a day and a night I find my way to another trail that leads out of the forest, to — well, I know no one will ever believe me when I tell them where it takes me. Still I hesitate to describe it, even to you. Who would believe it? A girl's hysteric dreaming. A sailor's tall tale.

But first there is cloud, nothing but thick cool cloud driven hard by wind but never clearing. I can see nothing, it's as though I'm wrapped in a sail, but I know I am high, higher than I have yet reached. Low bushes whip at my legs and suddenly the ground slopes down, so steeply I put my hands out to the blankness as though it will stop me falling. My feet are cut by tumbling stone unstable as a coal heap. And as I slip and slide down over rock and ferns and mosses the air clears and I see I have reached a place for the damned. I lie in a huge and shallow basin of rock, with mountains all around. It is barren, unpeopled as far as I can see. The air here is close again, thick, choking. But worse, much worse: the very earth about me steams. It rises in vicious hissing wisps and funnels taller than me. And from the cracks and fissures oozes an evil white fluid, bleeding on to rock that is coloured rose and yellow and indigo. There are pools of bubbling water stained inky black. Streams that flow yolk-yellow. And the air is thick with foul egg, with sulphur and sickness and fumigation between decks.

My limbs grow heavy with mortal fear: what creature can survive such an unnatural place? I tear strips from my skirts to bind my feet and make my way across as best I can. I pull up scraps of moss to suck them for moisture and it is torture to me to see all this flowing liquid but know it evil and undrinkable.

I walk for an hour or more, until I think this is the end, that I will die already in hell. I am sick to my stomach. There is a thundering in my ears as if my very blood is to boil.

Then, as suddenly as it began, the bleak basin ends. Some dozen yards ahead the rock disappears into steam. As I approach the stench grows stronger, the incessant noise in my ears louder. I slow my steps. There is no way around the whiteness. I inch forward, my bound feet soaking through like warm poultices with each step, until I find myself on the edge of a sloping cliff. The mass of swirling steam that presses against my face in a thick suffocating cloud rises from a huge cauldron below. I peer through the steam and see a sight that would stop my heart.

The cliff girds a lake of water, milky white. Directly below my feet, where it laps the rock, it appears smooth and calm. But as I look out and over, I see where it begins to tremble and spurt and shiver, smack obscene bubbles and heave about incessantly. I put my hands to my face and cry out, cover my eyes, then look again. Yes, see: the whole lake is boiling, as though heated by the fires of hell, as though alive with wickedness.

When I reach the outskirts night has already fallen, but the moon is shining full and fierce on the empty alleys and crowing cocks. I find a garden, thick with jasmine, and curl myself in the darkest corner. The lake boils red in my dreams.

A hand prods my back, shakes my shoulder. The voice is low and urgent and for a moment I think it him back from the dead to torment me, but as I sit up I see a nigger woman crouched over me. She speaks again as I stare at her. She is old, her face thin and dark and lined, but her eyes are terrifying: tiny chips of blue. I moan with fear and scrabble away and out into the alleys.

I walk and walk. The walls and doors heave about me, and everything I see seems not real. How long it is since I made my way around that pit of hell and down through the forest I do not know. That sulphurous air has seeped inside me, issues from me, I can smell it still.

Now the streets are filling, native women walking one after another into town. They carry baskets of corn cobs and fruits on their heads. I search behind them but they do not let anything drop. I creep along the walls like a shadow for I do not have the strength to stand upright.

Now there are no more walls but a wide open space of damp red earth. The stilted buildings on three sides and the fourth open to a sloping shore and a great wad of mist I know to be the salt sea again. I breathe it in, deeply, deeply, and grow dizzy. From a dark corner I watch as the women set up stick frames and toss over canvas shades; they squat down on low stools and lay out their wares: a ring of blue fruit, a pile of bloated green vegetable. Their chatter rises, mingles with the opening of shutters above my head, the cries of children. Now a nigger man strolls through, naked to the waist, with an earthen jug balanced on his pate. Now a broad, crisply dressed nigger woman brings a long chest of woven fibres. She sets up a low table and takes out folded linens to lay upon it; she is joined by another woman, and another, until a line of stalls fences the buildings that face the sea and the rising sun. The women's gold ear hoops glint and flare.

And now someone walks past with a basket of fresh bread and as its scent envelops me I begin to swoon. I remember the coin in my pocket and struggle to my feet.

She stares at my outstretched hand, her eyes wide. Then she shakes her head crossly and bats my hand away. I realise she has torn off the end of a loaf and tossed it into my lap. I hold out the coin again but she is staring over my head, impassive.

'*Merci,*' a voice says, and it is my own. But she must be watching me for after a while

500

she is holding a gourd of water out before me. I swallow at last. But when I thank her she will not see me.

'*Les anglais?*' I ask. She shrugs.

'*Ici? Les anglais?*'

She shrugs again. Then in one swift movement she has plucked up her basket and moved away into the crowds.

Now the sea is a glittering maze of silver and the marketplace threaded by processions of pale ladies come to buy. Each is an unbending, elaborate confection, all in white, each made still taller by a woven straw hat perched atop her head cloths. Bright parasols hover like giant butterflies above their heads, for behind them walk their nigger maids, bare brown feet slapping in the wake of their red and blue slippers.

And this is when my final hope dies, when I look at these maids, all a-trailing behind their mistresses.

The maids' linen is fresh and gauzy and crisp also, albeit without the flounces and fine-worked bodices, the escaping ringlets. They too wear ornaments in their ears. Their necks are clean and glistening, their feet well tended. I cannot read their dark faces. But I know their thoughts, I know what they do, the knacks they have, what needs they must anticipate. Ever since I saw

501

the women washing their ladies' clothes at the river I realise I must have been harbouring this same secret hope: that perhaps I might return to that world of women I should never have left.

As the trading commences, the bargaining and deference and narrowing of eyes, I see them all move before me like players in some elaborate and cruel masque, some dumb show. I feel a great pain in my heart as I understand what these costumes are telling me. The only costume a white woman can wear on this island is that of mistress. The white women here are rare birds indeed. Look at them: women of family, with friends and connections. I watch the ladies as they nod to a gentleman or two, stop and converse, and the maid halts too, stands silent and adjusts her parcels. All about these white women, tending to their every need, filling every other role, whether stallholder or maid, are natives.

I shrink back into the shortening shadows. Even if I spent all my coin on linen, went to the sea and washed myself clean and presented myself at some lady's door, why should she pay me to tend her when her husband can buy her as many shining black slave girls as she might wish?

I spend some of my coin, and I have a

lump of bread in one hand, am lifting my cup to my lips, when they all barrel into the square from the alley at my back. Six of them, arms about each other's shoulders, cocked hats awry, blind drunk. They are not redcoats, I hear straight away they are not British, but still the blood drains from my head. Before I can move, one of them jogs my elbow and when he whirls about on his heel I see he is a soldier indeed, armed with pistol and sword, his epaulet and half his buttons dangling, but of what nation I cannot tell.

They are a sorry lot, stumbling into the tables and sending the chickens squawking, but still I am afraid and think to leave promptly, to take my bread with me. But they settle themselves at the very next table, making a great hubbub. Danish, perhaps, or Dutch? I cannot make it out. They have hemmed me in. I will draw more attention to myself by leaving. I look about and see the others return to their talk. And I have not yet drunk my broth.

I am wary, though, watch them as I raise the bowl to my lips. I have to remind myself who I am, who I am not. They do not notice me, their eyes do not even rest on me. And here come the dark girls now, in any case, flitting closer, touching their hands to the men's shoulders.

When I look up again one of the girls stands before their table, her back to them all and facing me, her arms akimbo. She is flaunting herself, I think, daring them to seize her. Her woolly hair has been coaxed into stiff ringlets that stand away from her cheeks even as she bends forward. She wears a striped canary and white bodice, with her chemise pulled so low it can scarcely be seen. Her bosom is full and soft, her skin a clear sugar-brown, and I realise I am staring, transfixed, I cannot help myself. Because in her I see you. She has your smooth rounded shoulders, your long strong neck. She even moves like you, slowly, lazily, as though nothing could ever alarm her. She is at home in the heat, like you. I watch her turn her head to talk to them, even her pointed chin, her small white teeth, are like yours. She touches her fingers to a tight yellow ribbon about her neck and glances across, she has caught me watching her.

I am covered in confusion, forget myself entirely, because I am flooded with memories of you again, and the force is like that of a wave cresting the bow, it slams up against my heart again and again so hard I think it will splinter. I turn my face to the wall.

When I look back you are still there, nuzzling into a soldier's neck, seated on his right knee. He is laughing with his neighbour, and his hand rests idly on your breasts. His thick black hair hangs lank to his shoulders. He is large and coarse of body, heavier than me, not much older but far stronger. And now I find myself wishing for Nick's knife in my hand. The man is a pig, a drunken sot who must not lay another finger on you. I watch, agonised, as you shift your seat a little, fall back artfully so he has to catch you up and your head lolls back, your ringlets fall charmingly into your eye. I am willing you to look at me again so I can beckon you over, take you from him.

And then as though he can feel the force of my anger, my longing and loathing, he breaks from nuzzling your nose and looks over. His glance rests on me. The expression on his long florid face is sharp and questioning. He is no longer laughing. I feel his gaze like a weight in my own chest, dragging me down.

He looks away, but only to drink from his cup and again, he is staring at me hard now and the girl is arching her back and pouting at him because he ignores her. He puts his hands to her waist, as if to push her away. In a minute he will get up and come over and stand over me. I have done nothing to him, only looked. But, too late, I recognise his type. He is one of those men who are always in choler, who faced with a whore or a fight would choose both. I hear the scrape of his chair and make for the alley.

It twists and turns and after a while, though I press myself into a doorway and listen hard, I cannot hear him coming, his jangling harness or his heavy boots. I catch my breath. Indeed now, why would the fellow follow me? What sort of rival am I now?

The alley gives on to a dank passage ending in a wall and a set of steep stairs. I climb them, and find myself standing in a full warm breeze on the sea wall, not a dozen yards from the town's harbour and all its ships and men. I have kept to the back of the town as best I could, not wanting to risk another encounter with the British marine. Yet despite everything, my heart gives a great leap at the sight. It seems a sort of coming home, like seeing again a familiar garden where the trees have grown and the seasons changed. I look from ship to ship, trace the curves of the hulls, the patterning of the rigs, scan the fluttering pennants. That other world again, the floating world.

Then I spot a British cutter drawn up to the quay. There is a hoy, too, and several naval longboats. Out in the deep water lie one, two, three British warships. One, two, three. The heavy sun beats down upon my head as I count them again, to be sure.

I cannot believe the Navy is still at anchor here. Why do they not go? The cowards cannot lie in harbour for ever, I tell myself. The damned war is still to be fought, is it not?

That night it rains hard, and I sleep in a rank closet. I do not know how long I must guard my coin and so I dine on the fruit dropped from the trees. In the morning I wake suddenly to be sick. I count out my money, wonder how long it will last. Whether I will end my days here, in the gutter with the stray children, the starved dogs.

I make the closet my night home. I drink from the springs and save my money for bread, but I count three Sundays and then all my coin is gone. The woman who gave me her bread that first day throws stones at me now: beggars are bad for business.

There is a small stone and plaster church in one of the squares. The whitewash around the windows has been elaborately painted with curling strokes of green and yellow. Every morning before dawn a small line of black children has formed at the door and when it reaches to the bottom of the steps the door opens a crack and someone hands out bread. The children all shout at once and the line breaks up as they run to the door. If a pair of fine ladies happen to walk by they shake their heads sadly but do not stop. One day that fourth week I join the end of the line. I cannot stand long, I sit in the dust like the children.

When I reach the half-open door I hold out my hand but the bread does not appear. I peer into the darkness. A heady familiar smell escapes from within, of spice and earth and bonfires. I start when his large head appears above me. He is very tall in his priest's robes, his pate smooth and white. His small eyes stare without expression. But his thick pink jowls seem to tremble.

'*Viens,*' he says, and opens the door a little more.

After I have eaten his bread and drunk a little of his wine I rise and straighten my ragged skirts and tell him my story. Before I begin I apologise for my sore lack of French and hope he will comprehend if I speak in English. He nods, and takes the cup from my trembling hands. 'Please speak, my child,' he says. His accent is good. I take a breath and meet his eye. For I am Mrs Emily Hooper, I tell him, a clergyman's daughter of Saxtead in the county of Suffolk, who was embarked from Ipswich to join my dear husband here before starting our married life. I do not know why but dear Simeon never came to meet me. I heard there is much yellow fever in these parts? I do so hope that — I break off, wipe my eyes, recover myself — I have no other friend or relative here in these islands and find myself much reduced. I pause. Then, for good measure, to crack open his heart for his eyes are still impassive blue — I add that I was robbed of my trunk and all that I had on my first day, was even hit over the head and came to in the gutter, in the dark. I point to the ugly scar on my brow. 'I am shamed to stand before you thus but I must appeal to you, sir, to show me the kindness that befits your calling and reach out a helping hand to me.'

It is the most I have spoken to anyone since I left the *Essex* and my tongue moves ungainly in my mouth. But the fine phrases, well rehearsed, tumble out. Also I have watched those ladies well. I hope I have caught the tilt of the head, the elegance of the stance. And I hope against hope he believes me.

Father Jean proves as diligent in his care of me as he is of those dusty children, and of the bright fruits in his garden, that gives on to the back of the church. Indeed, the minute he has the measure of my destitution — the extreme distress of this unfortunate English gentlewoman — he becomes suffused with a vigour that becomes him greatly. He lunges tenderly towards me as if he would lift me into an invalid's bed himself. His voice cracks as he hollers for his maid and I thank him profusely, and gasp for air, and sigh, and shrink from the girl's leathery fingers.

He puts me in a dark high room, where I lie a-swooning like a lady as long as I can, making sure to sob quietly when I hear his tread outside my door, which comes at least every dusk. It is not hard to cry, once I let myself; it is hard to stop. When he has creaked away there is only the thud of ripe fruit falling, the faint trickle of a fountain.

She is very young, his maid Ariadne. She is plump all over, excepting her neck, a slender stalk that might snap under the weight of her woolly head. I do not talk to her, nor her to me; I watch her through half-closed lids as she adjusts the slats at the window. She has no fire to set, no milk to warm. But all else she does as I did: she sweeps the crumbs from the sheets, re-freshes the water in the jug, lays out a surf-green voile costume for me, that I recognise as my signal to rise. The dress is not tight and Ariadne fastens me in a trice, but I feel myself trussed, like a cocooned fly: the stuff is at once frighteningly fragile and as impeding as a sack.

Father Jean fusses over our first breakfast together.

'I gather you favour the mango most of all our tropical fruits,' he says, holding back his cuffs to push a dish towards me, and I wonder what else his Ariadne has noticed.

He sips at his china cup, I sip at mine. He clears his throat.

'Mrs Hooper. The ladies of my congregation have been impatient to meet you, as you might imagine. I wonder, if after mass today —'

I maintain my composure, straighten my back and attempt the expected platitudes. But I find myself stammering, because I know what such ladies are like, and I fear them. Father Jean is a kindly gull. But they will probe and question without seeming to, they will ream out all the truth of it within the hour.

'Good, good, very good,' he smiles, his cheeks red as apples. 'Forgive me, but I must note with satisfaction that your complexion is much improved, Mrs Hooper.'

He will be too polite to mention the scar to my brow, that will not be much improved by anything less than a veil. 'It will not be long, god willing.'

It will not be long, he means, until I am quite starved of light and air and freedom and turned snowdrop white, a true lady again. I do not know whether to laugh or cry.

I have told him I am Anglican, and so I evade churching at least. I cannot have the town gentry craning in their pews to see Father Jean's latest charity endeavour, this curious English girl whom no one seems to know. But the hours pass very slow. I sit on the side of the bed, swing my legs. The heat grows even more stifling. I peel the costume from my shoulders, wriggle out of the skirt and sprawl on my back, spread my legs, spread my toes.

Father Jean spoke of a lady who has expressed interest in my schooling her two young daughters, who she fears are running wild here. Another would like to improve her own English, I might pay visits to her villa up in the hills. And Father Jean himself has promised, now I am well, to provide me with pen and paper so I may write to my family at the earliest opportunity, to inform them of my unfortunate circumstances and implore their assistance. What an illegible missive that would be, scratched and blotted like a bird had walked all over it. I wonder, if I could write, what I might write to you.

The trickling fountain in the garden below is torture. I listen for the sound of the surf on the distant rock. But I am trapped. The bell in the hall trills and their voices pipe their advance, the clatter of their heels heralds the invasion. Then Father Jean's rumble, and a door muffles all but the occasional shriek.

I turn my face to the cool pillow, slip my hand inside and clutch your kerchief. I cannot see these ladies. I cannot speak to them. I cannot have them look upon me. These specimens of womanhood are as strange to me now as the flocks of island parrots that swoop and caw overhead. When Ariadne knocks I beg to be excused; tap my head and grimace, to pantomime a sick headache. She does not look impressed. I hear her descend, the arpeggio of regret. They will be gone soon, I tell myself. But what then? What then?

The hallway is dark. The only light comes from under the door of the parlour, at the front of the house. I tiptoe towards the kitchen. No light here. It is late, the ladies are long gone. Perhaps they have all gone to bed, Ariadne too. The passageway smells of stewed meat, and soft onion. I may faint I am so desperate for air. Cool, clear scentless air. At the back of the kitchen is a scullery, its stone floor cool underfoot. Moonlight beams into the garden beyond, bleaching the ground silver as an ocean. Almost out. Then I step into a large and pale shape, as high as me, that rocks and almost falls. I gasp. Only when I clutch it steady do I realise it is a drying horse made of canes; I have hold of one of Father Jean's shirts. The thin flannel is still a little damp.

Chapter Forty

I launch myself up into the branches and scale that wall as easy as the thieving monkeys, even with the surf-green dress wound about my neck like a noose. I am crouched in the alley in a moment, and up again, stumbling, hurrying, running ever downhill, towards the sea.

Ah the quenching joy of that soft night air. I sob with relief, for I can move freely again, move through that coolness in long strides that seem to skim the ground. I have slipped a short stubby kitchen knife into the pocket of his yellow trowsers. And I have your kerchief back about my neck, un-washed still and salted with my own sweat.

I catch my breath as I near the harbour. Here are lights in the streets and people. I slow my pace, fall in with a group of foreign tars, and drift in their wake to the door of a tavern. Inside they are all singing. The words are strange but I know this tune. And back it comes, that first blundering night quest through the streets of Harwich, following my own compass to the wide open door of the Three Squirrels.

The tavern sits right on the shore. I can hear the water lapping. There is the smell of fish guts, the sweet odours of tobacco and rum. I breathe it all back in, fill my lungs again and again. I linger a moment on the threshold. Until morning, when I can find myself a slopshop and exchange the dress, I have no coin. But I stand there a moment longer, longing to be in there, shoulder to shoulder with them all again, singing out. I look from face to face to face, all the many men of the oceans. There is a nigger woman too, seated on the counter, a soldier nuzzling at her neck. Reluctantly I move off into the crowds, to look for a quiet place to spend the night.

Even as I hear his long strides behind, his clanking sword, he has caught up with me. I run hard down one street, turn into another and another, and when I hear him no more I slow to a walk. But he comes up upon me again out of nowhere, I can see his boots flashing out of the corner of my eye. I walk faster, desperate to avoid a blind alley, thinking to gain the marketplace, or to lose him somehow. His pace quickens, until he is right behind me.

But he does not knock me to the ground, nor draw his sword or shout out. He does not even lay his hand on me. No, he falls in step with me, walking just a fraction behind so I cannot see his face, but I know he is there, at my shoulder, like my shadow. We walk like this the length of one dark, narrow and empty street, the windows all shuttered up against the night. I see lights further down, figures moving, and I take a breath, pace myself, thinking, let me just reach the end of the street, let him not make a move until then. We walk on. There are only inches of air separating us. It would be ridiculous were I not so unnerved. Five more paces. Christ, it is as though we are marching together, comrades in arms. I even find myself matching my stride to his: it's the rhythm of his boots and jangling sword, like a dance. Enough. Another ten paces and I will be at the corner, and I can break away from this madness. I finger my knife in my pocket. I am ready this time. And then I hear him chuckle beside me, a soft, throaty musical sound like the cry of some shy marsh bird.

He is laughing at me. He has chased me and terrified me and not even done me the honour of knocking me down. And so I turn

on him, turn all my courage and desperation and loneliness and bewilderment on to
him. All fear gone. I step in front of him,
raising both fists and crying out in a fury,
ready to beat him to the ground to make
him stop. But we are both walking at such a
speed and I stop so suddenly the whole padded bulk of him runs into me. He staggers,
then takes me by the shoulders to stop
himself falling.

I twist away. *'Arrêt!'* I cry out and I can
hear all the panic in my voice I've tried so
hard to conceal. 'Stop!' I back away, up
against the wall.

I can just make him out, bent over with
his hands on his knees, winded. Then he
crouches right down and comes up with
something in his hands. He hands it to me,
smiling.

'You drop this, I think?'

I am quite taken aback because I understand every word: he has spoken in English.
With a strong yet familiar accent I cannot
place. When the soft bundle falls apart in
my hands, I realise he is returning to me
the dress, the surf-green costume that must
have fallen from my neck as I ran. He stands
back, then gives a chivalrous little bow.

I cannot make him out at all. I had
thought him some sort of hector, chasing a

bob cull for the sport of it, and he plays games with me, acts the gentleman. He mocks me. But now I am entirely in his debt, for that dress is all the currency I have. How could he have panicked me so?

I feel an utter fool. And I realise too that now I have spoken to him, he knows me to be English. Are they looking for me still? I have no idea. But he says nothing, asks nothing, just stands with his head cocked, watching for my reaction. I clutch the dress to my chest and look at the ground, panting, churlish and silent.

'Why you run away?' he asks.

His voice is a little sad, but I barely notice this, so panicked am I by my own guilt and terror. Why did I run? I ran away because I had thought for some small space of time that I was free again, free to return to you at last, and free from the dark house and the gossiping women, from the barren basin and the boiling lake and the tangled forest, and from the dark cave and the man lying there still, from the long nights aboard the *Essex* always ploughing through the water on and on away from you. All I want, all I ever wanted, was to get back to you, but now I will always be running. I wish I could sink down to my knees, hide here in this dark place, and never move again. But here is this sweating man, this shambling foreign soldier, who has done me a kindness that may yet be a trick. I must not let him suspect a thing.

I tuck the dress tight under my arm and tug at your kerchief, clear my throat once, then twice, before I can speak. I say, as humble and fearless as I can manage: 'I must thank you, sir. Goodbye.'

Now I will nod, and walk away.

He rests a light hand on my arm. 'Stay,' he says. I stay.

We regard each other for a moment. He stands a little taller than me, but not much. Our breathing slows in unison. I notice our stance is the same, his belly is bigger, thrown out, but we set our feet at exactly the same angle, as though we learnt together. What is it, this mirroring? Our faces could not be more different. A dark down on his upper lip, fine as a child's eyebrow, thickens to a hint of moustache that licks the corners of his mouth. His nose is long and curved, horse-like, his red lips thick and full, but there is a look about his eyes I recognise.

Have I seen him before? For one alarming moment I think perhaps he sailed upon the *Essex* but I do not know his uniform, he cannot be a British marine. No, now I see it, he was the soldier I saw with the girl outside the tavern, the brown girl who was so like you I could not look away. He had caught me looking, but no, that makes no sense: that was when I had your kerchief about my head, a chemise and skirt about my body. Surely he could not know me again?

Somehow, though, the atmosphere between us is softening by the second, as though we were old acquaintances who had bumped into each other in a foreign port, and taken a moment to recognise one another. This is most dangerous, I must walk away now. We stand still and look at each another a moment longer. He is almost smiling. Despite everything, I want to smile back. And as I do, I realise.

CHAPTER FORTY-ONE

He calls himself Albert. But he was born
Childeberta, on a farm outside Outenarde
in the Low Countries. It was a wild, windy
place and Childeberta was a wild and romp-
ing girl; always out of doors, and addicted
to all sorts of mischief. Oh she was eager to
get away and so she married young, to a
sailor who took her to Lille. But he spent
all his money and abandoned her there. Her
baby girl died when she was seven months
old and Childeberta moved in with an aunt.
She earned her board spinning or scullery-
ing, but it went against her spirit so she
could not keep at it. She had such a passion
to be outdoors and fighting, to be up and
away and have her own coin in her hand.
Her friend came one day, while the soldiers
were marching by. She leant against the
doorpost and stuck out her hip, thus, and
said: Berta, it is so sad to see you here by
the spinning wheel when the drum is beat-

ing outside.

'I took up the small axe we used for chopping wood,' says Albert, 'and smashed that household devil up.' He is smiling when he says this, leaning forward eagerly over the table. He has slung his coat across his chair and turned back his cuffs. Sweat plasters his linen to his muscles and beads his high brow. He has my hand clasped warm in his and I'm smiling back, cannot stop smiling. I must look as though I lost my wits, for I am all a-tremble from head to toe, hysteric. I cannot believe he exists. But he does. She does.

Albert and I could not stand long there in the street, so close to the harbour. He found a tavern, a table in a dark room at the very back. And we are very, very drunk now. It is heaven.

Look at him, his lank black hair hanging about his face, stinking of baccy, stinking like a wet dog. Look at him smiling, smiling, to have found me too. To be telling his tale, at last, at long last. It is spilling out of him.

His cheeks quiver with suppressed laughter. He widens his eyes comically. 'There. All smashed. What is to be done?'

I wonder at Childeberta's spirit. Was I ever so headstrong, so incautious? Oh I was timid before. I have had to learn bravery. And caution — crushing, tedious, numbing caution — before all else.

'I said to my friend: I have no money and cannot earn any. But,' he unclasps me and the table rocks as he drums it with both hands, 'ta-da-da! My friend had a sum, enough to buy one suit. And she said, when we have that, we can sell this woman's garb —'

We both look swiftly to my dress, bundled on a chair at my side, and swiftly back to each other. Now I laugh, and lace his fingers in mine and squeeze them tight. I think to myself, I do not have to be cautious with Albert.

'That's what I did,' I say breathlessly, and glee and relief trill through me like a brook. 'What I was to do, when —'

'When I saw you.'

But of course Albert already knew that.

I fall sober again. Conscious all of a sudden that we are only two, that we are both far from home. Who are we? I ask myself suddenly. What do we think we are about? I rouse myself, look into his eyes. What did he see, when he looked at me that day?

I have to ask. 'What made you follow me? When you saw me, how did you —'

He cocks his head. Of course. Of course.

He was looking for a brother too.

'But no one else, not even —' Then I stop. I cannot talk of him, not ever, even to a brother.

Albert shrugs. His eyes are bright. I can see that he has never told another soul his story. That he too has been alone. I should reach out and press my hand to his cheek, to comfort him. But I cannot. The habit of offering comfort is gone. And anyway he is refilling my beaker.

'And when you had sold your costume?' he asks. 'What you spend your coin on, I wonder?' He winks, pokes out his thick tongue.

'No! No. Why, I thought to go down to the harbour to look for a vessel bound for England.'

'Ah, you would play the good old British tar!' He stuffs his hands in his pockets, sways in his seat and curses explosively.

I splutter. He sounds nothing like any British tar I ever met.

'You want to go home now?'

I nod.

'To England! But why?' He sounds incredulous.

I tell him I left my friend behind. That I was taken by the gangers, and that I jumped ship here. Nothing else.

Still, he grows sober for the first time. 'Then you must be careful,' he says frowning.

'I know.'

'You must go back?'

I nod. We say nothing for a while. We drink. When I ask him what happened to his friend he shrugs. 'I followed the drums and she came along a while. But then she grew tired of the life. Always moving from place to place. She missed her son, I think.'

He takes me back to his room. As we walk he puts his arm about me and I hide my face in his sleeve. No one stops us.

The cocks are crowing and the light of dawn shows green and orange at the low window. He sits on the side of the bed and smokes his last pipe as I let down Father Jean's trowsers. I stagger as they pool at my feet. I am so drunk now I can hardly see. Father Jean's shirt comes to my knees.

'Take it off,' says Albert, puffing away.

I don't know why but I do. What do I have to hide?

He stares.

'You do not bind?' he says incredulous. I do not know what he means, and then he guffaws again and tugs up his own shirt to show me linen strips, tightly wound about his breasts. They are brown with sweat. I finger them, curious.

'My breasts are not like yours,' he says, rubbing his hands up and down the bindings. 'They have made me great difficulty.'

I never thought to bind. I trusted to my billowing shirt. And as the muscle came about my chest and shoulders, I did not think much on my breasts, not until I first stood before those British marine. 'You do this yourself?' I ask.

'Why of course!' he cries, 'who else? I will show you, if you like. Though you do not need it so much, I think. Still —' and he winks.

It is so strange to be flirted with like this, by a man who I know is not a man yet still seems so like a man to me.

Then he roots about under his mattress and gives me also a sum of money. 'In the morning,' he says, 'we will go together to the market to buy you a set of slops.'

I shake my head. He has bought me jug after jug of rum. I cannot take his money.

But he insists. 'We sell the costume and you return me the sum. And now, I think, we must sleep.'

He lowers himself heavily to his bed and shifts over to the wall, leaving space for me. And that is how I sleep that night, cradled against his bound chest.

I wake to a sound of running water, and sit up to find Albert standing by the open window, his trowsers undone, pissing in a great arc out of the window and into the street. I cannot believe my eyes.

'Ha,' he says, his eyes dancing, 'I knew that would wake you.'

He shows me his curved horn, that is very like the bullock horn the sailmakers fill with tallow to stick their needles in. Only this horn he wears in a pocket inside his trowsers. He shows me how he takes it out when necessary. He has to show me several times before I see how it is done, so convincing that had I not known I would have had no suspicion.

'Very useful,' he says, sniffing it and making a face before tucking it away. 'Get yourself one of these, I think.'

He is so proud of his tricks, and I think suddenly: who else can he tell, who else could he show off to?

'No,' he says, retrieving the horn. 'You take it. I'll get another. Then we go find some girls!'

He begs some thread and a needle from his landlady and I sew myself a pouch for the horn. He take up some linen and tears it up and binds my breasts for me. Once I am dressed again he looks me up and down and smiles.

'Now walk.'

I walk to the window and turn and walk back. It is very different already. The linen is awful tight but I can swell out my chest without fear. And the horn, how it moves between my legs. I feel myself blush. He pokes me in the chest.

'Very good!' he says. 'Very good.'

We take ourselves off to find something to eat first. We walk arm in arm, keep to the shady side of the street. When I find myself at the head of the harbour, and see the land wind ruffling the bright blue water, the mass of masts and the rigging, something sinks in me and I slow my pace. Albert squeezes my arm, encourages me on, says he knows a good place across the bay, where the tars never go. Before we have gone twenty yards I stop dead.

There is my name. LUKE FLETCHER. On a torn and ragged flysheet attached to the doorpost of a sailors' slophouse. The words leap out at me. LUKE FLETCHER, loblolly boy attached to the warship ESSEX. Wanted for MURDER. By order of His Majesty's NAVY.

Albert catches at my arm, pulls me off down an alley immediately. He sits with his arm about me and I shake and I shake but I cannot speak. He takes me back to his room. Later he goes out, to a tavern by the docks, he says. For several days more I keep to the room and he goes in and out and brings me food. I will not speak to him, I cannot. I pull the blanket over my head and lie beneath it all day, not moving, breathing in my own fug. I sleep for hours. I know he is there in the room, but he does not ask me anything.

I cannot sleep when it is dark. If I do I dream and wake and must pace about a long while. One night I am crouched by the low window, waiting for dawn, when he gets up and comes over and takes my hand. I cry on his shoulder and he brings me back to bed and I must take drink after drink before I can confess what I could never have told Father Jean. I tell him what I did aboard the ship, what I did to get off it. And then I tell him what happened in the cave, and how I brought the rock down on that man's head again and again, how I twisted out from under him and hit him again and kicked him too and cursed him and I could not stop until he was all quiet and did not move again.

Albert speaks at last. 'It was no bad thing you did.'

I pull away, stare at him. He looks like an

engraving of a soldier, all grey skin and black hair.

'Believe me,' he says. 'May god forgive you. God forgive me too. I do not know how many men I have killed.' He shrugs and strokes my hair.

'What do I do now?' I whisper. 'They will kill me too.'

'No, no,' he says. 'I will not let them.'

He tells me to forget all about Gilles. Never tell a soul else, most especially not you. The man must lie buried here on this island for ever.

The next day when Albert comes back with the bread and some fruit he is smiling. Tells me to sit up and listen. Your navy ships are gone, he tells me. He reeks of rum and tobacco, his eyes are reddened and there is a big yellow flower in his lapel. I ask him if he is certain.

'Certain! Of course, I tell you.' He brings a fistful of the navy bills out of his pocket, throws them on the bed all crumpled. 'See, I took them all, all I could find. No one will be looking for you now!' He sits on the edge of the bed with me and offers me a swig from his flask. 'That's better, yes? Come, see with your own eyes.'

I dress and he takes me down to the harbour. The light hurts my eyes after so many days indoors. I scan and scan the bay, walk the length of the quay twice. He is right. I'll go to the top of the town, I say, check from there.

'No, enough!' he says. 'We celebrate. I can take you to a good place, the girls will love you.'

But I shake my head and draw back. 'No, Albert,' I say. 'Thank you, thank you very much, for everything. But no. I need to find a ship.'

He looks at me and bites his lip. 'That girl, heh?' he says after a moment, and screws up his eyes like a young boy.

I nod.

He looks down at the ground, scuffs it with the toe of his boot. Then suddenly he turns his back and walks rapidly away. I start after him but just as I reach him he turns again and takes a hold of my shoulders.

'You will be alone on the ship,' he says in a hectoring tone.

'Yes,' I say, quite bewildered now.

'You do not want to be another man's boy again, do you?'

Suddenly I feel sick. 'No,' I say. 'I don't.'

'You want to see her again,' and now he seems to mock me, 'you will have to learn a little something, don't you think?'

I swallow. He is right. 'Yes,' I say. 'I know.'

He slaps me then, hard on the left cheek.

Before I even feel it I have slapped him back harder.

He catches at my hand and holds it tight before I can draw it back. His eyes are bright, and a red patch is rising on his sallow cheek as I watch.

'That's good,' he says, and he's smiling. 'That's good.'

He takes me to a quiet place, under the shade of a spreading tree. There he picks up a handful of earth. 'I will give you some gunpowder. Keep it in your pocket, like this. Then you can throw it in his eyes.' He feigns throwing it at me and I dodge to the left. He brings the heel of his hand to my chin and puts his thick fingers over my face. 'And then you hit your hand so into his face.'

He makes me take a turn, throw the earth, heel his face. I feel his warm wet lips beneath my palm. When Albert bats my hand away, his face is stern. 'Use your shoulders. Don't hit his face, hit his brain.'

I try again, he ducks away, looks back at me incredulous.

'I cannot fight you,' I say to him angrily, my chest heaving. 'I am too small, and I need my hands to sail. I have a knife, see. Teach me how to use the knife.'

'Put it away,' says Albert. 'That's later.'

He explains how well armed I already am. You are small, he tells me. Yes, and this, he says, stroking my elbow, is the short fellow's best weapon. He shows me how to use it. An elbow can be like a bullet, he says, pointing to a scar on his forehead. That was an elbow, I bled like a pig.

You are slight. He shows me how to catch even a hefty fellow like him off balance.

You are clever. Surprise him then. Put up your palms so, and apologise, show you have no weapon, speak nonsense, confound him. And then he shows me how to drive my fingers into his throat.

You watch, all the time. You look past the noisy clown, you look if you can see their hands, you look for the little weasel at the back whose hands you can't see. You know where everyone is, even when the candle goes out. You do not go in anywhere without knowing how you will get out, you see who is blocking the way.

And now, forgive me, Luke, but you will be glad. And then he comes at me, with all his bulk and his hair flying and barrels into me, his fist drives deep into my stomach, and then a blow to the side of my head that knocks me off my feet. Everything is red: howling, shifting red. He catches me as I fall and I have not the strength to resist him.

'Now,' he takes my chin and forces me to look at him. I can barely focus, his eyes are fierce. 'Remember this feeling. Now,' he says, 'now when he feels you weak, now you use that elbow.'

I struggle away and he takes my head between his hands and kisses me hard on the forehead. He is bouncing about on his feet, he is as frisky as a lamb. All the pain and humiliation wells up in me and I drive my fists straight at his chest. I want to break his ribs. He lets me pummel him a while. I aim at his face and feel my hand crack. He winces. Like this, like this, he says, straightening my wrist, and use the heel of your hand if you can.

We sit down against the tree trunk and I nurse my hand. He puts his arms about me, strokes my hand. 'Good strong hands, they are,' he tells me. 'You'll be all right.'

Oh, the knife, he says, I had forgot the knife. I show it to him. Good, he says. Short, stubby. He stands up, shows me how I can conceal it in my hand, behind my thigh. And I must hold the end of the handle so, on my palm, wave the other hand in apology so he turns his head and I can drive the blade into his exposed neck, so.

'Now you don't get too confident. Don't say too much.' It's my turn to raise my eyebrow now. Silence is what I know best, after all. 'I mean it,' he says. 'Quiet is good. Talk too much, and they will see your weakness.'

For several days we go about, up and down the quay, to the customs house and the slop shops, to the market to sell the costume for a tidy sum, and in and out the houses for Albert wants to show me at least what I am missing. Many more days like this, I realise one afternoon, and I will be as any other feckless tar: my tidy sum will have slipped right through my fingers. But the girl starts to squawk that I owe her anyways and when the men come Albert gives me the look and so we start in. I am away through the back door soon as I can but I can hear Albert in there still, giving his all.

It is quite dark when he comes back to the room, and his eye is swollen like a fruit. He throws himself on the bed and will not speak to me, and it is not until the morning that I can get out of him what happened.

He jokes, as always, but I know he is worried. I think for a while, and then I get to my feet and tell him I am going to find out if the man lives. Albert scuffs the sole of his boot on the boards.

I find the house, but it is all locked up, they cleared out overnight. We lie low several days more, but eventually we must go out again. We move from tavern to tavern, but hear nothing. Still, Albert hangs his head, and drinks harder than ever. We have been sitting all day at the very back of a tavern on the water's edge when we overhear a British tar grumble that his ship the *Gemini,* a merchant ship, is bound for Ipswich, his is a poxy fate for sure because he likes the island women very much.

'Ipswich,' I say to Albert, unable to believe my ears.

He looks up. 'Where is Ipswich?' he whispers.

'England.'

'England, eh. Near where you want?'

'Near enough,' I say, laughing.

We follow the man who talked of the *Gemini.* But as we wait for him to emerge from a house, out comes a girl behind him, crying. Albert asks her who was that man who left now and she says that was Billy King gone to tell his captain. And then she starts up crying, for he was the best mate of her English boy, who lies upstairs dead after brawling. I glance warningly at Albert but his face is set in an expression of sweetest sympathy. He was to have sailed tomorrow, she wails.

'Aboard the *Gemini*?' Albert asks her gently.

'Yes indeed,' she says. She is crying too hard to suspect anything of us. Still, I tug at Albert's sleeve but he shakes me off. And when we have comforted her some time, he asks: 'And what was your poor lad's name?'

'Dear Tom Docker,' she says, 'and he was only a boy still.'

'Tom Docker?' says Albert, in his best wholesome manner. 'This boy here was previously a shipmate of your poor Tommy Docker, aboard the —' and he pinches me hard in the waist so I cry out and say the first name that comes into my head.

'The *Dolphin*,' I say. 'I sailed with him aboard the *Dolphin*.'

'How sad that poor Tommy is gone!' Albert says to me with one eyebrow cocked, and then he pinches me again so's I weep with him.

'Ah, alas!' she cries too and holds out her arms to me and she embraces me in turn while Albert winks. Then she asks us kindly to go on up and pay our respects, she's away to her mother.

We watch her hurry away down the street.

And once she has turned the corner, Albert hugs me and laughs and says: 'Save your money and stow your tale for now it is simple. The *Gemini* is a hand down, now's your chance. You shall present yourself at the muster.'

While she is gone we go up to her room. Albert will not let me look at poor Tom Docker lying dead on the bed. He tugs me into the corner and opens up Tom's sea chest. His coin is all gone but the chest is sound and he has a fine knife and sundry other essentials.

That night we spend most of our coin on rum. When Albert rolls atop me I let him kiss me a while and then must roll back atop him. Back and forth this goes a while. He will not let my tongue in his mouth and I cannot abide his. He rides me a while until I try to find his parts but he pulls away. 'You must be a girl again for me,' I tell him, vexed and frustrated, but he shakes his head and that is an end of it.

And so we sleep with our backs to each other, are awkward with each other when we wake, awkward all morning indeed, and though it pains me I can do nothing. We walk down to the dock in silence. But when we get there my heart lifts and I clutch Albert's arm, all distance forgotten. I turn to him and he pats my hand and says: 'Off you go, boy, off you go!' and I cannot but hug him to me.

For here are ships aplenty, any one of them big enough to take me home, and one of them the *Gemini.* The world opens up again before me, and for the first time since I was pressed a ship seems to me not a floating prison but a vessel of hope; the oceans full of possibility again.

For Albert has drilled me well, instructed me in all his tricks, and if he has passed for so many years then so can I. And I will be with you.

We look for vessels flying their flag of departure. There are three, but only one a frigate, lying some way out. The *Gemini* is a little red and white two-master, battered about for sure but she looks trim enough. Up and down the dock we go, until we find a bumboat bound to her. The bumboat is waiting on a poultrier so we find a tavern and drink off first one bumper and then another, for we find there is not much to say, and drinking passes the time.

And now we are saying goodbye here on the public dock.

'Well and off you go,' says Albert again, kicking at Tom Docker's sea chest that is his no longer since we scraped off his initials and Albert scored some device of his own in its place: to remember him by, he says.

I wish I had thought to say all I had to say back in his room. 'I never met another,' he had told me that first night. 'Not once, in all these years.' He had had many girls, he said, but still, he had grown lonely. I had not understood. Five years, he said, I think it is, since I began. That is a long time. Still I did not see it. God give me five years with Becca, I was thinking, let me pass as well as Albert has done and I would kill for a lifetime so with my Becca.

But now, as we are about to part, I understand a little. Now I too will scan a man's face, observe his walk, the swell of his hip, the set of his head upon his neck. Watching, waiting, just in case. I put my arms about Albert and hug him hard, like a brother. 'I won't forget you,' I whisper to the back of his head, half hoping he won't hear. After a short time he pushes me away. 'Ouch,' he says deadpan. 'Your arms are too strong, boy.'

I try to laugh but my eyes are filling with tears.

'You'll be all right,' he says. 'No big heavy rocks aboard a ship, to pick up by mistake. I think you will not get into too much trouble.' I wince a little but he is smiling and shaking my hand now and the bumboat woman is calling so I clasp him about the back of the neck and lay my forehead to his.

I mean to match his tone, make some sharp retort of equal intimacy, but the feel of his forehead against mine is soft and warm as a kiss, and what comes to my lips is 'god forgive us both.'

CHAPTER FORTY-TWO

And so here I am now by the main mast, awaiting the captain, and sweating hard in poor Tom's fine stolen reefer. I do not think much of the *Gemini:* the *Essex* would swallow two or three of her whole. I could cross her deck in ten paces, her main mast looks to be half the height. But she is daunting enough. Six or so of the crew are already on deck, another three in the rigging. I square my shoulders, steady my feet as I feel their gaze upon me.

Rapid steps sound below deck and out of the aft hatchway rises a great dark negro, so tall and strong and severe in aspect I take a step back. He looks me up and down as though I stand aboard his own ship, must account for myself. He does not speak, so I must.

'Luke Fletcher,' I say.

'English?' he asks. His voice is strangely high, and sibilant, for such a big man. 'Very good.' He introduces himself. His name is Orlando Rossito, he is the mate of this vessel, and in sore need of hands. Another man died ashore last night and three lost to fever, including the carpenter.

'You are not a carpenter too?'

I shake my head.

'Can you furl, reef, and stow?'

'Aye, sir, aye,' I nod vigorously.

Albert's rum is flooding warm through my veins, but my head is clear and sharp: somehow, now that I am afloat again, I feel fluent and strong and able to take on anything, even such a strange buck negro as this, with a chest like a barrel and fine manners.

'Steer and sound?'

I hesitate. I remember Nick's strutting speech to the lieutenant aboard the *Essex*. 'I would put myself under your instruction, sir, if you were so minded. I am most eager to learn, and learn fast, sir.'

'Manage a gun?'

I would be a fool to lie about this. 'I know its parts but have never fired one.'

'Where have you served?'

'First aboard a collier brig,' I lie. 'Two years up and down the east coast and the London River with Captains Foakes and Hamish and then a Captain Whittaker.' I stop, a little alarmed at my own fluency.

'In what vessels?'

I have to think hard. 'Lately the *Samson,* bound for Brazil out of Hull. She was wrecked.'

'Where?'

'Here, sir. Hereabouts. Which is why I need a ship.'

'I have heard of no wreck about these islands lately.'

'I was on the Holland packets too, for a while,' I say, to distract him. 'As a hand on the *Dolphin,* out of Harwich. You are bound for Ipswich, are you not? I know those parts well.'

'Hmm. The Medusa Channel?'

'Aye sir. And,' I venture, on a sudden inspiration, remembering your father now, his interminable stories, 'the Cork Sand. She's a tricky one, by god.'

He compresses his lips. 'How old are you?'

'I have been at sea many a year, sir.'

He nods. 'I'll take you on a boy's wages for a week, then we'll see.'

He offers me twelve shilling a month, double the coin I was promised aboard the *Essex,* and I sign the articles eagerly.

'You have a chest?'

'Yes,' I say, 'yes,' and point to it, there by my feet, with the strange pigeon-chested bird Albert has daubed on to its linen cover.

'Cocksedge is the bosun here. He will show you where to stow that.'

Cocksedge is a small brown man whose face is all of a slant: one eye set higher than the other, his mouth going one way, his nose another, like his face yawed about one day and his features never righted themselves. 'You look pleased, boy.'

'Twelve shilling!' I say, unable to stop myself. By god, I will shower you with coin, we will be set up good and proper.

'Sally raiders'll wipe the smile off your face,' he says over his shoulder as he leads the way down the hatchway. 'Still plenty of 'em off Africky. Danger money is what it is.' He smiles even more broadly when he sees my stricken face. 'Shall be spring storms up in Biscay. Like as not take us three month to tack up to the channel. Cargo'll be juice.'

I realise now he is joking with me but my heart is sinking with every word he utters.

'And if we dodge the rovers once we're in the Channel it's the navy bastards, fierce to press us out of our very hammocks they'll be now.'

I stop dead and he turns round.

'Don't fret. We're fighters, us *Gemini* boys. Come on, I'll take you down.' He unhooks a lantern and heads down the steps.

I take a breath from force of habit, so's not to have to take in the full force of the bilge, but what I smell instead is even more familiar, and far more disturbing. The sharp, penetrating sweetness bursts in my nostrils, set the juices running in my throat. I let my sea chest tumble, I'm doubled up, retching. That strange-shaped cabin up by the bowsprit. The stove burning hot and fast. Dominique crouched in a shirt too big for him. And Gilles's hand at my head, pressing the warm wet cloth gently against my wound. The scent of limes rising from his wrists, spreading in the hot, thick air.

Cocksedge holds his lantern high, peers back. 'God damn, lost your sea legs already?'

I spit, wipe my mouth with one hand. I have vomited into the other. 'What is that smell?' I ask, my chest burning.

'What's to turn your nose up at, I'd like to know? 'Tis the cargo, lad. Stowing two dozen barrel of limes we are, among other things. Get yourself down there.'

Four days out. My nose is peeling again and my palms are swollen tight as eggs, but young Luke is in his element. I've got the salt spray in my face, my heart is pumping, and I'm up and down pell mell, hands and feet moving like clockwork, she's still short

547

of hands and I never stop.

But I don't mind much. Don't mind at all. It's good to be moving, to have work to do and I'm good at it. I'm up the mast as often as I'm not and I'm happy up here, with the wide blue ocean about me, hearing the boys sing out at the ropes.

Never had no singing above decks in the *Essex,* weren't allowed under navy rules. But from the moment the *Gemini* set sail, the boys all started up with 'Haul Away Joe'. They've been good to me, these boys. Aboard the *Essex* they always said the merchant boys were cuckoo, for who'd go to sea off their own cock? But this lot love their work and it shows. Only eighteen of us crew and not half of them English, there's an Ethiope, two Irish, a Swedish boy, many Danes, even a lad from the Alps if you would believe it. I like their pigeon talk, their wild stories. No one pries, see? No quartermaster wanting you to touch your cap, setting about with his starting stick every time anyone swears. Best is, pulling on a rope, packed together up on the yard, we can sing out when we like. It's like church, it's better than church.

I milk the goats, make cheese, make myself popular. Jack from Dublin has sailed the south seas and offers to tattoo me. I ask him for a swan on my forearm. Don't think the lad remembers too well what a swan looks like, but he gets the long curving neck and beak right at least. The body's a mess, though: square and solid with feet like paddles.

Now that was a mistake. For I see it every day as I work, as I lay down to sleep. And it does something to my dreams, swims through them, the waters part and there you are, night after night after night.

And in the day too. After many weeks out I come to see as much in the clouds and the canvas as I had ever seen on land. For in the skies are landscapes, grander than any to be seen ashore. And to my eyes at least, the folds of the sails are peopled with figures varied enough for endless amusement.

One day, about eight bells, I lie back in the crow's nest and close my eyes. The night had been bad but the seas are calmer now. Wind's tugging her along nicely, she thrums like my aching muscles. I drift off. When I open my eyes again I cannot distinguish the whiteness of the topsail, furled above my head, from the glare of the sky, until what I took to be snaking clouds resolve themselves into runnels of shadow.

Idly, I follow the folds with my eyes. I

gasp. For there you sit. Your head bent, the narrowness of your neck. I follow the curve of your back down to your full seat, trace your bent leg up and down to where it tapers into your toe. The lines of you are so perfect, so exactly as I remember you, sitting naked on the sail, in the attic.

She is but a fold in the canvas, a tiny, crooked fold upon which the light lays aslant to raise a shadow figure. I know this. But she seems so alive to me, poised between sitting and standing. I feast my eyes, draw a sort of sustenance from the vision, a soft comfort like a dream of milk bread after sea biscuit.

And then, of course, the call comes, for the wind is freshening and we have much distance to make up. The ropes rattle, out crawl the others, and down comes the clotted canvas, in clumps and then billows. And I almost cry to see her go, for suddenly I know how much I miss you, and understand how far I have come from you and everything I loved. I can barely believe you still exist when even a shift in the sail means your shadow could vanish so sudden and complete.

It passes, that feeling. It has to. I could not live otherwise. I harden myself again, make myself work.

And so there are other days, many other days that merge into one another. When I am as much a part of the ship as the rig itself, lashed together, we are moving as one. To be any good you've got to be up there all day, every day, see. Live in her like her rope and mast are sinew and bone. And you're the life blood, coursing up and down, keeping her tight, making her move. Tighten a bit here, flex there, let her run a while. And all the time you're on the lookout. Toss the hair from your eyes, squint and shade your eyes and scan the horizon for something, anything, that's not sea, 'cos if you don't, and if some bugger on deck spots it before you you've had it, an extra watch and a whole load of grief when you hit the deck.

And I live among the boys, I can never forget them. I live like I'm one of them. We move as a pack: drink together, sleep together, fight together, work together. I thank Albert many times over. I lose myself in the pack and it works, it's a sweet release: there's nothing like it for forgetting. Sometimes I have to sing it out.

'Ridin' at my station! I love my occupation!'

If only he could see me. At these moments I am the finest fucking topsail man in all the jerry fleet. I'm full of spunk and hard as they come. Hear that? Eight bells on the finest spring morning the Atlantic ocean has ever known, she's cutting through the foam like a dick through cunt spume. Up here, look you, see me. No, not there you fool, that's Mal, the useless scum. No, up here, up the main mast. Keep on going, up up up, yes there, right up in the topgallant that's me. And to my right I've got Si and to my left Tizzer and we're all singing out yes we are. Here comes the chorus. And wait for it, I'll take this verse. Got a new one came to me last night. They love that, the lads, that's mine that is. Damn that Dodder yahooing, down below. He's a dirty scum he is. Hey, watch this boys: dick out, piss on his head why not? Only playing, only playing. Ha, see what happens? Gust of wind, some fucking dew spews off the lower gallant. He looks up face like a cross donkey, shakes his fist. Sail billows out and that's him forgot. We all laugh. He's just another broken-down hulk. Like Nick.

Remember Nick? To think I once thought that useless hector was king of the yard. I won't end up like him oh no, I'm going to ride this wave until I come crashing into a cliff, or Davey Jones calls me. Sir yes sir. I call out to Tizzer, we set too, working tight and nice. Si hauls up, the sail is drying nice now all that piss rolled off. Easy to handle.

And we pull, hard hissa! Here we go with all our beef. Sing out again this is the life all right. Here's a fray in the bunting, look. Give me a minute I'll get my knife out, tidy up. Down below the old man gives the order for the crowd to get to their stations and make sail. Howe! Hissa! Haul away! Hoist 'er up. Hey mate keep clear of me can't haul with you blowin down me bloody neck. A couple of deck boys climb aloft. Yo ho, tail on the fall! And we all sing out.

CHAPTER FORTY-THREE

Up we come smartly on a brisk south-
westerly that's carried us all the way through
the Thames estuary, a weak English sun at
our backs. I am high on the larboard fore-
mainyard, just me and the open singing air.
We've hugged the long low coast all the way
along from the cliffs of Walton; dun, sandy,
prickled with leafless trees, the odd windmill. But here we are, in the Medusa Channel, and up ahead the anchorage, the big
ships and the small. My heart beats faster.
Up we come.

Harwich. Yes, she's all still there, but tiny,
like toys laid out on a table. There's the high
light house and the low, both a bit green
about the gills after the winter. I can see the
gatehouse, the ditches and the walls. Two
new rows of saplings, the long shingle shore
and the last of the whelkers. And there at
last the sudden press of buildings right up
to the water, under a pale pall of smoke

pierced by the spire of good old St Nick's that I never knew so tall and fine.

Harwich. She's so close. There's Admiral Dunton's new house right on the east shore, plastered saffron now, stacks of buxom bay sashes all finished off and aglint with glass. I can see the steaming tar barrels at the navyard, the clean ribs of a ship and a half in dry dock. Tiny red coats and striped skirts and pennanted bonnets a dozen on the quayside. Then we round west and we lose the wind.

I curse, for the hulls and masts of all the hoys and brigs, frigates and schooners and lugs are moored up between us and the town. Damn them. Frantic now to spy the packet quay, there's two hoys tied up is that the *Dolphin*? I put my hand to my throat. For one beautiful moment I can see right down the length of West Street, there's a waggon stopped halfway, women walking. My god, you could be there this moment, back from the market with a basket on your arm.

Now we're into the channel and she's foundering because the tide is against us. My sail gaps and wallows. I glance away from the ropes for a moment: and see the wide, wide Stour opening up before us. She's in full flood, lapping into Erwarton

Bay and soaking the marsh at Wrabness. A mile or so beyond, past Wrabness point, where the river curves out of sight, will be the town of my birth, beyond that, the farm where I grew up, and my mother.

No time for that. It's up the Orwell we must go, and we need the wind to move round or we're going nowhere at all. Reef up lads. I work like a demon. Every muscle in my body sings with power. Damn, I could take a giant's leap from frigate to tender, shoulder through the thicket of masts, tack my way through the streets to West Street. Run up that fine curving five-stepped stair, grasp that thick gleaming brass fish and slam her down again over and over. Hear her echo in the dark hall, stream up the stairs, shiver the glass of the yellow-stained window, flood under the door of your room, thud against your heart, open your eyes.

I slide down to the deck, take a turn at the soundings, avoiding the others. I must keep you hidden in my heart a while longer, for now we sit here in the channel, till the tide turns or the wind moves, or both. All about us, and in clusters off Shotley and Harwich, the small boats ride at anchor in military formation, lying to the tide, their sterns to the sea. I watch them, without really knowing what I'm waiting for, until the line-up falters, and they begin to veer about and nod to one another as though guests at an assembly.

And then I remember, with a great flood of feeling that seems to choke my heart, that first time we walked west along the quay and upriver, to the sea wall and the marshes. When you stopped and pointed to where the estuary meets the sea, showed me how, when the tide is on the turn, the movement of the water stills. Watch, you said, for once they're equal, the salt water and the sweet, but they're still fighting, they're all in confusion. It's not going to last. It seems to go on and on, but it never, ever lasts. You took my hand then. Magical, isn't it? you said. Slackwater. We'd stood and watched, hand in hand.

Such a short time, the space between one bell and the next, one turn of the sandglass. And the flow has reversed again before I am fully aware, the tide has regathered its strength, streaming the little boats back into line, this time to face the sea. I take a deep breath, hold it as long as I can, let it out slowly.

Slowly, so slowly, we float up the Orwell dogleg. The wind has barely moved, it takes a lifetime to round Shotley point, and I stare back at Harwich, so close, so clear, receding imperceptibly. Just as the sun sets, as the land darkens and the water starts to glow, we reach Colliner point and I lose sight of St Nick's. The woods of Shotley point slide across, like a door shutting.

It's twelve miles up to Ipswich. Carcasses of two new ships gleam on the north shore. Then comes the stench of tanneries, lights winking on the shore, shouts over water, the rumble of wheels.

That first night on land again is a jangling blur. Paid off good, letter of service tucked inside my jacket, sea chest under my arm, across the gang we go and my feet land clumsy on the hard stone. A floating world no more. Together we visit a tavern, then a chophouse, another tavern and another, as the girls gather. One by one my shipmates pair up, go off, and when I awake, stiff and fat-headed, I am alone.

I take myself off to a slophouse, rap on the shutters until the door opens and I can show them the colour of my money. Tom's reefer is ripped to shreds and Ipswich in March is chiller than a galey topmast. I'm after a serious watchcoat, down to my ankles. I'm after a thick jacket with six brass buttons, fancy shoes with two silver buckles. Three cambric shirts. A sheeny straw hat that I tip to the back of my head. I'm tempted by the ribbons, red and yellow and blue, but I'm not an able top-man, not yet anyhow. Not ever, I realise. That's my seafaring days done now. Ashore for good now, Becca. Then I bundle my old rig up, with its lice and stains and rips, and follow the smell of lye to a street where steam comes out of the windows and there are suds in the gully.

The laundry girl looks me up and down, gives the ragged end of my kerchief a quick tug. 'You'll want that washing, too.'

She's a woman like any other, but to me that's everything. I can't help but stare, she fills my eyes, replenishes something deep inside. She's miraculous. All wide eyes and shifting shoulders. I watch her breasts topple softly inside her chemise. Her hair is like spun moss, beaded with moisture, damp tendrils cling to her neck.

She arches her back a little more. I smile back. I hold her gaze until she glances away. Oh, the thrill of it, the moment, I could have her. The knowledge goes straight to my nub and sets it throbbing. My knees swim.

'No,' I say. I see her face fall and know the sinking of her heart as if it were my own. 'No,' I say again, more gently. 'Take the rest of my rig. The kerchief I will wash myself.'

Next morning it's market day as I straddle

my way down the pavements of Fore Street, struggling still to keep my balance. Gentlefolk from all about are out in force. What a fine and thrusting set of merchants and traders Ipswich can boast. How ridiculous they look, to my sea-trained eye, like actors in a play. Rotund men in extraordinary wigs. Gaggles of lady wives whose hoops fair sweep the goods from the stalls. The women trumpet like geese on their way to market, the men strut among them like cockerels. And you thought Ipswich a superior sort of place. Only the naval officers brought any distinction to the streets of Harwich, you said, their balls and gatherings its sole redeeming feature. There's no navyard here, only tanneries, grain warehouses and ropewalks. No navy boys.

I stop dead then. I look down at my new shoes with their conspicuous buckles, my creaking white trowsers. I was grown so proud of the tar I had fought to become. I wanted to look my finest for you. Thought only of that. And made myself a target even a mewling midshipman could spot.

And worse recklessness, what sort of fool heads straight back to the naval port from where he was taken, where the ships and quays and streets swarm with men on the lookout for a bounty? For all I know Cathcart's ships are wallowing back up the channel this moment, their yards only half-manned and most of their crews dead of fever and worse. Ain't His Majesty's Navy desperate still to round up any man with so much of a hint of a rolling gait, let alone a spanking new rig and a jaunty straw hat. Won't Harwich jump with joy when they find they have Luke Fletcher, pressed man, and deserter, murderer, who has smashed open an officer's skull. They'll be anxious to make an example of him. Should they flog him, or hang him, or send him straight back out to sea?

But I have been travelling so long to get back to you. And you are so close. I remember the open channel of West Street, that squirrel stair that rises to our own nest. So swift and silent we might go. No one need spy us.

Up and down Ipswich quay I pace, until I find a likely-looking lighter, due to sail with the tide for Walton but yes, they'll stop off at Harwich. All it takes is a flash of a coin or two.

'Keen, ain't you?' says the grinning tiller-man, and I know then I offered too much. 'What's Harwich got that Ipswich ain't?'

It's still several hours to high tide so I fill my belly. I order new boiled ham and oysters, fresh butter, warm soft bread, all that I dreamt of at sea. But I find I have little appetite.

The tillerman comes in for a last drink. He's smiling still, gazing at me with gusto as though he's found himself a new drinking mate.

'Edward Trey,' he says jauntily and sticks out his hand. I shake it firmly, don't reply. I try to remember: is he one of the Trey boys my mother talked of? He won't know me, he can't, but he'll know of the Fletchers all right.

'Albert,' I say. 'Call me Albert.'

He's an easy-going lad, don't take offence. He's used to sailors and their secrets. But I search for something to say, to keep him sweet.

'I'm after work on the packets.'

'Aren't we all. Don't know as there's any to be had, mind.'

'Trade not good?' I say, by way of making conversation. And then, because I can't help myself: 'I hear the *Dolphin* is the one to try for.'

Trey raises his eyebrows. 'Handley? I'd hold off there. Had a bit of a run-in with customs, so he did. Right old stink. Come on, I'll help you with your trunk.'

He talks on as we board the lighter, wedge

my trunk in the bows. The black water slaps hard at the quay. 'Try the *Dispatch,* I would.'

'Don't the *Dolphin* still run?' I ask casually. But I'm thinking: if your father could not buy his way out of trouble once more, then what of you?

Trey sucks his teeth, prepares to cast off. 'Not a chance, mate. Handley's finished on this coast. Closed up that fancy house of his, too.'

'Closed up the house?' I repeat dully. A driving rain is coming on, smearing the lights of the town.

'That's right. Have a hold of this, would you? Blasted lantern's always on the blink.' He sits down and fiddles with the catch.

Do I ask him? Do I speak your name?

But Trey has hit his stride. 'Aye. Left in such a damned hurry he forgot one of his own daughters. Mind you, sisters, eh? Fight like cats in a bag. I got twin girls meself. Glad to be out the house.'

I'm holding the aft mooring so tight I feel the fibres squeal.

'Make room for someone else, that's what I says. Packet trade's overcrowded as it is. Wouldn't mind a stab at it myself, if I had the capital. Capital, see, it's all down to capital. Got any capital?'

'Trey,' I say slowly. 'Do you know which

563

sister he left?'

'Why, the little minx of course.' He laughs, fixes the lantern back on the mast. 'Fancy your chances do you? Right old gilflurt, I hear. Well, you're out of luck. My wife says as she's all set up here, married that bastard Francis Copdock.'

I tell Trey he can keep my money but he's grumbling still as he casts off again, says he'll likely miss the tide now. He gives me a hard blue stare as he eases her out. I heft my trunk up away from the quay as far as I can go, as far as the Spread Eagle, and there I sink down in the alley, put my arms about my trunk and sob my heart out. I near as vomit up the beer and bread and oysters curdling in my guts.

Next morning I'm out looking, asking. Amazing what a natty young tar can get out of shore folk with a nod and an easy smile. Francis Copdock. Oh yes. Owns a number of tanneries, has shares in half a dozen traders, lives in that great five-bayed house up by the Buttermarket when he's in town. Not the finest merchant in this town of merchants, not by any means. Not the richest, nor the grandest. But he's got a reputation all right. Everyone knows Francis Copdock.

Goes through wives like a hot knife

through butter, that's why. Wears them out, the slimy sod. Had three already, last one died in childbirth, shipped the little ones off to his sister at Belstead. Still, should see the females make up to him, for all that he's got a belly on him like a banged-up nanny goat. Wider than he's tall, that one. Comfy berth though, yes indeed. Two bastards that is public knowledge, who can say? You got a sister you keep her out of his sight. He'll bang her up and pox her good soon as look at her.

Happy to talk, these Ipswich folk, with a hot rum to nurse, on a drizzling grey day when it feels as if winter's going to go on for ever. I nod, and I smile, but they all sound as if they're talking through a fog. Every word is sharp, though, so sharp it hurts. I store it all away, hold each thought as carefully as a blade.

Finally I have to say her name. And even though I knew it must be her, it still hurts when they repeat it back. Miss Rebecca Handley? They frown. Shame, isn't it? Must have been a good-looking girl. Still, he'd never have had a chance otherwise, would he?

There are three churches behind the quays. Three square flint towers, looming over all the massive red tile roofs and Dutch gables like landlocked masts. And the bells of all of them are pealing out: three in a row, fast and high, one low and droning, the rest joining in a crushing, insistent assault as though god's calling the whole rotten town to account.

I start with St Peter's at the harbour bridge, stand by the font for a full half hour, watching the fine folk process in. They don't come.

Then St Mary-at-Quay, a little further along, but I never even go inside the door: the ground about is swampy, the stones swayed and the congregation sad and sickly and unpromising. No fine merchant and his wife would worship here. I stand alone in the street, I can hear the drone of the sermon inside, the streets have emptied, everyone's at church. But which church? There's only one more where the sea merchants go.

I run all the way back to Fore Street. The bells have long stopped tolling but St Clement's isn't hard to spot, bigger than the other two put together, huge and solid as a ship of the line. There's a sharp ferrous stink in the air, like brimstone. Bright yellow daffodils prance inside the boundary wall. I slip inside the gate. There are crowds and crowds of them, all got up in fur muffs and velvet hoods, clean white stockings and heavy capes. This must be the place. And there, among all the gentlemen, the merchants and ladies and children, standing at the side of an older woman, I see you at last.

Your head is drooping, your shoulders slumped, your blue dress is quite nondescript. Your face is covered by a veil. But I would know you anywhere.

And then, as I watch, a man approaches. A short man, with a wide hard belly, and dwarfed by his hat. The older woman steps aside, simpering, curtsies even. You stand motionless a moment, quite alone. You seem to be gathering your strength. I do not see you meet his eye. You incline your head and you hold out your hand. He steps up smartly and clamps your hand to your side, under his arm. I watch him doff his ridiculous hat to your companion and lead you away through the crowd. Mrs Francis Copdock.

Chapter Forty-Four

I could have called out then. Hailed you fondly from across the churchyard, with a raised hand and an open smile. You would have found your dear long-lost friend in the crowd and raised your hand also, coming up a little on your toes, your eyes brightening. We would have kissed each other's cheeks and walked away arm in arm, heads bent, conversing closely. Talked for hours, sat by the fire, or tucked up in a window seat.

I could have stopped a few gallant paces from you and removed my hat with a flourish, bowing deep and smartly. You would have lowered your head, but I would still see your smile. I would have uttered some refined commonplace, and offered my arm. Thrilled to the light touch of your fingers, the nearness of your scarcely veiled bosom. Remarked on the fineness of your gown. Then I would have called on you, enthralled you for hours with my tales of travel while our chaperone sat silent by.

Even now, I could have swung out to block your path with my tattooed arm and bellow some sentimental sweetheart ditty. Had the deep shameful gratification of seeing you clutch up your skirts, avert your head, as my shipmates shower us both with laughter. Snuffed up your ladylike scent, lusted after that soft and yielding flesh within its genteel carapace, all a-quiver at my insolence. How gratifying would have been your angered stare, your hot retort. The sweet, pulsing pause while you bid me let you by, the perturbed swish of your skirts. And then, the long lingering view of your figure, retreating until you were lost in the crowds but stored away for ever in my mind's gallery of most desirable females.

I was all of these — your intimate friend, your gallant wooer, your street admirer. And yet I was none of these. I could do as none of these did.

I followed you to your house. I saw Copdock open the wide old door himself and escort you inside. I went round to the back and saw there was a long garden but no gate in the wall. I went back and waited across the street, smoked pipe after pipe and the drizzle came on. I was glad of my watchcoat. About three o'clock by all the bells the sun came out again and I was watching the birds skit about the puddles when the door creaked open. You lifted your skirts and walked rapidly up the street, away from the harbour. I followed you, through a gate and into a garden and then I lost sight of you behind an outbuilding. I opened another gate and was in an orchard. Still I could not see you.

Then you came, walking back towards me straight down a narrow muddy path between the rows of bony trees. Nothing was in bud yet. You were deep in thought, walking alone still, your hands thrust inside your muff. You did not look up until I was fewer than twenty paces distance.

What did you see? I wonder. A common young sailor in his finest shore-going rig, rolling a little as he went, as they all did, and sucking on his pipe. Your heart sank a little, I'm sure. No doubt the lad will accost you in this solitary place, he looks the type, young and cocky.

At ten paces I slowed. I removed my hat, but I did not bow or move aside. You clasped your muff closer and your lips tightened. A little of your old hauteur returned, your eyebrows began to raise. The old Becca would have put this forward boy in his place with a single flashing glance, and both enjoyed it too. But your eyes were dull now. I could see how weary you had become, of delay and disappointment and insurmountable obstacles. You lowered your gaze. I thought I heard you sigh. You would not look at me. You would walk by without a word.

Closer you came, and closer, until you were only a couple of paces from me. I set one leg akimbo and sucked hard on my pipe, fixed you with an appraising stare, the very picture of a fired-up young tar fresh ashore.

Dull, flickering anger first, then a kind of mute puzzlement. You were pricked to curiosity, to intrigue, then disbelief. You looked quickly away, then back again, as though your eyes were tricking you.

I wanted so badly to speak then, to say your name, to make myself known. But I could not. All of a sudden it seemed important that you see me for yourself or not at all. After all, how could I say who I was? I was not your young Lou no more. Certain I was no longer the boy you had known all those months ago.

So I did not speak. But I could not stop myself touching your red kerchief, all softened and faded now. Despite all the starching, its two twirled ends would droop a little. You did not even glance at it.

'Let me pass,' you said impatiently and I heard your voice was not changed at all, so full and rich and penetrating I fancied the raindrops quivered on the branches.

I sucked on my pipe a moment more, and then before I knew what I was about I stooped to the ground to pick a snowdrop. As I held it out its heavy little head nodded wildly for my hands were trembling so.

You stepped back with a quick, disbelieving laugh, as though you thought the sentimental gesture quite pathetic.

'You looked sad, miss,' I said soft as I could, though the words came out hoarse and strange. 'I thought to cheer you.'

Again you looked at me, more closely this time; still you did not see me. Your expression lightened a little. 'Cheer me?' you said then, and I heard it in your voice, something of the flirt you had always been, buried deep, but still there. You glanced about us. We were all alone on that path, among the trees, there was no one to see. So you reached out to take the flower and as our fingers touched I said in a great tearful rush, as I had said once before: 'You are beautiful to me.'

I saw the blood leave your cheeks and lips,

you were as white as the flower.

'No,' you said in a great, shuddering breath, 'no!' And your face crumpled, your eyes widened, your mouth fell open, in utter dismay.

I caught up your hands eagerly, hardly daring to press your soft flesh. You only gazed at my fingers, that were thickened and rough, the blackened thumbnail and the grazed knuckles. You looked for my hair that was pulled back tight and tarred into a neat little cue. You scanned my face slowly, looking from my bleached eyebrows to my tanned cheek and my scarred brow, and at my mouth that was chapped and finally into my eyes.

You shook your head, slowly. But you did not pull away. And so I had to kiss you, take your head in my hands and take you to me, kiss you full on the mouth as I had been dreaming of all this time, your soft, warm little kittenish mouth. And your lips were softer and sweeter than ever I had imagined, your teeth smoother, the bones of your chin and the shape of your neck finer.

I wrapped my arms about you, feeling my watchcoat knock against your hoops. Then I was blind to everything but the touch of your flesh, the press of your bosom and I buried my face in your neck, the sugary scent of your skin. I wanted to take you then and there, let you down upon the damp ground and lift your skirts and strike about you, lose myself, forget everything, be as we were.

But you were pushing against me, twisting your head about. When I did not let go, you aimed a sharp kick hard at my shin. We broke apart and I stood, gasping, like a landed fish. You straightened your bonnet, put your hands on your hips and gazed at me, your bosom heaving. How fierce brown your eyes are, I thought. I saw the little white scars stand out livid against the red flush of your cheeks. You wiped your mouth, swallowed.

Then there came, like a trickle of cold water on the neck, the thought that perhaps you were not pleased to see me thus, to see me at all, despite your fervent kisses, your arms that had clutched about my back. That I had been too long away. That I had lost your heart. I held my breath.

'Well,' you said finally, your voice as stern as ever, 'And I had thought Ipswich a dull place after all.'

But your eyes were dancing.

CHAPTER FORTY-FIVE

We saw a little church on the rise, with a thatched roof, curled up cosy as a sleeping cat. It seemed a good sign. Oh, I've had enough of adventure, I told myself then. I just wanted us to be safe, you see. Safe and hidden and together and alone.

I paid off the cart and took down my trunk, shouldered your bundle. We walked up through the dripping trees past several houses and barns, and there was an inn, but it was nothing like the heaving tar taverns I knew. It was a low-eaved cottage, plastered a dull, mottled pink, with a steep tiled roof. Inside was one small room, quite dark and silent, and the fire banked right down. We heard voices out the back, a little girl chattering. She came through at the sound of the door, a mewsy-faced little thing carrying a light and swinging a dead mouse by the tail. She wrinkled her nose.

'That's five today. Shouldn't think there

none more left, where is he, the greedy bugger?'

Then a woman hurried through and took the light from her to look us up and down. She was short and beady-eyed, her skin shiny and dark. 'Good evenin't'ye,' she said straight off, cocking her head like a bird. 'Reckon you'll be needing a fire.'

As you peeled off your cloak I could see those beady eyes assessing the crumpled lace at your neck, the fine weave of your skirt. You kept your left hand from her. I'd full forgot this was how women looked at one another, combed each other over for signs like an animal looking for ticks. Then she turned her eyes on me, and it was all I could do not to hang my head.

She spoke to you, not me. 'Give over them slippers, why don't you,' she said, and she wiped them dry with her apron and hung them on a nail above the fire.

The woman Sarah showed us a room in the eaves, airy and clean. It was cold, and the linen was yellowed and damp, but had barely been slept in. We were together, that was all that mattered.

'Aw look at you now,' Sarah said gleefully. She had turned before I could slip my arm from around your waist. 'Not long married then, eh?'

You smiled encouragingly, said some light, female thing. Sarah giggled, seeming pleased as though we were her own kin.

I told her I was retired from sailoring and she laughed.

'Bit young, ain't you?'

I blushed and she reached over to squeeze my arm hard.

'Sensible lad. Wish my man had stayed home. Wouldn't be working my fingers to the bone here else, now would I? Gone and drowned himself off Newfoundland, foolish bugger.' She turned to you. 'You keep a tight hold of this fine lad.'

She didn't ask any questions, was more than happy to take my money for as she could well tell we had plenty. We had her best room, were her only guests.

The rain trickled through the casement where the latch was loose. I hung my coat over the back of the chair and went to fix it. All of a sudden I thought of our attic nest. I looked at the whitewashed walls, chill and blank as the canvas dividers aboard ship, and remembered the girls and the strange fruit painted inside that sea chest, how they had danced in the lantern light. But this is my room, I thought. A solid room with a window and four sturdy walls and I paid for it with my own coin. And this is my bed.

I pushed my trunk up against the door. I remember looking at you then, your hair damp and dark on your forehead, your skin fresh and still speckled with rain, and thinking: this cannot be true, you are not really here with me again. I had to put my hands to your cheeks, my lips to your lips, my hips to yours. And I steadied one hand against the wall by your head, leaned into you, as I rucked up your skirts and searched with my hand and found you at last.

It was all new again. You were very different, much diminished. I felt it when I lifted you and afterwards I saw it too, when you lay alongside me and I stroked my hand along your side, polishing the turn of your shoulder, your hip. The heft of your flesh, that I had so loved, was melted away again. You were lighter, almost frail, as you had been after you were ill. But you were not fragile, or timid. You arched beneath me, let me do what I would, closed your eyes and gave me everything. This was not play any more. It wasn't even delight. It was more urgent than that, more desperate. What was it?

Or was it I who was different? Did you feel so insubstantial, so pliable now, simply because I was stronger, bigger, braver? I rucked up your skirts with one hand like I was furling a sail, unpicked the knots of your laces with my eyes closed, turned and rolled you as easy as any barrel. We were both back where we belonged.

Everywhere I had dreamt of, you let me go, everything I would do, you let me do. But when you reached for my nub, though my thighs ran as wet as the streaming casement window, I nudged your hand away with my hip, just as Albert had done. When your fingers closed about his horn instead and you gasped I let you touch it a while but I would not use it. It was instinct, I could not help myself. It would have been wrong somehow. This was what I wanted now, to ride you like the ocean, to rig you and align you while the sheet billowed about our ears.

'I am thirsty,' you said when you woke, and for that one brief moment I was your maid once more, stirring sleepily to fetch for you, feeling guilty that I had not anticipated. I was halfway to the door, peering about for something to cover me for once I had left the bed the room was freezing. It was dark night already, but there was a little light from somewhere outside.

'Lou?' you said anxiously, pushing the hair from your eyes.

I stood very still, naked, shivering, at your command always. You could not see me, I was just a formless shape in the darkness. But I could not answer to that name. How did you not know that?

'Lou?' Your voice was cracked, hoarse even.

It seemed a long while before I could reply.

'I'll find us something,' I said.

I took the tray up myself, and set it down by the bed. I had found a lantern, and hung it from a beam. I needed light now. I could feel myself moving stiffly as I sat down on the bed, my face quite hardened as I poured out the pot of beer, and carved at the loaf with the blunt, inadequate little knife. I could not look at you.

For this was the moment, now that we were together again, had lain together, loved again. This was the moment I would have to woo you. Not that day long ago, the day of Henry and Hester, and the men who threw their beer over us, the day we had clutched each other in the attic, both overflowing with the injustice of it all and needing only to blot it out. Would you really have gone away with me that day, with no real idea of where we would go, what we would do, who we would be? Did I persuade you of anything at all? I had never known. I had taken you, as well as I could, hoping to make you see the realness of us; then we had slept, and then I was gone.

Could I ask you again, now, knowing what it took, what it would take?

But first we talked of other things. The bread in your hand never reached your mouth. You asked the most urgent question first, most urgent and hardest to say. But then, you never shrank from anything, did you?

'What happened to you? Where did you go? Why? Why did you not come back?'

I watched your eyes fill with tears, and felt sick with grief and guilt.

Should I have told you then? That indeed I had left your side of my own volition, that I braved the streets because some ugly old tar I had never met before told me I could find my feckless lost brother at the most notorious tavern in town? That I had left you alone and gone chasing after this figment through the dark streets, at the height of the harvest fair, the hot press, alone and abroad in my borrowed rig? That I had gone because — could I admit this, even to myself? — in that moment simply to lie with you had been not enough. I had to know who I was, find my compass, and my only sea mark had been my brother. And even when I knew he would not come — because I knew now he could never come — I had lingered on in that noisome place, drunk deep and sung out, and stayed there, stayed on because — and this I could not deny — because I had found something. Though I had not found my brother, he had led me to where I must be. And something had swung about, deep inside me.

But as I faced you that night in our own room, your hair about your face and your eyes bright with tears, saw how real you were at last after so many months of dreaming, I could not honestly recall how it had felt, how urgent that need had been. I could not tell you, any of it. It felt like a dream itself.

Should I have told you, then, what that old man Melcher had told me: that the reason my brother was stolen away, the cause of all my mother's tears, had been your own father, his mendacity and greed? That indeed I had only come to your home at all because of his guilt over how he had betrayed that long-lost brother of mine? Even, that he had brought me to you as a sort of penance to my mother. That he had betrayed her too, long before he betrayed you.

And then all that happened aboard the *Essex,* and on the island. What I had done, and what I had seen? Should I have told you that I did find a brother, of sorts, after all?

I could not have begun to make you understand. What good is the truth, I thought, when there are so many secrets already? I have survived it all, and I have found you again, that must be enough.

I told you only what I could recall of that night. It had taken so long to remember, I explained, and even now I was not quite clear in my head. 'They must have hit me here,' I said, touching the back of my head, where the scar was hairless still. 'I lost my senses for a while, and it must have addled my wits even longer for I recalled nothing, for days and days.'

'Who?' you said, all concerned and impatient at once, 'who hit you?'

I had to think hard to recall the sequence of the thing. 'I went down to the tavern,' I said. 'You were sleeping and I was thirsty.'

You grimaced, raised your tumbler.

'And I thought to myself, damn it, why not? How many hours had I spent in that room and never once ventured down and shown my face? If we are to do this, I said to myself, I shall start now. I shall roll on down there, a young tar banging in after taking a piss in the back yard. I'll pitch up at the counter to quest a pitcher to share. Hand over my coin, wink at the girl and back up again in the time it takes to light a pipe.' I feel a pain in my chest as it comes back to me: that lightness, that optimism, that cockiness.

'So I dressed ever so careful: put your kerchief about my neck.' I touched it now, limp and soft against my collarbone. 'Cued back my hair and plaited it, lashed it up. Pulled the Monmouth down low over my eyes. I think I even frowned into the window glass, drew my brows together, like this.'

You would not laugh. I don't know why I even wanted to see you smile if not simply that you looked so serious, so vulnerable. But this I did want you to understand: that it had still felt like a game to me then. A game that was easy to play, that we were bound to win. I had even bothered to tie my purse about my neck, like the sailors do so they do not lose it. Slung the prick of baccy over my shoulder and smiled at my own reflection in the little window. A complete costume. All I needed was a stage, to make my first entrance.

'The place was heaving, I had to press myself between an old porpoise and his woman even to get to the counter. They were scarce capable of seeing each other let alone me. I bought a jar of Canary, and was jostled so I thought I should sip some rather than spill it. And then a girl held up her can —'

'A girl?' you broke in harshly.

I had to laugh. 'Yes, a girl, but listen. So just to act the part I filled her can and then the songs started up again and she was watching me so I joined in. Hadn't we heard them so many times through the floor? I didn't even stumble.'

Now I remembered the words I had bellowed along with the rest.

'It was one morning, in the spring,' I had sung.

'I went on board, to serve the King.

'I left my dearest dear behind,

'Who oft times told me, her heart was mine.'

And I remembered too, with a terrible pang, what I had seen when I had closed my eyes, the clear vision I had conjured up for ourselves of the cottage, the sweet grass, the feel of your fingers in mine. Before I went on, I took up your hand again, to anchor myself.

'But then, it didn't seem any time at all, there was some sort of ruckus up the front, shouting and stools falling about. They had come, you see.'

'The hot press,' you supplied, grimly. 'I think I knew. But I could not allow myself to —' You paused, stared at me, 'I did not imagine for a moment that you would have gone down on your own, without telling me. I didn't once think what a hot-headed fool of a —'

You stopped, then, pressed your fingers between your eyebrows. Now you were remembering, and it was no easier for you.

'When I woke it was still dark,' you said, as if to yourself, your eyes still closed. 'I was quite puzzled when I found you were gone. Cross even. How could you leave me, after all that had happened that day? Where could you have gone? It was the middle of the night, but I could hear the fair still. I went back through the attic to the house. Everyone seemed to be asleep. I went to my room but you were not there. I waited for you. I even crept up to your room, Hannah was sleeping and your bunk was empty. I could not wake her, or Hester, and ask if either had seen you. I went back to bed, and waited some more. In the morning Hannah knocked at the door, said you were nowhere to be found.' You put your hands to your face again, covered your eyes. 'And by then it was too late, wasn't it?'

I remembered you at your dressing table after you had the pox, covering your eyes to blot out what you most dreaded.

'I went out looking for you and when I came to the Three Squirrels I saw the windows broken and some of the tables too. I thought it just the usual trouble at harvest time. But that's when I really worried. All sorts can happen to a girl in Harwich. So then I went looking for your sister.'

I sat upright then, full of alarm.

'You think I didn't know?' you said.

'I tried so hard not to let you —'

'Why on earth?'

'I thought you would not allow me to remain your maid. It would not be respectable —'

'Respectable! Every woman is a whore, had you not realised that? It's only a matter of degree. I whored myself for Henry, right enough. Your sister was a sight more successful. I found her eventually. Turned out Hannah knew where to find her all along. But Susie had no more idea than I where you might be. We thought perhaps you had headed up to London alone.'

'Run away? I would never have left you, never.'

You smiled at me then, stroked the scar over my left brow. 'I know, I know that now.'

'They hit me on the head before I knew it. I woke on a tender, we were in cuffs, and then we were out at sea.' I could not begin to tell you how it had been. 'At Spithead, and then St Helen's, and then — But I came back, Becca. I love you so, Becca. I had to come back to you.'

And then I did what I had planned to do that last night, when I had returned with the jug of wine to quench your thirst. It was to be our libation. First, though, I had to take that ring of Copdock's and throw it under the bed. I did it swiftly, roughly even, I could not look at it a moment longer. I glanced at your face after I did it, looked into your dark, wet eyes. You nodded. Then I took up both your hands and kissed them. I took off another of your rings and turned it about so the stone did not show and pressed it on to the ring finger of your left hand. I kissed it. Took a breath.

'See, Becca? We're married now. You forget him.' I could not say Copdock's name. 'I don't want to know anything about him. Forget him. You will be my wife always. I'll give you my name. Mrs Luke Fletcher. How fine is that? I, Luke Fletcher, do take this woman good and proper —'

'Luke Fletcher,' you said slowly. My heart turned over then. This was how you would say your new husband's name when we talked with neighbours and friends. I am Mrs Fletcher, and this is my wedded husband, Luke.

You tried to smile. But you cried then, properly. Cried as I'd never seen you cry before.

'I'm sorry,' you said between sobs. 'I'm so sorry for what I did. I thought you dead and gone. I thought I would never be happy again. But I would have waited, I swear. I did not care for Henry one jot, you know that. Hester is welcome to him. I would have sat there alone in my father's house and I would have waited for you. But then they came for my father. He had had trouble before, but this time — I don't know what happened — he could not buy them off.'

They had found contraband everywhere. They searched the *Dolphin*. They searched the house and they opened up the tunnels. They even went through the attic. No one would call on the Handleys, or receive them. Henry went back to sea and Hester up to London to Aunt Tabitha's. Eventually your father went to the farm to broker with his brother. You paused.

Your uncle's farm. Where my mother had taken us all to keep us safe, where she lay yet in her bed without either of her girls by her side.

I knew. As soon as I saw your face change I knew.

I made you tell me. How he gone to her sickbed and offered his help. Those receipts of Peter's. But she had struck out at his face. Sent him away. Then called him straight back. Asked for news of her children, any one of her three lost children. And he had no answer to give her.

Now she will never know. And there is no way back.

You stroked my hair, held my head, cradled me to you. The lantern burnt right down. I lay with my head in your lap. Eventually, just as the birds began to sing, you spoke again.

'While Dadda was away, that was when Copdock came calling. The whole coast knew my father was finished. And Copdock can smell a bargain, just like my father.' You paused. 'Lou?'

When I still did not answer, you lay down beside me. 'Lou, don't you see —'

'Luke,' I said quietly. 'My name is Luke.'

I kissed you hard, before you could speak, again, and again. I held you tight. I made you mine. No, Copdock didn't matter, none of it mattered, because your husband was here and could comfort you. Yes, Luke's kisses, my caresses, that was what you wanted, all you needed. You had craved my touch as much as I craved yours, and how glad I was to know it. I had given you my name. We would be each other's family now.

'You'll stay with me then?' I asked quickly, when I had wiped the last of your tears away, not daring to think that you might refuse me now, after all that had happened. I told you my dream again, the dream of the cottage and the green grass and the milking cow. I hoped it did not sound foolish to you this time. We would hide ourselves away, where the land was fertile and good, and live only for each other.

I watched your face. I had no sense at all which way you were turning. But you did in the end, you turned to me, lay alongside me. You nodded then, and you smiled, you could not speak.

And quickly again, to make you smile, before you could change your mind, I told you of my adventures. I made it sound so fine. About the sweet fruit of the island, the kind minister, about my fine work with a sailor's needle and the favours it earned me, and the dancing below deck on a Saturday night. 'You should have seen me!' I said, and scrabbled to the floor.

'I was tall and I was slim,' I cried, putting my hands above my head in the dim dawn light,

'and I had a leg for every limb!'

I capered so hard you had to laugh.

There were so many things I could not tell you.

I was too happy. I told you only how I had longed for you, dreamt of you. I kept fingering your clothes, smoothing your skin, stroking your hair to see how real you were. How warm and soft and clean. It was as though all the time that had passed was forgotten, almost as though no time passed at all. That we were close again as we were before.

You looked hard at me too now. Looked at your Luke. You felt my roughened cheeks, and my calloused palms. My hair that was frayed by sea water, and had tar in it to keep it from my eyes. You touched the scar on my brow, from that time in the orlop. Told me that my eyes you had remembered grey, were blue, a deep blue. You ran your hands over the new solid muscle in my shoulders and stomach and thighs. I could see how all this affected you, you could not hide your lust, and I was glad.

When you saw the tattoo, you rubbed at it, peered with an appalled fascination.

'What's this?'

It was the Handley swan, I told you, that had swum across all our butter pats, that had dissolved that first night in your house when I left my bundle by the fire in the hallway. It was to remember you by.

I did not tell you of the times I had put my hand to it and felt myself to be some such creature: all power and art aloft, gliding high up in the yards, but awkward ashore, rolling and ungainly on his feet, a fleet land bird no more.

I would find my land legs again. You would anchor me for good this time. For I was come back now, I told you. We would build another nest together. And swans, they mate for life, don't they?

How many days we kept to our room I have no idea. But when finally we ventured downstair, legs a little weak, hand in hand, I had to laugh. The inglenook was hung with rigid lengths of smoked eels, bronzed and pungent, strung through the gills on a kicklin string. The ground beyond the threshold was sandy yellow, the sky big and wide, and just over the rise, behind the church and the wind-bent trees, was a strip of sandy beach.

It was not the open sea. No, it was just a finger of her, snuck inland as far as she could go, and we had found the narrow tight notch where she could go no further. Where she slackened and the marshes took away all her force.

Still, it set me all wrong again for a while. I went back to our room and shut the door. You asked the name of the place, where was upriver, where down, how far was the sea and swore to me we would be safe. We had picked up that cart by the orchard out behind Tavern Street, where you had never seen another soul. The carter had not seen you come from Copdock's house, had waited for me and my trunk streets away from the Spread Eagle. I had paid him to take us far north of Woodbridge, distant from any town, well away from any port. We had been clever enough, you assured me. No one had even seen you go. Certain no one knew you here. No one would find us.

I knocked out the last of my pipe and watched the ash fall on to the bare earth of the yard below. There was only the sound of the river birds and the wind in the reeds. There was light still in the distance but the land was coal dark. I pulled in my head and latched the window and came to sit alongside you on our bed.

'It's so quiet,' you said eventually. 'No one bothers us, do they? We should stay.'

I turned. 'Here?'

'I like it. Sarah's all right.' You brushed off your skirt, snuggled in closer. 'No one to look at me. Even Ipswich folk was too critical. If I'm not to be beautiful then —'

'You are beautiful to me,' I broke in without thinking and you laughed. It had become our little joke by then.

'I know, Luke, I know. I'm the most beautiful woman for miles.'

It was true, though. There was no one to compare to you. Sarah had a face like a shrivelled berry, even at eight her daughter Emily was bent and awkward. The only other women we'd glimpsed were farm women, field women, all screwed-up eyes and rindy lips, like my mother. I should never see her again, I thought suddenly. She never knew what became of me, nor my brother.

'Don't look so solemn, Luke.' You were playing with my hand, splaying out my sea-swollen fingers like cards. It distracted my thoughts completely. I loved your touch, could never get enough of it.

'I'll never stop being vain, I know,' you said. 'But allow me some weaknesses.'

I swallowed hard. I tried to match my tone to yours: gently mocking. 'No hot baths here, you know. No chocolate.' I hardly dared remind you of what Captain Handley had given you and Henry Wilmington had promised you and Francis Copdock had ordered without a qualm. These were small things, I knew, but they had been your whole life. And the finer living of London, your entire aim and direction. I had not wanted to remind you of what you were leaving behind, for fear you would lose heart. I had kissed and fondled you, knowing at last my power over you, and hoping to ravish you into forgetting everyone and everything but me. Now, if you thought too hard about this, you might go straight back. But please, not to Copdock. Still, I had to be sure. 'No papers from London,' I went on relentlessly. 'No masques —'

'Heavens!' You put your fingers over my mouth. 'Luke, don't you see? I would never have made a gentleman's wife, whether the small pox had ruined me or not. Don't you see, I had to play the fine lady, first to snare Henry, then to impress you. And yes, to best my damned sister. Well now.'

And you kissed me hard, on the mouth. Your lips nipped mine, your tongue pushed between my teeth. You pulled back to watch my expression.

'You see?' you said simply. 'That man Copdock was good for one thing only. No!'

— you said hurriedly, when you saw my face change — 'If I hadn't known what I had lost when I lost you, by god I knew it after I married him.' You kissed me. 'I cannot tell you —'

'You will not tell me —'

'Don't be angry, listen to me. That man would have killed me within the year had you not come. He will not send after me. I know him. He will shrug his shoulders and find himself an easier lay. Why, he's gone through three wives already, one more won't bother him. No, he was good for one thing only.' And you jumped up to rummage in your bundle for a small bulging skin bag. You smiled as it grated and clinked. 'And I only took what he gifted me. If I simply cannot resist the lure of chocolate, why then, I shall send to London myself!'

But you realised your mistake immediately, and lay the bag down on the boards out of sight. 'Luke, please, please don't be angry. Of course I shall never touch a piece of it. I am yours now, entire. My Luke Fletcher, my dear husband. What else do I need?' You kissed me. 'Where else should I be?' You kissed me again. 'My Luke Fletcher! Who else do I need?'

Your tone was always so mocking, so stern. I'd learned to disavow it. But when I

looked into your eyes I could see the Becca
I first knew flaring there still. You had always
known your own mind. And if you knew me
to be enough then that was how it would
be. But I would keep you.

I kissed you back, felt your arms go about
my shoulders, clutch at my neck.

'Let us stay here, Luke.'

I pulled the wet tip of a curl away from
your lips, gentle as I could.

'Quite sure?' I said.

Now you were serious. 'Yes. Oh yes.'

CHAPTER FORTY-SIX

So we stayed on at the Anchor. I found work at a brickyard, that had a strong order on for a new kiln up at Snape. And we grew domestic so quick it made me laugh. Sarah was glad to let us the tiny one-room cottage behind the stable, which we could well afford now on my sea earnings and what the Rutters were paying me.

I watched your face that first day there, for there was not much to it. Sarah had very little to set us up and I would not have you send to town. But I cleaned it out good and proper, shipshape. Our bed was straw and blankets, we had a stool and a borrowed poker. I made us a broom, and braided baskets, a reed rug for your feet before the fire. I stuffed my ditty bag to make a bolster. There were nails enough in the beams and I knotted bags to keep our stuffs up and away from the vermin.

Properly alone, together at last, I sat you

down at the hearth and taught you all I knew about setting a fire, keeping a kettle on the go. You giggled, but you listened. Now it was you who were up before me in the morning, to bring me something hot before I rowed across to the yard. I couldn't quite believe it. When I came back the fire would be smoking and you'd be dozing on the bed with Sarah's cat on your lap, but when you heard the latch you'd jump up and come to the threshold to kiss me.

'Don't I make a terrible wife,' you'd say.

'What a fraud you are, Becca.'

'I'll tell on you too, Luke.'

It was a matter of weeks before I was doing it all again — the cooking and the cleaning — and I didn't mind a bit. I put on a tidy pot of pork and greens before I went out in the mornings, polished the kettle up with spit and a rag and sat up to strip the soiled lace from your sleeves and wash it and set it aside. I wanted to be the one to keep you, why should you lift a finger? I could not believe my luck. You had come away with me. I had you in my bed, every night, that was reward enough.

I started asking around about getting some goats, maybe a pig to see us through the winter ahead. When the time was right, a milking cow. I dug out a patch, dug deep with my spade just as my mother had. It was all coming true, I thought, my dream from long ago: you and I, man and wife, in our own cottage, able to do as we pleased.

We had another summer, just like our first. No, not like that. I'd been so lost before, despite our happiness; the truth of everything was secret, hidden, even from me. This was more peaceful. This was real. And no one could take it from us.

True, some days, if the tides were right, men came from downriver and stopped off at the Anchor. But we kept indoors then, waited until the voices faded across the water. Yes, we knew ourselves safe at last, far from press gangs, from fathers and sisters and husbands, from prying eyes of all sorts. Early mornings we walked out into the fields and rejoiced in the open space all about us, the birds free above our heads.

One day we found a nesting swan, sitting on her huge mound of twigs and weed among the grasses at a turn in the riverbank. She hissed at us, watched us coldly with one eye until we backed away. After that we walked out that way every day, to see her, but kept our distance. We looked, but we never saw her mate.

We thought ourselves quite settled, a regular married couple. Even had the occasional quarrel, words just sharp enough and silences just long enough to make Sarah smile and squeeze your arm. We'd lie in bed early of an evening, and even on a dull day, when the sky was pigeon-grey and heavy with cloud, the trees rustling and dark, there was light all about. We moved slowly, quietly, as though not to disturb the dusk.

Over time, though, we grew careless. I let myself curl up small next to you, nuzzle into your shoulder. I could feel my face opening again — my eyes widen, my brow clear, my shoulders loosen. It grew so hot I pulled off my binding altogether once I was home. You salved my underarms, where the linen had chafed my skin, swabbed me with cold water from the well. We were gentle with each other again. Put our heads together and whispered like girls.

And sometimes, it is true, you took to tracing my scars with your finger, lightly. The one on my brow, at the back of my head, another puckering low on my left shoulder, and a gash on my left shin that would not heal. And then, because they made me sad too, and to cover my fear, I would exclaim: What, you would have me milk-smooth as that young sop Lou? I would pin down your wrists till you lay still. Tug down your bodice to trace all your own pox scars, tell you this hard life was making them worse for sure, see here, and here — damaged goods! damaged goods! And you would always pout, and laugh, and wriggle, in the end.

One day after work I lay curled about you on the bed, stripped to the waist, my head on your bare shoulder and my fingernails still rimmed with clay. I saw a figure block the doorway, the light streamed in around her waist like arrows. We lay rigid. 'Becca?' she called shrilly. It was Sarah's daughter Emily. When you did not reply she folded her arms and tutted to herself and went away.

No doubt she was blinded by the strong sun, would have had to stand there some minutes before she could make us out in the gloom, but still. I wore my bindings every day after that. I had the boys at the yard shave my head close, so the scars flared out white as my scalp. Made you swear to speak no more of our life in Harwich, even when we thought ourselves alone. And I began to watch Emily, and saw that she watched me. When I set down my cup her squinting dark eyes were upon me still. As I straightened from the fire she was there, one foot inside the threshold. 'Make yourself useful then,' I would say, and then regret it for she was there for good then, like my shadow. I would stumble over my words, unable to meet her unblinking gaze. Sarah laughed at her seeming devotion, so did you. That girl knows a good thing when she sees it, you giggled, thinks she'll have you off me one day.

I smiled, but I saw the danger. Even here, in this most isolated place, we must guard against being discovered above all else, against our own carelessness. There was no one near by us but women, but I knew how much women can see and not tell, at least until they decide to, and all for their own secret reasons. Though there was no one could betray us we might still betray ourselves. I had thought myself practised at this, so inured to deceit I need not make extra effort. Now I knew I must never let up. I held myself stiffly away from you again. I must stay alert, be wary of them both. And then there were outsiders. They were few enough here for sure, but who knew what they might have heard, or what they might see.

So, when I walked round to take my pipe by the tavern door and found a stranger sitting on my own bench, availing himself of the warm evening air, I was wary, guarded. At first.

I stood looking at him a moment. He wasn't just brown and hardy like all the men who passed through. He had a sheen upon him. His face was so rinded and worn away by the ocean winds that he might never have been a soft-cheeked child at all. He had the huge shoulders, the battered hands and bulging thighs of a thorough-going top-man. He must have sensed me there and when he turned his long gaze went right through me, that eye trained to scan the horizon. His beard was bleached with salt and thick over his mouth.

I bit down on my pipe and nodded curtly.

He said his name was George Gowing, and he had sailed out of St Catherine's in Brazil some months previous and was now on his way to see his mother up at Saxstead. 'Make it by nightfall tomorrow I reckon, if I ship out early.'

It gave me a strange feeling, to hear again a boom like that, come rolling out his barrel chest right across to the water. But I took my pipe from my mouth and stuck out my hand. When we gripped hands he grinned. He had found the sea in me too. I was so glad to see him, this stranger, from that other world, that I had to blink and screw up my eyes. I pumped his arm hard.

Then he made room on the bench and we

talked over our times. I told him I'd never made it to Brazil and so he started in with the tales. I watched him while he yawed on: it was the sea burnish on him, how he was weathered all over, how the sun had reflected off the water for long weeks and months and got into every part of him, under his chin, into his eye sockets. His teeth were very bad, he'd had the scurvy many times I could tell.

You came out the door and when you saw this huge man there next to me your carriage changed, you could not help it. You were always happier when evening came, when the light dimmed. And at that moment you were like the old Becca again: the raised chin, the direct gaze. I had quite forgotten how you rose to male company — any company — like a stroked cat. You awed me all over again in that moment. You came near and I forget too what you said to him but he stood up, blushing right up to the roots of his hair and not knowing where to look.

'Meet my wife,' I said, looking from one to the other of you.

He's the picture of your father, I realised then, that wagging beard, the height on him. He towered over me, just as the Captain had that morning in the dairy. And when you saw how things stood between us, that he was not come to take me away, you flirted with him just as you had with the Captain, and with any man you ever met.

Did he flirt with you back? Course he did. You were the first woman he'd seen in weeks and months. Damn, he even tried it with Sarah later, when she dragged up some stools and we all sat out together into the night. He took Emily on his lap and squeezed at her knee till she ran away mewling.

He told us how he'd sailed off India, on a warship acting as escort for the East India Company. Had plenty of run-ins with the Maratha pirates, not been able to stop them plundering a ship called the *Derby,* and taking all the Company's gold for two years. I'd heard it was more like one year's supply, but I knew better than to spoil a good yarn.

'Were you over that way?' he gave me a questioning look.

I shook my head.

'Get yourself out there, boy. Worth it for the women. Strip everything off with hot honey they do, smooth as a suckling —' Then he remembered. 'Excusing me, madam, I'm sure.'

'No, I was bound to the Indies,' I said, to change the subject.

'With Ogle? To relieve Vernon?'

I nodded.

'Hear that was a terrible defeat.' He offered me his can of beer. 'You ever rounded the Horn?' I hesitated. Why did I want to lie, say I had? 'Did you see action, then?' he asked next.

'No,' I said, and wanted to hang my head.

'Did you?' you asked him. You had been leaning against my shoulder but you sat up then. Your hair fell forward over your right shoulder and you twisted it about in your hands like a rope.

'Oh yes,' said George.

He told us all about it. As he spoke you pulled slightly away from me, sat very still. I thought fiercely: I could tell you some tales. I could tell you anything you want to know if you would but look at me not him.

You laid a hand on his arm. 'You've killed a man?'

'Many men, I'd say, ma'am, many,' he said, barely restraining his pride.

I spun my can between my hands, not trusting myself to look at the pair of them.

'Let's have a tune,' I said then, slapping my knee. 'Hell's teeth, George, we need to clear our throats.' And then I spat a mouthful of beer at your feet and stood up.

I swayed and danced to a tune in my own

head at first, shuffling my feet to and fro, kicking up a little dust that was ghostly pale. I kept my head down, hummed to myself. After a while George took it up, drumming his feet before him until he seemed to be sitting on air. Then he yelped and leapt up and he was at it too. We joined hands, swung around, hammering the ground until we nearly fell and grabbed each other about the shoulders. On and on we capered and sang out in unison before you, but not for you now, no, for we had hauled about and we danced on, looking out and over your head to where the water was.

CHAPTER FORTY-SEVEN

Poor George Gowing. I kept him up so late he set off long after daybreak. No doubt he had to sleep in a ditch before he got to his mother. He had no idea what trouble he caused. But he was not the cause of it, not at all, he himself was not where the danger came from. He was a horrible boastful man, and no doubt you saw through him. He did not take you in. But everything he said had a terrible effect on me.

I tried to mask it. That night George and I drank hard and long together, the way we had at sea, knocking it back swiftly before the swell slopped it. It grew dark. Sarah and Emily went inside but you stayed there with us, Sarah's red shawl about your shoulders. You couldn't take your eyes from him; neither could I. He started up a ditty and then away we went till my throat rasped and we had to drink again and sing again. We sang 'Spanish Ladies', and 'Sally Brown'.

'Lowlands'. 'My Son John', over and over. We sang 'It was one morning'. He got down on one knee to you and I steadied my hand on his shoulder. After the first verse you stood up, brushed off your skirt where he had gripped it.

'Come on in,' you said to me. The wind had got up, we could hear it in the bushes and sweeping down the marshes from up-river. The sign rattled above our heads.

'Equinox near,' George said, for something to say. 'Damned glad to be off that bastard ship.'

I thought of the forty-day passage to Madeira. The contrary winds and the straining rig and the stinking, rolling life below decks.

'Aye,' I said, and raised my fist to his. 'Damned glad.'

We lay together that night as always. But I didn't want your kisses. It was done with and then I rolled away. You thought I was jealous and I was, but not of what you thought. You always were a terrible flirt. I wasn't jealous of the looks he gave you, but of what his eyes had seen.

A few days later I went up with the Rutters' barge to Snape. It was a wind-proud sky all right, and we went a fair old lick. It was the first time I'd been upriver and as the reedbeds slipped by, and the river narrowed, I began to feel muffled, smothered even, by the banks closing in, as though I was pressing my face into a pillow.

The day was hot and dirty, and unloading took hours. In between times I sat and wiped my face and watched the men swarm up and down the wooden scaffold that ran about the high and angular walls, adding slow course on slow course. When they let me off the barge at the end of the day, I watched her stern right round the rise until it disappeared.

It had been another scorching day and the cottage was unbearable close. Walking here, though, at the front of the inn, above the river and just beyond the mossy stink of the dried-out weed, the air moved like silk on the skin.

'You go with Sarah,' I told you again.

You didn't reply. Every day the tides had kept creeping up the shore, stranding the drift higher and higher until there was barely any beach to walk on. Grit stuck to the soles of my feet. The only freshness came off the water but the tide was going out now, the mud beyond the drift cracking already. I wasn't going anywhere, certainly not to the Dunwich fair with dull old Sarah.

We had very little to spend, anyhow. I'd given up the brick work. Turned my back when the Rutter fellows rowed up and shouted across the water. I'll end up like Jack in need of a beanstalk, I thought grimly. Everything about was flat and low and on the straight. The cloud was high above and far out of reach. What drinking there must be over at Dunwich this very minute, the packed taverns, the yelling and the singing.

'Do you good, Becca, see some life, some company.'

'No,' you said shortly. 'I don't want to. It's you who keeps on.'

'Look. Rats got the little one, d'you think?'

You glanced over at the three dirty-grey cygnets hurrying after their mother. Her huge white underbelly swayed awkwardly as she slapped down her feet.

We walked on in silence. I found myself listening to the voices of men over water: two old brothers who lived across the river. No one knew where they came from but they had lived together as long as anyone could remember. 'Can't help it,' one was calling out from inside the house, shrill as a bird, over and over. I could see the other, sitting in the doorway eating from a bowl. It seemed very important to hear the brother's reply. I slowed my pace to listen, but the geese came over again, masses of them this time, in a honking, ragged arrow, headed south.

Then Sarah shouted from the inn. I could see it was a relief for you too to break off from our walk. You took my hand then, as we turned back to the house. Squeezed it.

'What you got there?' you called out to Sarah. She was holding something.

'Look you, I've got you that piglet at last,' she said, her eyes bright. 'A girl too, so don't matter that it's a bit late in the year.' She held it up for us to see: its clean pink flesh rumpled up and its snout moist and whiskerless.

You both cooed over it as though it were a baby.

'You sure we got enough scraps?'

Sarah looked at me. She was expecting more gratitude.

'I'll pen her up then.' I took the squealing thing from you and tucked it under my arm.

'Luke, we could keep her about the house maybe, just for a while,' you called after me. I kept on walking.

It was cramped work. My shoulders hurt and I had not enough rope to lash the corners properly. I strode up and down to the beach, looking for combings. Feeling my muscles stretch and reach. When I'd caged her up good I went back down to the beach and strode up and down some more, kicking at the shingle. I listened to the bubble and churn of the little waves breaking and turned to feel the wind on my ears.

You came out and stood and watched me a while. You held a parcel in your hands. Then you came down and held it out to me. It was warm cakes wrapped in a cloth. You must have done them yourself.

You said my old name then, as you used to say it, fresh minted. And you watched my face, but I would not show you anything, anything at all.

You said it again, a sad, and hopeless question now.

I took the cakes from you and I set them down and you went away without speaking. In the morning I saw you pick up the empty cloth all limp with dew and tracked about with prints.

After a few days you threw down your bowl and cried: 'Why do you have to keep that thing mewed up like that. Listen to her.'

'Damned animal.'

'Can't you build her a bigger pen?'

'Can't you show some sense? That was space enough aboard the *Essex*.'

'Enough about the *Essex*. The damned

Essex, that's all you ever talk about these days.'

'Is it?' I hadn't realised. But you were right. It was not the *Gemini* I thought of all the time, where in all my time at sea I had imagined myself the happiest. It was not even Albert. It was that first shock of the sea that seemed now never to have left me, to have soaked me through to the bone.

Now, of course, when I think back, when I try to imagine how it might have been different, it's those first days with you at Harwich that I go back to, again and again. Girls stepping out on our first dance, feeling our way, without a thought of our destination. Perhaps I should have heeded you, when you poked your hand into the piglet's cage so's you could stroke her gummy snout and asked me to recall little Neptune. The day that a beer barrel popped its bands and Sarah screamed to split the skies, I should have repeated along with you what Skeggs said to Nels, the day the same happened to her. I should not have turned away when you held out your unworn gloves and asked, was the jessamy scent quite gone? Yes, I see now that you would have anchored us back in those days, if you could.

I recall your little cat Neptune. I remember exactly what Skeggs said. I can still smell that stunning jessamy scent.

But that year, as autumn came on, as husband and wife circled each other in that cramped little cottage, for me it was always the *Essex*. Again and again I relived the rhythm of those days, until I grew dizzy. The flex of the seas. The tug of the wind. Always, always, like there was a sea in my head.

'Oh yes,' you said harshly. 'It's old Nick this and Charlie that, who went to China and did you know there were monkeys with no tails —'

'Can't waste wood,' I said shortly. 'We need it for winter.'

'Can't waste wood. You're so mean now, you're even pouring water back from bowl into pitcher. How am I supposed to wash?'

I turned on you then. I bellowed in your face. 'It's me who's got to draw it! We wouldn't have water or wood or food to cook on the damned fire if it weren't for me!'

We had a proper row then. I said terrible things.

The next day Sarah wouldn't look at me. I took out the brandy I kept behind a brick by the bressumer, and as I went out to the sea wall I saw you both through the kitchen window, sitting close together. I saw Emily slip on to your knee when she saw me and you hide your face in her shoulder.

I sat out the front very late, on the bench where we had sat with George. I looked at the empty waiting water. I didn't come to bed until the fire was out and you were asleep in bed. You never could keep a fire going. Your face was wet when I touched it. I thought you'd probably cried yourself to sleep. I cupped your cheek and licked the salt tears from my palm. It only made it worse.

My dreams turned violent, with the weather. I saw Nick out on the yard; his beard was on fire and when he tried to bat it out he let go of the yard and fell back. I saw our pig roasting on a spit, her rind scored and sizzling and then the lash was falling, opening up long red gashes. I was back in the Three Squirrels, knocked to the floor, seeing water between the boards. Every night I dreaded seeing Gilles but finally he came too. There was a storm, the sails unfurled above my head, as fast as we reefed they came thundering down again, became the roof of the cave, became the boulder, came smashing down.

I woke up, gasping. I had banged my head on the beam but when I clutched my head there was no pain, no blood.

Or I would hear singing, loud in my ear. I'd wake up and listen but there was nothing there, nothing but the sound of wind through the grasses. It was blowing stronger, the weather more unsettled by the day. Big storms rolled up after noon and the sky stayed dark.

I planted my feet firmly on the ground, I wrapped my arms about the post, I spread myself against the plastered walls, but all of it refused to move; remained firmly, fatally still. I looked about the place and felt myself so firmly anchored I thought I might drown. I knew the tide to be soaking up through the earth all around me now, softening the soil, spreading herself out and rising up to me. And how I longed to climb up and away, into the wind and the air, to feel myself released once more into the elements and to know that the deep, clear water was there again at my feet to carry me away: open and liquid and unbounded.

I couldn't sleep more than four hours at a stretch, I was convinced I could hear the ship's bell, the bosun's whistle, and I would wake with a jerk. I'd lie awake and restless, eventually I'd turn to you and ride you till you woke. You didn't cry out even when I hurt you. You were happy that I had turned back to you. Could not understand why I was so short with you again in the morning. But it was only to rid myself of the rhythm that came to me in my dreams, the rhythm of the waves and the ship. I'd cast about you, fold up your legs, turn you over, but I always ended by riding you to the self-same rhythm.

One night I staggered outside, desperate to feel the wind on my face. There was a great orange moon hanging over the water, lighting a path. I don't know how long I sat there and wept.

When I looked up, the water had come up high over the drift, was reaching into the marshes. The skiff nearest me had been drawn up further than all the rest but she was still floating high, tugging on her painter. I could hear the tide ripple over her sides. It sounded like a spring.

I waded straight in, feeling the straws and weed scratch at my shins. I lifted a handful of water to my face and tasted it. Full salt. As I did, I felt the last of the tide come and the waters stilled about me. I looked over at the moon. It seemed to hang there motion-less, but I knew I had only the space of two bells. I went back inside.

I didn't wake you. I'm very sorry now I didn't wake you.

When I came back out the moon was

almost touching the shore and all the little boats had turned right around. The tide was pulling strong. The skiff was nearer now, so close I could reach out and touch it.

ACKNOWLEDGEMENTS

I am extremely grateful to Sarah Bower, and my fellow students at UEA (particularly Joanne Aguilar-Millan), Harriet Gilbert, Jonathan Myerson, Sarah Waters, Richard Woodman, Julie Wheelwright, Malcolm Ridley, Jenny and Will Taylor-Jones, Rowan Route, my fellow students at City University, Lisa Newman, Tony Peake, Veronique Baxter, Laura West and all those at David Higham Associates, Helen Garnons-Williams, Lea Beresford, Erica Jarnes and all those at Bloomsbury Publishing, Tobias Hill, and the sugarbowl circle for all their help, advice and support. But especially to John Wrathall.

ABOUT THE AUTHOR

Kate Worsley was born in Preston, Lancashire, and studied English at University College London. She has worked variously as a journalist, a massage practitioner and follow-spot operator, and has an MA in Creative Writing (Novels) from City University London where she was mentored by Sarah Waters. She now lives on the Essex coast. This is her first novel.

The employees of Thorndike Press hope you have enjoyed this Large Print book. All our Thorndike, Wheeler, and Kennebec Large Print titles are designed for easy reading, and all our books are made to last. Other Thorndike Press Large Print books are available at your library, through selected bookstores, or directly from us.

For information about titles, please call:
(800) 223-1244

or visit our Web site at:
http://gale.cengage.com/thorndike

To share your comments, please write:
Publisher
Thorndike Press
10 Water St., Suite 310
Waterville, ME 04901